# KNIGHTS

## OF

## MALTA

Last survivor of the great medieval Orders of
Chivalry, the Sovereign Hirosalamytan Order of the
Knights of Malta, the Knights of St. John, with its
Grand Magistral Palace in Rome and its associations in nearly every Christian country, is still rich,
still practising charity on a vast scale, still strict in
admitting only men of noble birth to the final
vows.

A certain powerful cardinal of the Sacred College
had ambitions to control this religious but independent order, for the sake of the power which its
ancient distinction and its vast property must
confer on its Grand Master. Readers of Peyrefitte's
*The Keys of St. Peter* will realize how uniquely
qualified this author is to unravel the intrigues
whereby the cardinal attempts to break the Order's
pride.

# KNIGHTS
# OF
# MALTA

BY

ROGER PEYREFITTE

*Translated from the French
by Edward Hyams*

*London:* SECKER & WARBURG: *1960*

# PART
# ONE

# I

ON SEPTEMBER 29, 1949, His Eminence Cardinal Canali, Grand Prior in Rome of the Order of Malta, his holiday being over, left his Umbrian villa, the Villa Quadrelli, and went to the Castello Magione, headquarters of the Order near Lake Trasimene, where he had arranged to meet the Bailiff and Treasurer Hercolani. On the back seat of his long blue motor-car the cardinal and his secretary, Mgr. Curatola, sat side by side, separated by a glass division from the chauffeur who was taking the route via Todi.

"A fine day, Don Giuseppe!" the cardinal said, patting the little monsignor on the knee with his large hand. "God is sending us sunshine after the recent rain; and St. Rita, my patroness, will send me success. With Hercolani in my pocket I shall be master of the Sovereign Council, whose best mind he is. The Order has been straying: I shall restore it to the bosom of the Church."

Mgr. Curatola shot a glance at his chief out of the corner of his eye, taking in the pendulous cheeks, straight nose, broad forehead, black wig, firm figure—everything, warts included. He was wondering why the most powerful man in the Holy See, in Rome, nay, in all Italy, was so determined to get his hands on the Order of Malta. He said, "I admire Your Eminence's industry. It is barely a fortnight since His Holiness appointed you Grand Master of the Order of the Holy Sepulchre, yet already——"

"You cannot suppose I take that title seriously?"

"Yet it is one of the most illustrious of the orders of chivalry, Eminence. You are in the succession to Godfrey de Bouillon."

"Succession? I succeed, alas! to a poor devil of a Franciscan who held the grand mastership as Patriarch of Jerusalem. Do you know who is the real Grand Master of the real Holy Sepulchre? Prince Chigi, in his capacity as Grand Master of Malta. My good Don Giuseppe, it is nearly five centuries since Innocent VIII abolished the Order of the Holy Sepulchre by combining it with the Order of St. John of Jerusalem, which became the Order of Rhodes, and subsequently of Malta. Later, the Franciscans, guardians of the Holy Land, announced that they had found

Godfrey de Bouillon's sword, and set about dubbing knights of
their own on the tomb of Christ. A series of popes fulminated,
reformed, declared themselves grand masters. Finally under Pius
XI, the Holy Sepulchre having proclaimed itself a sovereign order,
the Grand Master of Malta, Thun Hohenstein, Chigi's predecessor, complained to the Holy See and it was *my* predecessor as
grand prior in Rome, Cardinal Pignatelli Granito di Belmonte,
who, as arbitrator, pronounced in favour of Malta. Am I not,
then, obliged to revenge the Holy Sepulchre?"

"Ah, Eminence, the two grand masterships would be most
worthily united under your Hat."

"Well, well, it's true enough that some people believe Prince
Chigi will be the last lay grand master of the Order of Malta. But
we must not listen to flatterers; we must attend only to our
conscience."

"Surely Prince Chigi is hardly a layman? A religious, rather,
since the professed knights of the Order take the three vows."

"Yes, but not the vow of humility, for they make them conditional on being allowed to live their lives as men of the world. And
they've devised what must certainly be the most succinct religious
habit there ever was, since it consists in no more than the little
cross of profession they wear in their buttonhole. Thus, they dress
as laymen, belong to clubs, go to the theatre. Not having to say
mass, since they're not ordained, they leave praying for their salvation to their chaplains. We received a report, yesterday, on the
denizens of the Master's palace and we'll look into it presently.
Perhaps I've never told you that I have, moreover, a small personal account to settle with Prince Chigi?"

"Can so distinguished a man ever have been wanting in respect
towards Your Eminence?"

"He has indeed. When, last year, Cardinal Pignatelli was summoned to his Maker, it became necessary to appoint a new grand
prior. It is customary for the grand master to give the Pope a list
of three names, and for the Pope to choose the first on that list.
Chigi, being prejudiced against me, refused to put my name on
the list. And that despite the fact that, contrary to the case of my
colleagues, who are members of the Order only as princes of the
Church, I have been a member since my youth, as 'knight of

honour and of devotion,' that is to say, after giving proofs of noble birth. For, after all, whether these people like it or not, I am a patrician of Rieti. All that, however, did not give me the place of honour which my sacerdotal heart craved for. Fortunately I have, at the palace in the Via Condotti itself, a most valuable ally in my good friend Travaglini who, albeit *ex officio*—for he has no real business there—reigns in the lobbies—and over the grand master."

"Have I not heard Your Eminence call the Via Condotti the Via Travaglini? That is certainly a great honour for the Marquis Travaglini del Vergante, Viscount of Santa Rita."

"No need to roll his titles round your tongue like that. The marquis has no noble ancestor but himself; and it was I who procured him his viscountcy of Santa Rita from the Pope—in honour of my heavenly patroness. As for his marquisate del Vergante, it was his friend the Prince of Hesse who begged it of the King for him, I have never known why. At all events, he succeeded in persuading the grand master to include my name in the list of the three *porporati;* nevertheless, instead of being first on the list, I was last. Tantamount to excluding me while seeming to do me a favour. However, the Pope, breaking all precedents, chose me instead of the first named; and the grand master learned, that day, that he had Cardinal Canali to reckon with."

"I thought him a better psychologist, or at least more of a diplomat,' Mgr. Curatola said.

"He will soon be regretting that he is neither. He already knows that I have not strewn the path from the Via Condotti to the Vatican with rose petals. Now I am about to take decisive action: by insuring that their treasurer is on my side, I shall be attacking Malta by way of its exchequer."

"A very appropriate point of attack, Eminence. Does not history tell of the Magione plot hatched by Cardinal Orsini against Caesar Borgia?"

"Wretch! Cardinal Orsini was strangled in the dungeons of San' Angelo!"

Mgr. Curatola bit his tongue. It occurred to him that a critical attitude would be more effective than mere flattery in diverting attention.

"I confess to feeling surprise," he said, "at the weight Your Eminence is giving to the reliability of your Magione . . . interlocutor. He is generally considered a man of little substance, an idle clubman."

"I know him better than that. He it was who rehabilitated the Order's finances. As my representative on the Sovereign Council he is a shade too flighty. I shall require him to forego that flightiness in future, and shall know how to reward him for the sacrifice."

"Surely a gentleman of his rank will come rather dear, Eminence?"

"One does not offer such a man money, my friend."

"Incidentally, could Your Eminence not have met him in Rome? We go there tonight; and so does he."

"There are things I should not wish to discuss with him there; not, at least, for the first time. Magione entails but a trifling detour for both of us, since he is on his way back from Florence. I wanted to ensure a propitious atmosphere: an autumn evening in the country, a quiet backwater. Moreover I needed some pretext, and Magione is a dependency of our priory. For the rest—tact and—deftness."

And to illustrate the latter word the grand prior softly drew the end of his red belt, colourful against his black cassock, through his fingers; yet his fingers were too thick and clumsy to evoke the idea, and suddenly he clenched his fists: "Deftness to begin with, and then—woe to the Order of Malta! Not satisfied with stripping, as they once did, the Order of the Holy Sepulchre, the Knights of St. John received a part of the Templar spoils and Magione is a vestige of their loot. What the Church gave, the Church can take away."

"Her needs are so many!"

"This war I have declared upon the Order of Malta and which is about to break out, is the most passionately interesting business any cardinal has been involved in since the Renaissance. For who are our opponents? The last aristocrats, men from a single social and even religious caste formed into an order whose very existence is not suspected by the man in the street. The occasion is one where we can show our mettle, in which we can use all the recources of our diplomacy, the whole arsenal of the Holy Roman church, against all the superannuated finesse of the old Europe. And we have neither public curiosity nor history's judgment to be afraid of. Our opponents are bound, as Catholics, to keep within the limits of respect, especially since they are under our religious authority; and, as gentlemen, they will keep their mouths shut."

"But, Eminence, is there not a risk that the grand master may insist on equality of status in your dealings? He bears cardinal's rank, surely? He is the only Most Eminent Highness in the world, is he not?"

"A former pope's jest, no more, although it does, in fact, entitle the Grand Master of the Order of Malta to follow immediately after the cardinals in order of precedence."

"True; and Prince Chigi is hereditary Marshal of the Church and Guardian of the Conclave. That must bind him more closely to the Holy See. I can see him, in my mind's eye, closing the doors on that unforgettable conclave at which you elected His present Holiness."

The cardinal made no rejoinder. It was as if his secretary's words had reminded him of ambitions altogether more considerable than the ambition to be Grand Master of Malta, For the past few minutes the car had been running beside the Tiber which seemed, for all it was yet among the Umbrian hills, an annunciation of the Seven Hill'd city's pomp and splendour. Mgr. Curatola, guessing the effect of his allusion, again had occasion to divert the cardinal's mind: "Is there not a contradiction, Eminence, in the fact that the grand master, albeit sovereign, is under the Holy Father's patronage? The contradiction would be less if the grand master were a cardinal."

The Grand Master of the Holy Sepulchre's continuing silence showed that he saw no point in pretending modesty. Had he not, a few moments ago, half confessed his ambition? No doubt he was dwelling upon what the sovereignty evoked by his secretary would mean to him: he was already all-powerful; and in default of the papacy, he would at least be as sovereign as the Pope. And what a sovereign! The most enviable of all, since he would be without either territory or subjects, which did not mean without followers and resources. Cardinal Canali was, of course, above taking the twenty-five gun salute, which protocol allowed the grand master, seriously. But he would have liked to have his own diplomatic bag, a privilege which Prince Chigi had always waived; and to make liberal use of the right to import goods duty free. The vast business interests over which he presided were always in need of fresh outlets. Finally, he could estimate the sum of all kinds of services which would be rendered him by the most discreet of all diplomats, the members of a certain "international entity" who never drew attention to themselves and were, for that very reason, all the better placed to be of use. He concluded his interior monologue aloud: "In concerning myself with the Order of Malta I am following in the footsteps of a considerable figure of contemporary history—Stalin."

"Stalin, Eminence?"

"Certainly! Stalin. At the outbreak of war he made an indirect approach to the Comte de Pierredon, the Order's minister in Paris; he wanted to know whether the Order would not like to open a legation in Moscow. You can imagine the stupefaction at the grand master's palace. It became excessive when they discovered that there was a special department in the Kremlin to deal with the Order of Malta. Stalin, you see, was just picking up an old tradition: the Tsar Paul I was elected grand master—albeit improperly—after the conquest of the island.

"Our people in the Via Condotti jumped at the offer, which was accompanied by an even more extraordinary proposal: restitution of the Commanderies of the two former grand priories of Russia and Poland. Prince Chigi hesitated in the Russian case—the grand priory had been schismatic, but he was not going to refuse the Polish one, which had been Catholic. It was we who brought him to his senses, by threatening to impeach him before the Holy Office."

"I am unable to conceive what Stalin's motives can have been."

"No doubt, Don Giuseppe. The subject is beyond the sphere of a writer to the section for indulgences of the Sacred Penitentiary, such as yourself."

The car had passed through Deruta and crossed the Tiber. They were in sight of hill-poised Perugia's walls and belfries.

"Think of it!" the cardinal said. "It was there that the Order of the Holy Sepulchre took refuge when it left the Holy Land! It was there that its last general, Fra Battista de Marinis, was informed that he had become no more than a bailiff of the Order of Rhodes! However, let us glance at our report on the grand magistracy. Still nothing about the grand master?"

Mgr. Curatola, who had taken out a notebook, was unable to suppress a smile. "His Most Eminent Highness, Prince Chigi Albani della Rovere, is eighty-two years old, Eminence, and universally respected."

"A man may fall victim to the devil at any age. A couple of decades ago a certain Roman prince, Grand Prior of Lombardy-Venetia, being about to celebrate his eightieth birthday, had to be hurried into hiding to save him from the indignation of several outraged families. What of Hercolani? At sixty-five he is still a young man."

"His Excellency Count Hercolani Fava Simonetti is nevertheless and still—irreproachable. The rumour which attributed a natural daughter to that venerable bailiff has no foundation."

"A pity. We should have a firmer hold on him. His legitimate son was evidently enough for him: he took the vows, like Chigi, when his wife died."

"His Excellency the Marquis Rangoni Machiavelli, Chancellor of the Order, continues to lead his customary life. Not having taken the vows, he does not live at the Grand Magistral Palace. He spends his evenings at home designing coats of arms."

It was not merely for the pleasure he took in them that Mgr. Curatola pronounced these aristocratic names, together with style and title, in full. He wanted to show that he knew the customs of the Order by giving its bailiffs the "Excellency" due to them, and the title "Venerable" to those who had taken vows.

Meanwhile the car was cruising through the streets of Perugia and the cardinal pointed out the Church of St. Luke as they passed it: it had been the last to belong to the Knights of the Holy Sepulchre. Mgr. Curatola turned over a page of his notebook.

"His Excellency, Count Thun Hohenstein," he said, "former Secretary for Foreign Affairs to the Order——"

"No need to mention him; he is a saint. And like all saints, has been persecuted. He is another whom it will be my business to revenge."

"Forgive me, Eminence, but surely the venerable bailiff in question almost ruined his Order with his unfortunate Argentine wheat speculations?"

"You are repeating Via Condotti lies without any idea what you're talking about. The deal was a stroke of genius; a couple of book entries should have made the Order two million dollars of profit. Unfortunately it was taken out of Thun's hands. Moreover, we should be the last to regret it, for it was by way of protesting against the grand master who dismissed him from office as Secretary for Foreign Affairs, that Thun made his secret report to the Congregation of Religious which is going to enable us to explode our mine. But I'm not satisfied with his having merely shown us the fuse, I intend that Hercolani shall light it himself."

Mgr. Curatola assumed the modest air of one unqualified to meddle in such matters, and returned to his list:

"His Excellency, the Marquis Taccone di Sitizano, representing the Grand Priory of Naples and Sicily."

"You haven't told me yet whether Rangoni's behaviour leaves anything to be desired."

"Eminence, the Chancellor, Rangoni, is seventy-nine years of age."

"What of it?"

"He lives with nobody but an old serving woman and never entertains. As for the Bailiff Taccone di Sitizano, his only amusements are a game of cards at the Hunt Club, and an occasional visit to the circus."

"Have they checked on what seat he occupies?"

"Eminence, the Bailiff Taccone is eighty years old."

"Do you think I talk for the sake of talking? The devil is everywhere, even at the circus; and you notice that Taccone isn't too old to frequent it."

"I did not overlook your orders, Eminence: the footman who is in our pay has kept a sharp eye on the Bailiff Taccone, even at the circus, and has nothing—distressing, to report."

"Not a thing on any of them! But if we look close enough we'll find something on one or the other. The Via Condotti isn't paradise and its tenants aren't all angels."

"The Duke del Balzo di Presenzano, representing the Grand

Priory of Bohemia, Knight Commander Professed, is reported as above criticism. The story that he gives his money to the poor because he is a Communist, is untrue."

"Very questionable!"

"Adamovich von Csepin, Knight Professed, representing the Grand Priory of Austria, is distinguished by nothing but an inclination for brandy. It is said, however, that he drinks it medicinally. We have reports from the parish priest of the place where he spends his holidays in the mountains: they are favourable."

"Anything fresh about the young Austrian who comes to take his place from time to time?"

"Baron Gudenus, Knight of Justice: we have kept a particularly close watch on him, since he is only twenty-six. Our man, watching through the keyhole, has seen him performing penitential acts. As for the girl—that secretary who was seen coming out of his office with her cheeks flaming—it seems she had been the object of one of his rages: he's a choleric man."

"We can wait."

"His Excellency, Count Conestabile della Staffa, Delegate for the Department of Good Works, bears his eighty-seven years tranquilly, without the devil showing so much as the tip of his tail."

"Abraham was a hundred when he fathered Isaac; but that was by the grace of God."

"The Marquis Pallavicini, Knight of Justice, Master of Ceremonies, appears hesitant to take the vows, because he has not given up hope of contracting a rich marriage. Meanwhile, and albeit in his forties, his conduct is irreproachable."

"You've kept the titbit till the end—I mean Cattaneo, the one who was taken on by them last St. John's, and is already giving rise to talk."

"Count Cattaneo di Sedrano, not much older than Baron Gudenus. He is, indeed, a man of prodigious industry which drives him to exceed his functions as Secretary of the Chancellery. They say he wants to resuscitate the Order, that he is in correspondence with foreign knights, and that he has great personal ambition."

"And this is the man we have Travaglini to thank for! He brought him in under the impression that he'd be on our side. If it hadn't been for him the shanty—as its own people call the Grand

Magistral Palace—would have collapsed of its own accord, at the same time as its octogenarians. How long's he been married?"

"Seven years, Eminence."

"How many children?"

"One little girl."

"He's remiss in his conjugal duties."

Mgr. Curatola sketched a modest gesture.

"A man who's been married seven years," the cardinal went on, "should have seven children."

"There is a rumour, Eminence," Mgr. Curatola said shyly, "that it is not Count Cattaneo's fault that he has only one child. It is said that he only contrived to—make a mother of his countess by a trick, and that she made him swear never to do it again."

"He has a case for an annulment, then!" the cardinal exclaimed. "However, just let my lord count try and get one!"

"Has Your Eminence never thought of trying to win him over to us—I mean, to the Church's side? Young men are unaware of the real nature of their own ambitions."

"It's an idea, certainly."

The village of Magione came in sight upon its hill. Near it Lake Trasimene evoked historical memories, but as they were not much to Rome's advantage Mgr. Curatola avoided referring to them.

"Let us, though distant, pay our respects to the sweet city of Assisi," the cardinal said, half bowing towards the right and slightly raising his *callotta*. "We shall be there ourselves next week for the solemn feast of St. Francis."

"Eminence," Mgr. Curatola said, "you are mighty here below because you are strong in heaven."


# II


THE ANCIENT COMMANDERY of the Templars, which had become the Commandery of Malta, reared its imposing mass at some distance from the village. Its square tower and its round tower at opposite ends of the long façade; its few windows, just below the machicoulis which coped the walls; the crenelated stronghold within, all these were the very image of a feudalism still standing, but isolated in solitude. The car passed through a wide gateway and into the interior courtyard which was surrounded by three-story arcading. A black Fiat was already parked there.

Hercolani, who was chatting with his chauffeur and the glebe farmer, advanced to meet the newcomers. His expression was guarded. His slender figure and air of breeding were in contrast with the cardinal's burliness. His long face was lit by a pair of ironical eyes, and the nose was aquiline. Even the hanging flex of his deaf-aid had the elegance of a monocle ribbon. The little enamel cross of his Order glittered in his buttonhole. His grand prior had opened his arms to him, and planted a smacking kiss on each cheek. But this feigned outburst of affection could hardly have deceived either the bailiff, or Mgr. Curatola. The farmer came forward in his turn and kissed the cardinal's hand, and the cardinal asked him if the vintage had been good.

"The vats are full, Eminence," the man replied, "and the sacramental wine will be of the highest quality."

"Take particular care of it, for I want to give some to His Holiness. Monsignor, here, will go round the property with you in my stead. I have business to discuss with His Excellency."

He gave a little nod towards the farmer's wife and her brats, who were peeping at him round a door held ajar. Then, having settled his chain and pectoral cross in position, he took Hercolani's arm and together they went up the stairs into the great hall.

"Does Your Eminence really intend to give His Holiness some of our sour Magione wine?"

"I do indeed; in fact it's urgently required! Do you realize that he sometimes hasn't enough wine to celebrate Mass? Sister Pasqualina is so careful of his health that she counts it out to him drop by drop. But mass wine never hurt a priest."

"Our Paris colleagues, at least, are not likely to quarrel with us as to who is to have the vintage! I can still see Guy de Polignac's face the first time he took a mouthful of our Magione when he lunched with us here."

"He'd like us to drink nothing but his champagne. Our tastes are more modest."

The room they entered was very roughly furnished. But it wanted no help from furniture: it was sufficient unto itself. Its massive walls and dark vaulting seemed made to keep the secrets of the new Magione conspiracy. Several fiascos, glasses, and a dish holding grapes had already been set on the table, and a vase of oleander flowers. The cardinal and the bailiff sat side by side, in two large armchairs.

"You must know, Fra Antonio," the cardinal said, "that Fra Ferdinando is not pleased."

This exordium amused Hercolani: the cardinal was going straight for his goal, which had nothing to do with the Magione Commandery; and by calling Thun and himself by their Christian names, in the manner of professed knights of the Order, was giving himself the backing of the hierarchy.

"Nor are we, for our part, particularly pleased with Fra Ferdinando," Hercolani said.

And he waited for the cardinal to mention the appeal addressed by Thun to the Congregation of Religious, one of whose members had warned the grand master. By reason of its secrecy this appeal was without precedent in the annals of the Order, although they were not wanting in acts of indiscipline and even of revolt. Thun's colleagues considered his behaviour so treacherous that they could not bring themselves to believe in it; nor did Thun's protector now refer to it.

"If the Order of Malta were not a religious order," the cardinal went on, "I should be inclined to think a certain severity in dealing with Fra Ferdinando not out of place. But have you considered that his errors, or rather imprudences, were leavened by the yeast of charity? He was not alone in believing that the grand magistracy's good works were not all they should be, and his object was to procure the means to make them so. The refugee camp at Transtevere, in which he took an active personal interest, was swallowing immense sums of money."

"He might at least have consulted the treasurer and administrator general of our assets. They would have begun by reminding him of the clause in our constitution which prohibits an officer from pledging the Order without the concurrence of the Sovereign Council."

"That does not alter the fact that, considering his name and rank, you have been hard on him."

"Have you forgotten what he is costing us?"

"I shall continue in my opinion that it was a master-stroke to buy wheat from the Argentine at seventy dollars a ton, leaving a profit of twenty dollars per ton for our charities."

"Yes, Eminence; but the contract stipulated that we must pay in free-market dollars, and Fra Ferdinando was unaware of the fact that such currency was not to be had. He found it out too late, and when he came and told us, in June, that settlement for a deal concluded by him in the Order's name was due, and that we were bound to pay the Argentine 7,000,000 dollars and take delivery of 100,000 tons of wheat waiting for us in the Buenos Aires silos, you can imagine what we felt. The grand master had to call upon all his strength of mind to avoid taking the business as an utter disaster. God knows how we shall manage. It is true that we can get the contract annulled by sending a copy of our constitution to the Argentine government. But we felt obliged to honour the signature of a professed brother, a bailiff, and our Minister for Foreign Affairs into the bargain."

"General Perón is a gentleman," the cardinal said, "and will do the handsome thing. Do as much by Fra Ferdinando, and give him back his place."

"It has been abolished, and its functions assumed by the Chancellery, which is quite up to handling such diplomatic activity as we have. But the grand master has treated Thun very indulgently, since he has left him his membership of the Sovereign Council, as the representative of Lombardy-Venetia."

"I should not make too much of that indulgence if I were you. You know as well as I do that the grand master is keeping Fra Ferdinando only because there is nobody to replace him. It is not my fault, Fra Antonio, that the Order lacks professed brethren; it is not my fault if Knights of Malta are no longer willing to make vows of poverty, chastity, and obedience."

"It is nobody's fault, Eminence, and yours, assuredly, least of all."

The tone in which Hercolani had spoken the last words made it clear to the cardinal that the bailiff was well aware of his plan to

dry up the source of religious recruits, in order the more quickly
to get control of the Order. It was he who was holding in suspense
several requests from Italian knights that they might take the
vows. It was he who had recently prevented the re-establishment
of England's grand priory, a project made possible by the vocation
of five young English knights and the approval of Cardinal
Griffin. Weary of waiting for a dispensation which never came, the
five knights had married, and Cardinal Griffin was left mourning
his stillborn grand priorship of England.

"Fra Ferdinando's conduct was particularly inexcusable,"
Hercolani continued, "in that he had already landed us with a
pretty kettle of fish. Or, rather, of soda."

"Soda?" the cardinal said, flicking his fingers as if he were
shaking powder over the table.

"Caustic soda, Eminence. You know all about it."

"Ah, yes. An arithmetical error, I fancy."

"An error, certainly. It was designed to procure funds for our
charities; and it would have brought us into the law courts if the
English Colonel de Salis, a member of the Allied Commission
which had to deal with the business, hadn't been a Knight of Malta."

"Upon my word! Was there a hundred thousand tons of the
stuff involved?"

"No, twenty quintals improperly altered to two hundred, but
at a time when soda was fetching about the same price as cocaine."

"A religious spirit should understand and take account of good
intentions. I am beginning to feel surprised that you are not trying
to lay the business of the ten thousand eight hundred phials of
penicillin at Fra Ferdinando's door!"

"Neither at his door nor our own. The person who betrayed
our trust by pretending to get a gift of penicillin from America for
our hospitals, and then trying to divert it to the black market, was
unmasked in time, and the whole bag of tricks handed over to the
Ministry of Health."

"At least Fra Ferdinando was not involved in *that*. But should
we not change the subject? We must appear like characters in that
French play, where the grandees of Spain are squabbling over the
national assets—'*Donnez-moi l'arsenic, je vous cède les
nègres*'——"

"Well, I am not going to cede you Fra Ferdinando, Eminence, without first having asked you whether he has spoken to you of that other trifling matter, which only cost our Order a few wretched millions. When the Italian government repudiated all the Fascist government's drafts in payment, excepting those touching social welfare undertakings, Fra Ferdinando saw an unhoped-for opportunity to improve the pittance granted to the Transtevere refugees. On his behalf a number of these bills, issued in the Order's name, were presented for payment by the Bank of Italy, in Trieste. He had not noticed that they were forgeries. The bank, very civilly, did not lodge a complaint, but the intermediary who had advanced money on security of this paper had to be reimbursed. Fra Ferdinando's charity was—redoubtable."

"Ah, you've given me the key to his Argentine speculations," the cardinal said. "He wanted to make up for these inadvertencies by a really brilliant stroke. With a little address, Fra Antonio, you'll make something of all that Argentine wheat."

"God send that the nephew may not cost us the little left by his uncle!"

"What does that mean?"

"That his uncle, the Grand Master Thun Hohenstein, consumed a great deal of our substance during the First World War. He turned our possessions in Austria–Hungary into cash without so much as a by-your-leave, and invested the nest-egg in Austro–Hungarian War Loan. A fine investment!"

"He was doubtless forced to do it."

"He certainly would not have been had he remained in Rome instead of withdrawing to Vienna. Our Order was as indulgent with him as it has been, thirty years later, with his nephew. When the war was over he was requested to remain where he was for a few months, since it would have been difficult to save him from being arrested and tried. Subsequently, with his failing health as pretext, he was asked to nominate a lieutenant. He died in peace, our seventy-fifth grand master, and he appears in our records as Italian, his estates being in the annexed territories of Trent."

"Come, now, admit that neither the Prince Grand Master Thun, nor the Count Bailiff of the same ilk, have ruined you! I recently had a rough account of the Order's assets drawn up. You have between four and five hundred millions in stocks and bonds, thirteen or fourteen thousand acres of real estate, about a hundred commanderies of justice with which you endow professed knights —five times as many commanderies as professed knights!—and I am not counting endowments which are administered for a consideration by their founders' descendants. And then there are your legacies—marquises seem particularly apt to make wills in your favour. Admiral, the Marquis Cusani Visconti has left you a great house and a fine estate in the plain of the Po. The Marquis de Valva has made you his heirs to property in the neighbourhood of Salerno worth two thousand millions. In short, wherever you get it from, I see it as a great deal of money for a dying Order."

"The Order you pronounce to be dying is in tolerably robust health, Eminence: three thousand knights grouped in five grand priories and twelve national associations. More than there were in the Middle Ages."

"Too many, in fact! But what you're giving me is publicity handout language. I am concerned neither with your knights of honour and devotion, nor with your knights by grace of the grand master, nor with your donati of the first, second, or third degree. They are all no more than the honourific array of the Order. I am concerned with the knights of justice, who are candidates for taking the vows; and with the professed knights who have taken them. You, too, should be concerned solely with them, for they constitute the religious machinery of the Order. And what are their numbers, Fra Antonio? You number twenty-two, including the grand master. Twenty-two religious, in a religious order which was formerly the fine flower of all religious orders, so much so that it was called, simply, The Religion. And, at that, we really ought not to count the ten chaplains who are your priests. The Holy See, or, more precisely, the Holy Father, patron of the Order of Malta, scans the horizon in vain for more than twelve professed knights. This is a very serious matter, Fra Antonio."

"There was a time, during the nineteenth century, when the total of professed knights and chaplains was seven, yet the Order did not die of it."

"I confined myself to pointing out that it was dying; I did not say it was dead. France, the Church's eldest daughter, has an association, but not a single professed knight. Likewise, most Catholic Spain."

"Likewise Great Britain," Hercolani put in, allusively.

"At the rate things are going the five surviving grand priories—surviving thanks to the handful of professed knights and chaplains—are in danger of extinction, and the Holy See could never allow that. Nor could it allow a religious order to turn into a lay order."

"Do not cast our lay brethren in our teeth, Eminence. We owe them to Pius IX who granted permission for their admission into the Order. He was the father of our very flourishing national associations."

"Very well, but it is none the less true that your twenty-two professed members, rich as Croesus, should make better use of their wealth in supporting those charitable works which are the justification for their existence. Your Order—our Order—is an Order of Hospitalers, by foundation and by definition. Prince Chigi is Grand Master of the Hospital of Jerusalem——"

"—and of the Military Order of the Holy Sepulchre of Our Lord."

"I know it! You are the heirs of those Hospitalers who succoured and defended the pilgrims—and that, too, is a legacy to be vindicated."

"Perhaps I may give Your Eminence another publicity handout, by reminding you that in the course of the two world wars our several national associations succoured more than a million wounded? Perhaps I should enumerate our hospitals and hostels, our orphanages and crèches? We have a dispensary even here in Magione; indeed, we have one in the very palace itself, as a mark of our origins. And are you forgetting our missionary association, dear to His Holiness's heart, and which has, in its first few years, had thousands of pupils through its hands? And, finally—you must forgive what I am about to say—our great project for an international hospital of the Order of Malta, which was to be financed by America, and in which each association would have had its national ward, was opposed and prevented by certain people known to yourself who could not see enough in it for themselves."

"An odious calumny!" the cardinal shouted. "Moreover, I am certain that such projects would go through quickly enough if you were more directly dependent on the Holy See."

"I don't doubt it, of course; but surely we were sufficiently deferential to the Holy See? All the members of the Sacred College, led by yourself, were on the honorary committee. Prince Carlo Pacelli and Count Galeazzi were on the executive committee. Not, of course, that they were the only committee members."

The cardinal fidgeted in his chair. No doubt he had found the allusion a little too near home for his comfort, referring as it did to the two personages who, with himself, comprised that vast association of interests which all Rome called by the name of the Hindu trinity—the Trimurti. Offence to the other, the Holy Trinity, was thus avoided; and in any case the Holy Trinity did not seem always to be the inspiration of the trio which, composed of a cardinal of the Curia, a nephew of the Pope, and His Holiness's close friend, governed the Church's temporalities.

"Enough of the past," the cardinal said curtly. "I did not ask you to meet me here in order to be given a lecture in contemporary history. And for my part I have set forth my views of the present state of affairs by way of introduction to my proposals for the future."

He leaned forward in order to look the bailiff straight in the eyes. Hercolani met his look with a sardonic expression, seeing in it preoccupations rather different from those which his interlocutor had made such a parade of. He would not have dared to say that the grand prior was vowed to the three qualities attributed to certain nuns by the most famous writer of letters among Frenchwomen: pride, interest, hatred. But he might have gone so far as: ambition, duplicity, cupidity.

"What do you think of the grand master's health?" the cardinal asked abruptly.

"He was very active when I saw him in July."

"He is worn out, Fra Antonio. A reign of twenty years——"

"I had a letter from him only yesterday, a very entertaining letter in which he reminded me of tomorrow's reception in honour of the Catholic Medical Congress. During the holidays he made a tour of our charitable establishments and our houses all over the place. And at his own home, in Ariccia, his correspondence is as voluminous as ever."

"When the ant grows wings," the cardinal said, "it is a sign that she is near her end." (For he had a taste for proverbs.) "I am as much attached to the Order of Malta as you are, and have been a member longer. No man is more sensitive to the dangers which threaten it. All that money in your hands—it may well arouse a righteous envy in the Church, for she never has enough for her charity."

"Her needs are legion!" Hercolani said, more ironically than Mgr. Curatola.

"All your sovereign and diplomatic privileges would be very welcome to the Holy See, with its world-wide activities. And you must recognize that you are, at this moment, at the mercy of the Holy See, since it has never officially approved your constitution and would be entitled, on that ground alone, to take a hand in your affairs."

"You really must not exaggerate, Eminence. The grand master may have forgotten to ask Pius XI for the brief approving our 1936 constitution, but that constitution was nevertheless recognized by implication in the rescript of audience, as it was in all our dealings with the Secretariat of State. And we cannot help wondering who has suddenly discovered that oversight after a lapse of ten years, who prevented Pius XII from repairing it when we asked him to do so, and who inspired the Secretariat of State to propose unacceptable amendments to it as the price of the brief."

"Be that as it may, let me assure you that, if I were to make it my business, you would soon have your brief. But what is the point of my using my influence for a grand master who already has one foot in the grave?"

"Don't be in even more of a hurry to bury him than the Order of Malta, Eminence."

"I *would* bury him—as grand master, not as Prince Chigi. You have put Fra Ferdinando on trial before me here today; did it not occur to you that, indirectly, you were indicting his chief? If the Order were better governed Fra Ferdinando would have been kept in hand and his initiatives crowned with success. You have, very opportunely, reminded me of the faults committed by the

Grand Master Thun Hohenstein, and of their sanction; the faults committed by the Grand Master Chigi, or, at least, under his mastership, deserve the same treatment: let him make way for a lieutenant."

Stupefied, Hercolani stared at the cardinal who, with deliberate coldness, added, "Work with me, and you shall be the man."

The bailiff was even more astounded by this, but instead of replying that he had no ambition of that kind, he pretended to argue the point. "Don't make fun of me, Eminence. You maintain that we have no valid constitution. But even so we have the de Rohan code, which governed our conduct for more than a century and a half. The Grand Prior of Rome has certainly not the power to force a grand master to make way for a lieutenant. That is the privilege of the Sovereign Council, and no grand prior is admitted to membership."

"There is, however, a power superior to Grand Master, Grand Priors, Sovereign Council, and all: the Holy Father, your real sovereign. He can appoint a lieutenant tomorrow if he wants to."

"I doubt, Eminence, whether His Holiness would ever assume such a responsibility—in the case of an Order which loves and respects him."

"His Holiness owes it to himself to save an establishment which is dying before his eyes."

"But you, alone, see it so, and against all the evidence. The head of the Church is better informed."

"It is precisely because he is well informed that he is beginning to feel concerned. When complaints begin coming from within the Order itself——"

"We should very much like to know what and whose they are."

"You will shortly begin to feel their effects."

"Why not tell the whole tale, Eminence, and name Fra Ferdinando as the plaintiff? There, surely, is the lieutenant you want: big-hearted, charity personified!"

"The head of an order is not chosen for qualities of heart, but for those of his head. Everything points to you, Fra Antonio, to you; and you have no right to hold back. Not in vain did Heaven make you the representative of my grand priory even before I was grand prior. I have vast plans for the greater glory of the Order and the good of the Church, plans which already have the Holy Father's support. Thus, by joining with me, you join with him, you enter upon a league with the Vicar of Christ."

Hercolani shifted the flex of his deaf-aid. He said, "I am sorry, Eminence, I did not catch that. I'm afraid this machine is out of order." And he put both hands on the arms of his chair, as if seeking permission to rise. The cardinal leaned toward him and bawled in his ear, "Come back to Rome in my car. We can discuss the matter further."

Hercolani shook his head, signifying that he could not hear. He went to the table and offered the cardinal the dish of grapes. Both ate a few as they made their way out into the courtyard. Hercolani said, "If Your Eminence would give yourself the trouble of accompanying me to the cellar, you could bless the vintage."

# III

EVERY MORNING, Count Cattaneo went to Mass at the Church of St. Carlo on the Corso. The count, Secretary of the Chancellery, carried his height and his burliness well; his eyes were sparklingly blue and his fair hair had a distinct tinge of red. A native of Friuli, he looked more Teutonic than Italian; but his character was a blend of Latin subtlety and Germanic firmness of purpose.

When, after Mass, he walked the short distance back to the Via Condotti, the neighbouring great houses served as a kind of heraldic reminder of his Order's nobility: the Palazzo Borghese, across the street, was now the Hunt Club, the Roman aristocracy's club, of which the grand magistral staff were all members. On the right was the Palazzo Ruspoli, residence of the Grand Master of the Holy Hospice, a title which designated not the head of an order, but of a high Vatican office. Then came the Palazzo Chigi, now the seat of the Italian Foreign Ministry; it had kept its former name in honour of its builders, the Grand Master of Malta's ancestors. Via Condotti—the Palazzo Caffarelli and the Palazzo Torlonia.

About halfway down the street the outline of the Grand Magistral Palace stood clear cut against one of the most handsome townscapes in Rome: the dazzling Spanish Steps, the obelisk, and the Church of the Trinita delle Monte, that group of monuments which d'Annunzio called the "Catholic tepidarium."

Although contemporary life had invaded it, the Renaissance palace of the Order looked as impressively like a fortress as the Magione Commandery. A jeweller's shop and a gentlemen's haberdashery establishment were inserted into the massive masonry of its ground floor, and the dispensary which Hercolani had mentioned opened on to a side street. But despite these breaches, the haughty elevation of the façade seemed to conceal a mysterious life, the life symbolized by the three great heraldic shields of marble—white cross on red ground—placed, respectively, in scrolls at each corner of the façade, and in a panel above the balustered balcony of the porte-cochère; there was a fourth in a niche of the little interior courtyard, below a fountain. This palace, residence of the Order's ambassadors to Rome until the middle of the nineteenth century, now harboured the Grand Magistracy of Malta, the most ancient organ of authority in the city after that housed by the Vatican Palace.

Cattaneo, standing in the porch, exchanged a few words with the porter, Colonna, who had the right to a handshake from the prince of that ilk. He glanced at the rather meagre-looking palm tree which had been planted in the courtyard, near the fountain, as a reminder of those lands in which the Knights of Malta once had great possessions. He crossed the courtyard and went up the narrow, marble-faced staircase, past the first floor, where professed brethren had their quarters and their chapel. The second floor consisted of the two dining-rooms, the two drawing-rooms— the red room and the green room—the small council chamber, the grand master's apartment, the Chancellery, the Treasury (Hercolani), the administration general of property (Professor Rossi), the civic assistance offices (Bailiff Conestabile), and the heraldic committee offices (Bailiff Taccone).

Cattaneo, one of the first to arrive, nevertheless found his chief already at work. The fact was that the Marquis Rangoni came very early in the morning to avoid returning after luncheon. He was an old man, his hair and long moustache snow-white; a close friend of Prince Chigi since their youth. As chancellor, he was head of the Order's government. However, he looked upon his post as a pleasant sinecure, and spent his time in the office writing articles on former grand masters for the Order's monthly journal.

Cattaneo, making his way into the office on that October morning in 1949, was dwelling upon what Thun had said to him the evening before: "I should like a word with you. I'll expect you at my rooms tomorrow at eleven." Cattaneo was not so intimate with Thun as to anticipate becoming the recipient of the other's confidences. Their only link was one of the grand magistral charities—the Institute for Associated Emigrations—an undertaking excogitated by Travaglini and harmless enough for its chairmanship to be left to the Bailiff Thun. Cattaneo was its secretary. That post had, indeed been his entrée to the Magistral Palace and from it he had progressed to the Secretariat of the Chancellery.

In the latter post his functions were diverse if only because the chancellor left everything to him. Among other things they enabled him to understand, better than most, the real nature of the erstwhile Secretary of State's "inadvertencies." The speculations which Thun had embarked upon, with all the simplicity of a man of fashion crediting himself with capabilities quite beyond his sphere, were not undertaken solely to benefit the Order's good works, but to finance vast political projects. He wanted to get the Order recognized as sovereign by as many countries as possible. He wanted the Order to be appointed administrators of the Holy Places. He wanted the Order's flag to be flown over the International Court at The Hague. He wanted political refugees to be given Order of Malta passports. All this called for money, and the funds allowed his department were very limited. Hercolani, a veritable Cerberus at the Treasury, refused to subsidize undertakings which he considered chimerical, and it was in trying to escape his yoke that Thun had let himself be tempted by certain men of business.

Now Cattaneo had himself been fighting Hercolani at the Treasury, ever since he joined the Chancellery, albeit for humbler reasons. He had found himself consigned to an exiguous office containing a wooden safe, cupboards which would not shut, an archaic typewriter, a single telephone used by the whole floor, and a single secretary for a voluminous correspondence—true, it was one-way correspondence, since before his time it simply accumulated without receiving any answer. From this beginning he had contrived to progress: the office had been decorated, its gear brought up to date, its staff increased, and likewise, even, their salaries. But unlike Thun, who was at daggers drawn with Hercolani and accused him of being the author of his downfall, Cattaneo had earned the treasurer's good opinion and trust. However, the new white hope of the Order was about to call upon the old—for there were many who had once seen in Thun a future grand master, the second of his name.

At the time specified, Cattaneo went down to the set of rooms called "Lombardy-Venetia," Thun's rooms, since each apartment occupied by a professed knight was named for the grand priory he represented. Lombardy-Venetia, being placed midway along the front of the house, had the benefit of the balcony. Its decoration was sumptuous. The princely families to which Thun was related had sent him *objets d'art*, tapestries, and pieces of furniture worthy of his former position and of his aristocratic tastes. His noble brow, smiling eyes, straight nose, and pointed beard composed an attractive appearance reminiscent of his uncle, the former grand master.

"I take a great interest in you, Cattaneo," he said, after finding his visitor a chair. "It's natural, come to think of it, since it was I, in a way, who put your foot in the stirrup. And you've come a long way from our worthy little Institute for Associated Emigrations. You're young, intelligent, and hard-working. Anyone who knows anything about what's going on here is obliged to recognize your abilities. I should like to give you a few words of advice to help you in your career."

Coming from a man who had more than compromised his own career, this opening was certainly curious. Nevertheless, Cattaneo thanked him for his good intention: "Your Excellency must know that the post I occupy, humble though it be, is the highest I can expect. As I am married I cannot take vows, which means that I am automatically excluded from the Sovereign Council. An ambitious man might find that—discouraging."

Thun smiled and said, "Oh, we're not ready to let you go. You're already indispensable. Neither civil, canon, nor mercantile law have any secrets for you. You have brought order out of the Chancellery chaos. You speak and write several languages. In short, you are the man we needed."

"I am happy here, and I should like to stay, because I foresee what the Order could become. It will resume its pristine greatness on the day when its knights become aware of its grandeur."

"Such were my own ideas, and I am touched to find that you share them. I, too, thought of the Order as of something great. When we take the vows we are given a slap in the face, accompanied by these words: 'Awake, and do not sleep at your task'— I was more struck by the words than by the blow. The men I saw about me here were all asleep. I was the first to reawaken the Order, and especially to shake it out of the too Roman, too Italian atmosphere in which it was stagnating."

"There can be no doubt, Excellency, that the international task you tried to accomplish was magnificent, and we must all hope that one day it will be successful. But was there really much point in having us represented in San Marino, Liechtenstein, and Monaco in the hope of founding a federation of tiny states which could have been nothing more than a comic opera affair? How can it serve our purpose to have a minister accredited to Panama, where the only Knight of Malta is himself, so long as our ministers are not accredited in Italy and France? I will give you a symbol, Excellency: those two thousand passports you had printed for political refugees without ascertaining whether we should be allowed to distribute them—they're still undistributed."

"Of course! The grand magistracy gives diplomatic passports to King Humbert and the Archduke Otto, but it takes no interest in nameless exiles."

"It does for them what is within its competence. It feeds them, lodges them in two or three camps in Germany. The Italian government closed down our camp at Transtevere, but for reasons which did not touch us. As for the crowned heads, both their country of residence and their country of origin are glad enough to see the Order of Malta grant them a passport, which neither of them would be willing to do."

"That was no reason to take their diplomatic passports away from the people I had provided with them."

"We were obliged to make up our minds to it when the Italian Foreign Ministry asked us to. You cannot deny that you were not personally acquainted with all the people to whom you had granted that privilege: one of them had a record of sixteen convictions."

"I perceive that it is I who am to receive advice and *you* to give it. No doubt it will be to my advantage."

Cattaneo ignored the irony. "Advice? If I did have a word of advice to give your excellency it would be to get a new secretary."

"What! Another of you with a down on poor Gehlen, and all because he's a Protestant! Doesn't it occur to you that one may choose a secretary for his intelligence?"

"If all the Order of Malta with all Catholic Christendom to choose from could not find you a secretary both intelligent and Catholic, the case is desperate indeed!"

"You should respect him for having refused conversion. It proves that he is no hypocrite."

"On the other hand, Excellency, there is the little matter of his being brother to a general who happens to be one of the ablest intelligence officers in the West German service. You were even good enough to procure this same general our Grand Cross of Merit. Mark you, I say nothing against that and I am equally careful not to assert that the Roman Gehlen is passing our poor little secrets on to the Gehlen of Bonn. But, if you are aware of a certain uneasiness in the air about you, do please believe me that he has a good deal to do with it. I owed it to myself to mention this matter to you, since this is the first time I have been with you in his absence. True, had he been here, I should either have cut short this interview, or imitated Count Pecci."

"Ah, Count Pecci. Remind me what it was that our dear Minister to the Holy See *did* do."

"He called here, Excellency, after telephoning to tell you that he wished to speak to you in a matter both urgent and confidential. He arrived to find Gehlen sitting at that table with his back to the room, a pen in his hand, and a clean sheet of paper under it.

"'Beautiful weather,' said our minister. You waited for him to broach his urgent and confidential matter, but he went on, 'Though rather chilly yesterday.' You were thereupon obliged to agree that the evening had, indeed, been rather cool. Our minister then asked after one of your cousins, and whether the grand master's canaries, siblings of the Holy Father's, were still in good health. Whereupon, losing patience, you begged him to get down to business. 'Business?' he said, 'what business? The business you came to see me about. Ah yes, of course; well, I'll talk business when we are alone.'"

"We've talked enough nonsense, Cattaneo. This is what, between ourselves and because of the interest I take in you, I wanted to say to you. There are going to be some changes in this establishment. I shall benefit by them. I am suggesting that you—place yourself at my side."

"Excellency, I am on the Order's side, and I always shall be. Are you sure that you, at this moment, can say as much, and are not feeding a grudge?"

"That has had no influence on my decisions. There are certain matters which you cannot understand and which might make you change your mind."

"Excuse me, but I think I can understand everything."

"In that case, understand this. That to be with me is to be with the Church. Help me discreetly from now on."

"I am sorry, but I swore fidelity to the grand master and the Sovereign Council."

Thun rose and strolled over to the window; he said, "A fine day."

"But a little chilly, Excellency."

# IV

As WELL AS HERCOLANI, the Order of Malta's government included one other outstanding man: Raimondo del Balzo. It was, therefore, on good grounds that this professed knight commander, representing the shadow Grand Priory of Bohemia, was in

B

Cardinal Canali's bad books. Even so, to suspect such a man of Communism—he was a chamberlain of the cloak and sword to His Holiness Pius XII, an officer of justice of the Italian Republic, head of one of the seven families who are grandees of the Kingdom of Naples, and eleventh Duke of Presenzano into the bargain—called for all the cardinal's animosity and all the pettiness his spies could muster. Despite a frail appearance and the accident which obliged him to walk with a stick, his vitality was abundant and the lively eyes which illuminated his ascetic face were, so to speak, the symbol of his generous nature and brilliant mind. However, being much occupied by his official duties, he could do little more than support Hercolani at the infrequent meetings of the Sovereign Council, and applaud Cattaneo's juvenile efforts from afar.

Meanwhile, the Knights of Malta were protected on their most threatened frontier by an eminent diplomat, Count Stanislao Pecci. It would not have seemed likely that this great-nephew of Leo XIII could be destined to play a part antagonistic to the Church; yet such a part had been forced on him, albeit he played it within limits of discretion, by the fact that he represented the Order at the Holy See. It was, perhaps, some sort of inherited experience or family aptitude which had enabled him to hold his own with a combination of tact, intelligence, and energy. In any case, he might justify his attitude by considering that he was also following a family tradition in serving the Knights of Malta: that pope whose name he bore had restored to them not only the church and priorial villa of the Aventine, but likewise the office of grand master, filled by a mere lieutenantcy since Pius VII.

Short, distinguished, cultured and in some sort an artist, Pecci understood the Roman court and language. He had been struck by the apparently innocent remarks which he overheard there on the subject of the Order, and which he passed on, with his own glosses, though quite in vain, to the grand master. He had suspected that there was treachery afoot as soon as he had heard the Holy Father's 1940 speech at the annual audience granted to the Knights of Malta.

"The weight of ancient laurels gathered upon the fields and in the ports of Palestine, upon the beaches and ramparts of Cyprus,

Rhodes, and Malta, must not be allowed to lull the heirs to so much glory into an ecstatic dream of the past. . . . Our lives may not be dedicated only to a worship of our memories."

The Pope's words were, no doubt, very right and proper. For all its charitable works, the most glorious of the orders of chivalry was in need of revival. But Pecci immediately realized the manner in which this wise warning would be abused by the Pope's entourage. In this anxiety he was in a minority of one. Thereafter, the war had turned everyone's attention to other matters. And clearly Prince Chigi had not taken the words as a threat, since he had quoted them as a tribute at the head of the general roll for 1949.

Pecci had carefully sifted the staff of his legation. His counsellor, Baron Malfatti di Montetretto, was conscientiousness and integrity personified. A former army officer and half-Austrian by birth, he had a strong sense of discipline, and his wealth placed him above Vatican intrigues. The ecclesiastical attaché, Mgr. Hemmick, an American, was likewise set above such intrigues by his character and personal fortune.

Despite this judicious choice of staff an incident had disturbed the Malta legation during the previous year: the Secretariat of State had informed the Minister of the Order that, according to confidential intelligence, Malfatti's youngest daughter was a Soviet agent. In point of fact, her only misdemeanour was the frequenting of those artistic and intellectual circles in Roman society which play at Communism in reaction against the Church's predominance. But the visits which she was accustomed to paying her relations in Austria and Czechoslovakia rendered her suspect, which was quite enough for the Order of Malta's enemies, whose object was to dismantle the legation by forcing the counsellor, and possibly the minister, to resign. Pecci defended his subordinate, and the scandal ended in nothing worse than Malfatti's daughter being asked to do her travelling without a diplomatic passport in future. Mgr. Montini, substitute at the Secretariat of State, whose relations with the Order were formally cordial, anointed the threatened breach with balm, and the Pope honoured the slandered girl's father with the Cross of St. Sylvester.

The Thun business caused Pecci more serious anxiety. He had

been the first to guess the use which the Holy See would make of it. When he learned of Thun's secret plaint, he realized that the danger was getting nearer: but he had had no better success in his efforts to convince the grand master, who affected to shrug off his former favourite's treason and considered himself in no danger from Church intrigues.

Moreover, having a sharp eye on the manœuvres of the Trimurti, Pecci had also been the first to distrust Travaglini, its agent inside the Grand Magistral Palace. The two men were, in any case, natural adversaries: on the one hand was a man whose family was not, it is true, of the old nobility, but assimilated to it by having produced a pope; thus he stood, in his person, for the ancient "black nobility" but enlightened by fusion with the "white nobility"—the Vatican tempered by the Quirinal. On the other hand the newly made aristocrat was blindly obedient to the authors of his ennoblement. Pecci considered his conduct notably dishonest in that he boasted to the grand master of the Holy See's confidence in him, whereas it was Cardinal Canali only with whom he was hand in glove. Travaglini's ulterior motive was to make himself *persona grata* at the Secretariat of State on the grounds that he had the confidence of the grand master, whose officious spokesman he was tending to become. In view of which, the Order's minister had not been displeased when he had occasion, in this connection, to write to the Via Condotti asking, on behalf of Mgr. Montini, for "all relevant information concerning the capacities, character, past and present situation of the Marquis Travaglini del Vergante, Viscount of Santa Rita, Magistral Grand Cross of Malta." This muffled blow was aimed not only at Travaglini but at Cardinal Canali, whose secret rivalry with Mgr. Montini was thus underlined.

At the same time that at least one of "Nicholas's" eyes and ears were thus being put out of commission, a sudden opportunity to complete the task seemed to offer. There was, in Milan, a sincere and valuable candidate for vows, Angelo de Mojana, a man still young and bold, a jurist and barrister by profession. His appointment to the Council was expected to be in May, and hence Thun's replacement, since the chapter would be complete without him. Every precaution was taken at the Magistral Palace to ensure secrecy. It was unfortunately difficult to insist upon the same in the case of the Congregation of Religious, who had nevertheless to be informed.

Although Cardinal Lavitrano was prefect of this congregation Cardinal Canali was by far the most influential of the cardinals composing it. Its secretary was Mgr. Pasetto, Archbishop of Iconium, a peace-loving octogenarian whose resistance was negligible. However, the Grand Prior of Rome, wanting a man of energy, got rid of him by having him appointed Alexandrian Patriarch of the Latins. The assistant secretary was given his place, one Father Larraona on whom the cardinal could rely. A Spanish monk, and a missionary son of the Sacred Heart of Mary, he burned with such fires of fanaticism that he seemed to resuscitate the spirit of the Inquisition. Thun's secret plaint was in the hands of this new Torquemada.

# V

THE COUNCIL MEETING at the Magistral Palace that morning was clearly an important one. Yet there was no question of Father Larraona, new suzerain of the Order; nor was Angelo de Mojana, unhoped-for third professed knight, to be discussed; as for Thun, his business was only touched on.

It was what was called an "extended council," that is, certain "honorary and devoted" bailiffs, members of the great Roman families, sat with the members of the Order's government.

As they arrived they looked in at the Chancellery for news while waiting for the grand master. They all wore dinner jackets, with the white cross on the left lapel. Rangoni, the chancellor, and the secretary, Cattaneo, assumed a mysterious air. They did not, they said, want to spoil the surprise.

Surprise began when Thun was seen to arrive, for he had been cutting meetings, sulking in his tent, ever since his disgrace. He had even been cutting high table, and taking his meals in a restaurant. His greetings were warm, but the response somewhat chilly.

Somebody muttered, "Nicholas has sent one of his eyes and one of his ears back."

Presently, it was announced that the grand master was ready. The bailiffs hastened to the little council chamber. Pallavicini opened the door communicating with the grand magistral quarters and said, "His Most Eminent Highness the Prince and Grand Master."

The nobility of the old man who entered the room was striking. People who were in a position to know claimed that no king, of those who still survived, was hedged by such regal divinity. Although such distinction does not always depend on blood, nothing was wanting to Prince Chigi Albani della Rovere on that score. No member of the Roman aristocracy could conjure up the memory of so many tiaras; his three names recalled four popes; five, if you counted his deceased wife's name, since she had been a princess Aldobrandini. His white hair, imperial beard, and straight nose, the gentleness of his expression and his voice, composed a whole both majestic and suave, complemented by the elegance and simplicity of his manners. He greeted the assembly with a nod and took his place at the head of the long, narrow table, the chancellor taking the opposite end. He crossed himself, an example followed by the rest, and pronounced the invocation: "*Sedes sapientiae!*"

"*Ora pro nobis!*" came the response.

For a moment they stood with lowered eyes in silent meditation, then took their seats. It was remarked that Prince Chigi's smile at Thun had been full of benevolence; but all believed they knew the reason for this. The Prince had long since transferred his gratitude toward the Grand Master Thun, under whom he had been admitted to take the vows, to the latter's nephew. Moreover he loved, in Thun, a man who had himself taken the vows without waiting for decline into old age. Furthermore he saw in him the last scion of one of the greatest Austrian families, as he, himself, was the last scion of one of the greatest Italian families. In him he saw reflected his own distinction and breeding; even the beard was the same. And when the chancellor explained the object of this extraordinary general meeting, it was realized that the grand master had had yet another reason for that special smile. He had been trying to anoint, in advance, the wound which was going to be reopened. He pretended to have forgotten that Thun's wound had become the Order's wound, and that, although it was but a matter of money, yet it might prove fatal.

Rangoni stroked his long, white moustache and began, in his bleating voice, "My dear colleagues, His Most Eminent Highness has called us together to deal with the matter of the Argentine wheat, which has taken an unexpected turn."

"A turn," said the grand master, "which brings a frivolous note into a very serious business and makes it more serious than ever. But carry on, my dear Luigi."

Prince Chigi's use of the Marquis Rangoni's Christian name made by no means the same impression as Cardinal Canali's use of Hercolani's or Thun's. It recalled the fact that the men present composed not only an order, but a family and a caste.

Thun had bowed his head at the words "Argentine wheat," but he slowly recovered his assurance, for the chancellor made no allusion whatsoever to the responsible party. True, the responsible party might hold himself not responsible at all, like Cardinal Canali. But he was certainly, and even more gravely, responsible for his secret recourse to the Congregation of Religious, indirect consequence of the business in question.

"As you know," Rangoni was saying, "we have the Marquis Dragonetti de Torres in Buenos Aires as our envoy extraordinary and minister plenipotentiary, charged with negotiating this business on a new footing. But now it seems that the Argentine government no longer regards him as *persona grata*. We have just been informed of the reason for this change in their attitude: the wife of the President of the Argentine Republic is demanding that she be made a Dame of Honour and Devotion."

Everyone, excepting the grand master and the Bailiff Thun, smiled.

"The matter is complicated," the chancellor continued, "by the fact that Prince von Furstenberg, who had been dealing with the business on the spot, promised Señora Perón that this favour would be granted her."

"Tassilo von Furstenberg is not a member of the Sovereign Council," Hercolani said, "so that his promise involves nobody but himself."

"That," Rangoni resumed, "was also the grand master's opinion. Consequently we asked the Marquis Dragonetti de Torres to explain to Señora Perón that to be appointed Dame of Honour and Devotion, sixteen quarterings are required, according to the rules of the Spanish association which apply in her case and until we have an Argentine association. She received our envoy, unofficially, and told him that, according to her informants, her case should not come under the rule of the Spanish association, but should be considered under the rule of the association *in gremio religionis*, which answers directly to the Grand Magistracy, and in which cases the question of quarterings is at our discretion. The Marquis Dragonetti de Torres did not fail to point out that the rules of admission *in gremio religionis* were equally strict, and that even supposing she were only required to prove eight quarterings, as in France, or four, as in Italy, either way it amounted to having to prove at least two centuries of nobility, so that her case would be no further forward. Señora Perón replied to this that her husband had not been required to produce all this paraphernalia of quarterings in order to be appointed Bailiff Grand Cross of Honour and Devotion *in gremio religionis*. The Marquis Dragonetti de Torres made answer that His Excellency, General Perón, had been admitted in his capacity as chief of state, and showed her, on our nominal roll, H.M. King Humbert, King Carol, Admiral Horthy, and President Auriol, all *in gremio religionis*. Señora Perón, however, pointed out, in the same roll, among the dames of honour and devotion, Mme Vincent Auriol, and asked if she had proved her eight quarterings. The Marquis Dragonetti de Torres replied that the elevation of the wife of the French President to the category reserved for persons of noble blood was a unique error in the history of the Order of Malta, and that the Sovereign Council had solemnly undertaken never to repeat it.

"The Marquis Dragonetti de Torres tells us in his letter that Señora Perón barely listened to what he had to say and that her eyes flashed as she read over our nominal roll where, alone of her kind, she found 'Mme Vincent Auriol, *née* Ancouturier,' between 'Her Excellency Maria Christina de Sotomayor Luna, *née* H.R.H. Princess of Bourbon-Naples' and 'H.R.H. the Infanta of Spain,

Princess Mercedes de Bagration, *née* de Bavière et Bourbon.' I should explain that Señora Perón is waging open war on the Argentine aristocracy and they on her, and that she had looked forward to her appointment as a triumph over them, though she would seem to have had an inflated idea of its extent.

"The Marquis Dragonetti de Torres was not, however, sent to the lady empty-handed: he offered her our Cross *au Mérite*, which was the best we could do for her. She asked whether this cross would place her on the same footing as the ladies of the European aristocracy and Mme Auriol. Our envoy was obliged to admit that holders of the Cross *au Mérite* were not really members of the Order, and that this *onorificènza* had been created for the benefit of persons who had deserved an honour but were not of noble blood, nor even Catholics. She immediately and indignantly rejected it. It was in vain that the Marquis Dragonetti de Torres insisted that members of noble families also felt it an honour to receive the cross; in vain, too, that he proved that this cross, Latin in form and on its red shield, was even older than our octagonal white cross; in vain, finally, that he pointed out that its black and red cordon was more becoming than the plain black ribbon. Señora Perón consigned it to the devil. There the matter rests and that is the situation which His Most Eminent Highness wishes to discuss with you.

"I must beg you to take into consideration only the laws and the interests of our Order. Señora Perón's past is no business of ours. In deciding whether to appoint her a dame of honour and devotion, we need not inquire whether she has, or has not, been guilty of—lapses."

"It is not a question of lapses," Hercolani said, "but of quarterings."

"Our dilemma," the grand master put in, "is all the more trying in that Señora Perón is ready, if we do appoint her, to hand over the hundred thousand tons of wheat for a song—possibly, in fact, for nothing. Giambattista de Torres makes that quite clear."

"Paris is worth a Mass," the Bailiff Thun suggested.

"Take care, Ferdinando," said the grand master. "It was a Protestant who said so. Weigh your words well."

Rarely had the weights in any scales been so unequal. One

hundred thousand tons of wheat against a small enamelled cross. Yet the debate did not last long. There was but one opinion: better to ruin the Order than yield to blackmail. The Duke Caffarelli, dean of the bailiffs grand cross of honour and devotion, and the Marquis Alberto Theodoli, their vice-dean and a senator of the Republic, declared themselves ready to sacrifice their personal fortunes: and this was not in order to spite a president's lady as amiable as she was estimable, but to uphold the rule of the Order, and that all the more strictly in that there was a precedent for weakness, in favour of another president's lady, quite as estimable and equally amiable.

"I expected no less of you," said the grand master.

And these words, altogether improbable in any other council chamber than that of the sovereign and military Order of Malta, brought tears to the eyes of all present, including the Bailiff Thun.

"What a business it is!" Del Balzo exclaimed, looking at Thun.

"Yet it was good business, too!" Thun riposted boldly.

"Good business for Nicholas!" Hercolani said.

The grand master rose: "*Oremus, fratres . . .*"


# VI


GENEALOGICAL QUESTIONS stood for interests more substantial than mere vanity at the Grand Magistracy. Two princely families, Barberini Colonna Sciarra and Barberini Sacchetti, both descended from nephews of Urban VIII, were at loggerheads over the only bailiwick remaining in the Grand Priory of Rome: St. Sebastian of the Palatine. The bull by means of which the Pope had constituted it, and declared it hereditary in his family, was surely the most fabulous of all the monuments of nepotism, at least in former times.

In the first place it gave the Bailiff of St. Sebastian the right to take part in electing the grand master, thus flouting the traditional usage of the Order whereby no post carrying authority could be hereditary. In the second place it ensured the hereditary quality of the bailiwick by complementing the dispositions of an earlier bull which had established an entail: if there was no legitimate male heir, the bailiwick went to the eldest illegitimate son, in default of these, to sons, legitimate or illegitimate, on the distaff side. These failing, it must go to sons who "shall seem to be natural heirs, legitimate or illegitimate, in any manner whatsoever, even born of an incestuous union, fathered by a priest, offspring of monk and nun, of a married woman, of a nun and a married man, of a priest or monk and a virgin." As if this were not sufficient, Urban VIII's imagination had not stopped short at parthenogenesis and generation between males: in order to guarantee the bailiwick of St. Sebastian of the Palatine to his heirs, he willed it to "heirs deriving from any kind of coitus whatsoever happening with the permission of God and through human frailty." The year of this bull was that in which Urban had Galileo arrested for daring to claim that the earth revolved.

Yet not all his foresight had been able to prevent quarrels breaking out between diverse Barberinis in the course of centuries, a whole series of quarrels which, following the terms of the bull, had been submitted to arbitration by the cardinals. Since Urban VIII's nephews were likewise hereditary bearers of the golden rose, these cases involved the sovereign pontiff of the time. As to that, Pius XI and Pius XII had both come down in favour of Prince Barberini Sacchetti, who belonged to the family in which the office of Grand Harbinger of the Sacred Apostolic Palaces was hereditary. The Barberini Colonna Sciarras had accepted this defeat in the matter of the golden rose, but would not give way in the matter of the bailiwick.

The genealogical specialist on the Sovereign Council was the Bailiff Taccone de Sitizano, representative of the Grand Priory of Naples and Sicily. His weakness was placing the Neapolitan and Sicilian nobility above all others. Sometimes, by way of baiting him, a famous story concerning certain Siculo-Neapolitan barons would be mentioned. Some rich commoners were imploring the King of Naples to make them barons; they gave a splendid party for his entertainment, played cards with him, and cheated him in the most barefaced style, until he exclaimed, "*Fottuti baroni!*"— 'F—cheats!"—the word *baroni* having that unfortunate second meaning. Whereupon his hosts flung themselves on their knees and began to praise and thank him. "We have your Majesty's word! Your Majesty has spoken—'*Fo tutti baroni*'—'I make you all barons.'" The King was so amused that he made it so.

Taccone, by way of answer to such witticisms, would cite the case of his colleague Del Balzo, a descendant of the lords of Baux in Provence who had followed Charles of Anjou to Naples. As for the Carafas, their name threw him into ecstasies, and he never entered the red salon where hung the portrait of the Carafa Grand Master, twice victor at the Dardanelles, without bowing twice. On the other hand admission to the Order of any Roman prince, any "conscript nobles," any patrician from Milan or Florence, or any descendant of Venetian or Genoese doges, had to be dragged out of him. He regarded all their patents as suspect.

He had recently become very heated against the audacious Mgr. Fiorenzo Angeli, supernumerary secret chamberlain and central assistant to the Catholic Men of Action's Union. This prelate had tried to monopolize the publishing of an "official historical list" of the Italian nobility, which the government had just authorized and which, by mutual agreement, was to be published by the Order of Malta and the union in question. When Mgr. Angeli had had the dossiers of the 8,000 noble families of Italy, not to mention the portrait of the Holy Father inscribed to the Italian nobility, removed from the offices of the Consulta Araldica by main force, Taccone threatened to buckle on the spurs and sword he had received, duly blessed, when he took his vows half a century ago. He was ready to challenge, if not the Monsignor, at least any other member of the Catholic Men of Action, to a duel. He reminded his colleagues that profession of knighthood entailed furnishing not only proofs of noble breeding, but of "chivalrous conduct"—which meant never having refused to fight a duel: there was a Catholic morality, certainly; but there was likewise an aristocratic morality. The Grand Magistracy and the Union signed a treaty of peace; the 8,000 dossiers were returned to the Consulta Araldica, and Taccone breathed again—for the 8,000 noble families, not the least of which was his own.

*          *          *

All this nobiliary agitation was crowned, that year, by a picturesque initiative. The famous Neapolitan clown, Toto, a descendant of Byzantine emperors, had unearthed a genealogist to establish, and judges—Neapolitan judges—to recognize, him as a prince *jure sanguinis*, with the right to be addressed as Imperial Highness. When he had himself announced at the Magistral Palace by that title, he was warned that he would only be received there under his usual name, Antonio de Curtis; but that did not deter him.

The footmen made more fuss of him than of any other Imperial Highness on the Order's nominal roll. Love of Naples and the circus had made Taccone offer to receive him; that, and the expectation of being vastly entertained. Contrary to expectation, he was captivated by the good taste of the man's style and his look of breeding, in spite of his comical behaviour. He was accompanied by an attorney carrying a portfolio bulging with papers, who at once began to do the talking: "In memory of his ancestor Giau Tommaso de Curtis, who became a Knight of Malta in 1582, His Imperial Highness would like to become a knight of honour and devotion. We have, here, his genealogy all duly attested."

Taccone smiled, remembering Señora Perón who had wanted, so desperately, to become a dame of honour and devotion. The lawyer had opened his portfolio and was unfolding photostats of various documents and parchments.

"Save yourself that trouble," Taccone said, "it is superfluous."

"You are casting doubt on these proofs?"

"God forbid!"

"I am glad to hear that, Excellency, for His Imperial Highness has more titles to knighthood in your order than any knight on your roll. To begin at the wrong end, here is the ministerial order of 1941 which declares him to be a peer."

"That goes without saying," Taccone said. "We shall find the order at the Consulta Araldica, whose archives we have recovered. But it is one thing to be a nobleman, quite another to become a knight of honour and devotion."

"Of course!" said the lawyer. "Now, here we have the first part of the genealogy, from the beginning. The Emperor Phocas, called the Victorious, died 610, to Otho II, called Rufus, died 983. And this is the second part, showing the posterity of Leo Europalatus Nicephoros III, and Barde III. And then, here is the third part, showing the branches of the Griffeos, or Griffos. Finally, the fourth, with the two branches of the Curtios or Curtis, issuing in His Imperial Highness, here present, Prince Antonio de Curtis de Griffo Focas Gagliardi."

"We are less exacting than this in the matter of proofs," Taccone said. "All we require, as you know, are four quarterings, whether on the male or on the distaff side. Indeed, I am bound to tell you that a decree issued, much against my will, by the grand master, provides for a dispensation in the case of the maternal or paternal grandmother's arms, where the nobility of the father goes back at least three centuries."

"Three centuries! A wretched three centuries!"—the exclamation, accompanied by a sneer, came in chorus from Toto and his lawyer.

The latter resumed, "His Imperial Highness, for all the brilliance of his lineage on the father's side, might have need of a dispensation on the distaff side. But we shall not need any such dispensation. Let others invoke it on behalf of their grandmothers! We make our claim according to the decree which entails acceptance, 'as a knight of honour and devotion, upon proof of paternal nobility only, any descendant of an historical and illustrious family with a record of four hundred and fifty years of feudal or patrician nobility.' This decree opened your doors to the flower of Italian chivalry, and the proof, called the English proof, won you the flower of the English Catholic peerage; they can hardly fail, then, to let *us* in, since what we offer you is not three hundred years, nor even four hundred and fifty years of nobility, but one thousand three hundred years of imperial lineage."

"I claim no credit," Toto said, modestly.

"I can guess," went on his voluble pleader, "that proofs like ours are not offered to you every day of the week. But, if during too many centuries, the name which my august client is reviving has lain dormant in obscurity——"

Taccone raised a hand for silence. Putting on his glasses, he said, "I am going to read you the conditions established for taking proofs of nobility for the Order of Malta, established since the reign of the Grand Master Wignacourt at the beginning of the seventeenth century."

He turned to an old in-folio volume which he had brought down with him "in case," and opened it.

"'The commissioners will ask the witnesses——'"

"I am both advocate and witness," the lawyer interrupted.

"'—if the candidate for knighthood is noble by name and arms——'"

"What more do you want?" the lawyer cried, displaying a large coloured blazon on an ermine field, surmounted by the imperial Byzantine crown, while Toto turned a signet ring bearing his arms, on his finger; "'—if he was born in wedlock——'?"

The lawyer announced the date of Toto's parents' marriage, and that of his birth.

"Mark," said Taccone, "that 'the natural sons of kings, absolute princes, dukes and peers of France, grandees of Spain, and Italian princes who have struck their own coinage can be received as knights.' Emperors are not mentioned but are implied."

"A fig for your bastardies," Toto said.

"'—the candidate for knighthood can in no case be accepted if he is a descendant of Jews, Marrands, Moslems, or Saracens.'"

"My blood is pure," Toto said.

"Note, however," Taccone went on, "that the descendants of Jews converted two centuries ago can be accepted."

"I am glad to hear that members of the Orthodox faith are not excluded," the lawyer said. "As it happens, His Imperial Highness's ancestors have been Catholic for a thousand years. But if we go back further we find that an ancestress, the Empress Theodora, the second of that name, was canonized in the Orthodox church. I do not imagine that will count against us."

"Not in the least," the bailiff replied, "especially as Orthodox Christians can be accepted for knighthood immediately following their conversion, not to mention the fact that one of our grand masters, the Tsar Paul I, was Orthodox."

"We are aware of it," the lawyer replied.

"'The candidate for knighthood,'" Taccone continued, "'can in no case be accepted if he has been guilty of murder or has led an evil life in the world, or has been pursued by the officers of justice.'"

Toto and his attorney sketched a gesture of contempt.

"'Item, should he not be sound in mind and body.'"

"The first I prove every day," Toto said, "and can prove the second at a moment's notice."

"'Item, if either his father or mother or any grandparent be in possession of any land, property, jurisdiction, or any other asset belonging to the Order.'"

"Not as far as we know," the lawyer said. "I will not, however, conceal the fact that the founder of the Griffeo or Griffo branch of the family, having removed to Naples at the beginning of the twelfth century, may, in view of his high position at court, have profited from the Emperor Frederick Barbarossa's spoliations."

"A dispensation would not be out of the question," the bailiff said, "but I have not yet done with the reasons for excluding candidates. 'Item, if the candidate be indebted to any person for a large sum of money.'"

"My client has not a debt in the world."

"I will pass over the clause relating to candidates who have 'been engaged in any form of trading, banking, or money-changing,' since that impediment ceased to be one when the rule became obsolete, and even when it was in force there was an automatic dispensation for the principal mercantile cities. But unhappily, Signor de Curtis, there never has been and cannot be any dispensation in the case of the final rule, which touches you directly. 'The candidate cannot be accepted if either he or his parents have ever practised one of the mechanical, vile, abject, or prohibited arts.'"

Toto looked stupefied.

"How can that touch us?" the lawyer demanded.

"'The mechanical art'—that is self-explanatory; 'prohibited arts' has reference to witches, magi, magicians, fortune-tellers, astrologers; 'abject arts'—that refers to panders. 'Vile arts'—I'm sorry, but that means juggling."*

"Are you calling me a juggler?"

* *Jonglerie:* it presumably includes all the arts of a public "variety" artist. [E.H.]

"Nobody admires you more than I do, for we are fellow citizens. But my admiration cannot change the rules of our Order."

"Are you not aware," the lawyer asked, "that in England great actors are often ennobled?"

"Signor de Curtis might well have been our greatest actor, but he chose to follow a different course. The 'variety artist' is, at least according to our interpretation, the heir to those jugglers, ballad singers, and mimes who amused Signor de Curtis's ancestors in their palaces and castles. I bid you good day, gentlemen."

"We shall bring an action!" the lawyer cried. "It would be a little too much if a man who is pretender to an imperial crown cannot pretend to knighthood!"

"Come, my legal friend," Toto said, "do not let us make even bigger fools of ourselves."

They marched out of the room with their heads held high, after looking the old bailiff haughtily up and down. But for all the imperial dignity in the look and bearing of the illustrious "juggler," his mouth sketched the movement of that contemptuous noise which the Neapolitans call a *pernacchio*.

# VII

THE BAILIFF CONESTABILE DELLA STAFFA, Delegate for Charitable Works, was less active than the Bailiff Taccone, but his great age had not deprived him of his wits or spirit. As assistant he had a retired general who, with an ex-admiral in charge of the Order's monthly journal, and a former Italian ambassador in charge of the Foreign Office, composed the Via Condotti's general staff of retired officers.

When he had finished his duties in the Charitable Works Office, the Bailiff Conestabile, supporting himself by leaning against the wall lest he fall, would move into an anteroom on the second floor and sit down facing a model of the "Great Carrack." Passionately absorbed in the history of the Order, he seemed to find it symbolized or summed up in that fabulous vessel, taken from the

Turks by the Knights of Rhodes and, rechristened the *Saint Anne*, used to carry the Grand Master Villiers de l'Isle Adam to Malta when he went to take possession of that island. The old gentleman never wearied of looking at its silver cannon, its forest of rigging, and its red flags and pennants with their white crosses—Latin crosses emblematic of the Order, and octagon crosses for the grand master's emblem. Did he dream of the fleet which, for centuries, had been the West's rampart against the Orient? Represented now by no more than this toy, it seemed to have undergone much the same transformation as Malta's prehistoric elephants, which had been no bigger than a deer. But the Bailiff Conestabile could console himself with the thought that the historic fleet had been replaced by one more up to date—the seventy aircraft entrusted to the Order of Malta by Italy for life-saving in the Mediterranean.

That red flag with its white Latin cross, which had been flown at Jerusalem and St. John d'Acre, at Cyprus and Rhodes, at Tripoli and Malta—surely it symbolized the same spirit today as it flew above hospitals and almshouses? It was still the emblem of an aristocratic power at the service of Catholic Christendom. It had always been so, even at the nadir of the Order's history, when the Grand Master Hompesch, respecting his knightly oath never to bear arms against Christians, capitulated to Bonaparte. And the flag, the most ancient in Europe, had become the flag of two kingdoms, by a concession made by a grand master of Rhodes to the House of Savoy and to the Grand Priory of Denmark. When President Doumergue gave official recognition to the Order of Malta, the Comte de Pierredon flew the Order's flag, whereupon the Danish Minister, not so well informed as the French Ambassador, protested, invoking the law of nations which forbids any country to use another's colours. To which Malta's minister replied that the Order would be generous and not require the Danes to change their flag.

By such memories as these was the Bailiff Conestabile captivated. It was to them that he owed the privilege of remaining aloof from cares and intrigues of state. It was his belief that the Great Carrack, built for *l'alto mare*, ran no risk of shipwreck in mere *canali*. A long past of glory seemed to him to guarantee everlasting life to the Order of Malta.

The aged scholar was thus able to confine himself to perfecting his erudition. This had enabled him to rediscover a tale as pleasant as it was instructive, belonging in time to a period a year or two earlier than the capture of the Great Carrack. It was the only bravura piece in his repertoire, and he was forever adding a detail here, a refinement there, gathered from some old French chronicle or from the diary of some Venetian ambassador. It was his custom to tell this story to visiting knights as the best of all the Order of Malta's many stories. It may be that, thinking to amuse them, in fact he shocked them; but, unwittingly, he was preparing them for a new tale, one that was very soon about to begin.

# VIII

BAJAZET, THE ELDEST SON of Mohammed II, having ascended the throne, his younger brother, Zizim, who was then twenty years old, disputed his claim, and having been defeated in two battles, asked asylum of the Knights of Rhodes, who were at war with the Sublime Porte. The Grand Prior of Castille was sent out to welcome him. The prince arrived in rags, with two servants as his only attendants and the imperial seal as his only luggage.

Provided with clothes and a turban by the Grand Prior of Castille, Prince Zizim disembarked at Rhodes over a gangway with a cloth of gold awning, The grand master, Pierre d'Aubusson, who only two years before had driven off an attack launched by the armies of the Sultan, the prince's father, was there to receive him, mounted, among the Order's dignitaries. He greeted him with a compliment, to which Prince Zizim replied by placing his finger three times in his mouth, a gesture which, among the Turks, signified respectful silence. He was conducted to the French "inn," that is to the palace occupied by the knights of that "tongue", and was carried into it on the shoulders of his two servants, which was another Turkish custom. There followed a whole series of concerts, tournaments, and feasts in his honour.

Bajazet, appalled at the idea of his rival among his worst enemies, made them proposals for peace. They stipulated that he must pay them, at once and thereafter on the first of August every year, 45,000 Venetian ducats—about £100,000—by way of board and lodging for Prince Zizim, who was to become "guest in perpetuity to the Grand Master of Rhodes." Thus the defender of the Cross was to become a pensioner of the Crescent.

The Grand Turk, having garroted the Grand Vizier for reproaching him about this treaty, sent two relics to the grand master, by way of persuading him to be a good watchdog: one of the eight hundred thorns from Our Lord's crown; and the right hand of St. John the Baptist, patron saint of the Knights of St. John. This hand, which had baptized the Saviour, had its index finger, which had pointed to Him, still and forever pointing; it had been found at Constantinople by Mohammed II. Before installing it in the conventual church, the grand master decreed an inquiry into its authenticity. For it was known that apart from the head, which was kept in Rome, the Forerunner's remains had been buried at Antioch and there burnt by Julian the Apostate; and that the ashes were in Genoa. The Bishop of Rhodes, titular Archbishop of Colossus, learned that the right hand might, however, have been saved, thanks to St. Luke the Evangelist who, at Antioch itself, had piously stolen it. It remained at Antioch until Constantine Porphyrogenesis placed it in the imperial treasury. Miracles were attributed to it: one of the finger bones, flung into a dragon's maw, had killed the monster instantaneously; carried in procession up a hill on the day of the exaltation of the Holy Cross, and borne aloft, the hand opened or closed, thus indicating whether the year was to be a good or a bad one. Reassured by this information, the grand master had the hand set in a splendid reliquary and deposited it in the Church of St. John. Throughout all the time it was at Rhodes the Order celebrated the translation of its holy patron's hand every 5th of December. As for the Holy Thorn, it had been recognized as authentic without hesitation: it had been noted that it was green, like the thorns from the same crown sold by the Emperor Baldwin to the Saint-King Louis of France, and for which the King built the Sainte-Chapelle. More modestly, the grand master had the thorny relic set in a medallion of gold and rubies.

Prince Zizim, to whom Christendom owed these treasures, was "a majestic and regal youth who ate without chewing, drank highly spiced wines despite the Koran, went frequently to the baths and bathed daily in the sea, where he stripped without shame or respect." He immersed himself likewise in music and poetry, and corresponded, in Persian verse, with the grand signor his brother, with his mother the sultana, who had remained in Turkey, and with his wife, who had taken refuge with the Sultan of Egypt.

Bajazet did not confine himself to sending Venetian ducats, Christian relics, and Persian verses to Rhodes. He also sent several hired assassins with orders to dispatch his brother to the next world. They were seized; but the grand master, made uneasy by these attempts, decided that it would be desirable to remove a prisoner, who brought him such fine gifts and so large an income, away from Turkish waters. Prince Zizim was just as anxious to be gone: he was hoping to be handed over to the King of Hungary, called "the scourge of the Ottomans," who was offering to engineer his return, in victorious triumph, to Constantinople. Before his departure he was required to sign two treaties: in one he gave the grand master powers to negotiate on his behalf with Bajazet; in the second he promised that, if he recovered the imperial throne, he would grant the Order an alliance in perpetuity and 150,000 gold crowns "by way of defraying all the expenses he had given rise to." The vice-chancellor of the Order had proved to the most reverend lords in council and in twelve pages of Latin, that in removing their guest to a safer place than Rhodes, they were not breaking the promise they had made to the sultan.

The grand master entrusted Prince Zizim to his nephew, Guy de Blanchefort, Grand Prior of Auvergne and a future grand master, who assured his prisoner that they were setting off for Hungary. But instead of disembarking him at some Dalmatian port, the ship and its escorting fleet dropped anchor in the Bay of Villefranche in the Duke of Savoy's territory. There, Guy de Blanchefort awaited orders from his uncle, who had asked Louis XI for permission to entertain Prince Zizim at his fief of Bourganeuf

in Auvergne. The King's reply did not reassure him: Guy
de Blanchefort was instructed to avoid French territory. Remaining in Savoy he went first to Exiles, then in succession to Saint-
Jean-de-Maurienne, Chambéry, and Rumilly, Commandery of
the Order, where Prince Zizim was visited by the young duke,
Charles II, at that time fifteen years of age. He took pity on the
prisoner and wanted to contrive his escape. He would be obliged,
in that event, to cross Louis XI's frontier, but the situation was
critical: an ambassador from Bajazet had arrived in Provence,
with orders to claim custody of Prince Zizim. The King, unwill-
ing to receive an infidel envoy, instructed him to stop at Riez
and to make the bishop of that diocese his intermediary. That
prelate began by trying to convert the ambassador, with the argument that, baptized, he would be allowed to go at least as far as
Plessis-lez-Tours; but unable to persuade the other to hear him,
resigned himself to doing the listening. Bajazet's generous offer
was then conveyed to him: he would release several thousand
French monks who were prisoners of the Turks. The bishop
having given him to understand that he was impressed, the
ambassador added that there would also be a large sum of
money.

Alarmed at what was going on, the Grand Prior of Auvergne
called upon the Grand Prior of Saint-Gilles to help him, he being
the most powerful member of the Order in France, and Lord of
Rochinard in Dauphiné. Prince Zizim was taken to Rochinard,
an impregnable castle whence he was shortly delivered by the
death of Louis XI. The Lords of Sassenage and of Montchenu
thereafter entertained the august captive who, according to legend,
inspired an intense passion in the bosoms of their respective
daughters. Next, Guy de Blanchefort took him to his mother's
house, she being Souveraine of Aubusson, and finally to Bourganeuf where the tower which he inhabitated is still pointed out to
visitors. There he spent two years, composing an account of his
captivity in verse.

Bajazet's ambassador had gone home, but Charles VIII, the
new King of France, was aware of what the grand master's guest
at Bourganeuf was worth to him and expressed a wish that the
grand magistral hospitality might become royal. The Knights of

Malta hurried their prisoner into the better-defended castle of Monteil-le-Vicomte, which belonged to the widow of the grand master's brother, and subsequently, to be quite on the safe side, removed him again, to Morterolles, under the warranty of the Bishop of Limoges, Barton de Montbas. Thus the Church of France found itself defending a son of Mohammed II against the King of France, in order that a French grand master of the Order of Rhodes should continue receiving a Moslem pension.

Pope Sixtus IV caused the grand master to be warned that it was sacrilege to accept money from infidels, but that if the money were passed on to the Church, or better still paid directly to the Church, the sacrilege would cease. The grand master replied that the income in question was being used to repair the damage done by Mohammed II's troops to the Island of Rhodes. In order to soften the grand master and win over the knights, who were obliged to recite 150 paternosters a day, Sixtus reduced this quota, allowing them to recite no more than the minor office of the Virgin, "excepting when they were on horseback."

His successor, Innocent VIII, proceeded more energetically; he was hardly installed on St. Peter's throne before he summoned the grand master to deliver up Prince Zizim, "for the salvation of the Keys." It was in vain that the grand master sent the Pope "a balas ruby of 500 crowns and a vase of real balm": Innocent VIII again demanded that Prince Zizim be handed over to him. To this renewed demand he joined a bull, confirming "all the privileges, indulgences, and liberties conferred on the Order of St. John by the popes and maintaining all its franchises and immunities in the matter of tithes, novales, first fruits, quitrents, and other duties." But, the grand master having asked for a cardinal's hat for his younger brother, the Bishop of Carcassonne, the Pope informed him that the hat depended upon Prince Zizim.

Nor was he the only potentate to take an interest in Prince Zizim. The grand master hardly knew which way to turn. The King of Castille was requiring him to deliver up the prisoner, recalling the role played by the Grand Prior of Castille in the Prince's arrival at Rhodes; the King of Naples wanted him, in order to preseve Calabria and Sicily from the ravages of the Turks; the King of Hungary's ambassador asked for him, to undertake a crusade; the Sultan of Egypt's ambassador, likewise, to hold Bajazet, who was making war on him, in check; and Charles VIII's ambassador—on the grounds that the "guest in perpetuity" was in France.

These monarchs were aware that the grand master would be losing a considerable annual income if he agreed to their requests. They therefore had compensations to suggest: the King of Naples offered 20,000 crowns, a matter of £30,000 in our values; the King of Hungary, 25,000; the King of Castille, 30,000; the Sultan of Egypt crushingly outbid all these with an offer of 1,000,000 golden ducats—about £1,500,000. Charles VIII did not offer cash down, but was willing that the grand master should save money, by exempting the Knights of St. John from payment of "all custom dues, road tolls, bridge tolls, harbour dues, ship money." And by granting the Order "permission to load their ships in the kingdom and obtain provision of arms, munitions, horses,' gold and silver coin, woollens, canvas, corn, and other victuals for Rhodes without payment of tax, excise, custom, truce money, or any other exaction whatsoever."

The grand master judged that the moment had come to send two envoys extraordinary to Rome: the Bailiff De Morée and the Vice-Chancellor of the Order. They were under orders to make clear to the Pope the nature of the moral scruples and material interests which his demand called in question. Innocent VIII understood what they were getting at: he offered the grand master 12,000 ducats; and he drafted two more bulls, the first confirming the Knights of St. John in the privilege granted them by Gregory VIII and known as the Gregorian, the second "prohibiting under the severest penalties, any alienation, appropriation, or leasing of property belonging to the Order." Moreover he undertook never to act as if vacant commanderies of the Order were in his gift, an abuse practised by the Roman court and against which the Council of Rhodes had been obliged to protest all too often. But, in the very act both of defending and himself promising to respect the patrimony of St. John, he once again required the grand master to alienate Prince Zizim, over the possession of whose person the Pope, four Christian princes, and one Mohammedan prince were squabbling.

The Bailiff De Morée and the Vice-Chancellor of the Order were shrewd men: they advised Innocent VIII that if he wanted to come off triumphant, his best way was to show the knights favour. He therefore gave them a dispensation to ignore the prohibition against commercial intercourse with the infidel, authorizing them to trade with Syria and Egypt. The grand master having responded by complaining that the benefits of this were hypothetical and not to be relied on, the Pope offered something better—a sure and immediate benefit: he incorporated the property of other orders, which he had been about to suppress, with that of St. John, to wit, the Order of the Holy Sepulchre, the Order of St. Lazarus of Bethlehem, and the Order of the Maison Dieu de Montmorillon. Thus it was that Prince Zizim was at the bottom of the conflict which, in mid-twentieth century, was about to break out between the Order of Malta and the Holy See, over the Order of the Holy Sepulchre.

When Innocent VIII had thrown in a cardinal's hat for the grand master, as well as one for the Bishop of Carcassonne, the Bailiff De Morée and the Vice-Chancellor of the Order said that they had nothing more to ask. They called upon Cardinal d'Anjou, patron of the Order, to draw up a formal contract with the Pope. On the Order's part—cession of their "guest in perpetuity," rendering of an account for twelve years' hospitality, two letters from Bajazet guaranteeing payment, a large collection of Persian poetry, and the seal of the Ottoman Empire bearing Prince Zizim's name. The grand master wrote to the kings of France, Castille, Naples, and Hungary announcing that he was "obeying the Holy Father for the good of all Christendom."

Meanwhile, fearing that Charles VIII might intercept Prince Zizim between Bourganeuf and Provence, he required the Pope to ensure the prisoner's safe-conduct himself. A nuncio set off for France at once. Charles VIII was willing to be reasonable, but on certain conditions: the Archbishop of Bordeaux was to be made a cardinal; Prince Zizim was to be guarded exclusively by French knights; and the Pope was not to cede him to anyone else, or if he did, was to pay the crown of France 10,000 ducats.

Prince Zizim was embarking at Toulon in the Rhodes treasure ship while an ambassador from the King of Hungary and another from the Sultan of Egypt were dropping anchor in Marseilles. Their object was to propose to Charles what they had already proposed to the grand master—20,000 crowns and 1,000,000 ducats respectively. The Hungarian, as representative of a Catholic, and even Apostolic, monarch, was received with full honours at Amboise. He got no good of them, however, for he was imprudent enough to admit that he had the money on him. Charles VIII pretended not to know that Prince Zizim had left the kingdom, and pocketed his cousin the Apostolic King of Hungary's 25,000 crowns, and treated the ambassador magnificently until his archers returned to announce that they had arrived too late. The Egyptian ambassador who, according to the protocol of the most Christian court, had been allowed no farther than Riez, had been wise enough to bring nothing but promises.

He had hardly taken leave of the bishop, without letting himself be converted, when another infidel of consequence arrived at the episcopal palace. This was another ambassador from Bajazet, come to tempt Charles VIII as his predecessor had tempted Louis XI, albeit in vain. He proved as indifferent to the bishop's evangelical zeal as his two co-religionists, but the proposals he was charged to make were, certainly, such as to arouse episcopal, and even regal, enthusiasm: he offered in exchange for Prince Zizim or a promise that the prince should never quit the soil of France, "all the relics of the prophet Jesus, of His apostles, and of His saints, which were to be found at Constantinople; and the Kingdom of Jerusalem once he, Bajazet, had conquered Egypt." But Charles VIII was dreaming of other crowns; and the treasure ship of Rhodes, with its escort of royal galleys, continued on its way to Italy.

Prince Zizim having disembarked at Civita Vecchia, an escort of 12,000 horse bore him in triumph to Rome. The cardinals, to do him honour, sent their hats, mounted on their mules, to meet him. He entered the city by the Porteuse gate, preceded by the Lord de Faucon, Ambassador of France, and by the Viscount de Monteil, another of the grand master's nephews. Franceschetto Cybo, a natural son of the Pope, rode at his right hand, and Guy de Blanchefort at his left. And the people of Rome crowded to stare at the son of the redoubtable Mohammed II, "whose corpse, flung into hell, increased the sufferings of the damned by its stench." He was given a magnificent apartment in St. Peter's palace, near to that of the Pope to whom, on the following day, he was presented by the French ambassador and the Grand Prior of Auvergne in solemn audience. He refused to kiss the Pope's foot, but nevertheless the Holy Father received him well. After which Prince Zizim withdrew to add one more page to the poetical account of his life. Fêted by the cardinals and by Roman society, he declared himself to be better off than at Bourganeuf. Innocent VIII, faithful to his promises, immediately made the Grand Master of Rhodes and the Archbishop of Bordeaux cardinals— the Bishop of Carcassonne having died in the interim.

Meanwhile, the Pope had informed the Grand Turk that, as the new possessor of Prince Zizim, he expected to receive his pension. He had added to his message that he wanted three years' payments in advance as it displeased him to be in too frequent financial intercourse with the Grand Seraglio. Bajazet required a promise that Prince Zizim would not be given up to anyone else, and having received it sent his ambassador, Mustapha Bey, with 120,000 Venetian ducats. Innocent VIII expressed surprise: the sum should have been 135,000 ducats. The ambassador explained that according to a secret clause 5,000 ducats per annum were reserved "for the grand master's dish"—for which no substitution of "the Holy Father's dish" had been arranged. The Pope learned a great deal besides: that the grand master had received 20,000 ducats from Prince Zizim's wife and from his mother, "for the expenses of his journey"; 20,000 florins from the Sultan of Egypt; and even 10,000 crowns from the King of Hungary, whose good faith seems to have been put to the proof all round. Innocent VIII wrote the cardinal grand master a sharp letter. Be that as it may, however, the vicar of Christ was, thenceforth, among the pensioners of Mohammed's lieutenant.

The chronicle tells us that despite the pension in question, equivalent to £100,000 a year at today's values, Prince Zizim complained of not getting enough to eat. And the account books do, in fact, show that of the 40,000 ducats a year paid over by Bajazet, only 3,000 were applied to his brother's housekeeping. Doubtless, the sultan was afraid that the prince might escape and

stir up trouble, for he went to some lengths in conciliating his
new jailer. Just as he had sent St. John the Baptist's right hand,
and the Holy Thorn, to the Grand Master of Rhodes, he sent the
Holy Reed, the Holy Lance, and the Holy Sponge, sacred instruments of the Passion, to the Pope. Innocent VIII, not less prudent
than the grand master, had their authenticity investigated. In the
case of the Holy Lance some doubt was justifiable, since two were
already known to exist. It was ascertained that the one in the
Sainte-Chapelle, at Paris, was only the point; and that the one
at Moremburg was really the lance of Constantine the Great
embellished with nails from the True Cross. Satisfied, the Pope
gave orders that the Holy Lance, the Holy Sponge, and the Holy
Reed be deposited in the Church's treasury. It is thus thanks to
Prince Zizim that every Good Friday all Christendom can admire,
from a tribune erected in the basilica of St. Peter's, these three
invaluable relics, shown annually on that day. The inscription on
his tomb, whereon Innocent VIII is shown prone, clutching the
Lance in his failing hand, tells us that it was "sent as a gift
by Bajazet, tyrant of the Turks," but fails to mention Prince
Zizim.

Meanwhile the Sultan of Egypt was offering the Pope 60,000
ducats for the privilege of becoming *troisiéme larron*. Innocent
VIII consulted both his bankers and his casuists. Would he do
better to get his hands at once on the lump sum offered by Egypt,
or rest content with the income paid by Turkey? Could one yield
up a person one had promised to keep, and that to the enemy of
the recipient of the said promise? And if so, was he obliged to
return that part of the pension received in advance? To what
extent must undertakings given to unbelievers be regarded as licit
and binding? There was a Roman proverb which said, "He who
is not a good Turk is not a good Christian"; had the chief among
Christians the right not to be a good Turk?

At the same time the King of Castille's ambassadors, and others
from the King of Naples, were both at the Pope with the same
object as the Sultan of Egypt. And a new embassy from Hungary
had arrived in Rome with attractive offers. The argument, however, was determined otherwise: at short intervals following each
other the Kings of Naples, Hungary, and Castille, and Innocent

himself, went to join Sixtus IV and the Bishop of Carcassonne—unless it was Mohammed II they joined.

Cardinal Borgia, who had just become patron of the Order, was elected Pope as Alexander VI; and Charles VIII of France announced that he would lay claim to the throne of Naples in opposition to Alphonso of Aragon, and thereafter conquer Greece and other kingdoms. The new pontiff knew the interest which the French king took in Prince Zizim. He immediately sent the Nuncio Bozzardo to Constantinople to announce that he needed 60,000 ducats to defend the prince against that monarch, who would certainly not fail to try to capture him. Bajazet then sent Alexander the most unheard-of proposal that any nuncio ever had to communicate to a pope. Let him "withdraw his guest-in-perpetuity from the anguish of this world and dispatch him to the eternal rest of the next." Upon delivery of the body the Sultan would pay 300,000 ducats, "in order"—as he wrote to the Pope—"that Your Greatness may buy estates to provide for your sons." This proposal was sworn to "in the name of the true God"; Bozzardo had also had it sworn on the New Testament.

Upon receiving news that the French army had crossed the Alps, Alexander VI had Prince Zizim put under lock and key in the castle of St. Angelo. He sent the prince's French guards back to Rhodes with a certificate of faithful service, and replaced them with his own nephews, one of whom, it is true, was a Knight of St. John.

Shortly thereafter Charles VIII entered Rome and Alexander VI, fearful of being made a prisoner, sought refuge with Prince Zizim in St. Angelo. Negotiations were opened between besieger and besieged. Terms discussed stipulated not only that "the Pope would act as a good father to the King and the King as a good son to the Pope," but that "the Pope would deliver the Turk into the King's hands; that the King would return the Turk to the Pope when he had no more use for him; that by way of surety for his undertaking to deliver the Turk, the Pope would deliver the Cardinal of Valentino (to wit, Cesare Borgia, his natural son) to the King as a hostage; that, as sureties for the ultimate return of the said Turk, the King was to give hostages to the Pope; that the King would undertake to obtain from the Grand Master of

Rhodes consent to the Turk's transfer; that the Pope would continue to receive the pension regularly paid by the Grand Turk. . . ."
Finally, and not actually included in the treaty, the King was to receive a cardinal's hat for the Bishop of St. Malo, his military adviser. And Prince Zizim, surprised to find himself shifted from St. Peter's palace to St. Angelo, and from St. Angelo set at liberty, all in so short a time, kissed his liberator's hand and shoulder.

He asked, in all innocence, permission to go to Egypt where his wife had been waiting for him for thirteen years, with a son he had never seen. But Charles VIII had not liberated him to lose him, and Prince Zizim, composing poetic lamentations over his misfortunes, set out between the King of France and the Cardinal of Valentino.

Alas, and thrice alas! At Terracino he was stricken with a "mysterious flux of the stomach," and at Capua, shortly thereafter, he died. The Cardinal of Valentino having promptly taken himself off, it was assumed that he had poisoned Prince Zizim: some say that this was to enable the Pope to keep his promise to Bajazet that he would yield up the prince to nobody, and to receive his blood money; others, that the Grand Turk himself had paid for the cardinal's services, using the Venetians as intermediaries. Charles VIII, weeping with rage, had Prince Zizim's body enclosed in a coffin of lead; with it was coffined not, in his case, a pension, but the principal hope for his eastern ambitions.

In life Prince Zizim had been a thing at auction; he was in the same case for some time after his death. The Pope begged for his body, saying that he was responsible for it in the eyes of God. He had not forgotten the condition on which he might expect Bajazet's 300,000 ducats: his son, not himself, might actually have done the deed; but he was still Prince Zizim's owner, even by his treaty with Charles VIII, and therefore the only person entitled to hand over the prince's remains. Meanwhile he concealed the death from the sultan; as did Charles VIII, with a view to intimidating him. But Bajazet had the news by way of Venice and, only too glad to have done with the Borgias, father and son, asked Charles VIII for the body. He knew, of course, that the King would not deliver it gratis either. Charles, however, was satisfied with 5,000 ducats, which were paid over at Gaeta, where the sultan's envoys had been on the watch. Meanwhile Charles was forced to beat a hasty retreat, leaving the Kingdom of Naples to Frederick of Aragon, who seized Prince Zizim's body before the Turkish envoys could get it on board ship. An argument broke out again, this time between the Pope, the King of Naples, and the sultan. It lasted four years but the King of Naples held out against the Pope. At last, after many journeys undertaken by the Pasha of Valona and despite all the intrigues of the Nuncio Bozzardo, the coffin was shipped aboard an Ottoman vessel at San Cataldo and "the grand signor had the pleasure of beholding his brother Zizim's body."

It was a pleasure to which his son, Suliman the Magnificent, gave singular expression when he conquered Rhodes twenty-two years later: in the presence of his army he had Zizim's son and grandson, captured in the island where they had resorted to the protection of another grand master, sawn in two. Such was the unhappy end to the posterity of a Moslem prince whose own life had been so wretched, and who had given Christian Europe many precious relics, the Sacred College three cardinals, millions of money to two popes and a Grand Master of Rhodes, before his own sad end; not counting the immense sums which had been bid for his person or his assassination. A prince, moreover, whose name meant "Love."

# IX

THE ORDER'S ATTORNEY, the wily Gazzoni, having been sent to the Argentine, settled the business of the wheat after three months of negotiations. He arranged for a postponement of the delivery date, and in the time thus gained the Grand Magistracy persuaded the West German Republic to take the 100,000 tons off their hands. The Order would only have to pay storage and brokerage charges, which were, however, considerable. Crosses *au mérite* were lavishly distributed and the Marquis Dragonetti de Torres even persuaded Señora Perón to accept one.

It remained to discover the financial means which would enable the German government to pay in unblocked dollars. Cattaneo was sent to Paris to sound the French government, his suitcase full of crosses *au mérite*. The ground had been prepared by the higher-class decoration which the grand master had distributed in presidential and Quai d'Orsay circles two years ago. The Papal Nuncio had been instructed to make himself useful, and the Order's minister and its French association did all in their power to help. The mission was successful.

Before leaving Rome, the Secretary of the Chancellery had taken part in a piece of business which determined the fate of the author of the imbroglio he was going to settle. Prince Chigi had agreed to sign the Bailiff Thun's dismissal. All that was needed was ratification of the decree by the Sovereign Council— scrupulous fairness was carried so far that the Grand Prior of Lombardy-Venetia, the Bailiff Da Porto, was entrusted with calling for this dismissal. So that Thun's fate was settled barring some formalities which had to wait upon the more pressing business of the Argentine wheat.

In mid-April Cattaneo stopped at Vicenza, on his way back from Paris, to call on the Grand Prior of Lombardy-Venetia, who lived not far from there, at Trissino. At the foot of the hill on which the grand prior's villa was built was a private aerodrome belonging to the multimillionaire industrialist Marzotto, a knight and an officer of the Order. A number of small private aircraft were flying round the perimeter, suggesting a world very different to that of ancient nobility and coats of arms. Their owner had, however, been made a count by Italy's penultimate king: he was one of the most prosperous among those representatives of the business aristocracy who justified the Order's claim that it was open to talent, at least among the Maecenases of the age.

The grand prior, very old and broken, was sitting, wrapped in rugs, in the sunshine; his armchair was black, and the aircraft he was watching were white. He was dictating a long letter intended for the grand master, his valet acting as his secretary: it was a list of his complaints against Thun. When Cattaneo told him that the decree of dismissal was already signed, his face lit up. He asked Cattaneo to write three letters for him when he reached Rome—one for the grand master, one for the chancellor, and one for Thun, setting forth the terms of the decree, and to send them to Trissino for his signature.

The necessary having been done, the grand master decided to call an extraordinary meeting of the Sovereign Council, and fixed May 5 as the date. Letters were sent to all members, convoking the meeting.

On May 5, Thun, who was at Povo, his château near Trent, did not put in an appearance when the Council met. Maybe this was a source of relief, for the first business on the agenda was his dismissal.

During the meeting the news arrived that the Bailiff Da Porto had just died: thus the decreee of Thun's dismissal, officially moved by the grand prior's letter, was being ratified at the very moment when the man who had been so earnest in promoting it lay dying. The second item on the agenda was another decree appointing Angelo de Mojana to represent the Grand Priory of Lombardy-Venetia.

When Thun received the chancellor's letter informing him of his dismissal, he declared the decree invalid, his immediate superior having died before it was signed; and that he was, therefore, still a member of the Council. The chancellor informed him that the Sovereign Council had not needed the grand prior's signature to dismiss him, and that the decree was certainly valid. Thun replied that if he was no longer the representative of the grand priory in Rome, he considered himself to be the Bailiff Da Porto's successor in the grand priory itself, and that with the approval of the capitulary chaplain. This ecclesiastical reference made it clear that his bold attitude was not unconnected with the support of Father Larraona and Cardinal Canali. And he might well feel confident in his position, for he knew of nobody who could replace him. Thus the banner of revolt was raised in the Grand Priory of Lombardy-Venetia. But the grand master was now on the warpath. Carlo de Belgiojoso, an old knight of justice of the grand priory, had recently written asking permission to take the first vows of profession; the grand master appointed him Regent of the Grand Priory, by telegram. The capitulary chaplain was obliged to capitulate and Thun to lower the standard of rebellion.

Nevertheless, he again wrote contesting the validity of the decree of dismissal. The chancellor's only reply was to request him, on the grand master's behalf, to come as soon as convenient and remove his personal property from the Magistral Palace. Thun then alleged that Prince Chigi's real wishes must certainly have been misinterpreted. When these wishes were confirmed by Prince Chigi in person, Thun then demanded a sum of money to cover his moving expenses. It was thought that the alacrity with which the treasury, usually so cautious, met his demand, would surprise him.

But instead of his person, it was yet another missive which arrived: it announced that, informed of his case, Cardinal Lavitrano had ordered him not to remove his effects from the Grand Magistracy but to maintain the *status quo* "in order to assist the investigation which he had claimed from the Sacred Congregation of Religious into his private life, works, and the decisions taken concerning him." This was an open admission of the "secret recourse" he had long since presented to the Sacred Congregation.

Cardinal Lavitrano, being approached by the grand master, said that he had never given any such order, but had simply asked him to hold himself at the disposition of the investigating committee, when it was formed, wherever he might be. The grand master wrote to Thun curtly ordering him to obey. Thun replied in the most respectful terms, announcing his imminent arrival. To hasten his coming he was warned that the chapter of the Grand Priory of Lombardy-Venetia was about to meet in Rome, and summoned to attend.

He came, was affable, took part in the capitulary proceedings without batting an eyelid, made an act of submission to the Regent Belgiojoso, and wished his own successor, Angelo de Mojana, the best of luck in his new post. The grand master was in the seventh heaven: *this* was the Thun he knew and loved. His colleagues, being less confiding, had two explanations of Thun's accommodating manner: his secretary, Gehlen, had been away, in Berlin, for several weeks; and Cardinal Canali was up to his eyes in Holy Year ceremonies.

However, Thun had still not moved out. When the chancellor

reminded him that Angelo de Mojana was waiting out in the cold, he replied that he again had Cardinal Lavitrano's authority to remain at the Magistral Palace. This time the grand master did not take the trouble of referring this to Cardinal Lavitrano. Using the form of words which no professed knight could ignore, he wrote to Thun calling upon him, "in the name of his oath of obedience," to move out of the palace forthwith. The letter was dated June 5.

# X

ON THE MORNING OF THE 6TH a pious ceremony was taking place in the priory Church of Santa Maria del Aventino: a conventual chaplain of the Hungarian association in exile, Mgr. Gyula Magyari, was taking his final, solemn vows. The thing might be described as a sort of religious curiosity, for conventual chaplains very rarely made profession. The three vows seemed, in their case, altogether superogatory, since, as priests, they were already sworn to the same conduct. But these extra vows, which shifted them, in a way, from the ranks of the secular to those of the regular clergy, gave them the right to be invested with a commandery. It will readily be understood that the Order did not encourage vocations of this kind.

The grand master's flag was flying above the villa, signifying that he was in residence: he moved up to the Aventine early in May, which did not prevent him going down to the Magistral Palace when he had occasion to. Inside the church, where Piranesi had harmoniously married vestiges of the Middle Ages to all the grace of the eighteenth century, the congregation was hearing Mass celebrated by the *cura*, Mgr. Beretti, titular Archbishop of Leontopolis. The grand master, wearing his vast black cloak with its wide grey facings, and his great golden chain, was seated under his baldachin in the choir. His grey *soubreveste* and the big white cross which covered his chest were just visible. The Order's flag hung near him, and, at intervals, the banners of

the former "languages" of the Order.* The members of the
Sovereign Council sat near him, on benches draped in red:
they, too, wore their black mantles, with the cross of white wool
on the shoulder. Each bore, on the left arm, a wide yellow stole
embroidered with the instruments of the Passion; and through
the opening of each robe could be seen either the yellow tunic
of a bailiff or the poppy-red tunic of a commander.

The benches in the nave were brilliant with the uniforms of
lesser dignitaries: knights of justice with their white facings;
donati of justice with their green facings; knights of honour
and devotion whose facings were black, edged with gold, and
knights magisterial with plain black facings. There were also
some ladies of the Order—dames of honour and devotion—
with the little cross pinned to their dresses.

The Mass being over, Mgr. Magyari, escorted by his sponsors,
crossed to kneel before the grand master, who asked him, "What
is your request?"

"I ask to be received and admitted into the company of
brothers in sacred religion of the hospital of St. John of Jerusalem."

"The request you make was refused to certain others who
were not worthy. But trusting in your probity, we have decided
that it shall be granted to you. . . . You will be constrained to fast
when you desire to eat, to watch when you would sleep. . . .
Consider well whether you wish to strip yourself of your freedom,
placing it in the hands of the masters of our religion."

"I do so place it altogether in their hands."

"I require you, now, to say whether you have ever taken vows
in any other order."

"No."

". . . We therefore admit you with kindness, promising you
only bread and water, travail and toil, and a simple garment."

The light, ritual slap, which had so dangerously "roused"
the Bailiff Thun "to business," did not appear to worry Mgr.
Magyari. With his hands upon a Testament, the candidate
went on to speak the formal words of the oath: "I swear

* Knights were grouped in "languages" or "tongues" according to their
nationality. [E.H.]

to Almighty God, to the glorious Virgin Mary, and to the sieur
St. John the Baptist, my protector, to observe and keep obedience,
poverty, and chastity, as it is fitting that all good Catholic religious
should do."

The grand master took up a black cloak and, indicating the
eight-pointed cross, said, "This cross was given to us in white
to signify purity. The eight points which you see are a symbol
of the eight beatitudes."

He enumerated them, vested him with the cloak and, after
explaining its symbolism, with the stole. The kiss of obedience
completed the ceremony which, since the candidate was a chaplain, did not include the blessing of sword and spurs. Nor, for
the same reason, was the grand master's bull, naming the candidate a Knight of Malta, laid open upon the wide arm of the
throne—that is to say, the document attesting that the candidate
had produced proofs of noble blood, as was customary for
laymen making profession. Following the grand master and the
member elect, the congregation filed out. Several of them glanced
at the funeral monument to the grand master Thun Hohenstein
as they passed, and realized that his nephew had not been present:
he was still obstinately immured in the Magistral Palace, despite
the oath of obedience he, too, had taken.

The garden offered its shade, its flower-beds and bright sheets
of still water. The grand master looked very much at home in it:
one of the fountains bore the arms of a Cardinal Chigi, Grand
Prior of Rome, who had contributed to the restoration of that
priory to the Order. His fountain seemed a complement to the
ancient wellhead engraved with an inscription of the Templars,
for the house had been their Roman Commandery.

Not far from the villa, whose three stories towered boldly at
the very edge of the hilltop, a buffet had been set out in the
summerhouse. It did duty for that bread and water, formerly
served to newly professed knights, to symbolize the promise
made during the ceremony of admission. Each with a plate or
cup and saucer in hand, knights, ladies, and prelates stood
chatting on the terrace which commands one of the most famous
views in Rome. A sudden altercation breaking out near the
garden gate attracted attention to a motor-cyclist, clad and

helmeted in leather, who thrust aside the porter and shot his machine straight down the drive between its lines of bay trees. He stopped by the guests, and without dismounting took a large envelope from a strapped bag: then, in the tone of a quarter-master-sergeant in a barrack square, he bawled, "His Most Eminent Highness Prince Chigi Albani della Rovere!"

Cattaneo hastened forward to snatch the envelope, but the messenger would not give it up. "I have orders from the Sacred Congregation of Religious to deliver this message into the prince's hands."

Pale, disconcerted, the grand master stepped forward. Cardinal Lavitrano's messenger handed over the letter, turned his machine, and vanished in an uproar of open exhaust.

The prince, who was shaking a little, tore open the envelope, which had been handsomely sealed in yellow and white wax with the arms of the Holy See. He unfolded the large sheet of paper, read it swiftly, and passed it to the chancellor. It informed them that, by a decree of the Sacred Congregation. His Most Reverend Excellency Mgr. Ilario Alcini, titular Bishop of Diony-siad and Visitor to the Seminaries of Italy, had been appointed Apostolic Visitor *ad inquirendum et referendum* in the matters raised by His Excellency Ferdinando Thun Hohenstein, professed Bailiff of the sovereign Hierosolymitan Order of Malta.

The war, which Cardinal Canali had so long been preparing for, had been officially declared.

# PART
# TWO

# I

IT WAS NO LONGER a matter of defending merely the records of their members' noble pedigrees: for the first time the Knights of St. John were being driven to defend their very constitution.

The Order had always enjoyed the privilege of self-government, and if, from time to time, a sovereign pontiff had interfered to settle some "monastic revolt"—the last occasion had been during the seventeenth century under the Grand Master La Cassière—it had always been at the request of a grand master or of the Sovereign Council. The knights had even been exempt from the jurisdiction of ordinaries, for they had been given their own bishop, "the prior of the Church," responsible directly to the Holy See. Their religious history, in Rhodes as in Malta, was full of their struggles against the Inquisition. They had expelled the Jesuits from Malta more than a century before they were driven out of any other kingdom. In Rome they had never been subject even to a Sacred Episcopal Visitation: and now here they were required to submit to a wretched visitor of seminaries.

Hercolani and Cattaneo were no more surprised than Del Balzo and Pecci, but none of them wasted time on I-told-you-sos: the thing was, to close the breach. It was fortunate for Thun that he still failed to put in an appearance at the "monastery table" where lay members of the Grand Magistracy occasionally ate their meals: for bitter indeed would they have made the "bread and water" of his pittance. The Bailiff Conestabile recalled that it was a complaint lodged by two Templars punished by their superiors which had provided Philippe le Bel with the pretext he needed to ruin the Templars Order. And their present predicament was all the more redoubtable in that Thun's supporters were Father Larraona and Cardinal Canali. Not that their interest in him was anything but a pretext: he was useful as cover for their own purposes. The apostolic visitor with whom they were, in reality, threatened, was not this Mgr. Alcini who seemed to be taking their Order for a seminary, but a certain

grand master of the Order of St. Sepulchre whose dream it was
to become Grand Master of Malta.

The knights in Sovereign Council voiced diverse opinions as
to the line they should take. For the most part, they were for
resistance. They were for writing to the Congregation of Religious
that, since its decree was in violation of the Order's rights, it
must be held null and void. At this juncture the grand master
gave fresh proof of his subtlety and moderation: if, he said, they
rejected the visit out of hand, the Order would give the impression of being afraid of its outcome. It was surely better to receive
it, while insisting that its legality was questionable. And Thun's
expulsion should, in common prudence, be suspended.

The titular Bishop of Dionysiad appeared, in due course, at
the palace. His form was pyramidal: hips and flanks were vast
under the tentlike robe, the shoulders narrow, the head, chin, and
nose pointed. While awaiting his visit information concerning this
prelate had been sought, and it was known that he was altogether
under his principal's thumb; the fact was, he had been in a little
trouble which had been disposed of by Cardinal Canali.

Mgr. Alcini asked the grand master only three questions, and
those somewhat naïve considering the state of the case: were
those members of the Grand Magistracy who were hostile to
Thun worthy of trust? Were the said bailiff's errors undeniable?
And, if so, were they such as to have required his dismissal?
The grand master answered "Yes" to the first two questions;
as to the third, he said that Thun's behaviour since his removal
from office had done away with any regret which he, the grand
master, might otherwise have felt.

Mgr. Alcini established himself in the small council chamber
and there spent several days questioning the staff, while a youthful priest took down questions and answers in shorthand.
Cattaneo's turn came round. That fiery son of Friuli had promised to keep his temper. He knew that Thun's friends were
spreading a rumour that he had hastened to the bedside of the
dying Da Porto to get him to sign his *ultima verba*. He hoped
that so gross a libel would not have influenced so fine a mind as
Mgr. Alcini's, but he was reserving his opinion.

The Apostolic Visitor asked to be shown the files relating to

Thun's transactions, and studied them at length. Cattaneo, observing that the young secretary was only making extracts from these files, gave him a set of photostatic copies carefully numbered—there were about forty sheets. Among them were the papers relating to the knights and donati appointed by Thun and struck from the roll after his dismissal from office. Mgr. Alcini passed over the ones who had been convicted by the courts and such as were divorcees: the Order being Catholic, divorce entailed exclusion or expulsion. (Hercolani had walked into the Chancellery one day, put a paper on the desk, and said, coldly, "For the agenda of the next council meeting." The paper was a motion for the expulsion of his own son, who had just divorced his wife.) The Apostolic Visitor did, however, challenge the expulsion of a knight who had been convicted of sodomy.

"You had unquestionable proof?" he demanded aggressively.

Cattaneo smiled. "We did not rest content with the report of the Roman police, which you will find attached. Your Excellency will find reports of the evidence collected in other towns where the person in question had resided. They were obtained from a Milanese vicar general, a parish priest of Lugano, the Rector of Freiburg University; from Monsignor the Archbishop of Strasbourg, and from a commandant of the French Army of Occupation in Germany, himself a member of the Order."

"Five suspicions do not amount to proof," Mgr. Alcini pointed out severely.

On the second day of his inquiry Mgr. Alcini sent for Cattaneo, received him standing, and said, icily, "In the course of my interrogation I asked you whether there were not some irregularities touching the letters written by the late Da Porto. You assured me that there were none. You will forgive me if, in view of the gravity of the case, I felt obliged to submit the letters in question to experts——"

"We are sensible of Your Most Reverend Excellency's trust in us," Cattaneo interrupted.

"—Here are the results. First, the signatures are authentic. Second, the letters are apocryphal: they were typed on your Chancellery machine. It follows that the letters were written after the event, to justify the Sovereign Council's decision."

Thereupon they had to prove to the Apostolic Visitor that the letters had been typed in the Via Condotti at the grand prior's request; had been sent to Trissino for his signature; and been returned, signed, to Rome. In short, a major inquest, entailing examination of registers, questioning of servants, weighing of letters—operations which the Bishop of Dionysiad followed closely with his eyes keeping a sharp watch on Cattaneo—the eyes of a Philippe de Marigny, Archbishop of Sens, ready to send his first Templar to the stake.

However, the inquisitor was obliged to confess himself beaten; which did not prevent the Vatican from continuing to claim that the Grand Prior da Porto's letters were apocryphal and Thun's dismissal from the Sovereign Council unlawful.

# II

HARDLY WAS THE GRAND MAGISTRACY rid of Mgr. Alcini and still awaiting the outcome of his apostolic visit *ad inquirendum et referendum*, than Cardinal Canali tried another broadside at the Grand Magistral Palace. He wrote to the grand master that the Holy Father, patron of the Order of Malta, had been deeply pained to learn that the Order's minister in Paris was a Freemason.

Prince Chigi, albeit shocked, was unable to believe that this could be true. His natural goodness inclined him to suppose that people were often the victims of calumny. Was it not well known that even princes of the Church had been slandered in precisely the same terms? Cardinal Verdier, a former archbishop of Paris, had been accused of Freemasonry, and so, even, had the illustrious Rampolla, who had so very nearly become pope.

The file relating to Baron Marsaudon, who had recently succeeded the Comte de Pierredon upon the latter's retirement, was hastily sent for. There followed a sigh of relief in chorus: the baron had been appointed Magistral Grand Cross *in gremio religionis* at his predecessor's request; and minister upon the

recommendation of the papal nuncio in Paris. The Order was
well covered, and Pecci rushed round to the Secretariat of State
with the news.

"Cardinal Canali is a first-class shot," Mgr. Montini told
him, after hearing what Pecci had to say. "Only think how
delighted he will be at bringing down two birds with one stone."

"What do you mean?" the minister demanded.

"His Eminence has hit both the Order of Malta, which he is
not overfond of; and Mgr. Roncalli, whom he detests."

Pecci went on to see Cardinal Canali whose offices were in the
gubernatorial suite of the Vatican City. And since Count Galeazzi
and Prince Carlo Pacelli had their offices in the same place, that
superb marble palace gave the impression of being the Trimurti's
headquarters.

"Poor Roncalli!" the cardinal said, with an air of genuine
distress. "I would have done a great deal to avoid making things
so awkward for him. I only hope this business won't cost him
his Hat. Send someone to Paris at once to look into the matter.
And mum's the word! As you know, the Holy Father has a
horror of scandal."

Thus it came about that the Grand Magistracy, which had
just been subject to an investigation, was now obliged to conduct one: one, moreover, which it considered a great deal more
delicate. For it was necessary to handle almost everyone involved
with great tact. The Order was under a great obligation to the
nuncio for his invaluable help in settling the business of the
Argentine wheat; to the Comte de Pierredon for his long and
faithful service, first in Bucharest, later in Paris; to Baron
Marsaudon himself for his meritorious efforts in obtaining
official recognition of the Order by the French government.

The Grand Magistracy made a sound choice when it appointed
Mgr. Rossi Stockalper, Canon of S. Maria-Maggiore and
Professed Chaplain of the Order, as its envoy. He combined a
rare personal distinction and experience in diplomacy with
another and surely unique advantage: he was a friend of both
the grand master and Cardinal Canali.

The "magistral visitor" set out for Paris. It had been suggested
to him that he should begin his quest for information with Father

Berteloot, S.J., a specialist in all that related to Freemasonry. Mgr. Rossi Stockalper did not much care for the Jesuits for, as secretary of a certain nunciature, he had been victimized by them; nevertheless, he made up his mind to this encounter.

Father Berteloot confirmed the news which had reached the Order so belatedly: Baron Marsaudon was not only a Freemason, but had attained the thirty-third degree of Freemasonry and was a life member of the Grand Council of the Scottish Lodge. Until that moment Mgr. Rossi Stockalper, like the grand master, had doubted the news. The shock of hearing it confirmed caused him to get out his handkerchief, mop his brow, and polish his glasses: the month was July, but he would have felt quite as hot had it been December. He asked whether, perhaps, a homonym might have misled them? The Jesuit took a document from his file and read out their subject's complete civil status: Baron Marsaudon, Minister of the Order of Malta, was unquestionably Baron Marsaudon, Freemason of the Thirty-Third Degree.

"How does it happen, Father," Mgr. Stockalper demanded, "that you should have kept such a secret to yourself?"

"It is not my business to keep the archbishopric informed; nor the nunciature; nor the Order of Malta. My business is to keep the Society of Jesus informed."

"Very well. But why did the Society of Jesus not pass the information to them?"

"The Society of Jesus makes a practice of caution. It passes on information only if it considers that there is any point in doing so; and only, of course, if questioned. The archbishopric and the nunciature have their own intelligence services, and might be supposed to have more reason to place their information at your disposal. Mgr. Roncalli and Mgr. Feltin will be glad to go more fully into the matter."

The canon made a careful copy of Father Berteloot's civil status certificate of Baron Marsaudon, and went to the archbishopric. He had not yet lost all hope. Possibly, when he applied to more exalted levels, he would be told that Baron Marsaudon had broken his connection with a sect which was under the ban of excommunication; perhaps he had even abjured in the Cathedral of Notre Dame?

Mgr. Feltin was just back from Lourdes, where he had been at the head of the national pilgrimage. He could talk of nothing but the grotto, miracles, torchlight processions. Mgr. Stockalper interrupted him to ask whether he knew the Order's minister in Paris.

"A charming man," the archbishop said, "—a good table good manners, and good works."

Disarmed by this reply, the canon gave up all idea of explaining the object of his mission, for all it was quasi-apostolic. He confined himself to asking the archbishop one more question: Was there, among his colleagues, one who knew Baron Marsaudon really well?

"Yes. Mgr. Bohan, I fancy. He is one of my vicars general and occasionally passes on some little anecdote about Baron Marsaudon. Why not question him?"

Mgr. Stockalper rose to go and Mgr. Feltin became suddenly grave: he said, "Since you are a professed chaplain in the Order of Malta, you might mention to the grand master that he seems a little inclined to forget the French cardinals. He did make Cardinal Tisserant a bailiff grand cross in Holy Year; but Cardinal Tisserant is in Rome and not one of his colleagues in France can wear the black ribbon and white cross. You will understand that I do not speak for myself, since I am, as yet, only a cardinal *in petto*. Even so, Cardinal Canali did not wait for a consistory before appointing me—very generously— Honorary Grand Prior of the Order of the Holy Sepulchre in France. We have the really beautiful services of the Order at St.-Len-St.-Gilles, and even at the Sainte-Chapelle. God keep you, Monsignor!"

The canon had himself taken to Mgr. Bohan. Here, the atmosphere was no longer that combination of ecstasy, optimism, and worldliness which was Mgr. Feltin's. The vicar general opened a safe and took out a file which he handed to Canon Stockalper. The cover bore an inscription in red: "Baron Marsaudon." There were several documents inside: a copy of the *Journal Officiel de l'Etat français* published at Vichy during the Occupation and in which Yves Marie Marsaudon's name appeared in a list of adherents of Freemasonry; three or four numbers of the Masonic review *Le Temple*, which contained articles written by him; and a certificate of civil status identical with Father Berteloot's. There was, alas! no certificate of abjuration in the file. Rossi Stockalper said, "But this is appalling!"

"Have you seen Father Berteloot?" Mgr. Bohan inquired.

"Yes."

"And did he not show you these documents?"

"No, excepting for the certificate."

Mgr. Bohan's face lit up.

"I've always said that the Jesuits' intelligence service was overestimated. As you see, our archives are fuller than theirs."

"Alas!"

"Mark you, Monsignor, I can well understand Father Berteloot's not showing you the *Journal Officiel de l'Etat français.* We, at the archbishopric, faithful to the spirit of the Resistance, keep our copies of the gazette simply as historical documents, and would on no account regard them as reliable proofs of anything. But that Father Berteloot should not, like ourselves, be a subscriber—through an intermediary, of course—to so important a Masonic review as *Le Temple*, passes my understanding."

Mgr. Rossi Stockalper, who found his astonishment increasing every moment, asked why this extraordinary information had not been passed on to the nunciature. Mgr. Bohan smiled.

"Since the nunciature has a habit of ignoring the archbishopric, the archbishopric finds itself constrained to ignore the nunciature. When they do deign to come to us for information, we open our hearts and our archives to them. When they forget us, we forget them."

"But this business involves the Church!"

"The Church? Let us say, the Holy See and the Order of Malta; but since the Order of Malta has close ties with the Holy See, and the Holy See is here represented by the nunciature, there is nobody more fitting than His Excellency the nuncio to furnish you with an explanation concerning His Excellency, the Minister of the Order of Malta."

Although he considered his mission to be virtually accomplished, Mgr. Stockalper decided to follow the vicar general's malicious advice. Not that he expected to receive from Mgr.

Roncalli any addition to the information he had gathered from Father Berteloot and Mgr. Bohan. But it had become a matter of conscience with him to throw as much light as possible on the circumstances surrounding Baron Marsaudon's appointment.

He rang the bell at the door of the small mansion in the Avenue du President Wilson. The tiara and keys of the armorial shield put him in mind of the powers given to Peter, the radiance of the spirit. A footman, all Italian affability, conducted him to the nuncio. Like the Archbishop of Paris, the titular Archbishop of Mesembrya had his head in the clouds, could talk of nothing but Holy Year, Fatima, the future dogma of the Assumption. He mentioned a French figure of Christ which had taken to shedding tears of blood, like the Italian ones. He came down to earth only to talk of the cure he had been taking at Vittel. And when Mgr. Stockalper was able to edge in a word about Baron Marsaudon, the titular Archbishop of Mesembrya politely referred him to Mgr. Bruno Heim, the Secretary of the nunciature.

The canon only knew this personage, a supernumerary secret chamberlain, by name; but he felt well disposed toward him in advance. He knew him to be, like himself, a Swiss by birth, and the author of a book on ecclesiastical heraldry. He was convinced that he was, at last, about to find himself face to face with a man who would have a proper understanding of the importance of his visit and would give him the key to all these mysteries.

On the threshold of the secretary's office, however, Mgr. Stockalper halted in consternation. The man who was coming forward to meet him was dressed like an English clergyman, was smoking a pipe, and had the badge of some sports club pinned to his lapel. Mute with astonishment, the Apostolic Protonotary sat down in an armchair beside this very odd supernumerary secret chamberlain. The visitor, in his beautifully fitted cassock of fine cloth to which was pinned the little white enamel cross of Malta, appeared the very antithesis of this other and different representative of the Holy Father. But then, each stood for a different epoch.

"I should explain at once, Most Illustrious and Most Reverend Monsignor," the secretary said, "that I have an indult to dress like this. I move with the times, but I keep the rules."

Mgr. Rossi Stockalper made a gesture of indifference: nevertheless, he was not indifferent to the fact that a churchman who moved with the times knew enough to give him the two honorifics he had a right to as a canon of one of Rome's three patriarchal churches. However, wishing to emphasize his superiority and teach the fellow a lesson, he said, "Perhaps you will be good enough to put aside your pipe. Tobacco smoke distresses me."

Mgr. Heim put his pipe into an ash-tray. The canon, without further preamble, then said that he had found complete proof, at the archbishopric and elsewhere, of Baron Marsaudon's membership of a Masonic lodge; that Baron Marsaudon had been appointed Minister of Malta on the nunciature's recommendation; that the Holy Father, Cardinal Canali, and Prince Chigi had been deeply disturbed by the news of the baron's Masonic connection; and that, charged by Prince Chigi to investigate the story, he was under the painful necessity of confirming its truth.

While he was speaking he watched Mgr. Heim closely, to discover what effect this revelation would have on him. Mgr. Heim's smile did not change. He said, "Excuse me, Monsignor, but did the archbishopric reveal all this in the guise of a great secret which they had uncovered?"

"Hardly, since it is a secret published in the *Journal Officiel de l'Etat français*. But it was very wrong of them not to inform us."

"And you are, on the whole, a little bit shocked by our discretion in the matter?"

"A little bit shocked!" Mgr. Stockalper exclaimed, starting upright in his easy chair. "Say, rather, that I am outraged! And I think I have already made it clear to you that I am not the only one. If there is one thing in the world utterly incompatible with being a Knight of Malta, not to mention an actual Minister of that Order, it is Freemasonry."

"Oh, come, Monsignor! Why, in Malta itself, under De Rohan's grand magistracy, there was a lodge, the lodge of the Illuminati, forty of whose members had taken your vows. It was founded by Count Callourat of the Grand Priory of Bohemia."

"It was the forerunner of the revolutionary spirit," the canon said, harshly, "and possibly the reason for the fall of Malta."

"Yesterday's revolutionaries are tomorrow's conservatives. I have made a study of Freemasonry. Monsignor, and know it, I dare say, rather better than Father Berteloot to whom, no doubt, you were referred. It is one of the last bastions of social conservatism in the world, and consequently of religious conservatism. Let us banish our prejudices."

"Clearly, Rome is behind the times, and Paris the city of light—and enlightenment," said the canon ironically.

"What I have just said to you was made clear to me by Baron Marsaudon himself, and I count it to him for merit. As a result, the very fact of his being a Mason made us support his candidature all the more warmly."

"Can I be dreaming?" exclaimed the Canon of Sta. Maria-Maggiore. "Has the nunciature forgotten the very existence of canon law?"

"I can recite canon number 2335 by heart."

"Then I need not remind you, Monsignor, that it entails excommunication for all Freemasons, an excommunication of the gravest order, reserved to the Holy See."

"Excuse me, Monsignor, but that is not so: the text reads neither *speciali modo* nor *specialissimo*, but *simpliciter* merely."

"I see; so the word excommunication is not enough for you, you must distinguish one degree from another. I have heard that, in the same spirit, the Society of Jesus possesses certain anatomical diagrams to demonstrate the gravity of sins of the flesh, centimetre by centimetre."

"It is a sin of the spirit to close our eyes to the light, whatever its source. But why did you not apply directly to Baron Marsaudon, Monsignor? He would have told you openly and frankly what the archbishopric whispered as a secret. And he would have convinced you that it was in your Order's interest to have a Freemason as its envoy in Paris. He has quite captivated us all, and if you were to talk with him for a few moments, you, too, would be conquered."

"When you say 'us,' do you include His Excellency the nuncio?"

"To the extent of his confidence in me, yes; and to the extent that he is sensible of the—*respiro grande*."

"For my part," the canon said, "I am suffocating," and he mopped his brow again. Mgr. Heim opened the windows to let in some air, but his visitor rose abruptly and said, "Am I, or am I not, at the apostolic nunciature and talking with a prelate of His Holiness?"

"Calm yourself, Monsignor, I implore you!" Mgr. Heim said, reseating the canon and hovering over him with filial solicitude. "You have been a diplomat: there are certain necessities, certain professional exigencies. . . . I am going to throw all the light I can on this business—a business which seems to have disturbed the Holy See and the Order of Malta out of all measure.

"Cardinal Canali, although he knows a great deal, cannot know everything. He is absorbed in his financial operations— I saw a photo of him recently, with Prince Pacelli and Count Galeazzi showing him a big ledger with the word 'Accounts' visible on the spine. A real symbol of his all-devouring, but perhaps rather limited, activities. True, by their very nature, his hand is on the levers of power in Italy; but he is unaware of what goes on beyond his frontiers. He is not aware of what we are doing within these four walls, the importance of which must predominate over all other considerations whatsoever. For this great work of ours, Baron Marsaudon is essential to us, and the day will come, Monsignor, when his name will be honoured in the combined ceremonies of the Holy See and the Order of Malta."

He paused for effect, and concluded, "The nunciature, Monsignor, is on the point of reconciling the Catholic Church and the Freemasons."

It was Mgr. Stockalper's turn to smile. "A fine project, assuredly. But have you forgotten the fable about the reconciliation of the cock and the fox?"

"This is no fable, Monsignor, but History!"

"History can sometimes look uncommonly like a fable: for example, you may recall Stalin's offer, made by his ambassador in this very house, to restore its former Russian and Polish Commanderies to the Order of Malta."

"I am not concerned with the Kremlin, Monsignor: we are in France; and I speak only of what I know."

"Then perhaps you have never heard that the Holy Father put an immediate stop to these singular negotiations, and that the Order's negotiators came very near to being disciplined by the Holy Office. I would advise you, most earnestly, to go very carefully, and make quite sure of your position, before carrying your own negotiations any further. And in any case there is no reason why the Order should suffer for your *respiro grande*. And since, apparently, you did not consider yourself obliged as a Catholic, a prelate, and a diplomat to inform us of this state of affairs, you might at least have done so as a mere matter of courtesy. As for Baron Marsaudon, whom I have not the slightest intention of seeing even though I am not afraid of being 'conquered' by him, he might have had the honesty to add the three full stops after the signature to his first dispatch. He, no doubt, had his own reasons for not doing so. Whereas you, in failing to do what you ought to have done, have wounded the knights of a religious order of chivalry in their feelings, in their traditions and, I will add—in their honour."

"Their honour is certainly not involved, since the person in question is a most honourable man. As for the Order's feelings, they are as diverse as the countries in which it is represented. The traditions which you mention, moreover, are manifold: the noble Knights of St. John were not always at war with the infidels; they were often at peace with them and sometimes even in alliance with them. Even the Holy See itself grew weary of preaching crusades: its litanies included the prayer, 'Protect us, oh Lord, from invasion by the Tartars!' But it sent envoys to greet the Tartar chieftains as friends of Christendom."

"That was in times when the danger to be warded off was armed force: it is more difficult to defend ourselves against ideas. Has it not occurred to you that the Holy See is bound to feel uneasy if it be true that Freemasonry is seeking a reconciliation with the Church?"

"Let us drop the subject, since it is outside the scope of your mission, Monsignor—which does not mean that I shall forget what you have said. And let us also ignore the part played by Baron Marsaudon in this business, and consider his position in relation to the Order of Malta. Were you aware that, thanks to his numerous and powerful connections, the sovereignty of the Order is about to be recognized officially? Do not overlook that fact, in Rome. One false move, and all is lost."

"I fear that, henceforth, the grand master——"

"It would be madness, Monsignor! The fruit is ripe: give Marsaudon a chance to pick it and make you a present of it."

"Ripe?" Mgr. Stockalper muttered, rising to take his leave, "it's rotten."

"Dear Marsaudon!" Mgr. Heim said, taking up his pipe. "I know nothing of his barony; but that he will be made a papal count, like his predecessor Pierredon, I am convinced. Which reminds me, Monsignor—the attribute of Minister of Malta is surely under the sign of the reconciliation of irreconcilables: Pierredon's father was made a count by Leo XIII, though he was an admiral of the Ottoman navy and one of the Red Sultan's pashas."

"The fruit is rotten," Mgr. Stockalper repeated.

*         *         *

At the Magistral Palace there was consternation when it became known with absolute certainty that Baron Marsaudon was not only a Freemason, but a high dignitary of Freemasonry. Notwithstanding which, the prospect of the service which he was about to render gave the grand master furiously to think— far more so than his special envoy had anticipated. A gratification so flattering as recognition by the French government could not be ignored by the head of the Order. True, his ambition was to obtain recognition from the Italian government; but he hoped that this would follow. Thus, Baron Marsaudon was essential to his plans, as he was to the nunciature's, though for very different reasons.

This calculation, justified by policy if not by ethics, obtained, very unexpectedly, the approbation of Cardinal Canali. The grand prior, who was doing everything in his power to diminish the domestic sovereignty of the Order, was quite as anxious as the grand master himself to see it strengthened abroad. But that, as we know from what he had confided to Mgr. Curatola, was because he hoped to make personal use of it. But at least, during the respite granted to Baron Marsaudon, he would be prevented from exploiting the business by using it to influence the Pope.

In his capacity as grand penitentiary he was in no need of reminding that Freemasons were under the ban of excommunication, albeit only "simply reserved." However, he suggested to the grand master a plan which would ensure the triumph of morality after the triumph of policy was assured. They would wait for that recognition, which it was in the baron's hands to obtain, and immediately thereafter put him in the way of abjuring his errors, making use of the special Holy Year facilities. He was referring to the fact that the Indulgences office had decreed that throughout the course of that year, so fecund in mercies, the indulgences known as Jubilee Indulgences were applicable to Freemasons. A memorandum drawn up by Mgr. Curatola reminded the Grand Magistracy that Baron Marsaudon would have to make the pilgrimage to Rome "with a contrite heart"; solemnly to abjure his errors "in the bosom of the grand penitentiary"; deliver up to him "all books, manuscripts, and insignia relating to the damnable sect"—or a written declaration that he had destroyed them "with his own hands." Finally, he would have to "submit himself, with humbleness and compunction," to a heavy penitence—in practice it was to be a "spontaneous gift for the reparation of the evil." And in the event of his refusing to give up his Masonic trowel, he would be called upon to give up his ambassadorial cocked hat.

They all began to sing small, however, when Mgr. Heim, telephoning from Paris, informed Mgr. Stockalper that "for reasons of health," Baron Marsaudon was going to ask to be replaced. It looked as if the grand prior and penitentiary was not going to have the pleasure of hearing a Freemason, minister of Malta, and knight magistral grand cross *in gremio religionis*, abjure his errors in the grand penitential bosom.

"What about recognition?" he asked the canon.

"A matter of days, according to Mgr. Heim. His view is that Baron Marsaudon would like to do something splendid for us before retiring."

Days passed and there was no news and the grand master felt

his scruples returning. He could not bear the idea that, on the
pretext of doing the Order a major service, the Maltese Legation
in Paris was prolonging its career as a satanic agency. He sent
the former Ambassador Auriti, who was looking after the Order's
Foreign Office, to find out what he could as to the real chances
and imminence of recognition.

The new "magistral visitor" was as swift and thorough as
his predecessor. Upon his return within a few days, he handed
the grand master a brief report: "Considering it pointless to
go into the details of my interviews at the presidential offices of
the French Republic and at the Quai d'Orsay, I have only to
inform Your Most Eminent Highness that the French government
is as remote from any idea of recognizing the Order of Malta's
sovereign as the earth from the moon."

Events followed each other in swift succession. Baron
Marsaudon offered his resignation, which was accepted by the
Sovereign Council, he receiving the new title of "Minister
Emeritus." The Comte de Billy, whose connections were in oil,
not Masonry, was appointed in his stead—Cardinal Canali,
who disliked the French ambassador to the Holy See, having
opposed the appointment of the ambassador's brother, the
Marquis d'Ormesson. Mgr. Bruno Heim was recalled, severely
reprimanded, and sent to Vienna, leaving both *respiro grande*
and Freemasonry to manage without him. There was a move
to give Father Berteloot the Cross *au Mérite;* and Mgr. Bohan
was made chaplain of the French association.

# III

THE RESULTS of Mgr. Stockalper's inquiry had all been dealt
with; those of Mgr. Alcini were still unknown. Meanwhile,
however, either because the Congregation of Religious considered the facts less favourable to Thun than they had hoped,
or because they could hardly go on encouraging a knight to
rebel against his oath, they asked him to move out. And the

Grand Magistracy was at last rid of a tenant who had cost them a great deal of trouble and, although there was no question of his honesty, some tens of millions of money.

Prince Chigi felt obliged to mark this event by a letter to the Pope. He had another reason for writing it: having forgotten to send Mgr. Alcini a memorandum setting forth the Order's reservations in accepting the apostolic visit, he was determined to express them in as striking a manner as possible. He wrote a résumé of the whole business and then went on to say that the Order had decided to waive its prerogatives out of respect for the Holy See; changed the subject with a commentary, in edifying terms, on his knights' participation in the Holy Year festivals; and concluded in the grandest manner of the Order of Malta:

> Humbly prostrate to kiss the sacred foot,
> I am,
> Your Holiness's most obedient son.

Thun had left the Magistral Palace but he had not left Rome. He was soon harassing the Order from a new quarter, with the help of the Jesuit Castellani, director of the Marian Congregation of nobles and one of Cardinal Canali's henchmen. This priest appointed Fra Ferdinando chairman of the Nazareth Charitable Institution, a technical training school for the children of the poor, supported by the Marian Congregation, and occupying the outbuilding of the Grand Priory of the Aventine. Thun, who was living at the house of a banker, let it be known that, during the daytime, he would receive visitors at the Institute. This gave him the appearance of being still entrusted with the Order's business, and compensated for his eviction from the Magistral Palace. However, when the grand master, at last roused to fury, ordered him to vacate the Aventine premises immediately, Cardinal Canali did not dare to back his man and Fra Ferdinando was obliged to go and nurse his aristocratic grudge elsewhere than on the hill to which the Romans had once retreated. Throwing him out was not tantamount to putting him into the street: apart from his private fortune (professed knights had a dispensation from the vow of poverty, which allowed them to continue administering the family estates), he still had his commandery of justice of the Grand Priory of Lombardy-Venetia.

Cardinal Canali, meanwhile, wanted to show him that he was not being abandoned to his fate. Discarding Father Castellani, he played Father Larraona again, instructing him to ask the Grand Magistracy to accomplish "no action which might obligate, in a permanent way, His Excellency Fra Ferdinando Thun Hohenstein, initiator of a recourse to the Sacred Congregation of Religious." What could be the meaning of this bizarre form of words? Cardinal Canali, knowing that the Order had a thousand reasons for striking Fra Ferdinando from its roll, intended, perhaps, to forbid it without putting his prohibition into so many words. The message was the first indication they had had that Mgr. Alcini's report had not managed to conceal the truth entirely. The Order's most vigilant enemy needed to retain Thun's recourse as a weapon; but knew that he could only use it with caution.

The grand master, consulted in his summer retreat, replied tit-for-tat to Father Larraona, asking, "What could be the nature of an act which could obligate, in a permanent way, a professed knight and bailiff of the sovereign and military Order of Malta?" He added that he "had never been informed of the recourse to which allusion had been made, nor of the consequences entailed." This letter overthrew Father Larraona and infuriated Cardinal Canali. To answer it would be tantamount to confessing that the Order would have been within its rights in striking Thun off its roll, and that they had been trying to prevent this. On the other hand, if they did not answer it, they would be leaving the Order free to do as it liked. On the whole, they found it better not to send an answer, despite two reminders. True, if the grand master was still at Ariccia, Father Larraona and Cardinal Canali were, for their part, supposed to be *ad aquas* —the Holy See's traditional expression for the summer holidays. The cardinal was at his villa in Quadrelli; the father at the country house of the Missionary Sons of the Immaculate Heart of Mary; they could not undertake large-scale operations and were content, for the time being to keep the enemy guessing.

*       *       *

The holidays being over, Cardinal Canali, who had no interview at Magione that autumn, let the grand master know that he was desirous of serving on the Sovereign Council. It was, he said, his right, and he claimed it. Deprived of his eyes and ears within the Order, that is, of Thun and Travaglini, he was evidently resolved to rely on his own.

The grand master replied that the cardinal must have misread the constitution: grand priors did not have the right he was claiming. The cardinal answered that they had, at least, the right to attend when matters of moment touching their grand priory were under consideration; and that, for example, the Marquis Maresca, his Neapolitan opposite number, invariably did so. The grand master's reply recognized that, within the limits alluded to, grand priors did unquestionably have that right: let the cardinal indicate any business he considered of moment, and he would be admitted on the days when it was on the agenda. To which the cardinal made answer that, for him, any business touching his grand priory was important, and that he must therefore ask to be admitted to all meetings of the Council. The grand master pointed out that to grant him a permanent seat would entail doing likewise for all grand priors, which would be against the rules. They met. Cardinal Canali said, "I am sorry to be obliged to require you to grant a right which I expected to be offered with good grace. The Holy Father is aware of my wishes and has deigned to approve them."

The grand master knew the Vatican practice of putting words into the Holy Father's mouth. Employing the form of words used by initiates, he asked, smiling, if the cardinal meant the Holy Father—or the Holy Father in personal speech with the cardinal.

"The Holy Father in personal speech with me," the cardinal asserted peevishly. "Are you forgetting that I have no need of such—refinements? Carlo Pacelli, Galeazzo, and I see him every day."

Prince Chigi did not allow himself to be dazzled by this evocation of the Trimurti, even crowned with the tiara.

"I am surprised," he said, "that our august patron should be willing to contravene our constitution."

"Do not lean too heavily on that, Highness, for remember

that it has never been approved," the cardinal said. "Besides, you must admit that the contravention is a very trifling one, and one which His Holiness considers full of potential advantages. His Holiness has very wisely realized that I shall be able to bring enlightenment in matters spiritual to your meetings, thus giving you fresh evidence of his paternal interest in our Order."

"Eminence, are you trying to tell me that I am to make way for you?"

"No, no, Highness, *per carità!* You are grand master and will take precedence of me in the Sovereign Council."

"We are not discussing precedence, but the constitution, our Rule, to which I swore on oath, and which the Holy See has recognized, even if it has never approved it. This Order is finished the moment that Rule is no longer respected."

The cardinal seemed surprised to encounter so much obstinacy in a man he had supposed too well bred to offer any resistance at all. It may be, moreover, that the authority he claimed to have received from the Holy Father had not, after all, been given quite so directly as he had asserted; at all events, he suddenly softened his manner.

"Supposing we agree on a compromise," he said. "I will attend your meetings, but simply as an observer, with no right to speak. Hercolani, my representative, will speak for my grand priory, as before."

"You are agreeing to waive a right given to you by the Holy Father, then?" Prince Chigi said maliciously.

"He left it to me to use my discretion. Come, Highness, I do beg you not to labour the point any further."

The grand master knew his Cardinal Canali, and had just shown him as much; but he also knew his canon law, and therefore that he could not, in fact, gain his point and that further resistance could be no more than a matter of form. When a cardinal cites the pope as his authority, his word must be accepted —he is an "oracle of the living voice," even if that oracle is less reliable than that of Calchas.

Cardinal Canali, then, started putting in an appearance at Council meetings. He did not confine himself merely to attending: as his confidence increased he demanded, first that times and dates be fixed to suit his convenience; thereafter, that he be sent the agenda for approval. He listened, took notes, did not open his mouth, and no longer made much of Hercolani. This silent inquisition exasperated the grand master and a day came when he started the meeting without the cardinal, who was late. When he did arrive, the Prince did not rise, and all present followed his example. Standing, the cardinal pronounced the invocation; nobody responded. White with rage, he sat down, listened to the proceedings without meeting any man's eyes, and left without taking leave. He attended no more meetings.

Of course, the Curia included men of a very different stamp, and among them some whom the Grand Magistracy could count as friends. The knights were consequently hopeful that Providence would prompt the Holy Father to appoint one of them as head of the Sacred Congregation of Religious in place of Cardinal Lavitrano, who had died *ad aquas*. Their prayers seemed to have been answered, therefore, when the appointment went to Cardinal Micara, Sub-Dean of the Sacred College. He was on the best of terms with the Order, who had made him a bailiff grand cross; and on the worst of terms with Cardinal Canali, who had played him more than one dirty trick. But it was certainly surprising that Cardinal Canali had not been consulted about the appointment; was the Trimurti's stock falling? They were soon to learn that this was far from being the case: it seemed that Cardinal Micara, who had long wanted that post, had sold his soul to Cardinal Canali in order to get it.

As for Cardinal Canali himself, they had seen neither hair nor hide of him since the incident at the Sovereign Council's meeting. It seemed possible that he was washing his hands of the Order of Malta's spiritual welfare, albeit the Pope was supposed to have commended it to his care. But he had evidently not lost interest in its material well-being. For, *plus royaliste que le roi*, he decided that an end must be made of a certain fraudulent operation which had been carried out at the Order's expense, and which the grand master had treated with indifferent contempt. In short, the cardinal telephoned the grand master to tell him that the Grand Priory of Podolia should be handed over to the secular arm.

# IV

AT THE TIME IN QUESTION the Italian Republic had no decorations in its gift and, the Italians being fond of such toys, not for the ribbon but for the honorific which they could attach to their names, spurious orders of chivalry were springing up like mushrooms. There were literally hundreds of them—there was even a "sovereign and military Order of Santa Rita," but Cardinal Canali and the Marquis Travaglini had nothing to do with it. Honours conferred by the Holy See, the Order of the Holy Sepulchre, and the Order of Malta, were only the more sought after, particularly the latter, since noble blood was a *sine qua non*. Consequently the Grand Priory of Podolia, which was doing a brisk trade in Crosses of Malta, was flourishing.

The grand priory in question had been invented by an Italian who claimed to be the heir of a Polish prince, Carthy, and used that name and title, which was not to be found in any almanac of nobility or heraldry. He claimed that his ancestor had founded the Grand Priory of Podolia at the time of the Tsar Paul I. The details of the fraud showed a certain acquaintance with history, but revealed numerous serious lacunae in the rascal's reading. The hereditary commanders created by the Tsar as grand master had only twelve descendants, and they were grouped, in Paris, as the Russian Grand Priory of Malta, under the tutelage of the Grand Duke Andrei. These worthy gentlemen, being Orthodox, were not recognized by the Grand Magistracy in Rome; they devoted themselves to a cult of the past, but did not trade on it. As for the Polish prince Janusz, who had founded the Grand Priory of Ostrog at the beginning of the seventeenth century, he had certainly never given anyone the right to confer honours, that being the grand master's prerogative.

The pseudo Prince Carthy operated with superlative cleverness. He had created the nucleus of his clientele by giving away honours, before drumming up the paying customers: police commissioners and prefects, magistrates, and other public servants had accepted letters patent turning them, by a stroke of the pen, into bailiffs grand cross of Malta, albeit in Podolia merely. They perceived that the grand prior's signature was attested by enormous, very legal-looking seals and, naturally, maintained that the honour confirmed was authentic.

The Grand Magistracy tried, indirectly, to stir the Italian authorities into some administrative action, but the thing was not as simple as it looked. The defences erected by the Grand Prior of Podolia were massive. Commissioners of police turned a deaf ear, prefects of police recalled that since the Republic recognized no decorations, it could hardly protect them; and magistrates declared themselves unable to act, officially, even for a sovereign Order, unless the Order was ready to prosecute. They knew that Prince Chigi, Grand Master of Malta, would never drag the bogus Prince Carthy, bogus Grand Prior of Podolia, into court.

Meanwhile, the plot thickened: the Grand Prior of Podolia was giving rise to emulators. There was already a Grand Prior of the Holy Trinity of Villeneuve; a Grand Prior of Burgundy came close upon his heels. All Italy would soon be flaunting the eight-pointed cross. But at this point Cardinal Canali personally took a hand: he arranged for a donat to get himself made Bailiff Grand Cross of Malta by Prince Carthy, prosecuted the latter for fraud, and forced him to shut up shop. With that judgment in the records, a visit paid by the police sufficed to put an end to the Grand Prior of Villeneuve's career, while a single telephone call from the Chancellery nipped the Grand Priory of Burgundy in the bud.

\*　　　\*　　　\*

One consequence was that the Italian government concluded that even a Republic needed honours in its gift. It therefore resolved to found an Order of Merit, and at the same time to forbid its citizens to wear any other decoration without first obtaining the president's permission. This meant ruin for the swarms of bogus orders. The bill before Parliament made certain exceptions, however: under the Lateran treaty, honours conferred by the Holy See were excepted, and to these were added those of the Order of the Holy Sepulchre—at Cardinal Canali's instance; and the sovereign Order of Malta, whose headquarters were in Rome.

The grand master, who had connections among the grandees of the Republic, had hoped to gain official recognition for the Order's sovereignty at the same time. But Parliament must not be pressed too hard. The chance had been missed under the Fascist régime: the advances which the grand master had made to Mussolini in an effort to gain recognition were now among his evil memories; he had given the Duce the Grand Cross of Honour and Devotion, which was reserved for reigning monarchs and heads of state. Victor Emmanuel had been mortified at the spectacle of his prime minister placed on an equal footing with the royal family, without having produced proof of four quarterings. And Mussolini had not recognized the Order of Malta, confining himself to inviting it to build a leper hospital at Tselaclacla in Abyssinia. And yet the grand master had saved him from making himself look ridiculous by claiming the Island of Malta in the Order's name, as some of the knights were urging him to do.

It was on October 25, 1950, that the bill concerning decorations received its first reading in the Senate. A Communist, Senator Terracini, mounting the tribune, read aloud a document which seemed to prove that the Order was selling decorations. The effect was disastrous: the clause exempting the Order of Malta might be struck out of the bill. A group of friendly senators telephoned the Via Condotti, urgently demanding that someone be sent to explain to them what all this was about.

Cattaneo was sent, and in a handsome reception-room at the beautiful Palazzo Signora was received by two gentlemen in a state of painful excitement: Senator Cingolani, Knight Magistral of the Order and a former cabinet minister; and Senator Cerica, Magistral Grand Cross, one-time General of the Royal Carabinieri, who had arrested Mussolini at the time of the *coup d'état*. They showed him photostats of a letter, and an appended memorandum, both typewritten on the grand magistral writing paper, and signed Hercolani Fava Simonetti.

"I hope these signatures are forgeries," Cingolani said.

"I believe I can assure you that they are authentic," Cattaneo replied.

"*Madonna mia!*" Cingolani groaned, clapping his hands to his head.

"If so, the Order is damned," Cerica said.

The letter, which dated from 1945, was addressed to a donat who was leaving for the Argentine: in it Hercolani confirmed the grand master's approval of his project—to recruit a score of new knights. The appended memorandum recapitulated the financial, religious, and moral obligations which candidates must undertake.

Cattaneo regarded the two senators with all the calm of a Mgr. Bruno Heim regarding the canon who thought he was revealing an appalling secret. He said, "I perceive, gentlemen, that although you are members of the Order, you are not well acquainted with it. Do you imagine that formerly, in Palestine, the Knights of St. John sold honours? Of course not. And yet, before being admitted to the Order, they paid what is still called the '*droit de passage*'—the fare paid by pilgrims travelling in the Order's galleys. Since the Order has been requiring payment from candidates for membership for nearly a thousand years, it's rather late in the day to start feeling righteous indignation about it."

"Neither of us paid anything," Cingolani said.

"Because the grand master used his right to waive payment, in your cases. You cannot suppose, for instance, that he requires payment from the heads of states he decorates with an honour, or from ruined scions of the Hungarian or Polish nobility? But apart from these special or political cases, everyone pays. The amount varies from one country to another, according to their economic status. I see, from this, that in the Argentine, five thousand pesos was the fee in the case of a knight magistral cross."

"Those same five thousand pesos, falling from Terracini's lips, were like a shower of ice water," said Cingolani.

"The fare, for a citizen of the United States, is a thousand dollars, which is a great deal more. In Spain, it's only two thousand pesetas; in France, thirty thousand francs; here, it's fifty thousand lire. But you must on no account reverse the proper

D

order, and imagine that you can get into the Order of Malta by paying. The payment is made only if and when the other conditions for membership are fulfilled. The memorandum attached to this letter deals with the religious and moral references required, as well as the financial conditions to be fulfilled. Did Senator Terracini quote those clauses as well?"

"Why no, he didn't," Cerica said.

"But," Cingolani put in, "there's something I don't understand. You say that, in principle, everyone pays to get into the Order. Surely not knights taking the vows—after all, one of the professions they make is a vow of poverty."

"Those taking vows in the Order of Malta are not simply monks. They have first to be admitted as knights of justice, giving proofs of their nobility: it's at that stage that they pay their passage, as we say. And, incidentally, they pay twice as much as anyone else—for, in the Order of Malta, the greater the honour, the greater the sacrifices required. Even so, without the generosity of its members and the income from its own property, the Order would be quite unable to continue supporting its various charitable works merely out of passage money, which is paid only once, and a few thousand lire of annual subscriptions. And remember that these same charitable works are the latter-day equivalent of carrying pilgrims to the Holy Land, boarding them, and protecting them."

"You must," said Cingolani, "have read an article in one of the Communist papers pouring ridicule on the Order's hospital work. There was one sentence in particular: 'An institution which has discovered the most absurd and complicated means of doing a little good.'"

"All the articles in the world cannot prevent things being what they are. The Grand Magistracy maintains, of its own accord, twenty charitable organizations in Italy alone; and that takes no account of the work done by the three Italian grand priories, nor of the military charities managed by our Italian association on behalf of the Ministry of Defence. As for our overseas associations, they maintain at least a hundred different good works, from Japan to one wing of St. Louis' hospital in Paris, from Uganda to the hospital of SS. John and Elizabeth in

London; in Ireland, the St. John's Ambulance Corps is a veritable little army."

"During the war," Cingolani said, "I myself inspected and travelled by the Order's hospital trains, which went right into Russia, and I shall be at no loss for arguments on that score when I have to answer Terracini. All you need send me is a memorandum covering the civilian charities. That, and the explanation you have given us, will be adequate, I think."

At the Magistral Palace the file for the unfortunate correspondent to whom Hercolani's letter had been addressed was sought and found. It seemed that the grand master, who had a weakness for rewarding services before they were rendered, had made the man a donat first class. A little later, it had been realized that this ardent recruiting officer was no better than an adventurer. Hercolani's letter, if ill interpreted, could be used against the Order; the fellow had sold it. Further research revealed that he was, at this very time, serving a sentence of imprisonment for fraud. The Magistral Palace hastened to inform him that he had been struck off the roll.

Informed of these events, Senator Cingolani told Senator Terracini that if he rose to speak of that ill-fated letter again, he, Cingolani, would have something to say about its recipient. On the day that the bill was voted on, Senator Terracini was absent from his place.

*       *       *

While the Order of Malta was repelling the Communist assault in the Senate, Cardinal Canali was engaged in stabbing it in the back. He had started the traditional ecclesiastical war of attrition—calumny muttered behind the hand, string pulling, a word here and a silence there, whispering campaigns to discredit the adversary, and all carried on in the name of religion and the Church.

His first idea was to get his hands on one of Malta's good works, and hand it over to the Holy Sepulchre: the work in question was the missionary association founded by the grand master, in which the Pope took a loving interest. It was the cardinal's usual tactics: set up the Order of the Holy Sepulchre, which he governed, against the Order of Malta, which he weakened with a view to its ultimate submission.

The Grand Magistracy, warned in time, appealed to the Congregation de Propaganda Fide, refuted the calumnies, and at one stroke overreached the Grand Master of the Holy Sepulchre, who had anticipated involving the grand master in difficulties and using them to belittle him in the eyes of Pius XII

Beaten in this secret battle, Cardinal Canali publicly revenged his own Order, this time on the field of prestige. He was aware that Roman high society was hostile to him, as to his partners in the Trimurti. The biting witticisms uttered at their expense, in the best drawing-rooms and in the two aristocratic clubs were faithfully reported to him, by the espionage service of bribed flunkies he maintained in these circles, as he did at the Magistral Palace. He hit back by raising obstacles to the appointment of noble guards: His Holiness remarked—though without guessing the reason—that their battalion was melting away visibly; and he occasionally bewailed the etiolation of the Italian nobility. But indifferent to Cardinal Canali's intrigues, the great families, all connected with the Order of Malta, continued to despise his Order of the Holy Sepulchre and it was only by going far afield to France that he was able to find a Bourbon-Parma as his lieutenant. Then, suddenly, the situation of one of the first families of Rome gave him an unexpected opportunity.

What was at once the most enviable and least disputable place of honour which the aristocracy owed to the papacy was that of Prince Assistant at the Threshold: least disputable because it belonged traditionally, and alternately, to the Colonnas and the Orsinis. The strife between these two families had divided Rome during the Middle Ages and their reconciliation had been effected at the foot of the papal throne. The function of princes assistant was to pour water over the Holy Father's hands when he celebrated Mass; their privilege, to be censed with certain prelates. This great honour had been a constant drain on their resources: during the great festivals of the Holy See they were obliged to entertain on the grand scale. This had necessitated

their marrying rich wives: such wives were not of the highest
nobility, so that several generations of such marriages had, in
the end, closed the Order of Malta to members of their houses,
or at least prevented their aspiring to its highest ranks. In fact
it was to help the Colonnas and Orsinis that the grand master
had made that exception to the rules which Toto had tried to
take advantage of, whereby proof of four quarterings could be
waived if proof of nobility on the paternal side for 450 years was
forthcoming.

For some years the head of the Orsini family had failed, for
personal reasons, to press his claim to the place; and the Pope,
for other reasons, had not transferred the family's right to it
either to the Orsini heir-apparent or to the cadet branch of the
family, who would have accepted it with avidity. The Trimurti
called upon the young Orsini to claim the place: he was appointed
Lieutenant of the Order of the Holy Sepulchre by Cardinal Canali
and Prince Assistant at the Threshold by the Pope.

Thus and thus, by crushing a bogus grand prior on the one
hand, obtaining recognition for the Holy Sepulchre's honours
on the other, and by giving the Pope a prince assistant, did the
indefatigable cardinal press his point against Prince Chigi.

# V

THE FIRST TERM OF 1951 was occupied, at the Grand Magistracy,
by an inquiry which was no less delicate and a good deal more
instructive than those of 1950. It concerned Cardinal Spellman,
a personal friend of Cardinal Canali's and the American agent
for the Trimurti.

Apart from what may be called their mutual business interests,
the two cardinals had other points in common. Cardinal Canali
was Grand Master of the Holy Sepulchre and Grand Prior of
the Order of Malta; Cardinal Spellman, patron of the American
association of the Knights of Malta, and Chairman of the Society
of Knights of Columbus. The Grand Magistracy had certainly

no reason to interest itself in these latter gentlemen, whose chivalry consisted in wearing a red garment over their dinner jackets; but it took a keen interest in the first named, the "passage" of each new member bringing in no less than a thousand dollars.

Cardinal Spellman had imposed himself as patron of the association, had set an excessively rich gentleman, a Mr. Macdonald, over it as chairman or president, had persuaded the Pope to make him a marquis, and ruled the roost with a firm hand. He had been at some pains to find a suitable title for himself, one which would distinguish him from the other cardinals, all bailiffs grand cross, like himself; he had settled on the title "Protector." Wishing, however, to distinguish himself, further, from King Leopold and Queen Wilhelmina, protectors respectively of the Belgian and Dutch associations, he had taken the title "Grand Protector" and, what is more, "Spiritual Adviser," titles singular to himself. There were some other singularities connected with the United States association: he had renamed it the "American Chapter of the Knights of Malta," although there was not a single professed knight among its members; and he had rebaptized its chairman, "Master." He had explained to the Grand Master Chigi, who was somewhat taken aback at the creation of this lesser, Yankee master—this *petit-maître*, as it were—that there was no question of setting up in competition; the device was a means of making American knights, all magistral by nature, understand that they were responsible to a grand master. And the cardinal had gone on to request that, in order to avoid misunderstandings, the grand master should not take the initiative in appointing American knights. The cardinal proposed about fifty candidates for membership every year. But the grand master, when he came to look into it, made the strange discovery that nobody had ever seen hair or hide of an American knight at the Grand Magistral Palace.

When, some time between the two world wars, the association was founded, its officers had pointed out that if gifts—apart from passage money—made by its members, were to be exempted from taxation, it would be necessary to specify in the statutes of the association the charities which were to benefit by such gifts.

Mgr. Pizzardo, chaplain of the association, had got the grand master to agree that the single charity to be specified should be not one of the Order's own good works but one maintained by the Holy See—the Hospital of the Bambino Gesù, in Rome. Mgr. Pizzardo—a future cardinal—was its administrator. The Grand Magistracy had been unaware of the total, and actual employment, of the gifts in question, but believed the sum to be a modest one, a belief which the Holy See discreetly fostered.

Toward the end of Holy Year, Professor Rossi, administrator general of the Order's property, conceived the idea of having the Order recognized as a charitable organization, in the U.S., since this would carry with it certain fiscal advantages touching its American investments. An eminent American lawyer was consulted, declared the thing to be feasible, and offered to carry it through. The grand master asked the chancellor to inform the Marquis Macdonald, as a matter of courtesy, while he himself undertook to inform Cardinal Spellman. The master did not answer, but the grand protector and spiritual adviser replied with a very angry letter declaring the project to be madness, impracticable, and dangerous to the association. Prince Chigi was particularly shocked by the fact that the cardinal, to whom he had written in the accepted forms of courtesy—*Most Reverend Eminence . . . Stooping to kiss the sacred purple*—had replied in a style altogether more airy—*Dear Grand Master . . . Yours sincerely.*

In January, 1951, while Cardinal Canali was absorbed in arranging for the canonization of Pius X, restorer and one-time Grand Master of the Order of the Holy Sepulchre (the cardinal's name did not appear in the case, it was nominally delegated to Cardinal Micara), a French Knight of Malta, one of Hercolani's friends, came to Rome, having just returned from America. This visitor astonished the treasurer by referring to the millions of dollars poured into the Order's treasury every year.

"Millions of dollars? You're confusing dollars with lire or francs. About fifty thousand dollars a year, in point of fact."

"You're joking, of course," the Frenchman said. "I personally know one American knight" (he named the man) "who, on the day he became a member, last year, sent Cardinal Spellman a cheque for two hundred thousand dollars."

"If that's the case," Hercolani said, "the beds in the Bambino Gesù Hospital must be made of solid gold." And he explained the statutes of the American association.

Its appetite whetted by this piece of information, the Grand Magistracy made inquiries both at home and in the United States. It was discovered that upon becoming members of the Order, American knights gave Cardinal Spellman a minimum of 50,000 dollars; that most gave 100,000; and some 200,000. That, thereafter, the richer knights made further gifts, almost as generous, to Cardinal Spellman, destined, like the first payments, for the Bambino Gesù Hospital. That Cardinal Spellman gave the knights an annual banquet at the Waldorf-Astoria in New York at the conclusion of which he took the plate round himself; and that no guest would have dared put in less than 1,000 dollars. That Cardinal Spellman maintained no charitable institution in the United States for "the American Chapter of the Order of Malta," but that, in his own country, he passed himself off as the real head of the Order whose bulls happened, because of an ancient custom, to be signed by an old gentleman in Rome. That Cardinal Spellman had forbidden American knights visiting Rome to call on the aforementioned old gentleman, who knew no English and did not want to be bothered with them. That one of the clerks at the Magistral Palace had destroyed the copies of the monthly illustrated journal issued by the American association which reached the palace. That the project of obtaining recognition as a charitable institution in the United States was very alarming to Cardinal Spellman who feared that the Grand Magistracy would try to claim the money destined for the Bambino Gesù Hospital, for its own good works. That the money in question, which did, indeed, run into millions, was sent, for the Bambino Gesù Hospital, to Cardinal Pizzardo, Pro-Secretary of the Holy Office, although there was nothing out of the way in the equipment or running of the Bambino Gesù Hospital.

The grand master was not reluctant to answer Cardinal Spellman's letter once he was furnished with such splendid material. Nevertheless, he decided to graduate his attack. He began by cancelling his erstwhile forbearance: the "American Chapter of the Knights of Malta" should be known as the American association; and its "Master" Macdonald as Chairman Macdonald. He added that the Order would certainly have itself recognized as a charity in the U.S. since, far from being madness and impracticable, the project had been approved by a notable American jurist and was already on the way to accomplishment. The grand protector and spiritual adviser vouchsafed no answer.

The American jurist informed the Grand Magistracy that obstacles of a political nature had appeared in their path. Prince Chigi, suspecting their origin, again wrote to Cardinal Spellman, drew attention to his last letter, and by way of putting a flea in his ear, requested him to furnish the Grand Magistracy with a list of the American charities supported by the American association, "charities which must be of great importance in view of the large sums which, according to reliable information, American knights have subscribed to charities under the Order's aegis." The grand protector and spiritual adviser continued to hold his tongue.

Prince Chigi wrote him a third letter, recalling its two predecessors. And used the occasion to strike his final blow: he requested the cardinal to furnish him, according to the rules, with his association's accounts; and, since they had never been received, annual accounts covering the whole period since its foundation. The grand protector and spiritual adviser returned no answer.

*       *       *

The relations between the Via Condotti and Knights of Malta in all other countries were as cordial and inspired by mutual trust as they were remote and difficult with those of the United States. During the last several years they had, in fact, grown closer: and although the Grand Magistracy was composed, for the most part, of elderly men, they had made a special effort to get young blood into the various national associations.

In the case of those associations which had been forced into exile, the events which had recently shaken all Europe had helped. Thus, the Hungarian association was now only nominally presided over by the aged Archduke Joseph; the Silesian, by the old Prince von Hatzfeldt; and the Polish by Prince Czartorynski.

In France, things were somewhat stagnant: there, the chairman was the Comte de Rohan-Chabot, Duc de Ravèse, a man well stricken in years whose principal preoccupation was keeping the grand magistral knights at arm's length. Although they were all members of the association, according to its own statutes, and although Prince Chigi had reminded the count that they were knights of the Order like any others excepting in matters of precedence, they had been driven to organize themselves into an "association of French hospital charities of the Order of Malta." The Comte de Rohan-Chabot was even more hostile to political appointments to the Order, and had refused to include in his nominal roll the Herriots, Bidaults, Schumans *e tutti quanti* who had had to fall back on knighthood *in gremio religionis* for want of quarterings. It had been a black day for him when he had been obliged to confer the title of Bailiff Grand Cross of Honour and Devotion on President Auriol. The distant and icy expression of his face, in the official photograph of the event, had borne witness to his true feelings. But, since Baron Marsaudon was one of the party, it may be that the Comte de Rohan-Chabot, Duc de Ravèse, had caught a whiff of heresy. And perhaps, in the course of all that republican buffoonery in which he had been forced to play a part, he was recalling the Order's last great days in France; remembering the loan of 200,000 crowns made by the Commander d'Estournel to Louis XVI, to help the King in his unhappy flight to Varennes; the Bailiff de Virieu's protest against the august fugitive's imprisonment, with his family, in the Temple tower—the Commandery of Malta. The fact is, there was something almost heroic in the Comte de Rohan-Chabot, Duc de Ravèse, so obstinately defending the Order against intrusion by commoners; for he had married outside his caste and must, presumably, exclude his own sons from membership.

However, apart from this nobleman of the old school, there

were other gentlemen in the French association who were open to new ideas and ready to welcome grand magistral knights with open arms.

*         *         *

And Prince Chigi, despite his preference for the "Italian atmosphere," had done much to show the flag abroad. Elected in 1931, he had begun by visiting France in 1932. No grand master before him had ever set foot in the land which had given the Order nearly half its great captains and whose royal ships, under Louis XIV, dipped their colours to the Order's vessels without requiring a reciprocal salute. He had been received with sovereign's honours. And President Lebrun had decorated him with the Grand Cross of the Legion of Honour. He had opened the new wing of the St. Louis Hospital—he had also, a few years before, laid its foundation stone as representative of his predecessor in office. Thereafter, he had visited Belgium, Holland, and Czechoslovakia, and had later been to Poland, Hungary, Austria, Tripoli, and Rhodes, where Italy was succeeding to the Order's knights of yore. At Malta, his call had been discreet, yet marked by much popular and respectful enthusiasm. And if his courteous refusal to do more than take an informal cup of tea with the British governor of the island had been a matter for smilingly raised eyebrows, he had nevertheless refused to visit England since there he would not have been received in state, as a sovereign. But now, while England still occupied Malta, Italy no longer held Tripoli and Rhodes. And the Greeks, new masters of Rhodes, had even gone to the length of expelling the Italian residents, including the Order's delegate, who was there to feed the flame of two centuries of erstwhile chivalry.

His taste for travel reviving, the grand master had accepted invitations to visit Spain and Portugal during the following autumn. It seemed to him that the journey would serve a purpose: it would take him to two countries whose associations were among the most active, which, in view of the Order's circumstances, was important. For the time was not far distant when the Order, if it was to defend itself against its Grand Prior

of Rome, who had become its persecutor, would, in default of
those members who were kept in leading strings by Cardinal
Spellman, have need of all its European knights.


# VI


DESPITE THE HUMILIATION inflicted on him in Sovereign Council,
Cardinal Canali arrived to celebrate the St. John's Mass in the
priorial church. And he was all sweetness and light. His bene-
dictory gestures and unctuous voice preached nothing but
reconciliation and peace. It was, however, noticed that he did
not wear the Order's insignia on his chasuble. And this omission
seemed like a warning, so that his copious flow of meekness and
benevolence appeared in a different light, and served to confirm it.

The traditional reception was held that afternoon under the
shady trees of the garden, the guests as usual being the Sacred
College, Vatican people, diplomatic corps, and the aristocracies
both white and black. Later, the traditional grand magistral
dinner was served in the summerhouse. The entire staff was
present, from Prince Chigi down to the most junior clerk, and
they sat in an easy familiarity worthy of the patriarchal house-
holds of ancient Rome in which certain annual festivals brought
masters and servants together. Cardinal Canali was never of
this company, but the Order's chaplains were always pleased
to remain behind for the event, sometimes partaking copiously
of the Polignac champagne.

The day was a red-letter one for the Chancellery calligrapher.
He was proficient in writing the texts of the Order's bulls in
Gothic script, but it was also his business to paint the armorial
bearings of newly made knights on the walls of the palace salon.
With the freedom proper to the occasion, he did not hesitate to
assert that "his" coats of arms were quite as good as those which
had been designed by the chancellor for the Vatican library.
But his pride and joy lay in explaining, for the hundredth time,
as a Roman and a Papalist, that he was Prince Chigi's middle-

class equivalent. This was the invariable theme of the speech which he had the honour of making at the end of the banquet, in reply to the grand master's. He was a member of that *petite bourgeoisie* which had taken refuge in the Vatican City in 1870, by way of protest against the seizure of Rome. His people had, ever since that time, been in Vatican employment, either as clerks in the Congregation offices, or as craftsmen manufacturing religious objects or ecclesiastical haberdashery. As for the calligrapher himself, he had certainly not mistaken his path when he had made for the Order of Malta; but although he had been there twenty years his ambition was not promotion from the rank of donat to that of magistral knighthood; it was to receive a commission in the Palatine guard, in which he was actually a non-commissioned officer.

There was another red-letter day in his calendar—the Feast of the Purification of the Virgin. It was he who ordered and decorated the great candle for Candlemas, which was presented to the Pope in the Consistory chamber, together with those of diverse orders, institutes, seminaries, patriarchal and minor basilicas, collegiate churches, and privileged brotherhoods. The grand master would have thought himself past his work if the Malta *cero* had not been the longest, the stoutest, and the most handsome. Consequently the calligrapher resorted to bribery, corruption, and subornation to discover, in advance, the weight, length, and decoration of the candles to be presented by the Jesuits and the Order of the Holy Sepulchre, the only ones which might aspire to outdo his own. And when he had well and truly painted, illuminated, and varnished his candle, dressed it with pompons and capped it with a snuffer bearing the arms of Malta, he would go to Prince Chigi's suite without having requested an audience and proudly summon him thus: "Grand master, come and see our candle."

At the 1951 Feast of St. John he was able to hymn his latest triumph. For, that year, every record had been broken: Jesuits and Holy Sepulchre had been wiped off the face of the earth: the Order of Malta's candle had exceeded six feet in length, had been decorated with inscriptions in red, and had weighed sixty pounds.

"May the Blessed Virgin Mary reward you in like measure!"
the Holy Father had exclaimed, clasping his hands together in
admiration.

\*       \*       \*

Summer passed without incident. In autumn the grand master
set out for Madrid and Lisbon, arm in arm with Cardinal
Tedeschini, Pontifical Legate to the ceremonies at Fatima.
Before leaving, however, he had reminded Cardinal Spellman of
his existence in energetic language.

He returned to Rome at the end of October, delighted with
his journey. He had reviewed guards of honour, had been conducted over the Order's ancient castles, King Humbert had called
on him, and he had been made much of by the four other cardinals
present at Fatima, and notably by Cardinal Gerlier, primate of
the Gauls, who was hoping for the Grand Cross of Malta.

On the day following his return, Prince Chigi received a letter
from Cardinal Spellman: by way of reply to the grand master's
several letters, the grand protector and spiritual adviser requested
the grand master to let him know what became of the thousands
of dollars which the American association sent him every year.
The grand master was sharpening his pen to indite a stinging
answer, when two other letters arrived. The first was from
Cardinal Canali asking him for "an act of justice, wisdom, and
magnanimity" in favour of Fra Ferdinando Thun Hohenstein.
Prince Chigi replied by return, asking since when the grand prior
had become the ally of knights rebellious to their vows, and
administrators guilty of imprudence. The second letter was from
Father Larraona: it informed the grand master that "in view
of the special circumstances of the Grand Priory of Lombardy-
Venetia, the Sacred Congregation of Religious would consider
any new decree touching the said grand priory to be inopportune."
This was, as it were, in illustration of Cardinal Canali's letter,
since it suggested that the post of grand prior, to which Fra
Ferdinando had formerly had some pretensions, must be left
open for him. The grand master's answer to Father Larraona
was to the effect that the Sovereign Council would issue such

decrees as it thought fit in a matter which concerned an administrative division of the Order. On October 31 the Congregation
of Religious announced that it refused the request of Angelo de
Mojana, Sovereign Councillor for Lombardy-Venetia, to take the
final vows.

"I smell brimstone," Pecci told the grand master, and he
added, "Let us hope that the canonization of the Blessed Couderc
on Sunday will purify the Vatican atmosphere."

The Sunday in question being November 4, the *Osservatore
Romano* published the news that "The Holiness of Our Lord
received in private audience His Most Reverend Eminent Signor
Nicholas Canali, Grand Penitentiary, Chairman of the Pontifical
Committee for the Vatican State."

That same afternoon, in the Vatican basilica, The Holiness of
Our Lord proclaimed that the Blessed Marie-Victoire-Therèse
Couderc, founder of the Convent of Notre Dame du Cénacle,
had been admitted to the glory of "mounting the altars." The
*Excellentissime* relations of His Holiness, the *Eminentissime*
Sacred College, the *Excellentissime* diplomatic corps, thirty
lord archbishops and lord bishops, the *Illustrissime* body of
Roman prelates, the *Reverendissime* delegations of the Pontifical
Court and the Vatican City, representatives of the sovereign
Hierosolymitan Order of Malta, and of the equestrian Order of
the Holy Sepulchre of Jerusalem were present at the ceremony,
likewise a vast concourse of people.

# VII

ON MONDAY, November 5, following Mass in the Grand
Magistracy chapel, Prince Chigi, obviously very upset, placed
two letters before the Sovereign Council, both of them astounding, the first being from Father Larraona and the second from
Cardinal Canali, but countersigned by Cardinals Micara and
Pizzardo.

The two letters differed greatly in format, if not in significance:

the first was printed on eight large pages of ministerial paper, which were tied, with white and yellow cord, to thirty-one appendices; the other was only two pages long, and those type-written on ordinary paper. The printed letter was dated November 3 and had been delivered to the Grand Magistracy on the same day, but not until seven o'clock in the evening. As it was a Saturday, there was nobody in the offices and the grand master was going to the theatre. He did not, therefore, read it until the next day; and then he kept it to himself, as if it were an outrage which could be suppressed by hiding it. But he was so overwhelmed that he was unable to accompany his colleagues to the canonization of the Blessed Couderc. The typed letter bore the date of November 5 and had been delivered at seven o'clock in the morning, as if written at dawn. Thus it was that the Spanish monk and the three Roman cardinals who were at last openly unsheathing the sword against the grand master, could take credit for having let forty-eight hours elapse, by way of respite, between first thrust and *coup de grâce*, whereas in fact the two blows followed one upon the other.

The first seven pages of the letter from the Congregation of Religious contained a historical exposé, manifestly partial, designed to prove that the Order of St. John had always been closely dependent on the sovereign pontiffs. This thesis, backed up by the thirty-one appendices, was summed up in a final paragraph: "The Holy See, animated by the desire to render the noble mission of the Hierosolymitan Order more efficacious, has judged that it is expedient to assist and direct it, the better to ensure the sanctification of its members and the good of the community. Therefore, the Holy Father did, on July 9, following out the wishes expressed by the plenary congregation of June 21, deign to set up under the aegis of the said Sacred Congregation, a Commission of Cardinals charged with responsibility for the Order of Malta. As a gesture of courtesy the members of the commission have been chosen within the bosom of the Order itself: they are, their Most Reverend Eminences Cardinals Canali, Chairman; Micara; and Pizzardo. Mgr. Scapinelli di Léguigno, Undersecretary of the Sacred Congregation of Religious, is appointed Secretary to the Most Eminent Commission."

Father Larraona, who had signed this long message, printed on the secret Vatican presses, had in his haste forgotten to add the usual formula of courtesy, for which a blank space was provided. The three cardinals, on the other hand, had not forgotten to renew, albeit at seven o'clock in the morning, "the assurance of their most distinguished devotion" to the grand master. This, after notifying him of what they had already "decided in obedience to the wishes of the Holy Father." Minutes of all the Sovereign Council's deliberations must be submitted to the commission; "an exact inventory of the Order's patrimony" must be produced to it as soon as possible, likewise the budget for the current year. No expenditure, nor any act of administration beyond those of routine business, must be undertaken without the permission of the commissioners. Finally, Mgr. Ilario Alcini, Visitor of the Italian Seminaries, and newly made titular Archbishop of Nicea, would resume his visits *ad inquirendum et referendum.*

For all that they were themselves members of a religious order and familiar with Vatican manners, the members of the Sovereign Council could feel nothing but repugnance and disgust as they read these two missives. Of all the infamous hypocrisy! Their indignation at the wrong done to the Order was only less than their anger at the wrong done to the Church, whose name and authority were thus profaned. Here were a Son of the Immaculate Heart of Mary and three lord cardinals, appointed by the Pope "the better to ensure the sanctification of its members and the good of the community," making a bee-line for the cash, demanding inventory and budget—as if to avenge a demand of the same kind which the grand master had addressed to a certain Eminence among their friends.

The arch-conspirator had gained his point; and thought he was saving appearances by dragging two other cardinals into the business, of whom one, however, was under an obligation and the other his accomplice. But in any case, could he really hope to save appearances when what he was doing, in fact, was to preside over a commission contrived to stifle an Order to which he himself belonged? But that, of course, was the "gesture of courtesy," a delicate attention on the part of the Order's grand prior: it was worthy of the unctuous piety with which, three days after the Congregation had given him the full powers he wanted, he had celebrated Mass in the Order's priory church in the presence of the grand master and the Knights of Malta.

The Sovereign Council was in a parlous state; but its members seemed to be sorry only for themselves and their grand master.

"Poor Gigino!" the chancellor said, calling his old friend by his youthful nickname.

"That they should do such a thing to me!" Prince Chigi exclaimed. "Why, my brother commands the noble guards! They're forgetting that I, my brother, and King Humbert are the only Italians whom the Holy Father ever decorated with the Order of Christ."

"A fine mess the cardinals will make," Taccone said, "when it comes to examining proofs of nobility."

"Nicholas will have the Greek Carrack moved to St. Onuphre," was Conestabile's comment. Adamovich von Csepin said, "It'll end with them making Thun Grand Prior of Austria," and Hercolani, jesting even unto the canon's mouth, "Oh, well played, grand prior!"

Del Balzo was the first to protest; he said, "Can't you see that something much bigger than ourselves is involved? This is the end of the Order of Malta."

There was a silence at that. The grand master leaned his head against the back of his chair and said, "True, true, I should be thinking of the Order, not of myself."

"And it's not the end," Hercolani cried, "it's the beginning. Of war. Well, let's wage it, then."

A telegram was sent to Angelo de Mojana, who was in Milan, recalling him in haste, that he might add his learning in the law to Del Balzo's who, meanwhile, was instructed to draft a memorandum. And it was he who insisted, in the teeth of the grand master's reluctance which was inspired by false shame, that Pecci must be told at once.

\*　　\*　　\*

As soon as he was informed of the letters' contents, the Order's minister to the Holy See declared that they must have recourse to the Pope. By that means, and only by that means, Father

Larraona and the three cardinals might be disarmed. He was likewise of opinion that they had not a minute to lose; but first, they needed more information. Leaving his counsellor, Malfatti, and Cattaneo, to draft the appeal, he called on Mgr. Montini. Pecci, although it might be possible to catch him out occasionally, like anyone else, was a superlative diplomat; and when he was on a scent there was no keener hound. Yet this time he found himself well and truly at fault. Mgr. Montini, kept in ignorance by Cardinal Canali, was as amazed as he was mortified. Mgr. Tardini, Secretary for Extraordinary Affairs and as conscientiously "correct" as the substitute, also knew nothing of an affair which was surely sufficiently extraordinary. Pecci, making the rounds of other offices where he was *persona grata*, made one discovery: Mgr. Alcini, who lived at the Ethiopian College in the Vatican gardens, had just taken delivery of many sticks of sealing-wax, which he had joyfully enclosed in a bag together with the newly minted seal of the Cardinals' Commission for the Order of Malta.

It was a detail only, but it gave Leo XIII's great-nephew the key; he could learn more now. He did: it was to this effect— that on the following morning at 10 A.M., the Archbishop of Nicea would make his way to the Via Condotti, accompanied by a truck, *ad inquirendum et referendum*. In order to hasten his inquisition and referendum the Visitor to the Italian Seminaries proposed to remove, at once, all the Treasury books and Chancellery dossiers: he would then have the offices cleared and seal them.

"They have it all planned," Pecci said, "but they've made one mistake; they've left us twenty-four hours."

The whole day was spent on the appeal to His Holiness; every word, every comma, was weighed, for the Order's fate was in the balance. If the appeal failed—and failure might be due to the smallest scruple of a trifle—half a thousand years of history was over, the sovereign Order at an end.

It was Cattaneo who typed the final draft, on the so-called state parchment, which was embossed with the Order's arms in red and white and had gilt edges. It was in the form of a letter, written "in humbleness at the Holy Father's feet," and it is due to this letter that the Order of Malta still exists. Pecci had considered it advisable not even to mention the cardinals, but only the Congregation of Religious, with which their Eminences were covering themselves. Prince Chigi was represented as saying that "the venerated communication of the Sacred Congregation had deeply wounded and saddened him." In it he saw the culmination of a series of acts hostile to the Order and which, not sparing even himself, took no account of either his age or his name. His letter then went on to recall that the origin of these hostilities was an appeal to the Sacred Congregation on the part of a professed knight, an appeal whose terms had never been communicated to him, while the Congregation was refusing the requests of new candidates for vows. Prince Chigi expressed the fear that rumours of these new and questionable measures might well rouse comment in Italy and abroad. And while protesting the Order's submission, the letter asked the Holy Father to suspend these measures and allow the whole case to be tried "before a competent ecclesiastical court from which impartial justice might be expected."

However, while this missive was being so carefully written, the grand master, ashamed, perhaps, of having been so put out in the first place, had gone to the other extreme, and was now lulling his anxiety with a naïve optimism and, in his own mind, settling the business to his satisfaction. He drew attention to the length of time—since the plenary session of the Congregation on June 21—taken by the cardinals in making up their mind to attack. From this he argued that although they had required an inventory of the Order's property "as soon as possible," this meant that they could take their time. As for the difficulty touching major expenditure and extraordinary business, that was easily overcome: all they had to do was confine themselves to routine business, ordinary measures of administration and expenditure. How was the thing to be judged? Was the conferring of an honour on a chief of state, for instance, ordinary or extraordinary business? The argument could be prolonged indefinitely.

It was Pecci who convinced Prince Chigi of the need and urgency of an appeal to the Pope and, at eight o'clock in the morning, got him to sign it.

"Let's hope it will serve some purpose," the old man said.

But the signature was not all: the Pope must receive the letter in person and at once. There could, of course, be no question of the prince delivering it himself: an audience of the Pope took time to arrange. On the other hand a letter, however urgent, which was delivered to the Secretariat of State in the morning would not reach their august correspondent until the afternoon. Cardinal Canali was, of course, fully aware of these facts and had no doubt slept soundly that night, confident that at 10 A.M. on November 6, the commission's seals would close the Grand Magistral Palace and the Pope, whose real wishes the cardinal was obviously overreaching, would be confronted with an accomplished fact. The number and difficulty of the doors which must be opened to reach the only man who could prevent this constituted as good a guarantee for the success of the grand prior's scheme as the help of St. Rita, his patron. The possibility of a single, backstairs door had not occurred to him.

As a result of which oversight, at 8.45 A.M. the Pope was reading the appeal, delivered to him by Mgr. Nasalli di Corneliano, Canon of St. Peter's and Secret Chamberlain. This prelate was the brother of Count Rocca di Corneliano, Assistant Administrator of the Order's charities, who had married one of the grand master's nieces. Mgr. di Corneliano suffered for his part in this business: Cardinal Canali sent for him, made a violent scene, and threatened to appoint him Vicar of Frosimone. Be that as it may, Mgr. Alcini was seen sadly removing the sticks of sealing-wax from his bag, likewise the seal; and he was obliged to dismiss the truck which stood, its engine already running, outside the Ethiopian College.

# VIII

THE HOLY FATHER'S WISDOM had prevented recourse to extreme measures: but the principles and means of interference with the Order which he had approved, remained. The three cardinals and their henchmen, checked in their head-long course toward the budget and inventory, were soon making their presence felt again.

Father Larraona, to whom the grand master had sent a copy of his appeal to the Pope, answered on the following day and in the name of the Congregation of Religious, as follows: "It was with the keenest astonishment that this Sacred Dicastery received your letter, and the copy of the appeal which Your Most Eminent Highness addressed to His Holiness. This Sacred Dicastery is conscious of having acted with the most exquisite consideration in its dealings both with the Order and with the venerable person of Your Most Eminent Highness. When this Sacred Dicastery was obliged, against its own inclination, and acting upon complaints lodged by a professed member of the Order, to take action, it was careful to appoint as Visitor *ad inquirendum et referendum* a man of the highest standing, to wit His Most Reverend Excellency, Mgr. Ilario Alcini, at that time Bishop of Dionysiad, subsequently promoted to the titular Archbishopric of Nicea as a mark of His Holiness's gratitude. It is the traditional practice of this Sacred Dicastery to withhold from interested parties the contents of confidential documents touching their case. This Sacred Dicastery is not aware that it has ever put obstacles in the way of candidates for vows, unless such candidature involved a canonical impossibility. This Sacred Dicastery assures the Hierosolymitan Order that no indiscretion can properly be imputed to it, since its proceedings are always conducted in the most absolute secrecy. Your Most Eminent Highness must allow me to make a heartfelt appeal to his noble heart, that he may faithfully and generously accept whatever this Sacred Dicastery, interpreting the will of the Holy See, shall see fit to decide. . . ."

The steady drum-beat of the word *dicastery* to denote his Congregation with the utmost solemnity; his "exquisite consideration"; his assurance of "absolute secrecy" in preparing his stabs in the back; the pretence of having intervened, despite himself, because of Thun's complaints; the hint that Mgr. Alcini had been promoted as a reward for his services—all this proved that Father Larraona was not wanting in humour, despite the somewhat heavily scored music of his style. Incidentally, Mgr. Alcini was not the only one to have received his reward already: Cardinal Micara had been appointed vicar general to His Holiness for the City of Rome.

The Sovereign Council now persuaded the grand master to reinforce the legal lights of Del Balzo, De Mojana, and the Order's advocate, Gazzoni, by engaging an expert in ecclesiastical business. Here, again, Pecci gave good advice: he suggested—and the suggestion was adopted—Ferrata, advocate to the Consistory and, as such, a Vatican dignitary. By this choice the Order not only disarmed any suspicion that its attitude was irreligious, but avoided blunders which might involve canonical sanctions. Moreover, Ferrata, who had delivered the "peroration" at the beatification of Pius X last June, was on the best of terms with Cardinal Canali. But he was a man of the same stamp as Mgr. Rossi Stockalper, and like him could combine this friendship and friendship with the grand master. Finally, he enjoyed the personal esteem of the Pope whose permission he asked to accept the brief. In granting it, the Head of the Church showed that he did not regard the Order's case as indefensible. Cardinal Canali, consulted in his turn, could hardly do otherwise than agree. However, to avoid contacts which might have disturbed his good relations with the cardinal, Ferrata had another consistorial lawyer recruited to the Order's juridical college—a member of parliament named Corsanego, a man who boasted of being no friend to Cardinal Canali and who was likely, therefore, to take an aggressive line.

To these appointments were added certain measures of "public safety." The Sovereign Council was to be in permanent session, that is to say no member was to leave the Magistral Palace, or at least the city. All decrees and all letters were to be passed, in the first instance, by a meeting attended by the lawyers, the Sovereign Council's two jurists, Pecci or Malfatti, and Cattaneo. Finally, chairmen of any national association who happened to be in Rome was to be invited to Council meetings.

While Ferrata was mulling over the reply to be made to Father Larraona, the others studied the printed letter, which might be compared in its function to those "moving towers" which had been used at the siege of Rhodes, for it was Cardinal Canali's means of assaulting the Grand Magistracy.

The historical exposé included many details which were useful pointers to the ulterior motives animating Father Larraona and his associates. It did not confine itself to proofs of the Order's religious dependence on the Holy See, which the Order had never sought to deny: it tried to establish that the Order's property was of a definitely ecclesiastical nature and origin, in order to vindicate Cardinal Canali's appetite for it. Having begun at the Flood, or at least in the year 1113 with Pope Pascal II, the Sacred Dicastery recalled that the Order had inherited a part of the Templars' property, thanks to Church intervention; and the conclusion was that the Order owed the rain of charitable gold which had poured on to it for centuries, to Church patronage.

Obviously, Father Larraona, in his reference to the Templars' case, was considering it as an act which did honour to the papacy, or he would hardly have dared to mention it in a religious document. In the same spirit, later in the letter, he blandly quoted the words which Clement VI had spoken to the Grand Master Gozon, in 1346. Indeed, these words seemed to be the inspiration not only of Father Larraona's letter, but of the three cardinals' own, and even some of the things which Cardinal Canali had said at Magione: "Desiring that thou should'st tread the straight and narrow path, and that the Hospital flourish both spiritually and temporally, it is with regret that we have heard the evil which is spoken concerning it, both as to persons and goods. For it is the opinion of the clergy, as of the people, often expressed by virtuous men in Our presence, that thou, my son, and other dignitaries of the Hospital, do not practice such charity as you should, considering your innumerable treasures, both transmarine and cismarine. . . . The administrators of the Hospital ride large and beautiful horses, feed upon delectable victuals, wear magnificent garments, drink out of silver or gold vessels, keep hounds and hawks, go hunting, accumulate immense sums of money, and give alms only moderately and rarely. We summon you, therefore, to remedy all this, lest We and the Apostolic See, as many are urging us to do, be obliged by your errors and idleness to take other measures."

Clement VI, it would seem from this, would not have been averse to serving the Grand Master of Rhodes as Clement V had served the Grand Master of the Templars thirty years before. Cardinal Canali, even more eager to imitate Philippe le Bel and Clement V, short only of burning at the stake, must have relished that medieval prose. But Clement VI was unable to imitate Clement V because the Hospital had profited by the Templars' unhappy experience and had avoided putting all its eggs in one basket. The best part of the Templars' property had been in France, and their grand master lived, and had been seized, in the heart of that kingdom. The Hospitalers' property was distributed all over Europe, and it would have been more difficult to sweep all their great men into one net, as the Sovereign Pontiff and the King of France had done to the Templars. Now, however, the Order of Malta stood, to the Holy See, in the same case as the Templars: for although the property of the Order's overseas associations was out of reach, the best of its wealth was in Italy. And it could be seized by laying hands on the Palace in the Via Condotti.

These sombre memories of medieval times, which Father Larraona set up like a scarecrow, working himself up until he seemed ready, almost, to rebuke the Grand Master for keeping canaries, and that despite an august exemplar, reminded the older bailiffs of a piece of ancient history more moving than anything that Spanish monk had any idea of: it was secret history, never yet revealed, and recorded in the most precious document of the Order's secret archives. That document established that the Hospitalers had received the booty of a certain spoliation in appearance merely. The last Grand Master of the Temple, Jacques de Molay, hearing that the Knights of St. John were considering coming to his rescue, sent a message imploring them not to compromise themselves for a cause lost in advance; asked that their grand prior, Raoul d'Orléans, might visit him in prison; and there handed him his last will and testament which appointed the Hospital heir to the Temple.

# IX

On November 10 the grand master had a stroke. His doctors announced that it was not serious: but he needed rest.

While he kept to his bed, the jurists were drafting a new letter, which they considered it necessary that he send to Pius XII. Their object was to lay before the Holy Father the reflections inspired by Father Larraona's last letter, and add some precise details to their "humble" appeal. The "competent ecclesiastical court" to which they had referred, for example, was the Tribunal of the Apostolic Signature. The rectitude of Cardinal Massimi, its president, would guarantee "impartial justice." Since then, however, Ferrata had argued that the grand master should demand a special court. The advantage he saw for the Order in this move was as follows: by avoiding an appeal to any customary court of the Holy See, the Order would be asserting its sovereign character. The sort of tribunal he envisaged was of the kind which former sovereign pontiffs had sometimes set up, at the request of kings, to deal with differences which had arisen between the secular and spiritual powers.

"But supposing the court be composed of the same three cardinals?" both Pecci and Corsanego objected.

"You must not let your animosity mislead you," Ferrata replied. "Cardinal Canali would not dream of doing anything so iniquitous: and were he to do so, the Holy Father would certainly not tolerate it."

Del Balzo, De Mojana, and Gazzoni were of the same opinion saying that a man could not be judge in his own cause, and that consequently Cardinal Canali's presence on the special court's bench would be an impossibility in law.

The letter petitioning the Pope to set up this special court was dispatched on the 12th. As was customary, the grand master had a copy sent to Father Larraona, with a covering letter commenting on it in energetic terms. In this he adverted to his own unquestionable right to preserve the Order from measures directed against its patrimony, whether chivalric, political, material, or moral. He declared himself certain that the measures in question were in excess of those desired by the Holy Father. By treating the Order simply as a religious institution they were rearming those who, denying its sovereign quality, had sought, in the law courts, to strip it of its property. Its legations, too, would be abolished, since an ordinary religious institution could not be accredited. "Your Most Reverend Excellency," Prince Chigi concluded, "will no doubt agree that it was not merely my right, but my duty, to prevent so ruinous an outcome."

Feeling somewhat recovered, he had left his room that day. And to show his respect for Pius XII and the Sacred College, he had attended the Sistine Chapel to be present at the memorial service for those cardinals who had died in the past twelve months. Cardinal Canali watched him curiously, in sly, sideways glances from behind one of the large warts which marred his face, and muttered to his neighbours, "Our princely friend looks a very sick man."

Ten days before this event, the former Ambassador Auriti had been informed that a letter recognizing the Order of Malta as sovereign *de jure* was before President de Gasperi for signature. It was now or never, and consequently a matter of leaving no stone unturned. Recognition was a consecration which would be a redoubtable weapon in the quarrel with the Holy See; but a government composed of Christian Democrats would grant it only if it remained in ignorance of that quarrel. Auriti had been besieging the Palazzo Chigi since November 5, hoping that the fact of the Ministry for Foreign Affairs occupying the grand master's ancestral house might somehow be lucky. It was.

President de Gasperi's letter arrived on the 13th; without, for the time being, envisaging an exchange of diplomatic envoys, the Italian government recognized the sovereignty of the Order of Malta and agreed to receive an official delegate as from that day's date. The grand master's dream had come true; and such was his happiness that he sent a message to the British Minister to the Holy See saying that he would, after all, accept the invitation to the morrow's cocktail party, which he had felt himself obliged to refuse. Then, just before noon on the same day, he had a somewhat singular visitor.

Father Castellani had asked to see him. The grand master thought the call had something to do with the Marian Congregation of nobles, of which body Travaglini was chairman and himself honorary president. But the tortuous means taken to obtain an interview should have forewarned him: the Jesuit, avoiding Pallavicini who arranged audiences with the grand master, had approached one of the latter's footmen—the man had a Jesuit confessor. Thus, Father Castellani slipped into the palace like a shadow, glided along the corridors, spoke briefly to the footman who was waiting for him, and vanished into Prince Chigi's private quarters. Eleven o'clock was striking when he reappeared, to withdraw as discreetly as he came.

The skirt of his cassock had hardly swished round the turn in the principal staircase when a dull thud was heard from the grand master's bedroom. Servants came running. He lay in a dead faint on the floor. His doctors, summoned in haste, repeated that there was nothing seriously wrong with him. And an injection rapidly counteracted the effects of a cardiac seizure. But it was impossible not to connect this accident with the visit which had preceded it. What, when he was so elated by the Prime Minister's letter, could have happened to strike the old prince down so suddenly? Father Castellani had called to inform him, on Cardinal Canali's behalf, that he was about to be excommunicated.

During that afternoon, Ferrata paid his first visit, as advocate to the Order, to the Palazzo St. Calixtus, where the Congregation of Religious had its offices. Father Larraona informed him that he had been much impressed by the grand master's latest arguments. They had been like a religious enlightenment to him. His Sacred Dicastery was, therefore, laying down its arms; and was at peace with the Order. It was by such sudden changes of temper that the Congregation of Religious and the three cardinals designed to disconcert their opponents.

On the 14th the grand master decided to leave his bed and go about his business. Either he was resigned to excommunication, or he had convinced himself that a Prince Chigi could not be excommunicated, and that in a moment of depression, he had paid too much attention to an empty threat. Nevertheless, he appeared very low in spirits. He had never been so unwell as he had been on the previous evening and he was probably dwelling on the ordeal which the Order would have to pass through if it were deprived of the support of his name. The events and incidents which were crowding upon him seemed to show that the enemy had guessed at the decline in his strength. His death would be the decisive moment which Cardinal Canali was waiting for. The appeal to the Pope would have been no more, in that case, than a palliative, had not the Grand Magistracy already taken certain precautions.

As early as the month of May, when the grand master's health had been causing anxiety, the chancellor had been led to raise the question of succession. He was among the people who did not approve of the Pope's failure to appoint a cardinal camerlingo, whose business it is to act as regent for the Church during the interregnum between the death of one Pope and the election of another.* The Order's constitution laid it down that the oldest member of the Sovereign Council must assume the lieutenant grand mastership upon the death of a grand master. That meant Hercolani. Cattaneo therefore drafted telegrams, in readiness, addressed to all grand priors, chairmen of associations, ministers and delegates to foreign courts, sovereigns and chiefs of state. The telegrams were written in Hercolani's name and they announced both the grand master's death and his own "assumption of the lieutenancy." But although these preparations had been made without the knowledge of the lieutenant-designate, the chancellor had been troubled by scruples when it came to keeping his old friend Gigino in similar ignorance: he hesitated for several months, but at last the preparation for the grand master's Iberian journey gave him his chance. Prince Chigi then had to appoint Hercolani "Lieutenant during the grand master's absence," and when it was gently hinted that there was a logical conclusion to this temporary appointment, far from taking offence, he agreed at once and blamed himself for not having been the first to think of it.

* It will be recalled that when Pius XII died, October 8, 1958, there was still no cardinal camerlingo. The functions of that office were performed by Cardinal Tisserant, Dean of the Sacred College. The Pope thereafter elected, John XXIII, was the Mgr. Roncalli of the French nunciature, in Chapter II. [E. H.]

On November 14, the professed knights and some lay members of the Grand Magistracy sat down to luncheon without the grand master. The major-domo, who made a round of the offices every morning to find out who would be in for the day's meals, had told them that Prince Chigi would lunch in his own rooms. He wished to rest in preparation for the British Minister's party, where he hoped to meet some members of the government and receive their congratulations on the recognition of the Order.

Suddenly, a servant entered the room, crying, "The grand master is ill!"

They rushed to his room: livid, and fighting for breath, the old man was crouched down in his armchair, over the tray on which his luncheon had been served to him. His favourite man-servant—the one who had smuggled in the Jesuit Castellani—was on his knees, and in tears, at the prince's side; he was howling, "No, no, Grand Master, please don't die!"

A doctor, summoned from the dispensary, pronounced the prince already dead. Cattaneo muttered the first words of the Requiem, and slipped out of the room.

His first move was to close and lock the small room containing the palace telephone PBX. He went thence to the Chancellery, took the telegrams out of the safe, and gave them to one of the porters, a man whose loyalty was well known to him.

"Go directly to the St. Sylvester post office and send these off at once. It is now one-twenty. I expect them all to be dispatched by quarter to two."

Then he returned to the others in the grand master's room and left it shortly afterward with them, so that the dead man could be laid out. He asked the others to come into his office, and turning to Hercolani, said, "Excellency, I have the honour to inform you that, acting on orders from the chancellor and the—grand master, I have just dispatched telegrams announcing your assumption of the lieutenancy."

Hercolani protested, adding, "You're joking, of course. And in bad taste."

"Anyone would think," Taccone said, "that you'd never been lieutenant before. Well, you never will be again, I dare say."

Sententiously, Del Balzo summed up: "There is no point in arguing: it's done."

All the members of Council approving, Hercolani resigned himself to office. And such was the manner and sole ceremony of his investiture, in the secretariat of the Chancellery.

The PBX was restored to use and Cattaneo telephoned Nasalli Rocca, Rangoni, and Pecci. The first, being related to the grand master by marriage, undertook to arrange for the funeral with the dead man's family; the second, as executor of his will, would have to seal the grand magistral suite of rooms. Pecci alone did not confine himself to lamentations; he exclaimed,

"*Santo cielo!* This is the end."

"Not yet," Cattaneo said. "The venerable lieutenant would be glad to see your excellency at once."

"Ah! So we're in Hercolani's hands: God help us all!"

The lieutenant also sent for the Professed Bailiff Franchi de' Cavalieri, who did not live at the Grand Magistracy and no longer held office. He had held the lieutenancy in the past, when the Grand Master Thun had been obliged to retire; he had been elected in Thun's place but had declined the honour, using his influence to get Prince Chigi elected. He, very much a *preux chevalier* of the "good old days," had just entered the room when the telephone rang. It was Cardinal Canali, asking to speak to "the Bailiff Hercolani."

Pompously, Cattaneo said, "I will connect you with His Excellency the Venerable Lieutenant, Eminence."

Franchi de' Cavalieri whispered to Hercolani, raising a finger to mark each epithet, "Be strong. Be precise. Be brief." And all of them crowded round, curious to miss nothing of this first passage of arms during the lieutenancy.

"I've just received your telegram," the cardinal said, "it was phoned through to me. I am grief-stricken. Poor grand master! I shall pray for him. How did he come to die so suddenly?"

"A heart attack, Eminence. It struck like lightning."

"Ah. You are aware that the Commission of Cardinals is in being, and that the Order can do nothing without reference to it?"

"Yes, Eminence; but you, doubtless, are aware that everything is suspended pending our appeal to the Holy Father."

"As Chairman of the Commission, appointed by the Holy Father, I forbid you to assume the lieutenancy."

"I am sorry, but the matter is already settled. As my duty was, I have already informed not only the high dignitaries of the Order—yourself first and foremost—and its secular representatives, but all sovereigns and chiefs of state."

The members of the Sovereign Council admired the ease with which Hercolani had, in a few moments, assumed the tone and spirit of the office which he had tried to refuse. Pecci, who had arrived in time to overhear the telephone conversation, was even more surprised than the others. The cardinal was saying, "It's an abuse of authority, I tell you! You have no right to be lieutenant. I call upon you instantly to desist from this—this usurpation."

"Eminence," Hercolani said, curtly, "you are speaking to the head of the Order of Malta."

"The Order of Malta has no head but the Commission of Cardinals, and in the name of that commission I must remind you of your responsibilities——"

"For the time being, Eminence, I am quite equal to them."

The cardinal hung up abruptly. Hercolani was congratulated. Franchi kissed him on both cheeks. The Order of Malta was saved—provisionally.

# PART
# THREE

# I

THE FIRST COUNCIL MEETING of the lieutenancy, held on the day of Prince Chigi's death, paid homage to the deceased grand master, approved his policy, and resolved to continue it. It also decided to assemble a complete Council of State as soon as possible, so as to elect a new grand master. Finally, in order to have a record of his telephonic dialogue with Cardinal Canali, the lieutenant wrote him a polite letter recalling the terms of their conversation and seasoning them with the customary protestations of devotion to the Holy See.

A mortuary chapel had been set up in the red salon. The grand master lay on a catafalque, dressed in the habit of a professed knight, with the white cross on his breast and a white rosary in his fingers. The catafalque was placed between the portraits of two of his remote predecessors, Carafa and Paul I. Someone had had the strange notion of putting Capuchin sandals on his feet. None of his decorations were apparent. Two knights in uniform and two officers of the military section of the Italian association kept a vigil. The statutory seals had been placed on his apartments, but a few hours later they had to be broken and the formalities of closure repeated: the canaries had been forgotten.

A succession of Masses was to be celebrated in the chapel; Cardinal Canali expressed the wish to celebrate the first. The grand master's footmen had to be kept firmly in hand: convinced, like everyone else in that house, that the cardinal was answerable for their master's death, they were ready to make a scene. But nobody could prevent the younger Chigis from turning their backs and marching out as Cardinal Canali entered the chapel.

After the body had been placed in the coffin, the doors were closed, according to the protocol governing the obsequies of a cardinal—the grand master ranked as such—and the dead man's family shut out. The Grand Magistracy then carried out its last duties to the grand master. The chancellor began to read the parchment which would be placed, in a tube of lead, inside the coffin, as for princes of the Church: *Hic est corpus magni magistri Ludovici*—he could not utter the whole name, and was overcome by faintness. He was carried out of the room; Cattaneo read the rest of the declaration. Then the lieutenant, followed by the others, knelt beside the bier and kissed the dead man's right hand. This was symbolic of obedience, transformed, in the case of Hercolani, into a symbol of authority. But just as the Order no longer had a grand admiral, neither did it have a grand marshal to repeat the gesture of the last holder of that office, at the funeral of the Grand Master de Rohan, a year before the fall of Malta: he broke his marshal's baton and threw it down at the foot of the coffin.

In his will Prince Chigi apologized for being unable to leave all he possessed to the Order, since he had children. He did not want to be buried in the Aventine Church like his predecessor, but in the family vault at the Roman cemetery. He asked forgiveness of any man or woman he had offended or neglected. Finally, he asked that his funeral be as simple as possible unless the interests of the Order required something more elaborate.

Both the grand master's wishes and the Order's interests were served by having two ceremonies. The first was held in the priory church in the presence of the Grand Magistracy and the Chigi family. The coffin was placed on the ground, between two candles, like that of any obscure Knight of the Order. But as the body was borne out of the church to the hearse on the shoulders of four kinsmen, the Malta squadron of the Air Force performed a fly-past, nor was that the only visible sign of respect, for the Italian government had ordered all flags on public buildings to be flown at half-mast. Some days later the second ceremony was held in the Church of the Holy Apostles, the mourners grouped about a cenotaph surrounded by the hundred candles pertaining to a cardinal, representatives of all the authorities, and both diplomatic corps of the capital.

On the day after the grand master's death Ferrata visited the Congregation of Religious to spy out the land. He found Father Larraona in tears.

"A sad loss for the Order," the inquisitor said. "But, after all, there are men of parts in the Grand Magistracy who will take up the torch. For our part, we shall be careful to do nothing whatever which might intrude upon their grief. In any case, we are waiting, as respectfully as the Order itself, for His Holiness's decision."

In the circumstances these words, which made him forget Cardinal Canali's outburst, seemed perfectly genuine to Ferrata. Despite all his subtle shrewdness, it was to be a long time before he really understood the kind of minds and hearts the Order had to deal with in its adversaries. His convictions, even his profession, made him incapable of supposing that high Vatican officials could and would lie constantly and with effrontery. He believed that the Pope was fully apprised of the case, although the Order assured him that this was not so.

The grand master had hardly been placed in his family vault when Father Larraona informed Hercolani, on behalf of the three cardinals, that the election of a new grand master must be "temporarily postponed." The following morning Mgr. Alcini sent, likewise on behalf of the three cardinals, to say that he would arrive at four-thirty that afternoon to resume his apostolic visit *ad inquirendum et referendum*.

Despite the gravity of these two warnings the Grand Magistracy was entertained by the fact that Cardinal Canali had not dared to convey them in person. It was known that he was now regretting having acted too openly in assuming the chairmanship of the commission. It was likewise known that he had done so in the conviction that victory was already within his grasp so that he could afford to dispense with kid gloves. But his hopes had been set at nought by the grand master's resistance and it was a melancholy glance that he cast at the seals, which were not Mgr. Alcini's, on the grand magistral apartments, when he came to say Mass in the chapel. Henceforth, he was going to consider it both more decent and more expedient to work under cover and through his creatures.

The lieutenant was by no means inclined to submit to Mgr. Alcini, even if he was "a man of the highest standing" as Father Larraona had put it. He asked him to postpone his apostolic visit for twenty-four hours. This was the time needed in which to draft a really magnificent bull, the first of the lieutenancy; and this was solemnly delivered into the visitor's hands. It contained the text of a decree of the Sovereign Council to the effect that, pending the Holy Father's decision, the apostolic visit must be "strictly confined to spiritual matters and, as to the patrimony, to the commanderies of professed members." And, what made the greatest impression on the Archbishop of Nicea, and caused Cardinal Canali the most annoyance, was the fact that in the Latin text which preceded the Italian, all the lieutenant's titles were, like those of a grand master, attributed to the Grace of God—*Dei gratia*.

The Grand Magistracy had already replied to Father Larraona's letter, protesting that to prohibit the election of a new grand master was a fresh infringement of the Order's rights, which, accordingly, it must regard as null and void. It was Mgr. Alcini who, in default of having been able to carry out his *inquirendum*, was charged with the task of confirming the prohibition. The idea may have been to make him take a hair of the dog that bit him. The lieutenant repeated that it was out of the question to infringe or suspend the rules of their constitution. And he wrote to him: "The Order's first task is to elect a new chief. The Holy Father, who has so often raised his noble voice in defence of the Church's international character and of the personal integrity of others, will not leave the sovereign Order unrespected and undefended." Alcini then let it be known that in view of the impossibility of accomplishing the task set him, and the seriousness of the attitude which the Order had adopted in the matter of the election, he would refer all these questions back to the Most Eminent Cardinals and the Sacred Congregation of Religious.

Which was the last they were to hear of Mgr. Alcini, Visitor to the Seminaries of Italy, and, incidentally, to the Order of Malta.

# II

WHILE AWAITING THE POPE'S DECISION, the Grand Magistracy busied itself in assembling references with which to compose their answer to Father Larraona's historical exposé. It was decided to confine research to the last hundred years and not to follow his example back to the year 1113; for references to the Middle Ages had a frivolous air of mere learned trifling.

The Magistral Palace archives were in a state of appalling confusion, at least as regards recent years. As Cattaneo said to the chancellor, "You have, or claim to have, Jacques de Molay's letter to Raoul d'Orléans, yet you cannot put your hand on letters from the Secretariat of State received in the first years of this century!"

Gazzoni and he, however, made a discovery, in a manner which was positively novelettish.

They had for some days been spending their time in the attics where old files had been dumped. They worked steadily through the dusty cardboard boxes, with little return for their labour, lighting candles as the evenings came on, for electricity had never been connected to this uninhabited floor. Late one afternoon, when the atmosphere threatened a storm, a gust of wind blew open a shutter and extinguished their candles. A big register fell at their feet at the same moment as lightning struck a neighbouring street. And when they had relit the candles they found a letter, fallen from the register, which was for the year 1873, lying on the floor. It was impossible to guess how that letter had ever got into the register; for it was from Cardinal Gasparri, Secretary of State to Benedict XV, and it had conveyed to the Grand Master Thun a copy of the following declaration sent to the Czechoslovak government in 1921: "The Holy See recognizes the Order of Malta as an international, independent order, with sovereign rights, and as an order which glories in practising the Catholic religion openly and is bound by secular traditions to the Holy See whose sympathetic friendship and vigilant protection are thereby assured."

"*Saint-Jean Dieu aide!*" Cattaneo exclaimed, using the ancient war-cry of the knights. "Providence is on our side."

"Certainly," Gazzoni agreed. "But if Providence intends us to triumph over Cardinal Canali, we shall need more than a letter from Cardinal Gasparri."

Meanwhile rumours began circulating in well-informed Roman circles that differences had arisen between the Order and the Holy See. The Italian government did not seem to regret having granted recognition, but hoped that these differences would be settled. So did the Order. Nearly all the officials at the Palazzo Chigi were for the Order. The diplomats accredited to the Holy See, variously informed according to their ecclesiastical connections, were obliged to run with both hare and hounds. But the esteem which Pecci enjoyed among them, and his friendship with the Italian and French ambassadors, created a prejudice in the Order's favour. In Roman society the position had not changed: the two exclusive clubs, all the salons, and the aristocracy both "black" and "white" had become increasingly hostile to Cardinal Canali since the grand master's death. Prince Ruffo della Scaletta, chairman of the Italian association and former Minister of the Order to the Holy See, was the only man of his rank who was against the Grand Magistracy. This, according to Via Condotti gossip, was said to be because he bore Pecci a grudge for pinching his place during the war. And even he pretended that he was not backing Cardinal Canali, but supporting the Pope.

The Order could, then, count on a host of allies; but it was hoping that it would not be forced to carry the war into the newspapers. For the press was almost entirely covered by the shadow of the Trimurti; and the monthly illustrated journal which was the Magistral Palace's only organ of the press was hardly of the calibre required to take on the *Osservatore Romano*.

To offset the tendentious information already being spread by the nunciatures, Hercolani decided to give all the facts to his ministers abroad. Unfortunately, he no longer had the means to do as much for the Pope. Pecci could get no further than the Secretariat of State, where Mgr. Montini fed him soothing syrup. Mgr. Nasalli Rocca had no wish at all to be sent as vicar to Frosinone. True, he seemed protected against any such fate not only by being nephew to the Cardinal-Archbishop of Bologna, but by his own standing. His papal service had recently been changed and he had passed from the functions of the Wardrobe to those of Secretary of the Embassies; nevertheless, he had asked the Order not to be misled by that title, and to apply to him, as to St. Rita, only if the case was desperate.

Reinforcement appeared, however, in the person of the former minister-general of the Franciscans, hero of what the Sons of St. Francis called the "battle of St. Anthony's." That is, the defence of a fat legacy received by their basilica, St. Anthony of Padua's, which Cardinal Canali had tried to deny them. He was to be received in private audience by the Holy Father, and he promised to enlighten him as to the real state of the Order's affairs. However, he had already been waiting three months for his audience.

Then they thought of Cardinal Tedeschini. De Mojana, who knew him fairly well, went to call on him at the Palazzo della Dateria, where he lived. It was a long way from St. Peter's for the archpriest of that basilica; but the fact was his own *palazzina* was occupied, without justification, by Cardinal Canali—a fact which might—who could say?—be not altogether pleasing to the Fatima pilgrim. The Grand Magistracy's special envoy called upon him to help the Order with the Holy Father, whose decision, he said, was in danger of being affected by certain malign influences. He did not mention Cardinal Canali by name, primarily to show respect for the Sacred College, and in any case because he did not think it necessary. Cardinal Tedeschini warmly promised his good offices, and two days later telephoned De Mojana to come at once. De Mojana flew to the Dateria on wings of hope.

"As you may know," the cardinal there told him, "business connected with the Order is managed at the Holy See by my colleague, Cardinal Canali. I thought that the best and simplest thing to do was to report what you told me to him. I am delighted to tell you that I succeeded in convincing him. He was outraged to hear that malign influences were working on the Holy Father and he promised to see to the matter at once. So you can be perfectly easy."

De Mojana was too shaken even to laugh.

The Commission of Cardinals and the Congregation of Religious, in other words Cardinal Canali and Father Larraona, were only opposing the holding of an election for fear of seeing Hercolani made grand master. They could not stomach the idea of their principal adversary becoming a Most Eminent Highness— that is, a sort of cardinal. On the other hand they could not accuse him of persisting in his determination to hold an election simply in the hope of being elected, for it was no more than his duty to press for such an election. However, as it was not generally known that they were themselves holding up the election, they put it about that the lieutenant was doing so because he was in no hurry to drop the substance for the shadow.

Hercolani was greatly surprised when Cardinal Canali suggested that they should meet. But he did not think himself entitled to refuse. He called by appointment, was immediately conducted to the cardinal's office by Mgr. Curatola, and met by the cardinal advancing to welcome him with open arms. The lieutenant, to spare his host the farce of an embrace, confined his greeting to a bow. They sat down near the window whence, beyond blocks of buildings, they could see the dome and apse of St. Peter's. There was a large crucifix on the table; the walls, panelled with red damask, were innocent of all ornament excepting a portrait of the Pope.

"You are aware of the esteem I feel for you, my dear Hercolani," the cardinal began (no more "Fra Antonio"!). "I know that you are devoted to me, devoted to the Holy Father, devoted to the Church, and that the misunderstanding during the first moments of your lieutenancy was the work of the hotheads and troublemakers, especially the youngest, by whom you are surrounded. What I want you to realize, so that your future conduct may be guided by it, is that the Holy Father trusts me completely, that I have his entire confidence, at least in the matter of the Order of Malta. There is, therefore, no point whatever in imitating the poor grand master and sending appeals to the Pope, whatever the means of conveying them, since all he does is to pass them on to me, and it is I who make the decisions. Let us come to terms once and for all. Give me an assurance of personal loyalty, and not only will I obtain the Holy Father's permission for you to hold an election, but you, yourself, shall be elected."

Hercolani admired the effrontery which enabled the cardinal to reproduce the scene played at Magione two years before. And his ironic appreciation saved him from losing his temper at the idea of his being supposed capable of making a different answer on this occasion. Was the cardinal ignorant of elementary psychological laws? Or had the work of corruption in which he was so generally engaged convinced him that even men of high integrity would yield if one were sufficiently patient? Without troubling to point out the incongruity of the cardinal's offer, the lieutenant sketched a gesture signifying his indifference to the idea of being grand master; and picked out, for his answer, another part of the cardinal's speech which had really shocked him.

"I have too much respect for the Holy Father to believe that he hands our appeals over to you and leaves the decision in your hands."

The cardinal half-opened a drawer in his desk.

"Supposing I tell you I have the grand master's letters here?"

"I'm afraid I should ask to see them."

The cardinal slammed the drawer shut.

"Your doubt is an offence to my cloth," he said. "The audience is over."

But Hercolani was already on his feet.

"I beg your pardon," he said, "but it is I who choose to leave you."

# III

On December 8, Feast of the Immaculate Conception, the Sovereign Council decided to call a full Council of State for February 28, with a view to electing a grand master. The lieutenant had taken care to warn Father Larraona, some days before, that he found himself obliged to ignore the second prohibition, communicated by Mgr. Alcini. He quoted the case of the Tsar Paul

I, as proof of the Order's need to elect a chief in whatever circumstances. And he softened that reference to the schismatic grand master by pointing out that the Council had deliberately chosen December 8 as the date for its meeting in order "to place the subsequent election of a grand master under the Virgin's patronage." Pecci carried this news to Mgr. Montini, and did not forget to emphasize this pious detail, which was thought likely to touch the Holy Father.

On the day in question, then, the Council sent summonses *de eligendo magno maestro* to all the Order's electors. The recipients were members of the Sovereign Council, grand priors, professed bailiffs, and chairmen of the national associations who were electors in their capacity as successors to former grand priories of the Order. This, while excluding all non-European countries, brought in the old European aristocracy. In addition, the three Italian grand priories, and those of Austria and Bohemia, had the right to elect two professed knights to complete their delegations.

Two days later Mgr. Montini informed Pecci of the important decision for which the Order had been waiting more than a month. The Holy See had at last made up its mind to take this decision, to counter that taken by the Grand Magistracy. Was the act of equity for which they had asked the Pope all that they were entitled to expect? At the Via Condotti, nobody doubted it.

"The Holy Father," ran the text, "welcoming the filial instance presented by the Hierosolymitan Order of Malta in the person of its Grand Master His Most Eminent Highness Fra Ludovico Chigi Albani della Rovere, recently called to his eternal rest, thereafter in the person of the provisional Lieutenant His Excellency Fra Antonio Hercolani Fava Simonetti, has benignly deigned to set up a tribunal composed of five Most Eminent *porporati*, to resolve all difficulties." The substitute at the Secretariat of State, in undertaking to forward, as soon as possible, the pontifical chirograph in which the name of the judges was set forth, signified that in the same document, "His Holiness had benignly deigned to order that the election of a grand master be suspended pending the findings of the Court."

The Grand Magistracy read it through calmly. The word *chirograph*, to designate a brief bearing the Pope's signature, caused no more alarm than Father Larroana's use of the word *dicastery*. The Council members were touched by the granting of their request even though, while fulfilling their wishes in one respect, their fondest hope—permission to hold the election—was denied them. They were delighted to have the Commission of three cardinals disposed of: for though they would now have five to deal with, it was inconceivable that these should include the first three, especially their firebrand leader. For such an arrangement would have given the Commission a majority on the bench. Pius XII's high-mindedness was incapable of turning an act of justice into one of derision.

The Order did not instruct its minister to question Mgr. Montini concerning the composition of the Court of Cardinals: anything hinting at distrust would, in the circumstances, have been an outrage. An effort was, however, made to take advantage of the short delay to get the text concerned with the election amended. Pecci explained that the electors had been summoned and that if they were now to be told not to come after all, explanations would be necessary. He then went on to argue that to maintain the present state of affairs *sine die*, even though not indefinitely, hardly helped the Order "to ensure the sanctification of its members and the good of the community." He also said that the continuance of the prohibition hardly squared with "the interest which the Holy See had always taken in the religious Order of Malta"; nor with "the unforgettable words uttered by the sacred lips of His Holiness on the day when he, Pecci, had presented his letters of credence."

While Pecci was turning these fine phrases for the edification of Mgr. Montini, Cardinal Canali was working on the Pope. They heard, a little later, that he had not had an easy task, and that the discussion had been heated. The Trimurti had made much of the fact that the exclusion of the three cardinals would be "an offence to their purple." And this was judged more serious than an offence to justice. On December 12, Mgr. Montini dispatched the copy of the chirograph which contained the names of the five cardinals: the list included the original three commissioners and two new names. Cardinals Tisserant and Aloisi Masella.

The most astounded man at the Grand Magistracy was Ferrata. It was not only that his conscience as a jurist, a Catholic, and a man of the Vatican was disturbed. He could not help wondering whether the Order might not suspect him of treachery, since it was he who was responsible for the idea of asking the Holy Father to appoint a special court, instead of accepting the jurisdiction of the Supreme Court of the Apostolic Signature. When he protested that he had been doubly deceived, it was taken to mean that someone in whom he had absolute confidence had perfidiously suggested the idea to him. If he needed vindication as an honest man it was there, manifest in his sorrow and shame. And to his harsh strictures on Cardinal Canali, whose collaborator he had formerly been, and on Cardinal Tisserant, Dean of the Sacred College, for consenting to preside over a court so constituted, he added some sorrowful reflections on the Church's future.

Meanwhile it was impossible not to admire Cardinal Canali's cleverness in putting the Court, where his word would be the only law, under the aegis of that "great scholar" and "great Frenchman" who directed the Congregation for the Eastern Church. People who knew the real facts of the case were aware that the Dean of the Sacred College would be absolutely helpless. For he was in disgrace with the Pope and had only accepted this post in the hope of patching up some sort of peace with him, through Cardinal Canali. At least, however, one name out of the five might be a concession to impartiality; that of Cardinal Masella, Pro-Prefect of the Congregation for the Sacraments, and pacific administrator of his little Order of St. John-Lateran. It was obviously without knowing what he was in for that he had allowed himself to be embarked by the Grand Master of the Holy Sepulchre on his crusade against Malta. And one might wonder just what he would do in that galley.

# IV

CALM RESTORED, the Grand Magistracy studied the chirograph coolly. It was laid down that the Court would determine "the quality of the Order of Malta's sovereign and religious attributes respectively, with the consequences entailed in these findings for its relations with the Holy See." The Court was "invested with the fullest powers, even in respect to forms of procedure, excepting as regards guarantees for a legitimate defence. All the acts of the Court must be accomplished on the territory of the Vatican State and City."

A number of the bailiffs were for making one final effort to enlighten the Holy Father. The chirograph was not a public document and he might consent to amend it. But against this it was pointed out that he was hardly likely to change three members of the Court after Cardinal Canali had made their inclusion in it a matter of personal honour.

Another group was of opinion that the Order, while proclaiming that it did indeed "glory in openly professing the Catholic faith," should detach itself from the Holy See before the Holy See could crush it. But these radicals were denied: the foundation of the Order was religious, it could not run the risk of being condemned by the Church. Did not even the Venerable Order of St. John, an English parody of the Order, base itself on the Protestant religion? Surely the whole gravity of this business resided precisely in the fact that it concerned men who were only too anxious to remain faithful to the Church and its head. And this meant that they must appear before this singular tribunal and so contrive matters that it would be unable to perpetrate a denial of justice. This solution had the backing of the Order's able advisers, for these lawyers thought that they had found a loophole which ensured the safety of their case.

Meanwhile, by way of light relief, there was a personal duel between Cardinal Canali and the lieutenant. The cardinal, annoyed by the circular summoning the electors, expressed his surprise that the Sovereign Council should have discussed the matter without inviting him. The election seemed a sort of mania with him, for he could not leave it alone and must register his protest although the Pope, meanwhile, had suspended it. The lieutenant reminded him that grand priors were not members of the Sovereign Council and added that the grand master, in granting the cardinal the privilege of attending its meetings, had been using fuller powers than he, the lieutenant, possessed: a lieutenant, especially in the Order's present difficult circumstances, was bound strictly to observe the constitution.

In the face of this dismissal the cardinal accused the lieutenant of an "offence to the purple," always his *pièce de résistance* and *ultima ratio*. He angrily announced that Hercolani's mandate as representative of the Grand Priory of Rome was withdrawn. The lieutenant replied to the cardinal grand prior that following a deliberation by the chapter of the grand priory on February 4, 1950, the mandate in question had been renewed for three years and was therefore valid until February, 1953. To which the cardinal grand prior retorted that, renewed or not, it was not valid because not consistent with the office of lieutenant. Hercolani parried by pointing out that since the constitution said nothing of any such incompatibility, he was sorry he could not give way. The cardinal persisted, saying that in any case and apart from all other considerations, he held the mandate to be null and void; he even informed the chancellor of this "as in duty bound by his office." The chancellor drew his attention to the fact that the representative of a grand priory could only be stripped of his office by a vote of the priory chapter and then only if this vote was ratified by the Sovereign Council. He therefore invited him to submit the motion "in concrete terms," and assured him that it would receive prompt and deferential attention. This was too much for the cardinal, who knew that he would not get a vote for Hercolani's dismissal, and certainly not ratification. The last shot in his locker fell short: he stated that he would attend to the appointment of a new representative later and would, meanwhile, represent himself. It goes without saying that he never showed his face at the Magistral Palace where the lieutenant, mockingly triumphant, continued to represent him.

But there could be no doubt about the significance of this shadow-boxing: it meant that the fight must be to the death.

# V

CHRISTMAS GAVE PECCI the chance to exchange seasonal greetings with Mgr. Montini. He wrote to him: "In this season of peace and good will the Order is hoping that at least a preliminary to peace will emerge." At the same time he sent "for your exclusive information and use" a note calling attention to "a detail which the Holy Father seems not to have known." It was that, of the five cardinals, three had already delivered themselves, unquestionably, definitively, and in writing, of a judgment in the case which the special Court had been set up to try. The Order did not wish to trouble the Pope by drawing his attention to this "detail," but saw no harm in dropping a hint to his Secretariat of State.

When Pecci had been delivering the Order's acknowledgment of the chirograph, Mgr. Montini had tried to get him to alter its terms, by taking out a reference to the three cardinals which, he said, could serve no purpose.

"On the contrary," the minister had replied, "I believe it may prove very useful, both to us—and to you."

The substitute had the honesty to drop his suggestion at once: he had guessed the nature of the flaw which the Order's jurists had discovered and might use. If the Court forced them to do so, it would not be for want of warning.

The increasing incidence of rumours going the rounds of Rome convinced the Grand Magistracy that their adversaries were not exercising the same discretion as themselves. With Prince Chigi out of the way but still powerful by his name, they were putting it about that he had been on the point of submission and that his ephemeral successor was betraying his memory. This slander made some impression on people who did not know that the Sovereign Council membership was unchanged, and that it had decided to follow the grand master's line of conduct, and that the one and only instance laid before the Holy Father was the grand master's.

Pecci urged Mgr. Montini to publish the real facts in a

communiqué; but the substitute objected that the Pope had a horror of publicity in matters ecclesiastical. For its own part, the Grand Magistracy was extremely careful to publish nothing. The Congregation for Religious, which made such a parade of "always proceeding in the most absolute secrecy," would not have failed to make an issue of it. The Grand Magistracy had informed its ministers to foreign courts and perhaps one or two chairmen of national associations who happened to pass through Rome; but it had been very discreet with the majority of the electors, even when writing to explain that the election would not take place. Nor had it ever responded to journalistic curiosity. The more aggressively it was attacked, the more unattackably blameless it wanted to feel itself to be.

At this juncture the Grand Magistracy received an offer from Comte d'Ormesson. He, French Ambassador to the Holy See, had been created Knight Magistral Grand Cross by Prince Chigi. Being on friendly terms with the leading men of the Order, he persuaded Auriti that their silence was a mistake and that the man to break it was the Rome correspondent of *Le Monde*. It was decided to take advantage of this attractive offer, but there must be a condition—a very ingenuous one: the article must state that harmony reigned between the Order and the Holy See. This was to ask more than could, in the event, be granted.

The Foreign Affairs Office was told off to receive the journalist, to show him the palace from cellar to attics; to show him, as a signal favour, the imperial crown with its Maltese cross, worn by Paul I of Russia; to say something about the thirty-six or thirty-seven French grand masters; to speak highly of the heroism shown by the D'Aubussons, Villiers de l'Isle Adams, and La Valettes; to sing the praises of the Grand Master Gozon, who was elected for killing a dragon. They were even to concede that the Order's founder, the Blessed Gerard, was born at Martignes, as French historians had always claimed, and not at Scala near Ravello as was held by Italian chroniclers. Any question relating to differences with the Holy See were to be received with an air of innocent astonishment. But the correspondent of *Le Monde* knew, as was fitting, the world, and was not to be kept indefinitely in such calm waters, even aboard the Great Carrack.

"All this is very interesting," he said at length, "but there is talk in Rome of rather more urgent matters, in short of a complaint carried by a member of the Order to the Holy See, an appeal by the Order to the Pope, a Commission of Cardinals, an apostolic visitation, and a special Court of Cardinals."

To which they replied, "My dear Sir, in the course of many centuries the Order has often had little family squabbles with the Holy See and they may, from time to time, be revived, but their sole interest is historical."

"You admit, then, that there is such a difference?"

"Heaven preserve us from admitting anything whatsoever! When one is dealing with relations going back to year one thousand, one must go warily, you know."

"Come now," the journalist said, point blank, "you are not going to deny that something of great moment for the Order of Malta is in the wind—in fact, that its sovereignty is threatened?"

"No matter what happens, nobody shall lay hands on our sovereignty."

Three days later *Le Monde* published a sensational article in which this answer was printed. The Grand Magistracy trembled. And when, a week later, the *Osservatore Romano* published the text of the chirograph and Pecci protested strongly against this violation of secrecy at the Order's expense, Mgr. Montini smilingly replied that *Le Monde* was to blame.

# VI

ON JANUARY 25, 1952, Cardinal Tisserant communicated the Court's first decree to the Grand Magistracy. This was a list of the experts the five judges had co-opted; and a request that the Order's experts should attend a meeting with them to establish procedure.

The choice of the Promoter of Justice, Monsignor, subsequently Cardinal, Ottaviani, at the time Assessor to the Holy Office, could give nothing but comfort to the Grand Magistracy, well aware of his unbending rectitude. The choice had not been made easily, however: Cardinal Canali had tried to get Mgr. Alcini appointed to the post, which corresponded to that of public prosecutor. Fortunately, Pecci was warned by Mgr. Montini, who was trying to prevent things from going from bad to worse. The idea of again having to do with the ex-Bishop of Dionysiad, promoted Archbishop of Nicea for having nearly succeeded in seizing the Magistral Palace, was clearly intolerable. Exaggerating a little, Pecci asserted that rather than suffer any such insult the lieutenant would proclaim the Order of Malta dissolved. This gasconade was effective: Mgr. Alcini was left to his seminary visiting.

Cardinal Canali made up for this, however, by taking Mgr. Alberto Serafini as his historical adviser, that prelate being Apostolic Protonotary, and consultant to the Conciliar and Ceremonial Congregations. He was the Order's oldest enemy, having sworn undying hatred twenty years ago. At that time he had aspired to the honour of being its conventual chaplain; but Prince Chigi, unable to discover that he had any special qualification for the post, had refused him the appointment. Since when he was invariably to be found in any movement hostile to the Order.

Mgr. Serafini had grown grey in the service of his hatred, spending laborious days in the Vatican library collecting references designed to prove "the crimes of the Order of Malta" with the same industry as others had devoted to proving "the crimes of the popes." He it was who had provided the material for the historical exposé of November 3, which, in default of proving the Order's crimes, at least tended to prove its subjection to the popes. He had not been attached to the original Commission of Cardinals only because Cardinal Canali had needed a mere hatchet man, such as the Archbishop of Nicea. But the original attack having failed and the situation grown more confused, the cardinal was obliged to call up his reserves. It, had been hoped that Mgr. Mercati, the second historical adviser worthy brother of the cardinal who was patron of the Vatican library, would counterbalance Mgr. Serafini. But he had no sooner seen his colleague at work than he decided he wanted no part in the business; his discretion, rather than his valour, distinguished him in the event.

Finally, Cardinal Canali scored a notable point in his choice of counsel. In order to seem anxious to contribute toward a calm legal atmosphere, as the Order had done by choosing Ferrata and Corsanego, he also chose his advocate from the consistory lawyers. But *his* consistorial counsel was Prince Carlo Pacelli, no less. Thus while one member of the Trimurti was to sit on the bench, another was among the barristers. As for the third, Galeazzi was the special delegate of the Pontifical Commission for the Vatican City State, in which the trial was to take place.

Since the cardinals had created a precedent for addressing the Order in decrees, the Order decided to follow suit. And on the following day sent back a decree by way of reply. It contained the information that in addition to Ferrata, Corsanego, and Gazzoni, Professor Morelli of the University of Rome would appear for the Order; and that its historical advisers would be the Bailiff Franchi de' Cavalieri and the Chancellor Rangoni.

The prearranged meeting of lawyers and advisers took place in the court of the first instance in the Vatican City. The Order's counsel having been told that they must have a written mandate from their client, they made it serve their purpose in immediately establishing a point of the first importance: to wit, that they were appearing before an international court on behalf of a "being" which was sovereign in international law. If this point were not conceded, they said, their mandate became invalid, and they must withdraw.

"There can be no question about it," Prince Pacelli declared at once. "This court is international and the sovereignty of the Order goes without saying. Is it not described as such in His Holiness's venerable chirograph? The only question, according to the terms of the venerable chirograph, is to draw a frontier between what is sovereign and what pertains to the Order as a religious foundation."

Counsel were satisfied with this admission; but thereafter waited in vain for the record in which it should have been minuted. They were two months calling for it, and when, ultimately, the Court made up its mind to send them their copy of the day's records, they found, indeed, that "the ritual prayers were said"; but not a word of Prince Pacelli's assurance.

Another of the Court's caesarian devices had been earlier manifest: the Order's counsel were only given one month in which to depose their documentary references and deductions. They protested, unsuccessfully, that the time would not have been sufficient for the most commonplace trial before an ordinary court. They were obliged to agree, which entailed preparing their armoury in competition with Mgr. Serafini, who had been twenty years in training for this event. The only concession they could obtain was that they were not to be called upon to prove the sovereignty of Malta over the last 900 years, but only during a century and a half, that is since the loss of Malta itself.

Meanwhile Cardinal Tisserant had requested the lieutenant to call at the Court's meeting-place for an urgent communication. Hercolani, who had by then learned to go warily in dealing with cardinals, sent to know whether he was required "in his official capacity, or privately." He suspected an attempt to trap him into a public act of obedience. Informed that the matter concerned "a private communication of an official nature," he sent a message to the effect that he would not appear before the Court unless allowed to bring with him his chancellor, and his minister to the Holy See, in other words, as a chief of state.

Cardinal Tisserant did not insist on his personal appearance; instead he informed Hercolani, in writing, of the grave matter on which he had been summoned to appear. It was about the lieutenant's letterhead: the rubric described him, illegally, as "lieutenant" instead of "provisional lieutenant." The Dean of the Sacred College seemed to attach great importance to this detail of protocol; for, like Cardinal Canali's "offence to the purple," it became his leitmotiv.

# VII

At Candlemas the Holy Father seemed satisfied with the Order's first candle of the lieutenancy. But he took Mgr. Hemmick, one of the two conventual chaplains who had carried the offering, on one side and told him that "his paternal heart was bleeding" at the spectacle of articles being published all over the place about the Malta trial. These articles, he said, were damaging the Order's case; the Order, by countenancing them, was in error, and should be careful to distinguish the suggestions of the Paraclete from those of the Evil One. The Grand Magistracy, which had done all in its power to avoid indiscretions, and had stumbled through excessive simplicity into facilitating only one, was not surprised: they had expected to be held responsible for the lot.

Hercolani was, nevertheless, disturbed by the Holy Father's remarks, obviously made in all innocence, and he protested to Mgr. Montini that the Order had had nothing whatever to do with the campaign in the press. He was even more annoyed when Cardinal Tisserant called upon him to use "the most vigorous measures to correct or suppress the publication of tendentious articles in Italy and abroad." As he said, what power was he supposed to have to restrain *Le Monde*, *The Times*, *Newsweek*, the *Corriere della Sera*, *Il Tempo*, and the rest? And he urged that the Holy See might show the way by correcting tendentious articles in the *Osservatore Romano*.

Whereupon the Vatican newspaper did, in fact, publish a correction, headlined "Fantastic Absurdities," by way of describing what it called "the news maliciously spread by the international press," according to which Cardinal Canali was proposing to merge the Orders of Malta and the Holy Sepulchre. "This news," the article went on, "since it seems to imply blame of the Order of Malta and to pronounce judgment while its errors are *sub judice*, calls for an immediate contradiction." No doubt about it, the Grand Prior of Rome had the art of composing such contradictions at his finger-tips: whereas the chirograph had used terms no stronger than "filial instance" and "difficulties," he had succeeded in getting "blame" and "errors" into the very first official commentary.

The head of the Holy Sepulchre now shifted his attack to fresh ground. Being accustomed to behave as master in the Vatican, he set about depriving the knights of Malta of precedence in papal chapels, where they sat immediately behind the diplomatic corps. He had already contrived to slip the knights of his own order in behind them, thereby offending the dignitaries of the pontifical orders; and he did not propose to stop at that.

On February 9, a solemn service was to be held in the Sistine Chapel for the thirteenth anniversary of Pius XI's death. Arriving at the head of the delegation from the Order of Malta, Count Macchi de Celere was surprised to find a space left between his party and the ambassadors. The chamberlain on duty told him that, on Cardinal Canali's orders, the seats in question were to be held for the knights of the Order of Holy Sepulchre, who were late. But Count Macchi was very much a knight of Malta: he was titulary of one of the entailed commanderies which remained in the founding family, provided the reigning grand master had satisfied himself of the "purity of their lives" and had made them cough up a contribution to the funds. He turned on the secret chamberlain and said, "If you do not allow us to occupy our proper places, I shall pull off your ruff in front of all these people."

"Cardinal Canali——" the chamberlain stammered, glancing nervously toward the bench reserved for the Sacred College. The cardinal pretended to be praying, but was actually watching the scene with flashing eyes. Whatever that look might do to the chamberlain, it redoubled Count Macchi's boldness.

"We shall take our traditional seats and I do not advise you to try stopping us," he said, placing a hand on the pommel of his sword. "Go, tell your master that we will not leave them even under the threat of his pikes."

Although the chamberlain also wore a sword, no blood was shed in the Sistine. Cardinal Canali looked daggers at the chamberlain, who had saved his ruff, indeed, but possibly at the expense of his job. Nor did he look more kindly on the knights of the Holy Sepulchre, who turned up after the battle, their comic opera uniforms concealed under white cloaks.

*        *        *

The Grand Magistracy was not only obliged to defend itself in Rome; a second front was opened in Germany.

The two German associations—the Rhine-Westphalian and the Silesian—might well boast of preserving the traditions of chivalry above all others. The spirit of Lohengrin and the burgraves seemed still to inform their aspirations. Their country's taste for the feudal, the Gothic, for secret codes of honour and justice, as exemplified in the persistence of the Holy Vehm, all inclined them to take the Order of Malta very seriously. Whereas, for example, the French association no longer included the names which had formerly distinguished the three *langues* of Provence, France, and Auvergne—there was no Villeneuve, though there had been eighty-eight knights of that ilk, no Sabran, though there had been forty-three, no Forbin, though there had been no less than thirty-three in a single century—the three hundred or so German knights were drawn from the flower of the German Catholic *Almanach de Gotha*. They took great pride in the proof of nobility called "of Germany"—sixteen quarterings for a hundred years, which had been adopted by most associations and by comparison with which the French proof— eight quarterings for a hundred years—and the Italian, four for two hundred, paled into insignificance. And they were the stricter in their aristocracy for existing cheek by jowl with the Teutonic Knights, an offshoot of the Order of St. John, and the Protestant Knights of Malta, pertaining to the bailiwick of Brandenburg. Seven commanderies of that bailiwick, having broken away at the time of the Reformation, had survived, in titles, among certain families of the highest nobility, like the Orthodox Russian Grand Priory in Paris. Although the Grand Magistracy in Rome had no contact with them, it considered them legitimate, since there had been no discontinuity, whereas, for instance, the Protestant Grand Priory of England, where the Order had been suppressed by Henry VIII, dated from Victoria's reign. Baron Twinkel, Chairman of the Rhine-Westphalian association, and Prince von Hartzfeld, Chairman of the Silesian—quartered in Munich since the Russian occupation—guided these German knights and their charities, numerous as their quarterings. Discipline was perfect and relations with the Grand Magistracy friendly and sustained.

Toward the end of March, Prince Frederic von Hohenzollern-Sigmaringen, honorary chairman of the Silesian association, Bailiff Grand Cross of Honour and Devotion, wrote to the Magistral Palace to express his thoughts on the problems pending "between the Order and the Curia." He wrote that he had "defended the Order" in a recent letter to the Pope, but he added that, "the Pope being the Vicar of Christ, the primordial duty of the oldest Order in Christendom was to obey him." His conclusion being that the Order should make its peace with Thun Hohenstein whom the Pope had acquitted of blame. The present litigation, having, according to Prince Frederic, no other origin than the Thun affair, would be brought to an end by clearing that up, that is by appointing Thun Grand Prior of Venice. "Thereby," he concluded, "killing two birds with one stone."

The Grand Magistracy had long put the Bailiff Thun out of mind, but he had evidently found the means to draw attention to himself again. He was known to have family connections with this German Highness who, however, seemed to have taken his time over coming to his rescue. But they were not without a clue to his sudden zeal: Prince Frederic was said to be anxious to get the marriage of one of his sons annulled and to have asked Cardinal Canali to intervene on his behalf. He did not, apparently, know that the prelates of the Sacred Roman Rota turned a deaf ear to cardinalistic interference, and notably from that particular quarter.

Hercolani's first impulse was to write a sharp reply. But it was advisable to exercise tact with the head of the Catholic Hohenzollerns, several of the family being members of the

Order. He confined himself to giving the prince the true facts about Thun's conduct and its consequences.

The prince wrote to thank him for the information which would enable him "to reorient our German brethren, misled by gossip." The incident seemed closed. But the Grand Magistracy, not knowing what rumours concerning it might have reached the Vatican, whose favour Prince Frederic enjoyed, sent a copy of the correspondence to Mgr. Montini. Furthermore, not being sure that Mgr. Alcini's report on the Thun affair had ever gone any further than the Congregation of Religious, they had one drawn up by Corsanego, attached forty-five addenda, and delivered it to the Secretariat of State, who passed it on to the Holy Father. If it was true, as Cardinal Canali claimed, that everything which was sent to the Holy Father by the Grand Magistracy was handed over to him, he must at last face the fact that his protégé's cause had received a mortal blow.

But the brand which had thus been extinguished in the Silesian association suddenly flared up in the Rhine-Westphalian. No doubt about it, the German nobility felt themselves bound to demonstrate solidarity with Thun. Baron Twinkel arrived in person at the Grand Magistracy to assert that his knights had need of all their respect for discipline to keep them from revolting against the injustice suffered by the Bailiff Thun, who was related to several of their number. At least, they felt it must be an injustice, since they had never received a word of explanation. The Grand Magistracy, determined to have done with Thun once and for all, gave the chairman of the Rhine-Westphalian Association a carbon copy of Corsanego's report, with copies of all the addenda.

Baron Twinkel returned to Münster, called a council of his association, and showed its members these documents, letting each take his time. Out of consideration for the family of Thun Hohenstein, the papers were not to be shown to the other knights, however. The council members, having seen and believed and promised secrecy, were able to assure their colleagues that the Grand Magistracy was innocent of blame and the case of the Bailiff Thun was closed.

This man, who had erred in the Order's business with the best intentions in the world, had now, to his cost, erred in the conduct of his own. He had thrown the Order to the wolves; and then walked into their jaws himself.

# VIII

THE COURT OF CARDINALS was delivered of its second decree at the end of February. It granted the lawyers ten days to produce their instances, and, as already established, one month to depose their documentary evidence.

In the reply to the "Most Eminent Princes," the Order's jurists made all the reservations which were called for: the writ set forth the case made out by the Promoter of Justice, but not that of the defence; the ten days' grace was good canon law but that did not apply in the present case; the documentary evidence called for was not defined; finally, the Court had not indicated what procedure it had in mind for trying the case.

Mgr. Scapinelli replied that the defence was free "to develop its arguments over whatever period of time it chose, without prejudice to the decisions of the Most Eminent Court." Which was as good as admitting that the defence might work till Domesday, they would win their case when the moon was blue.

This did not prevent the lawyers from being thorough in drawing up the brief, they would argue, and delivering it within the time specified. The Vatican press was to do the printing; the Order's counsel informed the Court that they would require ten times as many copies as the sixty normally provided for the defendants. For, they said, since the Holy See had published the text of the chirograph, the least the Order could do was to provide its principal members with a copy of their plea; and there were 4,700 of them, spread over a score of nationalities. The Court provided forty copies: it was the clearest possible indication that they were not at all anxious that the Knights of

Malta be fully informed. The lawyers then applied directly to the Vatican press: the printers had orders that no more copies were to be printed. The Grand Magistracy thereupon had their own edition of the plea printed as a "white book," and sent it to their knights all over the world "under the bond of secrecy and under pain of the sanctions provided for." Nor did their cardinal-censors dare to protest.

The month of May came round and the Court had still not replied to the lawyers' requests to know what procedure was to be adopted. All it had done was to pass on the Promoter of Justice's "admonitions." The seasonal beatification activities seemed to have distracted its attention.

The Order was warned, by its friends inside the Holy See and at the same time by a nuncio's confidential hint to the chairman of an association, that a *coup de force* was about to be tried: it seemed incredible, but the Court was planning to deliver judgment without having first heard the lawyers, simply on the brief they had deposed. It cared nothing, apparently, either for the elementary principles of justice, or for the clause in the pontifical chirograph which guaranteed a fair hearing to the defence.

Pecci immediately delivered a note to Mgr. Montini informing him of the enormity about to be perpetrated and imploring him to pass this information to the Pope. But since, once again, swift action might be all-important, Mgr. Nasalli Rocca again hazarded his future, and all the more meritoriously on this occasion in that his uncle, the Cardinal-Archbishop of Bologna had died some months before and was no longer standing by to protect him. He courageously carried a copy of the letter to the Pope, which had an immediate effect: the Court was obliged to swallow its pride with its judgment.

Cardinal Canali, whose outbursts of rage were famous, suffered one which would go down in the Vatican annals. His invective against Mgr. Nasalli Rocca made painful hearing. And that was the last time the Order was to be able to count on their ally when the case was desperate: the Pope was so completely convinced by the Trimurti that the judges' intentions had been honourable that, while refusing to deprive Mgr. Rocca of his title as secretary to the embassies, he peremptorily ordered him to accomplish no more embassies for the Order of Malta.

Mgr. Serafini, who had very nearly lost the chance of parading his learning, now hurled 500 pages of "notes in illustration" of his argument at the Order's lawyers. These notes were no longer confined to proving that the Order owed submission to the Church; the claim now was that it had been created by the Church and that any sovereignty it might pretend to was merely "derived." Mgr. Serafini pretended not to know that the Order had existed as an order of hospitalers, with its own patrimony and complete independence, before it had been either a military or religious order. He was still quoting Pascal II and Eugene II; but he did not refer to Roger of Sicily founding the Grancia of Messina for the Knights of St. John and devoting whomsoever should violate its privileges to "malediction by the three hundred and eighteen saints of God."

Since these "notes in illustration" illustrated the thesis argued by Father Larraona in his letter of November 3, the lawyers found quite a useful counter-argument in this very fact: they pointed out that the Father's thesis had been set aside by the chirograph and by the setting up of the special Court. If this were not the case, how was it that several of the Most Eminent Judges had been present at the plenary congregation which had elaborated it? But when Mgr. Ottaviani and Prince Carlo Pacelli borrowed Father Larraona's historical survey in order to assert that the Order's property was, indeed, religious property, the value of Mgr. Serafini's "notes in illustration" became apparent. In seeking to show that the very origin of the Order was religious, they laid down the premises from which Mgr. Ottaviani and Prince Carlo Pacelli drew their conclusion. The Trimurti were still intent on taking the shortest cuts to the hard cash.

Mgr. Serafini next fired a second broadside of "notes in illustration": 250 pages this time. To them was added an explanation that since it had not been possible to print the documents quoted as references, they could be examined at the Court's Secretariat. The lawyers went to examine them and found that they were copies in longhand. They asked Mgr. Serafini if he was prepared to swear to their authenticity. He replied that he would take no such oath. They then asked him if he would at least swear that the documentation in dispute had been provided "for the truth of the cause" and not simply to support his own thesis: he again replied that he would take no such oath. The lawyers were aware that both their demands were insulting. But they could not help it; things had come to a pretty pass when Vatican lawyers defending the Order of Malta could not trust the word of a prelate, historical adviser to a Court of Cardinals and consultant to two Sacred Congregations. In view of his refusal they demanded that his "notes in illustration," together with a study as outrageously partial composed by the Congregation for Religious, be excluded from the exhibits. The Court refused, but consented to the exclusion of two supplementary studies whose author had nothing to do with the case: these, drawn up in aggressive language by a team of professors at the Gregorian University, had been signed by Father Castellani, Cardinal Canali's creature.

By way of administering a lesson in history to all these historians, the Order brought in a notable recruit to reinforce its jurists: this was Professor Snider, secretary to the *Institut International de droit privé* and counsel to the Congregation of Rites. The Professor wrote to the Court saying that, in the field into which Mgr. Serafini's notes in illustration had extended the argument, it would be necessary to consult not only Western law, but also Byzantine, and even Islamic, law. According to his own personal researches, which had been limited to Europe only, the libraries of various Moslem institutions contained more than 4,000 unpublished documents bearing directly upon the case, and therefore essential to it. This prospect routed Mgr. Serafini, who thereafter gave up writing notes in illustration.

On May 31, the Court met in the Plenary Congregations room at the Apostolic Palace and delivered its third decree. This reserved its right to examine the objections raised by the Order's lawyers in whatever light it considered expedient; called upon them to depose their conclusions within twenty days; and required payment, within one week, of a million lire "as a first deposit against costs."

The trial, in short, was like any other major trial: it had started with an exhibition of juridical chicanery; and with a demand for funds.

# IX

AND, ALSO LIKE any other major trial, it required time. The allowance of twenty days, due to an intervention by the Holy Father, was better than nothing but still absurdly inadequate. The lawyers, reminding the Court that canonical trials took two years in the first instance and another year on appeal, demanded at least six months. The Court was as deaf to their claim as it was still dumb in the matter of procedure. It was understood, however, that judgment would be delivered before the end of the summer: evidently the Court was determined to install Cardinal Canali in the Via Condotti before going *ad aquas*.

There was a dramatic meeting at the Magistral Palace. The Sovereign Council considered the possibility of withdrawing from the trial if the ordinary rights of defendants were not to be allowed them. The prospect frightened the lawyers, most of whom were connected with the Holy See. They pleaded that it should be possible to make some impression by an appeal to Cardinal Tisserant, who was lending his countenance to this farce. The letter they wrote to him, setting forth their point of view, concluded with the most warlike phrase which devout Catholics had ever used to an areopagus of cardinals: "In submitting the foregoing for your attention, with all proper respect, we feel ourselves encouraged by the conviction that the Court is jealous of its honour." It was a hint which might have been designed to illustrate Montesquieu's witticism touching the three tribunals which are never in agreement: those of law, honour, and religion.

Cardinal Tisserant's answer was a new decree granting ten days extra. It was said that Cardinal Canali had quoted an old saying, "Malta's boasted galleys will soon be laden with stones."

It was at this juncture that the Order put into operation a strategic manœuvre which they had been planning in secret for months. They had discovered an ancient custom in the De Rohan code of rules, "the assembly of venerable *langues*," which could be called on important occasion to affirm or throw light upon the nature of the Order's authority. True, no such assembly had been held for more than a century: but only because there had been no need for it. Whereas now the Order's only chance of avoiding defeat on the Roman battlefield lay in calling up its international troops. In short, the European associations, which had replaced the venerable *langues*, that is, the old administrative divisions, must be summoned to the rescue.

This summons had a fortunate outcome in Paris. The Comte de Rohan-Chabot, Duc de Ravèse, wrote that his advanced age and the state of his health did not allow of his travelling. The lieutenant replied that the summons was an order. The correspondent having pleaded that he would send a delegate, the lieutenant retorted that heads of associations must attend in person. The Comte de Rohan-Chabot, Duc de Ravèse, had only one resort: he resigned. Which was exactly what the Order wanted him to do. He was appointed Honorary Chairman and replaced by Prince Guy de Polignac who was given, as travelling companions, the Ducs Decazes and Morierre-Bernadotte, Knights Magistral.

The lieutenant was not so exacting with the Silesians: the Graf Henckel von Donnersmarck, who had long been the *de facto* leader of the association, deputized for Prince von Hatzfeldt in Rome. Out of special consideration for a professed member, moreover, the Baron Ludwigstorff, Grand Prior of Austria, was allowed to send the Graf Trapp, Knight of Justice, in his stead. The coming of this delegate was proof in itself of the Order's sovereignty: as an irredentist he could not enter Italy excepting by virtue of a certificate from the Grand Magistracy specifying the object of his journey. Finally, in the case of the Hungarian association-in-exile, the Archduke Joseph delegated his powers to Pallavicini, who was of Magyar origin.

F

As each foreign delegate arrived, Pecci informed the Secretariat of State, where surprise was unconcealed. From Mgr. Montini their sonorous names and titles passed to Cardinal Canali and the Holy Father. From England came Lord Iddesleigh, from Ireland, Captain Gaisford St. Lawrence, from Holland, Baron Voorst tot Voorst, from Belgium, the Prince de Ligne, and from Portugal, the Count of Alcaçovas de Lancaster.

The Spanish delegation was the first to arrive. Its leader requested a special audience of the Sovereign Council. Received at the door of the Magistral Palace by the Marquis Pallavicini, H.R.H. the Serene Infante of Spain, Don Fernando Maria of Bavaria and Bourbon, was conducted to the lieutenant and his colleagues who were waiting for him in great anxiety. Despite the grand master's visit to Madrid a year ago, and the excellent relations between the Grand Magistracy and the Spanish association, there was considerable doubt as to whether the very Catholic Spanish knights would take up a position against the Holy See. The Infante held up a vast sheet of parchment, headed by the arms of the *Sacra y veneranda Asamblea española*, and, like Don John of Austria setting sail for Lepanto as a Knight of Malta, cried, "Excellencies, here is the Spanish fleet!"

This parchment was a manifesto from the Spanish knights, proclaiming their solidarity with the Grand Magistracy and exhorting its officers to "continue to defend the sovereignty of the Order of Malta." Some of the signatures were interminable: the Duke of Medinaceli had only put a few of his titles, which occupied twenty-three lines of the Order's nominal roll.

The Infante went to see the Pope and left with him a petition which was quite as important as the manifesto: "Prostrate before Your Holiness, *cuyas sagradas plantas beso*, I give expression in all reverence to the joy and gratitude of the Spanish association at the supreme goodness which deigns to allow our sovereign Order to put forward the case for its legitimate defence."

A select committee received the chairmen and delegates of the other associations in the small council chamber, explained the Order's difficulties, and consulted them as to possible remedies.

This parliament, which held no plenary session, nevertheless had a suitable meeting-place: the dining-room of the Magistral

Palace was reopened in their honour. It was decorated with magnificent Bohemian tapestries, which had been hurried out of Prague before the Soviet troops reached that city. The dining-table had even more moving associations for all members of the Order: it had come from the flag galley of the Order's admiral. The silver dinner service bore the Maltese escutcheon. And even the French agreed that the food was exquisite, without going to the same lengths as Clement VI when he reproached the Order with living on "delectable dishes." And if they could not care for the wines of Magione, they could admire the list of one hundred wines in the Grand Master de Rohan's cellar, for it was framed for the purpose. At the time when that cellar had been full the luxury of it had roused the ire of the Capuchin Zammit, a precursor of Father Larraona, whose pamphlet, published during the Revolution, had compared the Grand Master to Sardanapalus.

Once all the delegations had seen the committee it offered them two resolutions, which they accepted. The first urged that the defendants' request for six months in which to prepare and depose their defence be granted. The second, that if it were not granted, the Order would repudiate the Court. Not all the delegates had supported this second resolution, in the first instance, for there were some who, like the lawyers, considered it overbold. The English and Dutch delegates were forward in helping to bring over these waverers. The Englishman showed that a judgment of the Court which gave grounds for attacks on the Vatican would be harmful to the Roman Catholic cause in Great Britain; the Dutchman echoed his argument which would also apply to Catholic evangelism in Holland. A German delegate read out a report on a meeting held by the Masonic lodge of Berne at which the conduct of the Holy See toward the Order of Malta was welcomed as carrying Holy water to the anticlerical mill. But even if none of this had happened the attitude of the Spaniards would have put heart into the delegates: for the Infante tabled a new manifesto proclaiming that the Spanish association would not hesitate to break away and declare itself independent if the Order was mulcted of one jot of its sovereignty.

The Grand Magistracy submitted the two resolutions to the Italian grand priories, which likewise approved them—in Rome, where conditions made a vote by the chapter impossible, votes were collected from the individual professed members.

The unanimity and fire with which the resolutions were supported gave the lawyers more courage at the prospect which had made them so timid. Nevertheless, they still urged caution and were given a respite while Ferrata wrote to Mgr. Scapinelli that "he was overjoyed to hear that the Court had granted six months' delay, whereby the Order was spared the experience of finding itself placed, in some sort, outside the Court's jurisdiction." This was using a white lie to give warning of what would happen in the event of a refusal. Nor did the Grand Magistracy fail to sound the same note at the Secretariat of State by informing it of the two resolutions.

The Court affected to be unmoved: it had sworn not to go *ad aquas* without having delivered judgment and declared that nothing should prevent it. The original time granted, plus Cardinal Tisserant's ten days, expired on July 24. But the assembly of venerable tongues had served its purpose: once again the Holy Father intervened, and the cardinals were obliged to yield. On the eve of the very day when they had expected to have done with the business, they were obliged to issue a new decree postponing the day of judgment to December 31. The cardinals added that since the Order had not deposited the million lire called for by the due date, it must pay a million and a half into court on or before October 31. It became increasingly evident that their solemn imposition of secrecy was not solely owing to canonical reasons: they wanted no revelation of their want of indifference to temporalities in their spiritual mission.

The visit of the foreign delegations had another outcome: it set the Grand Magistracy on the way to reform. In the course of many meetings at which the foreign knights were for the first time consulted as to the running of the Order, they did not conceal their opinion that its best guarantee must lie in reforming its own constitution.

And above all something must be done about recruiting men prepared to take the vows, for the basis of the Order's existence was its professed brethren. But since the Order's modern activities did not really call for the kind of vows which had formerly been entirely fitting for the military life of knights fighting far from their country, some other formula should be found, less rigorous, though maintaining the religious character to which, in spite of the cost, the Order still clung. It was also considered essential that henceforth the foreign associations be represented in the central government. A committee to study the whole question of such reforms was set up under the chairmanship of an eminent jurist, Massimo Pilotti, Procurator to the Court of Appeal, and a judge of the International Court at The Hague. The Congregation for Religious was asked to provide a canonist, and it could hardly refuse: Father Larraona caused Mgr. Pavan to be appointed, believing that prelate to be devoted to him; however, Mgr. Pavan saw the light with disconcerting rapidity, and thereafter remained as firm as a rock, despite a storm of threats.

While this committee was getting to work and elaborating a "charta," grave and mysterious things were happening in the Via Condotti. There was an uneasy feeling that despite the discretion of all working in the several offices, the other side were often informed of their activities. On one occasion a register vanished, to reappear two days later. On another occasion a man was seen in the central courtyard stooping to pick up a letter thrown from one of the windows. Cardinal Canali was openly boasting that the Sovereign Council's decrees were in his hands on the day they were issued, likewise the association's cables and even the lawyers' notes. It was at first believed that certain details were reaching him by way of servants in his pay, and that he was using them to pretend to know everything in order to spread alarm and despondency in the grand magistral ranks: in short, a war of nerves. But it was soon realized that they were not doing His Eminence justice: his information was far more thorough than could be accounted for by backstairs gossip.

Could there be a traitor in the Sovereign Council? Out of the question. In the Chancellery? Rangoni and Cattaneo answered for their staff. For a short while there were doubts of the consistory lawyers' loyalty, torn as they must be between the Order and the Holy See. But when Mgr. Montini read Pecci the agenda for a deliberation which he had had from Cardinal Canali, and which had been drawn up by Cattaneo and was as yet unknown to both the Sovereign Council and the lawyers, it became manifest that the leak must be sought in the Chancellery itself. Was it the classic case of a servant finding a rough draft in the wastepaper basket? Or had the spy read the document on Cattaneo's desk while he was out of the room? Could an intruder be getting in, from a neighbouring house, after dark? The case was submitted to a specialist, an officer in counter-espionage: he had the locks changed and the windows barred. Cardinal Canali continued as well informed as ever. Cattaneo tried a ruse: he drew up a bogus decree and placed it in a filing-cabinet to which he alone had a key. As soon as he learned that Cardinal Canali was aware of the text, he knew that some-body else had access to his papers. Remembering that the cabinet had come from a purveyor to the Holy See, he had the lock changed.

While all this was going on, one of the clerks fell ill, his life was despaired of, and he asked to see Cattaneo.

"Count," he said, "can you ever forgive me?"

"As far as I know, there is nothing to forgive. Tell me what wrong you have done me."

"I cannot tell you, but I implore you to forgive me. A dying man has a right to be forgiven unquestioningly and uncon-ditionally."

"My poor friend, I am not your confessor. Have you confessed?"

"Yes, but that isn't enough. All my life I have believed in God, and so I do now, more than ever. Well, despite the priest's absolution, I feel that there is something God has not yet forgiven me."

"If it will set your mind at rest and help you to recover, I forgive you."

The man died next day, but at peace.

Cardinal Canali received no more secret information.

# X

CARDINAL TISSERANT, sacrificing himself to his responsibilities as the presiding judge, let his colleagues go *ad aquas* and took the waters in Rome.

The post of chancellor falling vacant by the death of Rangoni, and Cattaneo being too young to hold the office, Pecci set forth the conditions which in his opinion ought to be fulfilled by the new chancellor. He should be a foreigner, which would eliminate excessive Italian influence; but a national of a minor power, which would eliminate too much foreign influence. Baron Apor of Altorja, Magistral Grand Cross, formerly Hungarian Minister to the Holy See and whose brother, a bishop, had been martyred by the Bolsheviks, received most votes, was appointed chancellor, and Cattaneo promoted vice-chancellor.

The new leader of the Order's government was a short, lively man with Mongoloid features, Impatient to display his abilities, he sought an audience of the Dean of the Sacred College. He was received at once, but "in his private capacity." The cardinal asserted that he could not possibly have received him in his official capacity, since he had been appointed by a lieutenant, and a provisional lieutenant at that. The powers of a lieutenancy had been limited by a brief issued by Urban VIII. Moreover, the Order's constitution of 1936 forbade a locum tenens to undertake any extraordinary act of administration, in which description the appointment of a chancellor must be included. Returning to the Magistral Palace with his tail between his legs, Apor read the texts justifying his appointment, sent the cardinal an outline of his findings, and instructed the lawyers to produce a more complete, in fact definitive memorandum on the subject.

Ferrata established the following conclusions: the attribute "provisional," associated with the lieutenancy, was not to be found in the De Rohan code of rules; it had not appeared until 1936. A provisional lieutenant's powers were identical with a lieutenant's. Urban VIII's brief, which limited those powers, envisaged the normal case of an interregnum between the death of the grand master and the election of another. The election having been postponed against the Order's will, the case could not be considered normal. The distinction between ordinary and extraordinary acts of administration was, in the present circumstances, devoid of meaning, since it was a question of ensuring the ordinary running of the Order. The 1936 constitution had been adopted for the sole purpose of bringing the De Rohan code into conformity with the new code of canon law, and was only concerned with the religious side: the office of the chancellor was so far divorced from that side of the Order's activities, that the 1936 constitution did not even mention it. Finally, and quite apart from the constitution in question and Urban's brief, the Court of Cardinals had itself recognized the lieutenant's power to transact extraordinary business, since it had subpoenaed him and accepted his lawyers' right to plead in the most important piece of business which the Order had been engaged in since the capitulation of Malta. Pecci delivered this memorandum to the Secretariat of State and Cardinal Tisserant stopped quibbling. And as if to complete his conviction that the lieutenant's powers must, after all, be valid, the new ambassadors of Argentina and Spain to the Holy See were, on the same day, also accredited to the Via Condotti.

There remained the small matter of the million and a half lire demanded by the Court. The time granted for payment was running out; Hercolani informed Cardinal Tisserant of his reasons for withholding payment. In international trials, such as those of cases referred to The Hague Court, the Court's expenses were never charged to the parties involved as principals. If the Order paid these costs it would, by so doing, admit its subjection to a court of common pleas, thereby abdicating the sovereign attribute insisted on in the lawyers' mandate. The lieutenant added that in order to be cleared of any suspicion that he was acting from motives of parsimony, he would place 2,000,000 lire at the disposal not of the Court, for its costs, but of the Holy Father, for his poor. The cardinal's answer confined itself to pointing out that the lieutenant had again forgotten the qualification "provisional."

*          *          *

Nearly halfway through December, the Court had still not indicated what procedure it proposed to adopt. It looked as if Mgr. Scapinelli, in ignoring the lawyers' instances, was kindly avoiding putting them to useless trouble. Prince Pacelli had smiled at their making a point of Cardinal Gasparri's declaration to the Czechoslovak government, shrugging it off as "an act of complaisance designed to save the Order's property."

Refusing to be discouraged, the defendants once again tried to make it clear that it was a shameful thing for any judge to pronounce judgment before the case he was to try had started; to point out the danger to the Order's diplomatic standing inherent in any attack on its sovereignty; to emphasize that such treatment of a religious order by a special Court of Cardinals must be regarded as scandalous, especially after the Holy Father had promulgated three apostolic epistles and an encyclical all stigmatizing the parodies of justice meted out to churchmen by the Communist countries.

All these observations remaining unanswered, a dead letter, the Grand Magistracy made up its mind to throw the bomb which it was holding in reserve. The deafness or indifference of their judges facilitated its use. Scrupulous to the last, the lawyers sent a final appeal to the Court, once again asking that the historical study prepared by the Congregation of Religious be withdrawn from the documents in the case. Their appeal was rejected. Whereupon the defence proclaimed that, the study objected to having issued from a plenary session of the Congregation of Religious, Cardinals Canali, Micara, and Pizzardo, being members of that congregation, had no right to sit on the bench of judges.

The Court was shaken to its foundations. The three cardinals, recovering their wits, then affirmed that they had not been present at the plenary session. Pecci called on Mgr. Montini and proved, from cuttings of the *Osservatore Romano*, that no plenary session of the congregation in question could be held without the Roman cardinals, since they composed it. Having done which, he asked whether Cardinals Canali, Micara, and Pizzardo wanted to hear themselves given the lie by three consistory lawyers in open court.

The reply communicated by the three cardinals was to the effect that even if they had taken part in the plenary session, it made no difference. For, that whatever they might then have decided, they did not thereby disable themselves from coming to a new and different decision, since their ecclesiastical rank and dignity rendered them "exempt from prejudice." In support of which contention they referred to commentators on canon law—notably the famous Cardinal de Luca—all of whom agreed that cardinals are *ipso facto* "above suspicion."

The Grand Magistracy retorted that they were obliged to raise an even more serious objection to the three cardinals: not only had they given their opinion before judgment had been pronounced; but, as members of the original committee of cardinals, had done so even before the special Court was set up. The only honourable explanation for their agreeing to judge a case they had prejudged was that they were anxious to revise their opinion; whereas they had done nothing but confirm it and seemed unable to depart from it. Consequently the Order found itself obliged to object to them as judges.

All this was, of course, expounded with the customary euphemisms. Never had flowers of rhetoric, diplomacy, and academic language concealed a keener dagger. The Order did not merely "take exception"; it declared the objection prejudicial, which must prevent the delivery of any judgment until it had been resolved. And in two successive instances, designed to reinforce a position already impregnable, it also claimed the question of payment of costs to be prejudicial, since it was linked with the whole question of sovereignty; and likewise the question of procedure, which had still not been determined.

With an arrogant contempt for mere justice the Court made answer, in a decree, that all these questions would be resolved in its sentence. It added, not without irony, that the manner in which it had conducted the case was sufficient indication of the procedure. And it reminded the lawyers that their conclusions must be deposed before St. Sylvester's.

Mgr. Montini asked Pecci to urge the Order not to do anything foolish, to depose its conclusions, in short to do nothing apt to annoy the Holy Father. His good faith in giving this advice was not to be doubted. But it was possible he might be deceiving himself when he went on to invite the Order to have faith in the judges' magnanimity. Some weeks ago he had been promoted Under Secretary of State, and was inclined to optimism.

The Grand Magistracy had reason to be less so; it realized that it was now up against a blank wall. It did the only thing left to be done in its own defence: on December 23, a solemn decree signed by all the members of the Grand Council announced that the Order of Malta was withdrawing from the trial. This was the measure which had been envisaged by the jurists from the beginning, and which had been approved in advance by the grand priories and associations—the measure which Ferrata had hinted at to Mgr. Scapinelli.

In justification of this act, the Order did not fail to invoke the pontifical chirograph guaranteeing the rights of the defence. It was even shrewd enough to quote an article of canon law which permits any party to a case to withdraw from the trial. The chancellor sent a message to the Pope explaining the reasons for what was being done. In it he said that "his (the Pope's) eminent learning, high juridical conscience, and fatherly affection for the Order" would assuredly enable him to understand the imperative need for it.

Certainly Pius XII needed all these qualities, and more, not to mention his knowledge of men's souls, to resist Cardinal Canali. That Eminence had suggested appointing Prince Ruffo, whose fidelity to the Holy See was well tried, as Commissioner of the Order of Malta. He insisted that the Order as a whole would throw over the Grand Magistracy upon finding at its head a presiding bailiff whose name would inspire confidence. The Holy Father, however, declared that he could not bullyrag people who had canon law on their side. In the same spirit, he readily granted them the apostolic blessing which Pecci solicited on their behalf on Christmas Day.

On December 29, the Court issued a new decree. This repeated the claim that it had, by its acts, clearly indicated the mode of procedure; it rejected the objection raised to the three cardinals as "devoid of foundation"; as for the Congregation of

Religious historical study, it now claimed that this was the
work of two specialists. For the rest, it would be dealt with in
the Court's judgment, to be delivered in its own good time.
It considered the Order's withdrawal from the case as invalid
on the grounds that there could be no escape from an ecclesiastical
tribunal. And it granted the lawyers another ten days' grace.

Snider, who was on terms with Cardinal Tisserant, had already
tried one personal approach, but it had been ineffectual. Thinking to touch a chord in the cardinal as an Orientalist, he had
sent him a memorandum giving him an idea of the Arabic
documents which had not yet been consulted and which he
considered of capital importance: the Chronicon Syriacum of
Abu Faradj; the Annals of Abu Feda; the Two Gardens of
Abu Chama; the Kamel Altevarykh of Ibu el Athyr; the Chronicle
of Ibu Ferat; the "Account" of El Aïni; the Life of the Sultan
Almalik Alnasir Saladin by Beha ed Din, etc. etc.

Ferrata wished to join with Snider in a second attempt, and
together they wrote the cardinal a noble letter. They turned to
him, they said, "as Christian jurists who had formed their rule
of conduct from their religious convictions, under the eye of
God." They reminded him that they had accepted the mission
of defending the Order "since here was a case which might
bear witness before the world to the wisdom and learning of
the Roman ecclesiastical courts." They did not conceal from
him their surprise at the "want of serenity" which, however,
had been manifest in "certain persons assisting the Court";
nor their fear that this "want of serenity might, in the event of
the facts becoming known outside, be attributed by the world
to the judges themselves.

"We do not here allude," they continued, "to that section
of public opinion represented by the enemies of our Mother
the Church, who will not fail, who already are not failing, to
make use of this matter in their attacks on her, and even on
the papacy. We may ignore such people. But we may not ignore
others, people worthy of consideration, prelates, priests, religious,
as well as jurists and scholars in every country where our faith
reigns—who are already giving expression to their sorrow and
amazement. This fact is all the more significant in so far as

the people in question are men who have often had no connection, or indeed even sympathy, with the Order of Malta. They have been led to take sides with the Order because they are convinced that an attempt has been made to impose a verdict in advance of the trial and that the task of the defending lawyers has been made impossible. Your Eminence, whose sensibility is well known to us, will understand our perplexity in this situation——"

But ever since he had hitched his wagon to Cardinal Canali's star, Cardinal Tisserant's "sensibility" had become rather less than the lawyers supposed, and he confined himself to trying to persuade them to disobey their clients by deposing their conclusions. He appealed to *their* sensibility, as advocates of the sacred consistory, citing in example their colleague Pacelli, His Holiness's nephew; and on seeing them smile at this, expressed great surprise.

# XI

THE CHANCELLOR'S LETTER had made the Order's reasons for withdrawing from the case clear to the head of the Church; but the Vatican took no less stern a view of that decision. Those of its members who had hitherto been favourable to the Grand Magistracy now felt themselves obliged to support the cardinals. Mgr. Montini declared that such a withdrawal was the last resort of a litigant whose case was going badly; Pecci was able to show him that the Order's case would have gone well enough before any other bench. Ferrata had just discovered two documents which, he said, would long since have put an end to the case if they had come to light sooner; but they had not figured among Mgr. Scapinelli's "notes in illustration." The documents were bulls of Popes Pius IV and VI respectively exempting the Order of the Knights of St. John "from all jurisdiction lay or ecclesiastical whatsoever and from all tribunals even those composed of pontifical legates or most eminent cardinals."

Ferrata sent copies of these bulls to Prince Pacelli and at the same time wrote to say that "the instance of the late lamented grand master to the Sovereign Pontiff, the effect of which had been the setting up of the Court of Cardinals, was no more than the voluntary act of the head of a sovereign Order who was willing temporarily to renounce his rights in order to establish that they were well founded." And the illustrious advocate, knowing just where the shoe would pinch, pointed out that these two bulls, enacted *in perpetuum*, covered the Order's property, since they declared any alienation of it to be null and void. Prince Pacelli replied that the popes being the source of canon law, what one had done another could undo. Pius XII was therefore in no way bound by anything decreed by Pius IV or Pius VI, *in perpetuum* or otherwise.

To enlighten its representatives in Italy and abroad the Grand Magistracy sent them not, indeed, notes in illustration, but notes in explanation. They set forth the reasons for the withdrawal, which they themselves had approved in case it should become necessary, and asked them to inform all members of the Order. Nor did they fail to refer to the bulls of the two Popes Pius which Prince Pacelli was treating with such scant respect. Thick as hail, in response, came telegrams of solidarity. Prince Ruffo had forbidden the regional delegates of the Italian association to communicate the contents of the grand magistral note to their members; but he was not obeyed; and in reproof of his attitude his office staff resigned in a body. That was a blunder, since it enabled him to fill their places with the handful of Roman knights sharked up, in the interval, by Cardinal Canali. The cardinal found only one ally in the Grand Priory of Lombardy-Venetia, apart, that is, from Thun: this was the Knight of Justice Flavio Melzi d'Eril who, taking, as it were, the words out of the cardinal's mouth, announced, in a letter which was made public, that the Grand Magistracy's withdrawal from the trial was "an act of rebellion against the Vicar of Christ." Still young, this knight, a brother of the Duke of Lodi, brought all the dash and fire of an ex-officer to the expression of his convictions, a boldness well worthy of a family in which a First Empire title still survived. His submission to the hierarchy of the Church was as abject as Prince Ruffo's.

The Trimurti, growing impatient, now had recourse to its most powerful weapon. Prince Pacelli was entrusted with the task of telephoning Hercolani to threaten him with excommunication. This threat, thus delivered by telephone for the first time in history, was received by the lieutenant with more phlegm than it had been by the grand master.

"I did not know that you had been seconded to the Holy Office," he said. "But even so, I have done nothing to be excommunicated for either by the Holy Office or by the Pope. If I am to be excommunicated by you, it will be an honour."

The retort sufficed to lower the Trimurti's tone, and the next day Mgr. Scapinelli was threatening nothing worse than an interdict.

The same threats were addressed to professsed knights. With lay officials another means was tried: they were offered place, money, and honours to abandon the rebellious magistracy to its miserable fate. And Cardinal Canali, anxious to minimize the effect given to the Order's decision by the support of two consistory lawyers, put it about that the decision had been taken without their knowledge and against their advice.

To demonstrate that it was conducting the business at diplomatic level, the Grand Magistracy started carrying on its correspondence with the Holy See in ambassadorial style: Pecci delivered two *notes verbales* to Mgr. Montini. The first drew attention to the fact that the Court was continuing the trial in the absence of the defendants; the second reverted, as had become necessary, to the bulls of Pius IV and Pius VI.

Realizing that their adversary was still eluding them, the Court modified its attitude and let it be known that it would deliver a verdict taking account of all the Order's interests on condition that the Order agreed to plead. This ruse was judged a trifle crude, despite the assurances given to the lawyers by Prince Pacelli. It was too reminiscent of Mgr. Montini's suggestion that the Order should trust itself to the magnanimity of the judges. However, this time Ferrata thought he could sense an accent of truth in Prince Pacelli's assurances and insisted that he be taken at his word. With the result that Apor wrote to Mgr. Montini saying that the Order would put in an appearance if it was informed of the verdict in advance and considered it acceptable. No more was heard of that.

The system of *notes verbales* had had no useful results. Instead of entering into negotiations the Secretariat of State had replied that 'convinced that it was taking the best course it had transmitted the Legation's notes to the Most Eminent Court." It had, in short, followed Cardinal Tedeschini's example when he had passed on the Order's complaints to Cardinal Canali.

The Court sent the Grand Magistracy a new decree which fixed the time and date for delivering a verdict—9.30 A.M., January 24, 1953. Hercolani acknowledged its receipt to Cardinal Tisserant but pointed out that since the Order had, by decree of December 23, withdrawn from the trial, it considered everything which happened in the Most Eminent Court as *res inter alios acta*, "a thing happening between third parties."

The experience of having their mouths shut with four words of Latin infuriated the five cardinals. They instructed Mgr. Scapinelli to require Ferrata, whose style they had recognized to withdraw the phrase at once if he did not want to be struck off the Sacred Consistory's roll.

The advocate returned to the Via Condotti looking thoughtful, called a meeting, and said, "I know that I am right; I know that we are right. But I also know, now, what you do not— what Cardinal Canali is capable of. I am not concerned about being struck off the Consistory roll; my career does not depend on my Consistory title, honourable though it be. What does trouble me, trouble me in my soul as a believing Catholic and a nephew of the man they call 'the famous Cardinal Ferrata,' is that I have just been called a miscreant and a wretch for having inspired the use of the words *res inter alios acta*. Could not the Grand Magistracy, therefore, attest that, its counsel's mandate having terminated with the decree of December 23, they were not consulted in the drafting of the lieutenant's latest letter?"

Hercolani, with general approval, said that he would draft the attestation immediately. And if it gave the impression of a split between the Order and its legal advisers, which was exactly what Cardinals Tisserant and Canali wanted, it could not be helped. It would also serve to protect Corsanego, who had likewise been summoned to attend at the Court's secretariat where, no doubt, he would be the victim of some similar threat.

"So then," somebody said to Ferrata, "you feel guilty because you committed those four words of Latin? It follows, you know, that we, all of us here, feel most shockingly guilty too, since we approved the words and are all, like you, believing Catholics."

And they called on him to be so good as to explain, for the deliverance of their consciences and the peace of their souls, wherein their culpability resided.

Ferrata's face flushed with anger.

"Culpable!" he exclaimed, "culpable, because we used and approved those four words? If any are guilty, it is the men who forced us to make use of them."

And after a moment's thought, he smiled and said, "On second thoughts I don't feel in the least guilty. And I want no such attestation from you. Forgive me, gentlemen: any man can have his moment of weakness; mine is over and done with."

# XII

SOME TIME BEFORE this event the Order had set up a press bureau. The curiosity provoked by the case had become all the keener for the fact that practically nothing was known about it, and the Order could not continue indefinitely in the attitude of the god Harpocrates, finger on lips. If the journalists did not get what they wanted at the Magistral Palace, they went round to the Vatican where the information they were given might not always be to the Order's advantage. A prudent use of the same weapon seemed necessary. The Marquis Sersale, a Neapolitan knight of the Order, was appointed director of the press bureau, and that he was devoted to the cause was unquestionable, since the office was an honorary one.

But in this field, too, the Order had to defend itself against the Holy See with inferior weapons. In fact it discovered that it was dealing with an opponent who had a thousand means of attacking it while himself beyond reach of attack. It was the Vatican practice to hand out information without assuming responsibility for it. There was a sort of voluntary and unofficial representative, a man of lugubrious aspect who toiled round the editorial offices of newspapers leaving a trail of typewritten sheets, "flimsies" which came to be called by his name. They were known to originate in the Vatican but were supposed not to, so that a bold attack could be followed by a strategic withdrawal. These operations were directed by Cardinal Canali and his two Trimurti colleagues.

No sooner had the Grand Magistracy set up its own press bureau than the Vatican volunteer became twice as zealous as before. Articles favourable to the Order were readily accepted by editors: but thereafter they were cut to the bone "for reasons of space" or were unaccountably "lost" by the printers. Such were some of the little games so skilfully played by the Grand Prior of Rome. The Sovereign Council was obliged to vote funds for acquiring the good will of compositors and proof correctors.

The lieutenant had the idea of getting one of the leading Roman dailies to publish an article on the day before that on which the verdict was to be delivered, an article designed to influence the Court's decision in so far as that was possible. During the last several weeks a perfect snowstorm of flimsies had been falling from the Vatican, or at least from the hands of its volunteer, upon editorial desks, with the result that public opinion had been misled. The public, in fact, was further than ever from understanding how the Order could be loyal, as it proclaimed itself, to the Holy Father, and yet repudiate a court set up by him. The time had come to set this right. The Grand Magistracy chose the *Giornale d'Italia* for its purpose, since one of its regular contributors was a friend of Sersale's. This journalist undertook to write the vitally important article himself and to answer for its publication uncut and unaltered. He let it be known that the director of the newspaper himself had passed the article, fixed the date, and reserved the front page for its appearance.

Sure enough the article appeared, intact, on the front page and on the right day, but with the following headline across four columns: "The Order of Malta Will Not Recognize the Verdict of the Five Cardinals." Sersale almost fainted when he read it and believed that he had been betrayed by his friend. Pecci, confined to his bed by influenza, telephoned Hercolani to say that all was lost.

The inquiry at once instituted by the *Giornale d'Italia*, where the indignation was quite as great as in the Via Condotti, revealed that the Vatican volunteer had been warned by his spy on the premises that an important article, favourable to the Order, was about to appear.

"Suppress it!"

"Impossible. It's been passed by the director."

"Then change the headline."

"Difficult, in view of the context."

"You are to change it, understand? Put something which will make the Holy Father angry. When you're dealing with scoundrels you've got to fight dirty."

However, to everyone's surprise, the day so pompously decreed for the passing of sentence brought forth no utterance from the Court. Not that it had decided to modify it; but at the last moment it had hesitated to promulgate it.

"If," the Pope had told one of the cardinal judges, "there is a public outcry, the Order of Malta will be damaged by it; but so will you."

These words were a vindication of what the Order's lawyers had said when trying to persuade the Court to see reason. But the Court was only reserving its verdict in the hope of forcing the Order to put in an appearance, or with a view to striking at it in some other way.

The Promoter of Justice, Mgr. Ottaviani, having been made a cardinal at the January Consistory and appointed Pro-Secretary to the Holy Office, his improved status seemed likely to be a new trump card in Cardinal Canali's hand. Both Cardinal Canali and Cardinal Micara were members of that congregation, but his standing in it was not high and its secretary, Cardinal Pizzardo, was not ready to place the Church's final recourse completely at his service. The Grand Prior of Rome believed, however, that Cardinal Ottaviani would agree to condemn the Order on the spiritual side, thus opening the way for the secular verdict of condemnation: in short, that he would give canonical substance to the telephonic menaces of Prince Carlo Pacelli. But the Pro-Secretary of the Holy Office refused to avenge the injuries suffered by the Promoter of Justice, much less Cardinal Canali's. He declared, as the Pope had done already, that in the canonical sphere there was nothing whatever to be said against the Order. And he added that as for the rest, it was none of his business now.

Twice did Cardinal Tisserant then summon the lieutenant and the chancellor to his presence; not to revert to the questions of the latter's appointment and the former's title, however. His purpose was to flatter and threaten them alternately in an effort to persuade them to change their attitude. He invoked earth and heaven; he told them that the responsibility for leaving the Order undefended would lie at their door, and be a stain upon their honour. But whereas the lawyers had found it necessary to remind the Court of its own honour, neither Hercolani nor Apor required any such reminder; both knew their duty.

Cardinal Canali having been unable to budge either the Holy Father or the Holy Office, and Cardinal Tisserant either the lieutenant or the chancellor, as a last resort the Court sent the Grand Magistracy, on February 6, a letter dated February 4, informing it of a decree passed on January 24 in substitution for the verdict: "In consideration of its own forbearance, and in so far as the attitude of the sovereign and Hierosolymitan Order of Malta constitutes an act of distrust toward it, the Most Eminent Court is determined, before pronouncing sentence, to record how deeply it deplores the attitude of the Order's leaders and their legal advisers."

Although Cardinal Tisserant's covering letter reiterated his regret that the lieutenant and the chancellor had not come to a better frame of mind, the victims of the decree were tempted to laugh: the cardinalistic mountain had brought forth a mouse.

Such, at least, was the Grand Magistracy's first impression. But the word *deplore* had been used in a substantive form—"profound *deploration*"—which was as new to the professed as to lay members, and to which they had not, therefore, given the tremendous meaning it had for the Holy See. It was no mere expression of resentment at their attitude, given a nobler term: it expressed despair of their salvation.

However, after the Secretariat of State had given its own opinion, "the Order's attitude could not be considered as anything less than an offence to pontifical authority," a more serious matter than offence to the purple, the decree had to be examined more closely. Mgr. Montini, furthermore, issued a warning as to "the measures which the Court would adopt if the Order's attitude was not modified."

On the following morning an "intimation by courier"—to wit, a dispatch-rider on a motor-cycle—arrived from the sacred apostolic palaces, and proved to be reassuring: Mgr. Callori di Vignale, Pro-Master of the Bedchamber to His Holiness, had issued his customary invitation to the Order for the papal chapel to be held on February 10. It was the fourteenth anniversary of the death of Pius XI "of sainted memory," and recalled the incident which had nearly led to bloodshed in the Sistine, a year ago.

On the morning of the 9th, Mgr. Quirino Paganuzzi, secretary to the master of the bedchamber, arrived at the Grand Magistracy in the guise of a courier, to cancel the invitation. This was tantamount to putting the Order of Malta under the ban of the Church. Pecci called on Mgr. Montini to discover whether this cancellation was "authorized." The Pro-Secretary of State replied that he would seek information about it. Cardinal Canali had the idea of reversing last year's defeat: the Order of the Holy Sepulchre would take unquestioned precedence, and the Order of Malta be made to seem ashamed to show its face. Had not a bust of Pius XII sculptured by Prince Lancelloti

and hitherto decorating a Vatican antechamber been removed
to punish the sculptor, a Knight of Malta, for not rallying to
Prince Ruffo's standard? The whole day was spent in marches
and counter-marches. It was discovered that Mgr. Paganuzzi,
won over by Cardinal Canali, had carried his morning message
unknown to the Pro-Master of the Bedchamber: that that prelate, annoyed as he might be with Mgr. Paganuzzi, could not
repudiate him. At last, Mgr. Montini, breathless, no doubt,
after hours of feverish activity, left Mgr. dell'Acqua, his subordinate, to telephone Pecci with the information that "the
cancellation was authorized." Mgr. dell'Acqua lost no time in
carrying out the commission; it was the first chance he had
had to interfere in the Malta affair. Like Mgr. Paganuzzi he had
been won over by Cardinal Canali, to whom he was looking
for his appointment as substitute; thus, like Mgr. Scapinelli, did
he justify his title of Prelate Domestic.

Nevertheless, the way was not closed to an accommodation
with the powers of light. Mgr. dell'Acqua had not confined
himself to announcing that the cancellation communicated by
Mgr. Paganuzzi was authorized. The Order, he had added,
could get it withdrawn if the Sovereign Council would issue,
before midnight, a decree "regretting the deploration of the
Court, instructing its advocates to appear for judgment, and
undertaking to abide by the verdict." And Mgr. dell'Acqua
had also made it clear that it was not merely the right to be
present at papal chapels which was involved: unless the decree
was issued the Holy See would, on the following day, appoint
a pontifical commissioner; and he had no need to add that the
man in question would be Prince Ruffo.

Mgr. dell'Acqua issued his ultimatum at 9 P.M. The lieutenant
retorted to the effect that Mgr. dell'Acqua's thunderbolts were
as powerless to move him as Prince Pacelli's. At 11.45 Pecci
called upon Mgr. dell'Acqua, who was reading his breviary
and expecting him. The Order's minister had brought only a
*note verbale:* the Sovereign Council had been unable to meet;
but those of its members who managed to assemble wished to
protest their attachment to the Holy Father and their respect
for the Most Eminent Court. And that was all: Mgr. dell'Acqua's

attempt at intimidation had been no more effective than Prince Pacelli's "excommunication" and the five cardinals' "deploration."

Their zealous servant had had very good reason for the haste he had made on their behalf, and the Grand Magistracy an even better one for shrugging off his threats with a smile: the "rescue fleet" was once again on the way and Pecci had announced the fact to the Secretariat of State. "The Order," he had written, "wishes to strengthen the decisions which will enable it to fulfil the wishes of the Holy See by taking a vote of its foreign members." It was well known that, in these circumstances, the Pope would be opposed to any extreme measures; and the Court had therefore been trying to break the resistance of the Grand Magistracy before the overseas delegates arrived.

On the morning of the 10th the first of these gentlemen arrived in Rome. There was no delegation from the Order of Malta at the Sistine. The Order of the Holy Sepulchre's delegates occupied the front seats under the doting eye of their grand master. But no pontifical commissioner arrived in the Via Condotti.


# XIII


CARDINAL CANALI had spread a rumour that the Spanish association, in the grip of remorse, was about to make an *amende honorable*. Nobody, at the Grand Magistracy, had believed this: for they did not know that certain important negotiations between Rome and Madrid had involved the Order of Malta.

Pius XII and General Franco were equally anxious for the signing of a concordat, but the Vatican requirements were such that Spain, with all the good will in the world, had been unable to accept them. The Caudillo had been blaming his ambassadors for failing to overcome Vatican intransigence, and recalled them angrily, one after another. The latest, Castiella, having applied himself to the task with exceptional determination, had suddenly found the Holy See much more accommodating. They offered to sacrifice three clauses of the concordat, hitherto the stumbling block to agreement, provided the *Asamblea española* of Knights of Malta would withdraw their support from the Grand Magistracy.

From the very beginning of the conflict between the Order and the Vatican Franco had seen in it a means to his own ends. Suddenly recalling that he was himself a bailiff grand cross of the Order, and not having forgotten that the Infante don Fernando Maria, chairman of the *Asamblea*, had been instrumental in getting the royal family to accept the conditions on which he was willing to restore the monarchy, he had stimulated the zeal of the Spanish knights; and then accredited an ambassador to the Via Condotti at the very height of the struggle. The fruits of these tactics had not been long in falling into his hand, to the benefit of Spanish interests. When the Generalissimo sent for the Infante and told him that he was relying on the knights to smooth the path to signature of the concordat, love of chivalry had to give way to love of country.

This deal, initiated in Rome, was consummated in Madrid by the Nuncio Cicognani, titular Archbishop of Ancyra, and had earned him a Hat. So that once again, as in the fabled times of the Grand Master d'Aubusson and Prince Zizim, the Knights of St. John had played their part in the creation of a cardinal. The Infante's scruples were set at rest by an undertaking that "the privileges and character of the Spanish association would be protected." Thus the nuncio had succeeded, at one blow, in detaching the Spanish association from the Grand Magistracy and forcing it to be as good as its word—that it would declare itself independent if the Order suffered any diminution of sovereignty.

When the telegraphic summons to the second and urgent assembly of the venerable *langues* arrived, the Spanish *langue* was evasive in conveying the answer that it would not be represented. The Infante was unwell; the other members of the council were prevented from coming by this or that difficulty. Rather than be obliged to make a poor showing for reasons of state, the caballeros preferred not to appear at all. The Grand Magistracy tried to console itself with the thought that their absence was preferable to their hostility. But Cattaneo and De Mojana were not of this opinion: they asserted that the participation of the Spaniards was all-important; their defection might well be the forerunner of secession. Moreover, this change of front must be explicable by some hidden reasons, and the only chance of getting to know them, and perhaps refute them, was the presence of Spanish delegates.

This view of the matter having carried the day, Cattaneo telephoned Madrid, insisted on the attendance of a Spanish delegation and offered to send one of the Order's own aircraft to fetch it. Finally, the Spaniards agreed to come, but said that they would make their own way to Rome.

While waiting for the Spanish brethren to arrive, the other overseas delegates called on their respective ambassadors to the Holy See where they were regaled with cautious speeches in flowery language. Nor did they fail to call on such cardinals as they were acquainted with. The Belgians were received at the Vicariate by Cardinal Micara, who had been nuncio at Brussels. Pink, bepomponed, and cooing like a dove, he exhorted them to allow the Court "to accomplish in peace its work of love, mercy, and justice."

"What have we done to the Grand Magistracy?" he added. "Nothing. It is they who have insulted us by withdrawing from the trial, and our only possible retort was a solemn deploration."

He was, however, happy to be able to tell them that the beatification causes of which he was the ponant were all going well, among the rest being that of the Barnabite Schilling, of such great interest to the city of Bruges; the Picpus Veuster, so dear to the good burghers of Malines; and that of the worthy priest Poppe, a son of Ghent. He called upon the delegates to be thankful for all that the Holy See was doing for Belgium in this field, not to mention the recent contribution made for the relief of flood victims; and to keep away from the highly charged atmosphere of the Grand Magistracy: "Go, rather, and visit the workshops of St. Peter's, where you will see the recently discovered remains of the Grand Master Zacosta, the only Grand Master of Rhodes to be buried in Rome. He was Spanish, but at that time Belgium was a jewel in the Spanish crown."

The French were received by Cardinal Tisserant in his majestic office in the Convertendi Palace. He said to them, in that gravelly voice which seemed to issue from a dictaphone which stood upon the table, "What have we done to the Grand Magistracy? Nothing. It is they who have insulted us by withdrawing from the trial and our only possible retort was a solemn deploration."

More discreet than his colleague, he said nothing about his praiseworthy efforts on behalf of the French candidates for beatification. He did not even reveal that his negotiations with the Congregation of Rites was going to result in the proclamation of St. Symphorien as patron of Pamiers. He rejoiced with Prince de Polignac at the presentation by President Auriol of the *berretta* to the Nuncio Roncalli, made cardinal at the last Consistory; and at the similar promotion of the Archbishop of Paris and the learned Bishop of Le Mans. Finally, he recommended the delegates to visit St. Louis-des-Français and there pay their respects to the epitaph on a compatriot, the Grand Master la Cassiere, the only grand master of Malta buried in Rome; it would, he said, prepare them to cast their votes as good Christians.

But such little courtesies did nothing to conceal the apprehensions of the judges, nor those of the Order's members.

# XIV

THE LIEUTENANT HAD DECIDED to do things with all the ceremony becoming a sovereign Order. An opening Mass was celebrated at the Aventine in the presence of all the delegates. It was, fittingly, the Mass of the Holy Spirit. And when it had been said the congregation remained for some time at prayer in the silent church. Their consciences, as knights and as Catholics, were about to wrestle with a grave problem. The fate of the Order of Malta was in the balance.

Everyone was wondering what the two Spanish delegates would do. The Infante had sent a very young knight, the Marquis Prado de Carvajal, and had given him, by way of chaperon, a Spaniard who lived in Bologna and who was not known, in Madrid, to be a personal friend of Hercolani's.

Whereas, on the occasion of the last assembly, the delegations had been welcomed separately in the small council chamber, this time they all forgathered in the green salon. Behind Hercolani's high-backed armchair was the great Malta coat of arms, and beside it the Order's flag, transferred from the priory church. When the door opened and the words "His Excellency, the Venerable Bailiff Lieutenant!" rang out, the members of the Sovereign Council, and the vice-chancellor who had been granted the right to attend all meetings henceforth, had their hearts in their mouths. They were immediately reassured; Hercolani was greeted with acclamations.

Hercolani delivered a speech of welcome, and then withdrew, as it was customary for the head of the Order to do on the occasion of these assemblies. The first business was the sending of a telegram of respectful greeting to the Pope, signed by all the delegates, and asking for an apostolic blessing on their labours. This was generously granted.

An incident disturbed the calm and cheerful atmosphere during the evening session of the meeting, which was dedicated to a preliminary exchange of views. Pecci had expressed a wish to meet the delegates himself and explain his personal opinion and feelings about their situation: it had been granted in the belief that he would strengthen their determination, but in the event his visit seemed to have weakened it. Dinner, in the great dining-hall of the Magistral Palace, was a very dismal affair. The Sovereign Council, much alarmed, could only suspect Pecci of some jiggery-pokery. Next day, however, the delegates' brows were no longer clouded: night had brought council. But some of them seemed to have taken warning from the Order's minister to the Holy See, though without revealing what he had said to upset them. That, meanwhile, was unwittingly revealed when the Prince de Polignac was overheard remarking that the excommunication of *l'Action Française* had shown them, in France, what a Roman excommunication meant. The threat which had killed Prince Chigi and made Hercolani smile had had its effect on the foreign delegates, but only for the space of a night.

How could Pecci have been guilty of such a blunder? Had he felt it his duty to show the delegates the sword of Damocles which had been hanging for so long over the Grand Magistracy? A man of strong religious faith who bore the name of a pope might well have a moment of weakness among all the problems besetting him. When, some weeks later, he honourably delivered to the Grand Magistracy a copy of a letter written to Mgr. Montini on the day of his talk to the delegates, the mystery was at an end. The letter informed the Pro-Secretary of State that he "had acquitted himself of his mission to the delegates." It was decided to overlook the matter; Pecci's obvious delight in the fact that the firmness of the delegates was unimpaired earned him immediate forgiveness. He had obeyed the Church: and was happy that his act of obedience had made no difference.

Two motions had been put before the assembly: the first expressed a wish to accept any verdict which "reaffirmed the Order's sovereignty and privileges"; the second demanded the election of a grand master.

The Spanish ambassador had done his best to tamper with the Spanish delegation, but they knew perfectly well that the Grand Magistracy was right. As they had been instructed to conform to the will of the Pope, a third motion was drafted and put first on the agenda: it reiterated a "profession of absolute obedience to the Holy Father." It was an implied vote of thanks for his secret support, without which the Order would have ceased to exist. And it served to take the sting, though only in appearance, out of the other two motions. All three were passed unanimously.

Next day, however, the Spanish delegates returned from a visit to their Embassy looking very hang-dog. The Infante had telephoned from Madrid to insist on their withdrawing their signature, at least from the second motion: obviously the ambassador himself had realized that to express readiness to accept only an acceptable verdict was to reject the five cardinals' verdict in advance. The young Prado was pale and dejected, the Bolognese Spaniard stunned and moping. Their embarrassment showed the strain which their loyalty was undergoing. Apor, very much the great nobleman, said, "A gentleman, sirs, *never* withdraws his signature."

"We have no choice," they replied.

The chancellor had a brain wave:

"All is saved! You will put forward your demand to withdraw your signatures, we will make it a motion, vote on it, and reject it."

It was done; and by this ruse, whereby the proof of the Spanish retraction was confined to the secrecy of the archives, the Order could still present a united front to the world.

They might just as well have saved themselves the trouble. The cardinals who had been urging the delegates to visit the graves of their former grand masters, had meanwhile been lightheartedly busy digging the Order's. That they were about to be shown that the Grand Magistracy's parade of international strength no longer impressed them. The ceremony at the Aventine, motions, speeches, and subtle manœuvres produced no modification of their decision and may even have reinforced it.

On February 19 at 12.30, Pecci called on Mgr. Montini and delivered the Sovereign Council's decree embodying the three motions. He was given time to have his luncheon; at 2.30 Mgr. dell'Acqua sent him a copy of the Court's verdict. It was dated January 24, to show that the judges had kept their word and also, that having reached a verdict, they had, in their wisdom, meditated on it for a month before pronouncing sentence; they had let much water pass under the bridges of the Tiber, the Rhine, the Seine, and the Danube.

As the lieutenant's decrees never forgot to give him his title "by the Grace of God," the five cardinals claimed to pronounce sentence "in the Lord's name," *in nomine Domini*. What the sentence could have been in its original form must be a subject for wonder, since the final version had presumably been modified by the Holy Father's several interventions. The Court, answering the question propounded in the chirograph, declared that the Order, although enjoying certain prerogatives which had caused it to be recognized as sovereign by the Holy See, did not possess all those which are proper to sovereignty; that, its religious and sovereign attributes being interdependent, its sovereignty was merely "functional"; that it was in two senses a dependency of the Holy See—being dependent on the Secretariat of State in so far as it was a sovereign, and on the Congregation of Religious in so far as it was a religious, order; and that all its members, whoever they might be, including the holders of honorific distinctions, were likewise so dependent.

Never had princes of the Church so betrayed the good will of an Order determined, from conviction and in the name of tradition, to maintain its religious form. There had been no need to strip it of its property in so many words, since they were taking away all its rights. They were even braving ridicule by claiming that the sovereigns and chiefs of state who had been decorated by the Order had, unwittingly, made themselves dependents of the Holy See.

The Grand Magistracy had believed that by withdrawing from the case they would prevent the judges from pronouncing any sentence. But all its cleverness, combined with the support of its foreign members, had served only to delay the sentence. Nevertheless, it received it unmoved. Like the Grand Master de Omédès, the lieutenant's motto was "Constant in adversity."

It was thought that the cardinals would take care not to publish such a judgment: the harm it would do the Order was offset by the harm they would do themselves if, at least, it became known under what circumstances it had been arrived at. It was also noted that it had been passed on to them by the Secretariat of State "in agreement with the Congregation of Religious" but that, for the time being, that was all that had been done: it was not accompanied by any new threats. True, it was qualified as "immediately operative." True, also, however, that Mgr. Montini went to the trouble of sugaring the pill. He told Pecci, "You must grasp the fact that from your point of view something very important has been accomplished. The whole business is settled. You are rid of the Court of Cardinals, free to continue your usual activities, and free to elect a new grand master, which was what you wanted more than anything else."

Sceptical, Hercolani's retort was a gasconade: he would study the sentence in relation to the Order's decree announcing its withdrawal and to the motions passed by the assembly. Mgr. Montini was unable to regard this as a satisfactory acknowledgment: it implied reservations in acceptance of a judgment which he described as "not unfavourable to the Order." And it expressed no contrition arising out of the cardinals' deploration. The Secretariat of State added that it would be very much in the interests of the Grand Magistracy to initiate talks with the Pro-Secretary at once, since otherwise the Holy See would be obliged "to resort to the measures it had proscribed in such an eventuality." The phrase projected an image of Prince Ruffo's elegant person knocking at the Grand Magistracy's door.

As on the last occasion, none of the delegates had been able to ask for an audience with the Pope, who was suffering from a mild attack of influenza, and was seeing nobody. However, Hercolani got hold of four of his most faithful allies and sent them to call on Mgr. Montini: the Pro-Secretary had heard the voice of the cardinals; let him now hear the voice of the world.

Count Hutten-Czapski, a former Polish Ambassador to Rome and the new chairman of the Polish association in exile, an organization spread over fourteen countries, was the first to bear the good word to Mgr. Montini. He was just returned from Canada where he had taken part in the last International Congress of the Red Cross as representative of the Order of Malta, a signatory to the Geneva Convention. He could bear witness to the flourishing state of the Canadian association, recently formed in Montreal, whose social service courses were already being attended by hundreds of students. He had won over the Canadian Minister for Foreign Affairs to the idea of entrusting the care and administration of the Holy Places to the Order of Malta. The dream once indulged in by the former

Bailiff Thun had not been abandoned and had weighty backing, but backing conditional on the Order maintaining its sovereignty. Mgr. Montini listened to the count with interest.

Baron Van Voorst tot Voorst, next to call, pointed out that the Dutch First Aid Society, comprising 20,000 members, was proud of having obtained the patronage of the Order of Malta, whose insignia it now bore and used, but would certainly put an end to the connection if the Order lost its sovereignty. Mgr. Montini listened to the baron with interest.

Wing-Commander Grant-Ferris, barrister and former M.P., Privy Chamberlain of Cloak and Sword, gave it as his opinion that the threat to strike an advocate off the roll of Consistory lawyers for defending the Order would shock all Britain if it became known; that the Venerable Order of St. John which had hitherto refrained, out of deference, from calling itself Sovereign or its principal Grand Master, would do both if the Order lost its sovereignty; that the judgment would kill the British association, which was engaged in broadening its scope and was raising £250,000 for its Hospital of SS John and Elizabeth. Mgr. Montini listened to the Wing-Commander with interest.

Graf Henckel von Donnersmarck brought out the fact that the efforts of both German associations in the field of charitable works depended on the Order's sovereignty; that in the past year the camp at Ulm, managed by the Silesian Knights of Malta, had received 134,000 refugees; and that the Flensburg Hospital, managed by the Westphalian knights, had provided hospital service equal to 120,000 patient-days. Mgr. Montini listened to the graf with interest.

To these four pleaders a fifth was suddenly added: Prado had received fresh instructions from the Infante, who was now urging him to place himself unreservedly at the disposal of the Grand Magistracy. The Holy See, irritated by the Spanish change of front, was again showing Franco its teeth, who promptly unleashed his knights. Prado saw Mgr. Montini and demanded, in the name of the *Asamblea*, of its missionary school and its recently rebuilt clinic, that "the rights of an order whose fame was intimately associated with that of Spain herself" be respected. Mgr. Montini listened to him with interest.

But his silence had proved that his interest was wholly assumed. The Order was forgetting that it was under the ban of a solemn deploration and a cardinalistic judgment; that the tribunal which had issued them had been set up by the Pope; and that the verdict had been delivered "in the Lord's name."

# PART
# FOUR

# I

THE COURT OF FIVE CARDINALS was not satisfied with having pronounced an iniquitous judgment, long deferred but decided upon from the beginning; it was bent upon getting it accepted and humiliating its victim. Torn between their duties as Catholics and as defenders of their Order respectively, the members of the Grand Magistracy were about to pass through a period of ordeal and tribulation.

There was no longer any division of opinion at the Secretariat of State: Mgr. Montini and Mgr. dell'Acqua were henceforth at one in their determination to force the Order to give way, at whatever cost. The personal interests of Cardinal Canali were not involved: now, even more than at the time of the Order's withdrawal, it was the authority of the Holy See that was in question.

Mgr. dell'Acqua told Pecci that the Pope, whose health required the utmost consideration, was much affected by the Grand Magistracy's attitude, and especially by its silence in the matter of the solemn deploration. The members of the Sovereign Council would have died rather than apologize to their judges; but the lieutenant hastened to write to the Pope saying how deeply sorry he was to have grieved him, albeit unintentionally, by an act which he had been unable to avoid.

Prince Pacelli, who happened to be with Mgr. Montini when Pecci arrived with this letter, insisted that the expressions of regret which it conveyed were not explicit enough and that this might delay the Holy Father's convalescence. The minister replied that his instructions were to deliver the letter and that such as it was, he must do so.

Next day Mgr. Montini telephoned the Via Condotti to say that the lieutenant's letter had not been delivered to His Holiness and that he was sending round a draft of a more suitable one. The chancellor asked whether the *quid pro quo* for signing it would be the opening of negotiations. Mgr. Montini replied frankly that he could do no more than send round the draft

and that it contained what the cardinals required the Grand
Magistracy to write. This remark was an eye-opener, and when
the draft arrived it was submitted to an expert in canon law:
his opinion was definite: the signatory of that letter would run
the risk of being placed under an interdict.

Having avoided this trap, Hercolani seized the opportunity
offered by the anniversary of the pontifical election to send the
Pope not only his good wishes, but an expression of the "spiritual anguish in which the Knights of Malta, the eldest sons of
the Church, were sunk." Meanwhile Pecci wrote to Prince Pacelli,
and using the eloquence he reserved for great occasions, conjured
him to put an end to "this grievous litigation, which has been em-
bittered by obscure influences and the settlement of which would
be a jewel in the crown of glory of an enlightened pontificate."

Prince Pacelli was presumably unable to get the upper hand
of the said "obscure influences": five days later Mgr. Montini
let it be known that if the Order would not accept the judgment,
the Holy See would break off diplomatic relations with it. The
pontifical directory being actually at press, there would be
time to effect the requisite changes in it. Furthermore, the
judgment would be promulgated, with whatever commentary
was deemed necessary.

This, then, was the real ultimatum at last. And the "rescue
fleet" had gone home. Cardinal Canali, in the character of
Bonaparte, lay off the grand magistral fortress in St. Peter's bark
and was calling upon Malta to surrender.

It is said that the Grand Master Hompesch had not sur-
rendered merely to force; by the same token it was Christian
feeling in the Grand Magistracy which led it to capitulate.
The meeting which decided upon it, however, was a stormy
one. Contrary to Mgr. Montini, the lieutenant could not convince himself that anything but Cardinal Canali's personal
ambition was involved. It did not seem to him possible that
the Church would adopt such a judgment as its own, albeit
delivered *in nomine Domini*. Only Gudenus, however, supported
him, but he did so with fire and conviction. It was precisely
because one was a Christian, said this youthful representative
of the Grand Priory of Austria, that one had a duty to rebel

against injustice. The cardinals' judgment was another *Anschluss* and never would he subscribe to it. The majority was more accommodating and found unexpected support in Cattaneo. The man who, for two years, had been the very spirit of resistance, was no more inclined than Ferrata to wonder if he had been mistaken; but it seemed that he had been wondering whether the time had not come to give way: the interests of the Church, henceforth deeply engaged in this quarrel, must come before those of the Order.

In fact, on the morning before the Sovereign Council's meeting, he had drafted a note in which he explained his reasons: to accept the judgment would be disastrous; not to do so would be worse. The very principles of the Order entailed the duty of never doing anything to strengthen the hand of atheism and materialism in their strife with the Holy See, which was the greatest moral force in the world. He hoped, however, as he wrote in conclusion, that the Holy See would not go to the length of requiring pure and simple acceptance of the judgment, and that the Order would find means to reconcile an acceptance with its own interests. This document, which was read aloud at the meeting, moved Hercolani and brought him round. Thereafter, despite the protests of Gudenus who did not regain control of his temper until he had passed some time in meditation at Santa Maria dell'Aventino, it was resolved that the lawyers should try to work out some kind of compromise.

On the day after the ultimatum Cardinal Canali gave himself the pleasure of summoning the chapter of his grand priory, Hercolani's mandate as his representative having expired. He had not forgotten the way the lieutenant had flouted him when he had tried to withdraw his mandate before its term. He had devised a ruse which would cut the ground from under Hercolani's feet.

The cardinal grand prior opened the proceedings by announcing that the first item on the agenda would be a vote declaring the appointments made by the provisional lieutenant to be illegal, as laid down by the tribunal. The professed members did not know that the Order had met and refuted this thesis, already put forward by Cardinal Tisserant, and it must be difficult for them to refuse their spiritual leader a vote required of them in the Church's name. The cardinal had no candidate of his own in mind, the whole chapter being hostile to him, but still, it would be vengeance sweet to prevent Hercolani's re-election by having him condemned by his peers.

This manœuvre was frustrated by the presence of Franchi de' Cavalieri who combined the prestige of a former lieutenant with that of being considered a saint by the Pope.

"Eminence," he said, "the constitution requires that the capitulary agenda open with the most important business. Our most important business today is the election of a representative on the Sovereign Council."

"As I see it," the cardinal replied, "nothing is more important than deciding whether our present representative has or has not done what he had a right to do."

"You are not, I believe, criticizing his behaviour as representative of our grand priory? Because that is the only criterion by which we can decide whether or not to re-elect him. The problem which Your Eminence has thus suddenly placed before us is one calling for mature reflection. It cannot, therefore, appear on the agenda of this meeting."

The other professed members hastened to agree with this. Rather than see Hercolani re-elected in spite of his teeth, the cardinal rose and withdrew. No doubt he consoled himself with the thought that though this small satisfaction had been denied him, there were great consolations in store: despite his wish, Hercolani remained his representative: but what, shortly, would remain of the provisional lieutenant? Or, for that matter, of the Order of Malta?

# II

ALTHOUGH the Grand Magistracy had resolved, in principle, to accept the judgment, there was still much hesitation as to how that resolution was to be put into practice. De Mojana re-read the long letter in which the Secretariat of State had communicated the Holy See's ultimatum. He knew exactly the worth of the phrase which described the judgment as "an act of kindness"; that was polite cant. And he could have wished "a chance of writing finis to the events of the recent past in order to restore to the Order the vitality of its historic past" rather more propitious. But he had been struck by the fact that Mgr. Montini considered the Order's "anxiety" inexplicable and its apprehensions "exaggerated," since the Holy See had "in manifold conjunctures and diverse ways" always been prodigal of its "marks of benevolence."

He was still studying this text when Mgr. dell'Acqua telephoned, asked him to call on him at once, and begged him to say nothing to anybody about his visit. De Mojana guessed that the Secretariat of State had in mind some "mark of benevolence" designed to make the act of authority which they called an "act of kindness" easier to swallow. In point of fact, Mgr. dell'Acqua, having been appointed substitute as promised by Cardinal Canali, felt himself quits with the cardinals and could turn his attention to pleasing the Pope.

"I asked you to call," he told De Mojana, "because I know of your friendship with His Eminence Cardinal Schuster; I was one of his favourite pupils. Also, I know you were the nephew of the late, lamented Cardinal Nasalli Rocca di Corneliano, with whom I had the honour of working."

De Mojana acknowledged these cardinalistic allusions with a bow, while wondering what the substitute was up to now.

"I have to tell you—quite between ourselves—that we are unable to convince Pecci that the judgment of the tribunal is excellent for the Order."

"He is not alone in his opinion."

"It is not the text which counts: it's the interpretation of it. 'The letter killeth, but the spirit giveth life.' Properly interpreted. the judgment is a guarantee of your sovereignty."

"But who interprets it in that sense, Excellency?"

"The Holy Father and the Secretariat of State. Can it be that you are less subtle than ourselves?"

"In other words, you are allowing us to accept the judgment conditionally?"

"Please! The Holy See could never admit of a conditional acceptance. But it might admit of interpretations, which is quite a different matter. Write to us saying that you accept the judgment interpreting such and such a word in such and such a sense. Your lawyers, and you yourself who are a master of legal subtlety, should have no difficulty in giving a favourable gloss to a verdict which, as we have already told you, is by no means unfavourable in any case. Bring me your rough draft and we will cast it into its final form together."

"Naturally, the Order will then be free to proceed to the immediate election of a grand master?"

"On the honour of a Dell'Acqua!"

This assurance, added to that formerly given by Mgr. Montini, seemed convincing. Once negotiations had opened, Mgr. dell'Acqua agreed that Pecci should again take a hand. That minister was very much put out to learn that he had been over-reached and that his hand had been forced. Consequently he was all the firmer in the final negotiations, so much so that it was he who had the last word.

The agreement concluded, christened "concordat" at the Magistral Palace, affirmed that the Order's sovereignty was none the less so for being "functional" and that its religious character extended only to the *professed* members who "composed" it. *Composed* was the word adopted by the Grand Magistracy and its lawyers, whereas the Secretariat of State had insisted on the word *constituted*. Everything else had been settled without much delay, but the argument over this point had lasted three days, until finally Mgr. Montini had risen, approached the Order's two representatives, and, in a voice full of feeling, said, "Do not be obstinate about this. I must tell you that if I cannot, by one o'clock tomorrow, March the twelfth, anniversary of the Pope's coronation, deliver your letter of acceptance, then the matter will pass out of my hands, and he will be persuaded by certain people to sign the brief appointing a commissioner."

It seemed that the numerous papal fêtes must all play a part in this business. But Pecci and De Mojana returned to the Via Condotti, proud of having hardened their hearts against this appeal. The Council, less heroic, considered that it would have been foolhardy to run the risk described by Mgr. Montini, and De Mojana was instructed to telephone the Secretariat of State and agree to accept the substitution of their word in the "concordat."

"I was just going to call you," Mgr. Montini said without giving De Mojana time to speak. "I have succeeded in persuading the Holy Father to accept your version."

The letter of agreement, drafted by Pecci and Malfatti, was sent off at once. It was accompanied by a letter from Hercolani to the Pope, conveying the Order's good wishes on the occasion of his coronation anniversary and informing him that "the Sovereign Council has dispatched a letter to the Secretariat of State accepting the judgment delivered by the Most Eminent Court of Cardinals." And, to complete the consolation of Pecci for the way in which negotiations had been opened behind his back, the Council session was concluded by passing a decree prolonging his ambassadorial mandate by five years.

On the evening of March 12, a great nobleman of the city was entertaining guests. The Order's negotiations with the Holy See were known to nobody. De Mojana was accosted by a fellow guest who said, "I hear you're being turned out bag and baggage?"

"Not to my knowledge."

"I've just heard Cardinal Canali, over there, telling someone it's all over, in the bag. He said the brief was before the Pope for signature this morning. Prince Ruffo is to take over tomorrow."

"There's many a slip——" De Mojana quoted, conveying a glass of *Asti spumante* to his own lips.

The Grand Prior of Rome sat on a couch at the other end of the room, his eyes flashing triumph and defiance. He was quite likely telling himself that the arrival of the foreign delegates had, in the long run, been to his advantage; by encouraing the rebels in their resistance, it had completed their downfall.

On the following day, however, it was Prince Ruffo who had to unpack bag and baggage. It had one singular consequence:

albeit a proper respect requires that no man walk too fast in
the Vatican's many corridors, Cardinal Canali was seen making
for the Holy Father's apartments out of breath and at a brisk
canter. In the course of the same day Cardinals Tisserant,
Micara, Pizzardo, and Aloïsi Masella all came running on a
like errand, to the government offices. Prince Pacelli and Count
Galeazzi also ran.

Meanwhile, a new uneasiness began to disturb the atmosphere in the Via Condotti: still no answer from the Secretariat
of State to their letter of March 12. The Grand Magistracy's
acceptance of the judgment as interpreted by it in agreement
with Mgr. Montini would not entail mutual agreement, a valid
concordat, unless and until approved by the other high contracting party. Pecci was besieging Mgr. Montini, who told
him, "There are five personages, all more important than I
am, who have been quite unhinged by this business. A grave
matter, since they are all, by etymology, themselves the hinges
—*cardines*—of our mother the Church. They are trying to
prevent me from obtaining the visa which I need for the letter
you are expecting. But tell your friends that when Montini
has passed his word, he keeps it. If need be, I shall threaten to
resign."

The letter came at last, on the 23rd. It was so phrased as not
to constitute a validation of the agreement arrived at. In it,
Mgr. Montini expressed thanks for the good wishes offered
to the Pope and the latter's joy at the Order's "filial" acceptance
of the tribunal's judgment, whereby it had corrected "its disrespectful attitude toward pontifical authority." These discreet
reproaches were designed to repudiate the idea that the Holy
See would, for its part, accept any special interpretation of
the judgment. It had drawn the Order into an engagement
while, despite its promise, avoiding any such engagement on
its own side. The Grand Magistracy's defence, in respect to
the states, was still no more than its own letter, laying down
the conditions under which it was entering into the engagement.
However, an agreement had been concluded at last, and if,
for the Holy See, it was a mere matter of form, the Order had
clearly defined the limits of its substance.

This apostolic and Roman treaty was reminiscent of the ancient Lacedaemonian scytale—the wand on which certain messages had to be rolled before they could be read.

# III

CARDINAL CANALI'S ANGER—or rather rage—was proof positive that despite all the caution, not to say perfidiousness, of the Secretariat of State's letter, the Order had won a victory. The scenes he made quite overshadowed those to which he had treated Mgr. Nasalli Rocca. Not wishing to make a spectacle of himself, he cancelled all his audiences for several days. Moreover, Mgr. Montini was obliged to do likewise, for the cardinal never left him, but, in a state bordering on hysteria, loudly and constantly reproached him.

The Grand Magistracy thought it had signed a peace. It did not last a week. On March 28, the judgment of the Court, in the form of flimsies distributed by the Vatican volunteer, was issued to the Press of Rome, Milan, and Naples, enriched by appropriate explanations: the Order had lost its case and the cardinals had branded its leaders as men of bad faith. All right-thinking people must hope that the Sacred Congregation of Religious would "make wholesome use" of the powers which the judgment attributed to it, to put Malta's house in order.

Pecci urged Mgr. Montini to publish a communiqué in the *Osservatore Romano*, in which, saying nothing about the interpretation since the Secretariat of State required that to remain secret, it would at least be made clear that the business had been concluded "to the entire satisfaction of both parties." And a communiqué shortly appeared: it was an official announcement that the Court of Cardinals had delivered its judgment and the Order of Malta accepted it; the sentence requested by Pecci had been blue-pencilled by Cardinal Canali.

The lieutenant decided to send a copy of the "concordat" to all chapters of the Order and the chairmen of overseas

associations, together with a résumé of the negotiations which
had led up to it. He received answers assenting to the agreement from all but the Belgians and the Dutch, who protested
vehemently. By what right, the respective councils wanted to
know, had the Order accepted a judgment which the assembly
had instructed it to reject? And how could they have agreed
to a dependence of a religious nature when the vast majority of
the members were laymen?

The chancellery sent them a more circumstantial account and
the matter was dropped.

Meanwhile, Graf Henckel sent to the Magistral Palace a
copy of an anonymous libel which was circulating in Germany.
Its fictitious date—October, 1952—was designed to give the
impression that it was not published by way of revenge for
the Order's recent, partial victory. Its title alone—"Communist
Infiltration into the Catholic Church by Way of the Order of
Malta"—produced a certain amount of excitement, not only
in aristocratic and religious circles, but in the Bonn government and among American officials in Germany. At the very
moment when the Grand Magistracy was hoping to initiate
official relations between the Order and the Federal Republic—
Chancellor Adenauer had been decorated with the Magistral
Grand Cross by Prince Chigi—an attempt was being made to
stab them in the back.

The "scandals" which had flourished under the Bailiff Thun
—the business of the Argentine wheat, the deal in soda, and
the affair of the diplomatic passports—were explained to his
advantage and attributed to "the Hercolani gang." They were
given as the motives for the Holy See's interference, and Mgr.
Montini's "crypto-Marxist" sentiments as the motive for his
indulgent handling of the Order which, thanks to Cattaneo,
a "lackey of the Communists," was controlled by Moscow.

The Grand Magistracy having stood firm under this igno-
minious and childish assault, a more violent one was launched
a few weeks later. It was another anonymous broadsheet, but
this time written in French and printed in Berne "by the good
offices of a committee for the moral rehabilitation of the Order
of Malta." An impression of some thousands of copies was

printed, and sent out not only to members of the Order but to leading political and religious personalities in the countries concerned. Its red cover bearing a white Maltese cross gave it the look of an official publication, and the bibliography which concluded it, a pleasing air of scholarship. A sealed band bearing the words, "Confidential: for the addressee only," had the appearance of being copied from the similar band which sealed the Order's "white book," on which was printed, "*Under bond of secrecy*." At the head of each chapter was a text drawn from Scripture, in the Protestant manner. The work was twenty-four pages long, and its "historical introduction" looked for all the world as if it had been derived from Mgr. Serafini's "notes in illustration." Dithyrambs in honour of Cardinal Canali, represented as the Order's good angel, betrayed the origin of an effusion which concluded with a hymn to the Holy Father and was, for the rest, a revised, corrected, and augmented edition of the German libel.

Mgr. Montini was not overlooked, although this time the attack on him was less blatantly worded. What secrets, the author wanted to know, connect him with Hercolani, Pecci, and Malfatti? The tribunal's judgment was printed, together with a gloss worthy of the Vatican flimsies. There was even a novelettish account of Mgr. Alcini's interrogations at the time of the Commission of Cardinals: according to this the Bishop of Dionysiad, seeing an arras move, had risen and pulled it aside, revealing the grand master seated on a chair, ears pricked and full of anxiety. Whoever had borrowed this scene from traditional melodrama was evidently not aware that there was no arras in the council chamber, where Mgr. Alcini had held his sessions. Yielding nothing to this in farce was the tale of a typist who had burst into tears when the investigator had called on her to swear that she had been telling the truth, and admitted that she had been forced to lie by "Hercolani and his *âmes damnées*." Mgr. Alcini also received praise for having justified Thun against an accusation which, it was claimed, Malfatti had brought against him—to wit, that he had a mistress. The Seminary Visitor had, it seemed, smilingly asked if he could meet the lady, to which the baron had replied, "Whenever you like, Excellency," only to be confounded when Mgr. Alcini produced the poor lady's death certificate.

Cattaneo was made to pay dearly for his part in the battle. He, too, naturally, had admitted something to Mgr. Alcini, to wit that the Grand Prior da Porto's letters were, actually, downright forgeries to which the dying man's signature had been obtained by force. Moreover, Cattaneo was no longer a mere "lackey" of the Communists but one of their picked men. All of which was accompanied by malignant nonsense about his family, personal life, and even appearance.

Nor were the other heroes of the struggle any better treated. The lieutenant was depicted as a devil incarnate and the pamphlet even accused him of the heinous offence of omitting the adjective *sacred* when referring to the Congregation of Religious. Though Cardinal Tisserant had not thought of blaming him for that, the pamphlet never failed to use the epithet whose omission had caused that Eminence so much distress; it went further, referring to Hercolani simply as "the provisional." And the discourteous terms applied to Prince Chigi proved that not even death itself entitled the former grand master to forgiveness for having dared to resist. Much was made of Senator Terracini's questions in Parliament, as a means of accusing the Order of selling honours; and of the cardinals' objections to the lieutenant's powers, as a means of invalidating all his acts. The chancellor was represented as a political adventurer, whose real business, *sub rosa*, was to push the interests of the Archduke Otto, who had rewarded him with the Golden Fleece. Nothing was said about Baron Marsaudon; but the reader was seriously asked to believe that the Comte de Pierredon had sent the lieutenant 20,000,000 francs, as a contribution from the Grand Orient Lodge "in your struggle against the Church." Also that Senator Cerica who, ever since the passing of the law relating to decorations, had been supporting the Order, was a Freemason. Professor Rossi, administrator of the Order's property, and the lawyer Gazzoni, were, so to speak, only flayed in passing.

As in the German pamphlet, Thun's dealings were related so

as to do him credit, but more subtly. The "document of exoneration" which Prince Frederic von Hohenzollern had demanded was mentioned. There was likewise mention of letters which Prince Chigi was alleged to have written to Thun restoring him to his good graces and confidence, and which had been "spirited away by Cattaneo."

These untruths, these wild explanations of matters about which the only authentic documents were to be found in grand magistral archives, the clumsy disclosure of things touching Thun's private life, showed that the authors of this pamphlet, which became known as "the book of Berne," were using his name but not in his interest: they were working in Cardinal Canali's interests. Their object was to strike at Hercolani who, now that the way was open for the election of a new grand master, was the obvious candidate. In much the same spirit had the old inquisitor of Malta been used to spread slanders, on the eve of an election, against any candidate he did not happen to approve of.

Thus, the men responsible for this booklet revealed themselves doubly inimical to the Order, since they sought to injure both factions. The Grand Magistracy contrived, in due course, to identify them: they were a German Protestant who had had several long talks with somebody at the Vatican Government Palazzo, and an Italian who had been sacked from the Via Condotti; they had provided the raw material. A French political refugee had done the writing; a German prince, himself a Knight of Malta, had put up the money.

*       *       *

The Grand Magistracy had a memorandum written to enlighten the grand priories and associations of the Order in the matter of these two libels. The fact that they were anonymous must discredit them in chivalrous circles: nevertheless, if enough dirt be thrown, some will stick, so that "the twenty-six soldiers of Gutenberg" are always dangerous.

The Belgian association, as if to make up for its recent

chivalrous touchiness, was the first to react: its "indignant sympathy" was reinforced by that of the Cardinal-Archbishop of Malines. The Silesian association had a more practical means of bearing witness to its solidarity with the Grand Magistracy: the octogenarian Prince von Hatzfeldt having at last made up his mind to resign the chairmanship, Graf Henckel, hand in glove with the Grand Magistracy, was elected in his place. The Council of the Rhine-Westphalian association struck one of its members, Schall-Riancour, off its rolls for having loudly abused Hercolani.

In France, for some inexplicable reason, the Comte de Pierredon echoed the book of Berne, albeit it did not spare him; but he was the only one. His aberration went so far, indeed, that he approached the Grand Chancellor of the Legion of Honour with the assertion that decorations conferred by the lieutenancy were invalid, and that wearing them should therefore be forbidden. His standing as a former Minister of the Order, and his Cross of Profession, an honour which he shared with only two other laymen, King Humbert and Prince Frederic von Hohenzollern, gave weight to his opinion, so that General Dassault, himself a bearer of the Maltese Grand Cross of Merit, was in some perplexity. But although he had received his Grand Cross from Prince Chigi, Marshal Juin held his Magistral Grand Cross from Hercolani. Even so it took the Prince de Polignac two months of hard work to prevent the publication of an order which would, in the circumstances, have been a catastrophe. The clinching argument was that President de Gasperi had accepted a Magistral Grand Cross within the last few months. The Comte de Pierredon had done the Order too much service in the past for any official notice to be taken of his conduct.

In Rome, the book of Berne had not for long been confined to members of the Order: Cardinal Canali's henchmen were soon hawking it through editorial offices as a work as salutary in matter as it was savoury in manner. They deceived the good faith of numerous journalists, by no means the least of their kind, who, under the common illusion that "a cardinal is above suspicion," set about exploiting that mine of inanities. To crown all, it was the right-wing nationalists, inclined to see the hand of Masonry and Communism more or less everywhere, who fell most readily into the trap. The anti-clericals, quite unaware that they were helping a cardinal, applauded these "revelations."

When the uproar subsided, the flimsies were used to revive it. In order to prove that the Order was no better abroad than at home, the flimsies made an atack on those chairmen of associations whom the book of Berne had spared. For the Prince de Polignac, the Order was simply a means of selling his champagne; for Graf Henckel, a cover for his dealings in coal; Baron Twinkel's aim was to secularize the Order so that he could become grand master and appoint his wife grand mistress. Lieutenant-Colonel Elwes was trying to make the Order a tool of the Intelligence Service. Count Czapski had a brother in the Kremlin. And the Infante of Spain had a mistress.

That part of the Italian press which could be reached by the *longa manus* of the Trimurti published articles which turned the true facts of the conflict inside out. One of them went to the length of asserting that Prince Chigi had died of a seizure upon discovering the malversations of the "Hercolani gang."

Certain propagandists were not even satisfied with that: they haunted the corridors of the Chamber of Deputies and the Senate, trying to recruit members who would ask parliamentary questions. They flaunted photostats of apocryphal documents which gained, in that form, a spurious air of authenticity; or of genuine and insignificant ones which they paraphrased to suit themselves. Although it had no wish to take a hand, the Grand Magistracy saw itself obliged to get some kind of statement into the Italian press. A number of articles giving a clear and intelligent explanation of the whole business appeared in several journals of repute, and put an end to the rubbish which was being printed.

The Order of Malta must have represented very powerful interests, thus to have provoked its enemies to such excesses that they had dishonoured themselves. But despite Beaumarchais'

witticism,* none of the dirt which had been thrown in an
allegedly religious cause stuck; for the public had become
convinced that religion had nothing whatever to do with this
business.

# IV

WITHOUT ALLOWING ITSELF to be disturbed by anonymous
libels, the Grand Magistracy pressed energetically on with
its negotiations with the Secretariat of State. As soon as agreement had been reached in the matter of the judgment, it reminded
the Pro-Secretary of the Holy See's promise to permit the election of a grand master, a promise which was, in any case,
implicit in the pontifical chirograph. Mgr. Montini could not
deny it, but said that the Holy Father was hoping that the
Order would first proceed to certain reforms. This hope, as
the Grand Magistracy pointed out, had been fulfilled in advance:
the Order's reforms committee had already worked out a
"charta" which would rejuvenate the De Rohan code. Mgr.
Montini retorted that this charta was a unilateral product,
whereas the Holy See was determined to take a hand in drafting
the new statutes: thus the only viable charta would be one which
was the work of a joint committee. The Grand Magistracy was
forced to make up its mind to go through with it on those terms.

The Grand Magistracy appointed as its representatives Graf
Henckel and Don Ettore Carafa d'Andria. The Vatican took
so long to choose its own delegates that it was difficult not to
suspect it of deliberate procrastination. After six weeks' delay,
unaccountable in view of the final choice which can hardly
have been difficult, it was announced that the Holy See's representatives would be Mgr. Scapinelli and Prince Carlo Pacelli.
When the Grand Magistracy, anxious to emphasize the parity
of the parties to the committee, proposed that its meetings
be held at the Magistral Palace and the Apostolic Palace alter-

* *Calomniez, calomniez, il en restera toujours quelque chose!"* [E. H.]

nately, the Secretariat of State replied that all meetings would be at the Apostolic Palace. When the Grand Magistracy inquired in what manner the two sides were to take turns in the Chair, the Secretariat of State replied that Mgr. Scapinelli would be the permanent chairman.

After such preliminaries as these and with such ready co-operation, the least that could be expected from the committee was a series of structural reforms which would adapt the ancient order of chivalry to the atomic age.

At the first meeting Henckel read a memorandum from Prince von Hatzfeldt in which it was proposed that a decade of the rosary be added to the knights' special daily prayers; and that the red habit of the Order be replaced by a black cloak. The Holy See's representatives were immediately anxious to show that they had not come empty-handed to the meeting: they tabled a "plan of daily pious practices" in the following terms: (1) Holy Mass (obligatory); (2) the Holy Eucharist (advised); (3) a holy meditation (15 minutes); (4) a visit to the Holy Sacrament (10 minutes); (5) the Holy Rosary (entire); (6) a holy examination of conscience (10 minutes). The joint committee, satisfied with these beginnings in fields of religion and chivalry, appointed two sub-committees to study the possibility of more substantial reforms.

Battle, and that fierce, was joined about the oath of conjugal chastity. This oath was not a vow of absolute chastity, but entailed a promise not to indulge, even in holy wedlock, in practices forbidden by Catholic morality. It was but half-heartedly encouraged by the Church, which was afraid of placing ecclesiastical celibacy in danger. But Cattaneo, its advocate at the Grand Magistracy, had discovered, in Sicily, a community in which it was canonically in force. Its opponents objected that, in Latin countries, the morality of the senses was more latitudinarian, even as between spouses with four, eight, or sixteen quarterings. (They might have quoted, by way of example, his own wife who, weary of the vow of conjugal chastity, had just had their marriage annulled.) He assured them that many German knights, husbands austere and *sans reproche*, were ready, hand in hand with their wives, to take this vow.

And he showed the advantage this would entail in augmenting the religiousness of the Order and so creating a category of members who, without being professed religious, would, as it were, reinforce the professed knights of justice. The representatives of the Grand Magistracy adopted the proposal and tabled it; Mgr. Scapinelli opposed it violently, and in face of his adversaries' persistence, adjourned to seek Cardinal Canali's advice.

That Eminent man exploded. Could he, who for years had been trying to discourage the recruitment of members anxious to make profession, countenance a reform which would tend to the opposite effect? The idea of this oath of conjugal chastity inspired one of his famous broadsides of Italian proverbs: "You cannot ring the bells and walk in the procession," he cried, "you cannot be both cape and cowl, nor flesh and fish. You cannot be both cooked and raw, black and white, in the oven and at the mill! That would be altogether too much, *Madonna mia!*"

Despite the cardinal, the oath of chastity triumphed. It was one of the resolutions which were finally carried. The others were concerned with simplification of proof of nobility, the right of knights of honour and devotion to participate in the government of the Order, although not to become grand masters, and the "plan of daily pious practices" tabled at the first meeting.

Modest though it was, this plan of reform took a month to complete. The traditional date for the annual departure *ad aquas* was approaching, and the Secretariat of State considered that the election of a grand master could not very well be held in the dog days. It was therefore decided that the complete Council of State should be summoned for October 25, "Feast of Christ the King."

In September, the Secretariat of State announced that the Holy See would only authorize the election of a "provisional grand master" and then only after it had approved the list of candidates. Hercolani agreed to the first condition but declared that to agree to the second was not within his competence and that it would have to be discussed by the electors: this was one more reason for summoning them all to Rome. Mgr.

Montini asked for a further postponement of the election until November 21, to allow time for this necessary debate, November 21 being the "Feast of the presentation of the Virgin."

The Grand Magistracy immediately sent out the writs calling upon its electors, in order to prevent yet another postponement. Whereupon Mgr. Montini informed the Grand Magistracy that the Holy See no longer wanted them to elect a "provisional grand master" but a "lieutenant of the grand magistracy" to be elected by the complete Council of State and thereafter to "carry through the reforms." Having made up his mind to accept whatever was constitutional, Hercolani at once agreed to this, too. Whereupon Mgr. Montini said that the Holy See no longer wanted a lieutenancy, but a regency. It was to be composed of the three Grand Priors of Rome, Naples, and Austria, that is to say Cardinal Canali, the Marquis Maresca, and Baron Ludwigstorff. As the latter could not leave Vienna and the second would have frequently to return to Naples, the real regent would be Cardinal Canali.

The maze through which the Secretariat of State had been leading the Grand Magistracy by the nose from month to month and one feast of the Church to another had, of course, been contrived solely to that end. Having failed to get his hands on the Order by force, failed to obtain all the advantages from the judgment which he had anticipated, failed to swamp the Grand Magistracy under a flood of anonymous libel and slander, failed to ensure the election of some creature of his own as lieutenant or grand master, Cardinal Canali had been reduced to the idea of a regency to accomplish his purpose.

The delegates arrived in Rome, the project of a regency was rejected unanimously as unconstitutional, and the right to elect a grand master loudly demanded. Mgr. Montini pointed out that the reforms must come before the election: some few had, it was true, been adopted at the suggestion of the Holy See at the beginning of the summer, but the whole De Rohan code had to be overhauled.

The delegates saw no point in persisting. They did not wait for the opening ceremonies of the Marian Year, to which the cardinals had invited them, but packed up and went home after having appointed a reforms committee and discreetly contrived an audience of the Pope.

The Head of the Church received them and repeated Mgr. Montini's words: the Grand Magistracy's attitude, now happily modified, had been considered, and could only have been considered, as an offence to pontifical authority, represented by the Court of Cardinals. One delegate, a Dutchman, had the courage to speak up: "Most Holy Father, in my country we have a sense of justice, and the idea that a man can be judge in his own cause, as were three members of the Court, is quite out of the question."

"Cardinals——" Pius XII retorted curtly, hesitated, smiled rather weakly, and went on in a tone without conviction, "cardinals have the privilege of being above suspicion."

*       *       *

The reforms committee set briskly to work: they were in haste to have done with the eternal shufflings and evasions of the Holy See. Meanwhile, the Order had re-established its own domestic tribunals of justice, which had been suspended with the loss of Malta. Cardinal Canali had moved heaven and earth in an effort to get such knights as were Italian magistrates forbidden to sit as judges in these courts. He did not want some new Thun being prevented from having recourse to the Congregation of Religious; but he had had all his trouble for nothing.

The committee began by laying it down that the basis of the Order's code must still be what it had always been—"defence of the law and service of the poor." Thereafter it carefully sifted the old De Rohan code, which was neither more nor less than a book of history with legal glosses. Of its twenty-two chapters, fifteen were obsolete, being concerned with hospitality, the maintenance of "inns,"* military dispositions, the Order's galleys and other shipping. The remaining seven chapters, clarified and explained, were retained.

For the edification of professed knights the rules concerning concubinage, laid down at the beginning of the fifteenth cen-

* These *auberges* were the hostels in which pilgrims to the Holy Land were housed, under the Order's protection. [E. H.]

tury by the Grand Master la Rivière, were retained. "With excellent reason has it been determined that it is in no way licit for our brethren to foster concubines or to have commerce with them. If, after having been thrice warned, a culprit shall persevere in sin for more than forty days, he will, without further warning, be deprived of his commandery should he be a commander, or unfrocked (that is, banished from the Order), even the Castellan of Emposta, after warning by the grand master."

Prado smiled at the severity of a law which did not even spare that worthy of the Aragonese *langue*, the richest in the Order. Yet, in defiance of all such threats, the knights persisted in their sin; for, a century later, the Grand Master Villiers de l'Isle Adam was again denouncing these practices, and fifty years thereafter the Grand Master Garzez was appointing special officers to put them down. And between these two events there had been the famous "cloister revolt," in which the Grand Master la Cassière nearly lost his life, and which had been provoked by the banishment of courtesans.

The articles relative to sodomy were dropped; it was no doubt considered that the practice was less common than it had been at the end of the thirteenth century, when the Grand Master Lorgne punished it by unfrocking; and then at the end of the fifteenth when the Grand Master d'Aubusson threatened to punish it by burning at the stake; and then at the end of the eighteenth, when the Bailiff De Suffren, Knight Grand Cross of the Order of St. John, one-time General of the Church's armies, Knight of the Holy Ghost, Vice-Admiral of France, and Ambassador of the Order of Malta to the Court of Louis XVI, practised it openly without losing any of his titles or offices.

The admission of ladies was regulated with discreet gallantry, but their role was firmly restricted. Wives of members of the Order could be admitted whatever their age; the wives or widows of non-members only if they had passed their fortieth year. A new category of magistral dames was created, which would have made it possible to meet the wishes of Señora Perón had she not gone to her reward.

Often, in the course of committee meetings, the young Prado allowed his eyes to wander from the crucifix which was placed upon the table, to a window on the far side of the street: the daughter of a Roman prince had smiled on him and the reform of the Order's constitution very nearly ended in a wedding. It would have been its only positive outcome.

# V

WHILE THE EUROPEAN KNIGHTS were doing great things in and out of the Grand Magistracy and, beyond Europe, the number of associations was multiplying—there were now nineteen, with a total of 6,000 members—Cardinal Spellman and the Marquis Macdonald had been as silent as the grave. The lieutenant, constantly busy defending the Order, had not re-minded the Archbishopric of New York of Prince Chigi's letters, still unacknowledged. Hercolani knew of the close ties between the American cardinal and Cardinal Canali and was consequently certain that the American association would make no sign of life until the litigation was over. For had not Cardinals Canali and Pizzardo precipitated that same litigation when Prince Chigi had uncovered the very profitable operations which were being carried on at the expense of the Bambino Gesù and the Order of Malta?

At the very worst moment of strife during the preceding year, a note from Mgr. Montini had caused great surprise at the Grand Magistracy: "It would greatly oblige this Secretariat of State if His Excellency the provisional lieutenant and the Sovereign Council would, as a mark of the deference they have always shown it, be good enough to bestow the Magistral Knight's Cross on Mr. So-and-so, a citizen of the United States, for whose honourable reputation, good name, probity, and religion the Secretariat of State will vouch. Herewith a check for 1,000 dollars in payment of his passage."

The lieutenant replied that he would be very happy to oblige the *Excellentissime* Secretariat of State, but felt obliged to point out that Cardinal Spellman, "Grand Protector and Spiritual Adviser" to the American association, had emphatically demanded that no proposals in favour of American citizens be initiated in Rome "for particular reasons." Mgr. Montini assured the Grand Magistracy that "the bestowal of the Cross on Mr. So-and-so would raise no difficulty of the kind referred to." This could mean only one thing—that the request emanated from the "Grand Protector and Spiritual Adviser" in person. Amused to discover that, despite Cardinals Canali and Tisserant, Cardinal Spellman evidently recognized his, the lieutenant's, powers, Hercolani sent off the necessary bull.

Three weeks later Mr. So-and-so arrived in Rome, and telephoned the Magistral Palace asking if he could meet the Order's "boss," and visit the villa on the Aventine. It was the first time that the Via Condotti had heard the voice of an American knight, and might even hope to see one. He was warmly welcomed and a few questions were put to him, the answers to which revealed that he had been raised to the chivalry by a letter from the "Master," Macdonald, long before the Secretariat of State had asked "the old gentleman in Rome" for the Sovereign Council's bull. But Cardinal Spellman, hearing that Mr. So-and-so was going to Rome and insisted on meeting "the old gentleman" and seeing the villa on the Aventine, had hastened to get the position regularized in order to avoid a scandal. The Order, fully occupied in fighting for its life on the Tiber, was not inclined to open a second front on the Hudson.

But it happened that in December of the same year another citizen of the United States, who was passing through Rome, also telephoned the Magistral Palace: he introduced himself as a Texan and a Knight of Malta, desirous of meeting the "boss" of his Order, and seeing the villa on the Aventine. He was a friend of Mr. So-and-so's. He was given an appointment; but it was Pallavicini who welcomed him.

"We are sorry," Pallavicini told his visitor, "but we are unable to find the decree admitting you to the Order."

The Texan knight flushed with anger.

"What's that? I was admitted two months ago."

"Are you quite sure? You see, between November, 1951, and today we have admitted only one United States citizen to knighthood, your friend Mr. So-and-so, whose admission was requested by the Holy See."

"I don't know what you're talking about. I'm only one of sixty-seven men recently made knights by the Master Macdonald and Cardinal Spellman. I gave fifty thousand dollars for a hospital right here in Rome and another thousand for the Order of Malta in Rome. Just let the boss here try to refuse me recognition and see what happens, mister!"

"Have you your bull?" Pallavicini inquired, appalled.

"No. We were told that it always takes a long time for the bull to arrive from Rome. But I have my letter of admission back at the hotel, and I'll be right back with it."

He was as good as his word, returning at once with a magnificent letter, signed by the "Master" and countersigned by the "Grand Protector and Spiritual Adviser." While Pallavicini kept him occupied, this interesting exhibit was hastily photographed. Its owner said that he had left Texas without mentioning his plans to the "Master," which explained how he had slipped through Cardinal Spellman's hands and been overlooked by the Secretariat of State. He knew nothing of the Order's troubles and there seemed to be no point whatever in enlightening him. He was told that probably the "Master's" office had forgotten to send the list of these new knights to Rome; as soon as this had been rectified, the bulls would be dispatched. He was then taken to shake boss Hercolani's hand and conducted over the villa on the Aventine; thereafter, he took himself off, happy as a pope.

The lieutenant was now well provided with material for a letter to Cardinal Spellman—the letter which Prince Chigi had not had time to complete. But the time fixed by the tribunal was approaching and he had other fish to fry.

However, he was not willing to forgo the pleasure of writing to inform Mgr. Montini that the Archbishop of New York appeared to have created *proprio motu* sixty-seven Knights of Malta in the year 1952, of which creations the Grand Magistracy had proof of at least one. And Pecci was instructed to add, by word of mouth, that the Sovereign Council would be within its rights, if it wished to insist on them, in striking Cardinal Spellman's name off the Order's nominal roll; but that they did not, in the Via Condotti, forget the respect due to the purple.

This forbearance was all the more praiseworthy in that an article in *Time*, entitled "The Knights Chastised," and hostile to the Order, was believed to have been inspired by Cardinal Spellman. Convinced that the collapse of the Grand Magistracy was imminent, the "Grand Protector and Spiritual Adviser" had not bothered to have his abuses regularized; after all, Cardinal Canali would soon be master, if not grand master. But, being warned by his crony that the plot had failed, and by the Secretariat of State that the cat was out of the bag, the cardinal-archbishop hastened to ask for the requisite bulls. This happened at the time when his five colleagues had just pronounced their judgment in a matter which, perhaps, involved his interests quite as much as theirs.

However, the Secretariat of State had not, in the circumstances, the face to forward his request immediately: moreover it did not want to put new weapons into the Order's hands until the Grand Magistracy had made the required act of obedience and submission.

Some time after the exchange of notes which comprised the "concordat," Mgr. Montini wrote to the Grand Magistracy that he "had the honour to forward a list of sixty-seven names proposed for membership by Cardinal Spellman, which had been accompanied by a remittance for $67,000. As, however, the Order of Malta was indebted to the Most Eminent Court to the extent of 1,500,000 lire in legal costs, the Secretariat of State was withholding $4,000 which it was hastening to remit to the secretary of the Most Eminent Court aforesaid."

"Short reckonings make long friends," was Cardinal Canali's comment.

# VI

THE NOVEMBER ASSEMBLY had fixed February, 1954, as the date for its next meeting, thus leaving the Holy See and the Grand Magistracy three months to come to terms. It had also set up an international committee to prepare a complete overhaul of the De Rohan code, thereby showing the Holy See that it was determined to remove the eternal pretext of reforms to be undertaken which the Order had been constantly beguiled with.

The Grand Magistracy's arguments during that respite had been a mere waste of breath. With the delegates about to return, permission to hold the election had still not been granted. Pecci tried to sway Mgr. Montini by informing him that while the Holy Father's approval of the election was required, his authority to hold it was not. To which Mgr. Montini retorted that if the Holy Father failed to approve it, it would be as if it had never taken place. At the Grand Magistracy, however, it was held that this would not invalidate the vote of tried and trusted Catholics belonging to thirteen European countries. And as precedents they quoted, apart from the case of Paul I of Russia, the election of the Grand Master Redin in the seventeenth century contrary to the will of the Holy See but subsequently approved by it. The occasion for confronting Mgr. Montini with this example did not arise, however, for he was already raising another objection.

"The Holy Father has been asking me for 'the rose of candidates' for the grand mastership. There were only a couple of names I was able to mention. His comment was, 'It seems to be no golden rose: it is somewhat short of petals.'"

Hercolani sought a way round this new difficulty, which had not been overcome by the project for reforms prepared under the highhanded chairmanship of Mgr. Scapinelli. He, certainly, had put forward his own solution: he had tried to persuade the Order to rely, for the choice of a chief, "on the wisdom of the Holy Father." The Order stood in no need of Mgr. Scapinelli's advice to trust to the Holy Father, whose benevolence it had so often experienced. But it was obliged to face the fact that beside the pontifical throne loomed the shadow of the Trimurti.

The constitutional code of 1936 required that a candidate for the grand mastership must have made profession not less than ten years before the election; on the other hand the De Rohan code required only that he be "*gentilhomme*, of legitimate birth, and a professed knight of justice." The Grand Magistracy, estimating that there must be more candidates viable for the grand mastership than for the papacy, set about drawing up a list. It began by questioning knights of justice who had made profession, and thereafter certain knights of honour and devotion, unmarried or widowers, and among the more distinguished, with a view to obtaining the requisite dispensations from the Pope should any of them be willing to take vows.

No Frenchman or Englishman was forthcoming, but one Hungarian (the Chancellor Apor), two Austrians (Adamovich and Trapp), a Pole (Czapski), a Spaniard (Don Luis of Bavaria and Bourbon, son of the bailiff-chairman), a Dutchman (Baron Speyart Van Woerden, a judge of the High Court in The Hague), and eight Italians, Hercolani, Del Balzo, De Mojana, Belgiojoso, Maresca, Thun, Melzi d'Eril, and Paterno, who, on the recent death of the aged Taccone, had replaced him as representative of the Grand Priory of Naples. Thun's name, since, after all, he was eligible, had been included as a proof of good will. But it was to beguile Cardinal Canali that Melzi d'Eril was put on the list. He was already the cardinal's candidate for succession to Hercolani as representative of the Grand Priory of Rome. He had arrived too late for the capitulary meeting of last February; but the Grand Magistracy had already been approached with a view to his transfer from the Grand Priory of Venice.

The February assembly of this year was short: the list of candidates was the only item on the agenda. It was adopted as a motion, incorporated into a decree of the Sovereign Council and sent to the Secretariat of State: "Unanimously the assembly begs the Holy Father to grant such canonical dispensations as

will enable the fourteen following knights to become candidates
for the grand mastership——"

Alas! the Holy Father was very ill and Mgr. Montini deso-
lated that it was out of his power to present this many-petalled
rose for his attention. In reality, the list had not had the good
fortune to please Cardinal Canali. The delegates, realizing that
they were to be once more choked off, did not linger, albeit
their expenses were being paid by the Grand Magistracy.
Cardinal Canali had sneered at the loyalty of folk who were
assembled by an offer of "a free visit to Rome, good board
and lodging, a seat at the opera, and an audience of the Pope";
they were anxious to prove that they had no intention of abusing
the privilege.

As soon as they were out of the way, he resumed the offensive.
Out of the fourteen knights disposed to become grand master,
he found strong objections to twelve. Realizing that neither
of his two liegemen had any chance of election, he declared that
the candidature of knights who had not made profession was
an attempt at secularization under cover of dispensations.
However, never afraid to contradict himself, he proposed another
layman, a widower and a member of the Order, who was not
on the list but whose name was sure to please the Pope: the
Marquis Sacchetti, Grand Harbinger of the Sacred Palaces.
The cardinal did not know that Hercolani had already, and
unsuccessfully, sounded him. However, when the lieutenant
had told him that the Holy Father favoured his election, the
grand harbinger questioned Mgr. Montini to make sure of
it.

"Nothing is impossible," replied the Pro-Secretary of State.

"It goes without saying that my standing for election would
be approved by the Grand Magistracy?"

"The Grand Magistracy would approve it provided you do
not appear as Cardinal Canali's nominee, put up in opposition
to their own candidates."

The grand harbinger realized that he would be sticking his
nose into a hornets' nest and invited the cardinal to seek his
requirement elsewhere. He did so, approaching the Bailiff Franchi
de' Cavalieri. Not seeing his name on the list, he was hoping

that there had been a quarrel. He was not aware that this bailiff, like the grand harbinger, had refused to allow his name to be put forward. The cardinal had no sooner explained his project, than the former lieutenant of the Order rose and asked permission to withdraw.

"What!" the cardinal exclaimed, "don't you want to be my grand master?"

"Do not insult me, Eminence."

From time to time, the all-powerful cardinal did receive such smacks in the face, as if to remind him that he, too, was only a man. Some months before, Lupi de Soragna, Italian Ambassador to the Holy See, paying his farewell visit, had said, "Eminence, if you did not already know of my retirement, you would guess it at once from the home truths I must ask you to listen to."

And His Eminence had heard some cruel ones.

Next, the cardinal tried to corrupt Maresca, whom he had thought of getting appointed co-regent with himself; there, too, he failed. And not knowing where to turn, he once again had the bullheaded stupidity to tempt God Himself. He sent his crony Travaglini to see Hercolani; Travaglini, since his misfortunes in the Via Condotti, had been extremely discreet in his relations with the Grand Magistracy.

"Now for heaven's sake don't imagine," this gentleman told Hercolani, "that I'm here on behalf of Nicholas. I have come straight from the Pope, who is much better. My instructions are to say that, if you like, you can be appointed grand master at once, by a pontifical brief, without the farce of an election: there'll be no protests from the Order, since they all adore you."

"I do not know whether they adore me," the lieutenant replied; "but I do know that if I want to be shamed and detested, I need only do what you suggest. Do not involve either the Church or the Holy Father in your gerrymandering. And give my kind regards to Nicholas."

H

# VII

THE ALARMS in which it was involved did not prevent the Order from fostering a very grand project, whose accomplishment would have done a great deal for its prestige. This was the question of the Holy Places, and it involved not only Christendom the world over, but that great power which had declared religion to be "the opium of the people."

Just after the war, Stalin, who had already resuscitated the Metropolitan See of Moscow, had set about bolstering up the Orthodox Church in the Near East. And just as he had tried to dazzle Prince Chigi with the prospect of reviving the two ancient Commanderies of Russia and Poland in an effort to get a Maltese legation opened in Moscow, he had started by offering the monks of Mount Athos resumption of the pensions formerly paid to their monasteries by the tsars, not forgetting the arrears. Some time later he had proposed to rebuild the Church of St. Sepulchre's, which, having once been restored by Alexander I, was falling down again. The dictator's death had not put an end to these mirific plans. Western diplomatic circles were concerned, since the projects conjured up visions of the Soviet government slipping into a Jerusalem which was already a bone of contention between Moslems and Jews. The Holy See had suggested that the perfect solution lay in internationalizing the Holy Places, but the State of Israel, and even the Jordanians, had reacted with violent hostility.

When the Order learned that a United Nations mandate was in prospect, it could hardly contain its joy: for it seemed to the knights that the Order of Malta was the obvious mandatory "power." The mandate could only be entrusted to a sovereign state without any political role in the world. The Order was Catholic, but its Cross for Merit, whose prestige it was inclined to exaggerate, could traditionally be awarded to both Moslems and Jews, which would surely entail the support of those two peoples. And as to its long strife with the infidel, it had been all over for two centuries. The old prescription, to be found in the Order's archives, according to which "the knights, sword in hand, must assail, crush, and trample upon the blood of Mohammed," now possessed a merely historical interest. When, in 1952, the King of Jordan, being in Rome, called at the Grand Magistracy, the lieutenant had given him a pair of golden spurs, the gift which former grand masters had made to the sultans whenever the sword was sheathed between them. It was symbolic of the final reconciliation between the Knights of St. John and the people who had driven them out of the Holy Land. The Order also claimed to be on good terms with the Orthodox Church: from the Euphrates to the Dead Sea it wooed her sectaries, and boasted that its list of knights magistral had long included many Rumanians and a number of Greeks. Finally, it asserted that it could count on the Protestants, thanks to the Venerable Order of St. John of Jerusalem, whose support it would purchase by granting the recognition solicited by that venerable order.

These negotiations were cleverly handled by a valuable newcomer to the Grand Magistracy, General Giannantoni. In charge of Arab affairs, he had been appointed Minister of the Order of Malta to the Lebanese government, but resided in Rome. His great merit lay in having won over to the Order's side Father Acacio Coussa, of the Basilians of Aleppo, Assessor to the Congregation for the Eastern Church and Cardinal Tisserant's *alter ego*. Thus, at one remove, the Dean of the Sacred College was secretly backing the Order's claim to the Holy Places mandate, while at the same time hurling the tribunal's thunderbolts at its devoted head.

Giannantoni won another supporter for the mandate, none other than Mrs. Luce, United States Ambassador to Italy. He had begun by curing her of a bias against the Order which Cardinal Spellman had caused to be vilified in her husband's weekly magazine. He next gave her the pleasure of surprise by taking her a copy of a document which was, indeed, far from ordinary: the draft of a treaty of friendship and navigation between the old Order of St. John and the young United States of America, at the time of the French Revolution.

As soon as the Grand Magistracy considered the negotiations

sufficiently advanced, it thought itself—ingenuously enough—
entitled to the Secretariat of State's congratulations, and maybe
even its help. Mgr. Montini delayed answering for several
months. At length, at the end of February, 1954, he announced
that "the question of the Holy Places comes within the competence of the equestrian Order of the Holy Sepulchre." As
this order had none of the attributes requisite for holding an
international mandate—the whole project was, in any case,
suspended as a result of subsequent international events—it
was apparent that Cardinal Canali, who had dictated Mgr.
Montini's answer, preferred sacrificing the Holy Places to
assisting a project which would have enhanced the Order of
Malta's status. He was indulging his spite or serving his ambitions
at the expense of the Church.

# VIII

THE MONTH OF ROSES had arrived, but not the dispensations
for the "rose of candidates." The Order's only consolation
was that although their own candidates had not been approved,
their enemy had not been able to find one of his own.

Then it suddenly became known that the intrigue with Maresca
had been secretly resumed and that the brief appointing him
lieutenant or grand master would be signed on June 20. Cardinal
Canali wanted the Order's new chief installed in time for St.
John's Day. Whatever might be the merits of his nominee, this
appointment was nevertheless a subversion of the Order's prerogatives, which even the judgment had recognized.

Meanwhile, Mgr. Montini had had enough of being made
to blow hot and cold. He told Pecci that he now regretted having already gone too far, that he was no longer prepared to
act against his own conscience and that he would no longer be
receiving him on the Order's business: henceforth it would come
into Mgr. dell'Acqua's bailiwick. He had shaken off Cardinal
Canali's yoke. A dark cloud of disgrace hung over his head.

Deprived of this defender who, if he had not always been able to parry the blows struck against the Order, had at least softened them, the Grand Magistracy could do nothing but resign itself and await the *coup de grâce*. The long struggle had eroded its will and worn down its strength. There was no point in recalling the delegates. However, a last manœuvre was tried: it succeeded.

The Grand Magistracy had proofs of the frequent visits which a certain German Protestant, principal author of the book of Berne, had paid to Cardinal Canali. It might be worth while getting them into the hands of the Pope: and it might be possible to overcome all the obstacles to doing so if they were accompanied by a threat to divulge the true facts. On June 17 a short memorandum was delivered to Mgr. dell'Acqua; on June 20, no pontifical brief arrived.

The Order was not very proud of the means it had been forced to use, nor of having been obliged to enlighten the head of the Church in such a manner. Once again, renewing their pledge of gratitude, the knights admired the skill with which, at the critical moment, that unfaltering hand always gave the right touch to the tiller of St. Peter's bark.

Meanwhile, as if nothing untoward had occurred, Cardinal Canali came to celebrate the patronal feast of St. John the Baptist at the Aventine Church. With a view to reminding him that the Order had friends in the Sacred College, the Grand Magistracy had invited several cardinals to the Mass, most of whom accepted the invitation. Cardinal Tisserant did not take that trouble, but a few days later the lieutenant received the following missive from him: "In my capacity as Dean of the Sacred College, Bishop of Ostis, of Porto and of Santa Rufina, it has come to my attention that my colleagues, the Most Reverend Lords Cardinal who honoured the Mass of St. John in the priory Church of St. Mary of the Aventine with their presence, were not separated from the crowd by a symbolical grille, although they attended in red. I should be glad to know why the Sovereign Hierosolymitan Order of Malta does not observe a custom which, in Rome, is required by the respect due to the purple."

The learned Dean of the Sacred College, and sometime Vatican librarian, seemed feigning, in this instance, to put off the purple in favour of the white bands of an Ignorantine friar. The Grand Magistracy, in all humility, undertook his instruction. The custom of concealing any *porporati* present at a religious service, behind a curtain called a "grille" or, vulgarly, a "cage," had been adopted in Rome after 1870, by reason of the fact that cardinals, being subjects and officials of the Holy See, were no longer on Vatican territory when in Rome, but on Italian territory; and they were not yet protected by the Lateran treaty. The custom persisted in Roman churches out of respect for tradition; it had never existed in the sovereign Order's churches, which were its own sovereign territory, on which the purple had always been respected.

# IX

TO BEAR WITNESS to its sovereignty in the religious, as well as in the judicial and constitutional, field, the Order had hoped for restoration of the ancient office of "Prior of the Church," a prelate of the Order who was not answerable to any bishop. This was desirable not only for reasons of prestige nor upon spiritual grounds merely: for in such conditions professed members would be less dependent on the Congregation of Religious, since the prelate to whom they would be responsible would be answerable directly to the Pope. This wish had been approved by the joint committee and submitted to the Secretariat of State. Pecci brought out the fact that nothing could be more calculated to sanctify the Order, one of the improvements called for by the pontifical chirograph.

Cardinal Canali rejected the title of "Prior to the Church" on the grounds that there were already several grand priors. He demanded that it be changed to "Prelate to the Grand Magistracy." He then had Mgr. Ferrero di Cavallereone, titular Archbishop of Trebizond, preferred to the post, without hav-

ing consulted the Order, in the hope that they would consequently
be at daggers drawn from the start.

This archbishop had hitherto been chaplain-in-ordinary to
the Italian army; but having quarrelled with a general, he had
to be replaced. Faithful to his policy of always doing prelates
in trouble a good turn in order to have them under an obligation, the cardinal had been busy on the archbishop's behalf,
but had seriously misjudged the man's character: the Archbishop
of Trebizond was no Archbishop of Nicea.

Appointed at the beginning of the Marian Year, Mgr. Ferrero
had soon come to realize that despite its bitter strife with the
Holy See, the Grand Magistracy had never forgotten the religious
principle of its functions. The missionary association, snatched
at the last moment from under Holy Sepulchral claws, received
its most devoted care. Count Nasalli Rocca, in charge of civic
charities, did not spend his days looking at the Great Carrack,
like the nonagenarian Conestabile della Staffa, whom he had
replaced. The Grand Magistracy might not always be in good
odour with the Congregation of Religious: at the Congregation
*de Propaganda Fide* it was the white-headed boy: reason sufficient, that it provided not only active aid but even money for
RAPTIM—*Romana Associatio pro Transvehendis Missionaribus*
—which transported missionaries and nuns to their posts by air;
and for the Society of St. Paul, which "intensified, by radio,
Catholic propaganda in Japan."

The stately bearing and majestic stature of Mgr. Ferrero
enhanced all ceremonies in the magistral chapel. When, at
Easter, he preached in St. John's Church at the Palazzo of
Rhodes, headquarters of the Italian association, he expressed
the knights' affliction at no longer possessing their traditional
relics, particularly, in this Marian Year, the miraculous image
of Our Lady of Philermo, attributed to St. Luke.

"Where now," cried the Archbishop of Trebizond, "where
now is Our Lady of Victory who once appeared in the sky above
Rhodes with St. John the Baptist, and put a Turkish army to
flight?"

And he sketched the peregrinations of that much-travelled
Virgin and of the two relics which kept her company, the right

hand of St. John the Baptist, and the Holy Thorn, presented
to the Grand Master d'Aubu'sson by the Sultan Bajazet, in the
matter of Prince Zizim. Villiers de l'Isle Adam having received
permission to take them with him from Rhodes when he sur-
rendered to Suliman, they distributed their mercies at every
stage of his long course—at Candia, Cythera, Messina, Baiae,
Cumal, Civita Vecchia, Viterbo, Corneto, Nice, Villefranche,
and Syracuse—before Charles V had given him the island of
Malta. From Malta they followed Hompesch to Trieste, and
later joined his successor, Paul I, in St. Petersburg. They were
saved in the nick of time from the Bolsheviks by Alexander
III's widow, who took them with her to Copenhagen, and
carried thence to Belgrade by her daughter, who gave them
to Karageorgevitch. Was Our Lady of Philermo to be found
there still, shedding her blessing on the stricken, silent Church?
Or was she, as had been said, locked in the safe of some American
collector?

But although the Knights of St. John had not recovered
Our Lady of Philermo, the right hand of St. John the Baptist
had made its way to the famous *Comendadores* of San Juan,
the Order's last convent of nuns, who kept it jealously in Bar-
celona. As for Bajazet's Holy Thorn, it passed from one princely
Russian to another until finally one of them piously gave it to
Benedict XV.

In reviving the memory of these relics, the Archbishop of
Trebizond did not fail to emphasize that they bore witness to
the singular favour in which Providence had always held the
sovereign Order.

\*       \*       \*

The loyalty and zeal with which Mgr. Ferrero fulfilled his
duties were not long in exasperating Cardinal Canali. Their
relations were already strained, and the paschal sermon in which,
mingling history with piety, the prelate of the Grand Magistracy
spoke favourably of Paul I, brought the strain to breaking
point. The cardinal held that the tsar, being a schismatic, had
not been a legitimate grand master. And, maintaining that the

Order's sovereignty was linked with the continuity of that title, concluded that it had come to an end with Hompesch. Mgr. Ferrero having retorted that, according to the Order's secret archives, Paul I had been converted by the Jesuit Grüber, Cardinal Canali set Father Castellani at him. That Jesuit thereupon took up his pen to attack the imperial grand master by denying a Jesuit the honour of having converted a monarch whose imperial mother had given asylum to the Society of Jesus when it was dissolved and persecuted.

A trifling incident completed the breach between Mgr. Ferrero and the man who had aimed to embroil him with the Order. The question of lodging the Prelate of the Grand Magistracy had arisen: he was given the grand prior's apartment in the villa on the Aventine, since the grand prior never used it. From that day, Cardinal Canali declared that never again would he speak to an archbishop who had the effrontery to sleep in his bed.

\*       \*       \*

The Prelate of the Grand Magistracy had a brilliant opportunity to distinguish himself, since his appointment had been made in the Marian Year. He suggested to the Sovereign Council that they should hold a vast demonstration to make manifest the rich spiritual life of the Order, while enabling him to make the acquaintance of its principal members. In June, a decree was promulgated announcing that a "Marian forgathering" of the Knights of Malta and their families would take place at Rome in October. A copy of the decree was sent to the Secretariat of State, which acknowledged it with congratulations; and to Cardinal Canali, who did not acknowledge it at all.

However when, in September, the Order started sending out thousands of circulars, accompanied by a form on which recipients could signify their intention to be present, Cardinal Canali, who was *ad aquas*, returned post-haste to announce that he was opposing the whole scheme for a Marian forgathering, which he described as a political demonstration. Mgr. dell'Acqua entreated him to authorize the assembly, if only out of respect for the Pope, who had initiated the Marian Year. His Eminence weakened at that, but demanded that the gathering be postponed for two months, by way of punishment.

It took place on the date originally fixed and, to the cardinal's great vexation, its success was complete. For the first time in the Order's history, delegations from Canada, Cuba, Mexico, Nicaragua, and Peru appeared in Rome, not to mention the Filipino delegation whose members, a little out of their depth, turned up at the Magistral Palace wearing dinner jackets and spurs. Likewise came several members of the Italian royal family and car-loads of *mitteleuropan* highnesses complete with wives and children. Never before had five hundred Knights of Malta, all in uniform, been seen in Rome.

The ceremonies were so arranged as to bring out the Order's international character. They took place in divers churches in every quarter of Rome, and both celebrants and servants of the Masses were representative of Catholicism in every quarter of the world.

The Secretariat of State had suggested that as a gesture of courtesy Cardinal Canali be invited to sing Mass in Santa Maria Maggiore on the anniversary day of the battle of Lepanto. He replied that he was otherwise engaged. The Order had solicited the presence of other cardinals: all of them, afraid of arousing the ire either of Cardinal Canali, or the Dean of the Sacred College should they not be "caged," sent excuses.

Although Nicholas did not come, his representatives were ever present, circulating misleading information about the arrangements made for the pilgrims, with a view to disgusting them with the Grand Magistracy. It became necessary for the organizers to address their noble flock every evening before it dispersed, explaining, for example, that the morrow's Mass was to be in the catacombs of Domitilla and not, as had just been passed round, the catacombs of Priscilla; or that it was to be at Santa Maria Maggiore and not, as someone had just been telling them, at Santa Croce in Hierusaleme.

The delegates approved the plan for reforming the code, and asked for an audience of the Sovereign Pontiff. They were less fortunate than the delegates to the International Flax and

Hemp Convention, received in private audience a few days earlier. They were summoned, with two thousand other people, to a general audience in the Castel' Gandolfo courtyard; but the Holy Father, high on his balcony, spoke a few kind words to them and expressed his good wishes.

The Grand Magistracy celebrated the end of this holy month of October by taking a little revenge on Cardinal Canali. He had excluded the Knights of Malta from the procession which, on May 30, bore the mortal remains of the newly canonized Pius X from St. Peter's to Santa Maria Maggiore. He argued that, Pius X having been grand master of the Holy Sepulchre, his escort should be composed solely of knights of that Order. On October 31, thanks to Cardinal Verde, Archpriest of Santa Maria Maggiore, whose heart did not warm toward the present Grand Master of the Holy Sepulchre, Knights of Malta only escorted the Madonna *Salus populi romani* to St. Peter's, where she was crowned by the Pope on November 1: the Order's tit for the cardinal's tat.

# X

VERY EARLY IN NOVEMBER the Marquis Pallavicini was startled by a telephone call. It was the Marquis Macdonald, calling him from the Grand Hotel to announce that he was in Rome, and that he wished to visit the priory villa and meet His Excellency "the old gentleman": at least he did not say, "the boss."

Curiosity at the Magistral Palace was keen. At last they were to see, in the flesh, the famous Chairman of the American association, who persisted in calling himself "Master" despite the late grand master. There was general astonishment that Cardinal Spellman should have allowed him to come without leading strings. It was very imprudent, surely, since there was a risk that somebody might refer to all those millions which vanished so mysteriously somewhere between New York and the Bambino Gesù Hospital. As the "Master" had not had the common courtesy to announce his visit by letter, it was decided that he should be received ceremoniously, rather than as a friend.

He had, as a matter of fact, half hinted at a visit, but the Grand Magistracy had not expected him, feeling he must be rather ashamed of his sixty-seven bastards, legitimized after the event. They had sent him the circular about the Marian gathering and he had replied that as his knights had already made a pilgrimage to Rome and it had been very expensive, they could not come a second time, but that he might come later.

And he might well have an ulterior and important reason for putting in an appearance in the Via Condotti. The Grand Magistracy had found means to cut the American cake in two: some months since a handsome letter had been dispatched announcing to the "Grand Protector and Spiritual Adviser" and to the Chairman that the association they directed would henceforth be known as either "The Association of the Eastern United States," or "The Eastern United States Association." The Western United States association had just been founded in San Francisco, thanks to the support of the archbishop, Mgr. Mitty. A Mr. Lynch had accepted its chairmanship; fifteen knights had already been enrolled and three members of the Eastern association had asked to be transferred to the Western. The Archbishop of New York wrote furious letters to the lieutenant and gave the poor Archbishop of San Francisco such a dressing-down that the three lost sheep were returned to the fold and Mr. Lynch, fearful of being lynched himself, hardly dared stir a finger. Nevertheless, the Marquis Macdonald might still have something to say on his own account.

The group of men getting ready to receive the visitor before passing him on to Hercolani were chatting in the red salon: the chancellor, the vice-chancellor, Pallavicini, Sersale, and Prince Pignatelli de Montecalvo, the Order's minister to the Panamanian Government, who, passing through Rome and married to an American wife, was anxious to do the honours for an American knight.

There suddenly appeared in the open doorway a sort of human mastodon wearing a ten-gallon hat and with an enormous cigar sticking out of one corner of his mouth. With shoulders squared, arms rigid at his sides, and legs perfectly stiff, this portentous figure advanced into the room without looking at anybody. The tight mouth and powerful jaws hardened a face which was not without a certain beauty, the head crowned with a mane of white hair. At last, he lowered his eyes to the short figure of the chancellor, who had gone forward to meet him, and handed him his cigar and his hat. Baron Apor, smiling, put the cigar into an ash-tray and the hat on a console table.

"His Excellency the chancellor," Pallavicini said, in his stentorian voice.

The Marquis Macdonald shook his hand absent-mindedly and did not apologize for his mistake. Nor did he show any more interest in the others when the chancellor introduced them, but collapsed on to a couch under the portrait of the Grand Master Thun Hohenstein, where, rolling his eyes, he said, "I guess you know I'm a Catholic, a great Catholic, a very devout Catholic."

"Well, so are we, you know," the chancellor said.

It was an opening which recalled the story of Mrs. Luce and the Pope: she had talked to him of Catholicism with so much authority, so much force and warmth, that His Holiness was obliged to remind her, gently, that he, too, was a Catholic. There was no longer any mystery about Cardinal Spellman letting the "Master" loose on his own: he would only have had to remind him that he was going among ex-rebels, men reproved by the Church. Prince Pignatelli, who had imagined himself providing a bond between the Order and America, was betraying his consternation.

"Did you have a good crossing?" the chancellor asked the Marquis Macdonald.

"My private aircraft is a good one."

"You flew directly from America?"

"No, from Cairo, where I left the forty friends who are travelling as my guests. They're following by air liner."

The Grand Magistracy had not realized that the Marquis

Macdonald was so rich. Cardinal Spellman had made a wise choice.

"You're not making bad use of the money we send you from America," the "Master" said, looking about him, and waved a hand toward the portraits of Carafa and Paul I, the vases of Chinese porcelain that Catherine II had given to the Grand Master de Rohan, and a bronze presented by Eugénie de Montijo, Empress of the French, Dame of Honour and Devotion. And he added, "The fact is, Cardinal Spellman and I send you money by the bucketful, eh?"

Nobody dared to tell him, as Hercolani had told the French knight just back from America, that the Grand Magistracy received neither more nor less than 1,000 dollars per American knight.

"I hope you make as good use of our money in your villa," the American Marquis went on.

"The Marquis Pallavicini will take you to see it," the chancellor said.

"His Excellency ought also to visit the Bambino Gesù Hospital," Cattaneo put in.

"What hospital?" the Marquis Macdonald inquired.

"The Bambino Gesù, here in Rome, which is maintained by your association, Excellency," the chancellor said.

"Oh, sure, I guess we do a lot of good with our money. We're so generous that Cardinal Spellman calls us 'super-knights.' Without our money and Cardinal Spellman, the Order of Malta would be dead broke."

These constant references to money and to Cardinal Spellman revived the idea, in some of the company, of revealing the curious discrepancy which the Order had discovered, to their visitor. But their distaste for the subject, as men of breeding, was reinforced by their conviction that they would be wasting their breath.

"You should just see him," the "Master" continued, "you should just see the cardinal taking the plate round our table at the Waldorf-Astoria! And all for you! But I wouldn't advise you to go on trying to compete with us in San Francisco."

The chancellor considered that these civilities had gone on

long enough. He conducted the illustrious American to the lieutenant, who did not keep him long. The Marquis Macdonald reappeared, disappointed.

"Cardinal Spellman was right," he said, as he took his departure, "when he said not to trouble the old gentleman."

# XI

THIS SAME MONTH of November was distinguished by an even greater event: the Order of Malta and the Italian Republic proceeded to a solemn exchange of decorations. With much pomp and ceremony a cortége arrived at the villa on the Aventine and bore the lieutenant off to the Quirinal, where he was received with military honours and the playing of the two anthems. He presented President Einaudi with the Order's Collar for Merit; and, albeit only provisional head of the Order, received in return the Collar for Merit of the Italian Republic, which was reserved for chiefs of state. His principal collaborators were likewise honoured with the highest distinctions. The Italian government had used this means to consecrate the Order's sovereign status, which it had recognized two years ago; and to give the lie to the calumnies industriously propagated against its leaders by foreign libels and flimsies originating not a thousand miles from Rome.

The flimsies took their revenge by jeering at a president and a government ready to accept decorations from people "who had no right to bestow them."

The Malta Collar for Merit, with which President Einaudi had just been invested, had been devised as an innovation by Prince Chigi, just before his death. Its purpose was to enable the Order to avoid making chiefs of state Bailiffs Grand Cross of Honour and Devotion, since that implied that they were both Catholics and aristocrats of ancient lineage. There was already a Cross for Merit, with the same series of ranks as the Cross of Malta itself, so that it was only necessary to add a superior grade, the Collar, on the analogue of the Grand Magistral Collar. The lieutenant had tried it out on the President of Costa Rica; he had then raised his sights, as it were, and conferred it on the President of Peru, which made it feasible to offer it, thereafter, to the President of Italy.

On the other hand it had proved difficult to convince the Prince de Polignac that any future president of France would have to be satisfied with the same treatment. He was not told that the Italian protocol authorities had also insisted that, while the Collar for Merit was all very well, the Grand Cross of a Bailiff of Honour and Devotion was even better. President Einaudi could hardly accept an honour inferior to that conferred on President Auriol. He was willing to accept a new decoration, but only after having received the old one. The Order was faced with the probability of having to confer two decorations in future, where one had sufficed. It bowed to the inevitable, but an unpublished decree conferred the Grand Cross on President Einaudi a few days before the public presentation of the Collar. Thus, on the big day, it could be pointed out that he was already a bailiff grand cross, so that no precedent was created which would have had to be followed in the case of President Auriol's successor, who would thus come under the new dispensation.

Although it had had to give way in the case of President Einaudi, the Order was firm in the matter of his wife: Donna Ida, less ambitious than Señora Perón and less fortunate than Mme Auriol, received the Grand Cross of Merit, with plaque and cordon. What she did not know was that the cordon in question, a bare few millimetres wide, was the result of a mistake. The meeting of the Council which had decided on this decoration, to be conferred on a woman for the first time, had been a long one: to decide on the correct width for the cordon the meeting had consulted several works of reference on matters of chivalry, and after reducing the measurement thus arrived at to centimetres, the order to the jeweller had accidentally been placed in millimetres. This was not discovered until the cordon was delivered, on the very eve of the ceremony. Which was why the lieutenant showed a certain embarrassment as he placed about Donna Ida's neck a cordon of the Grand Cross of Merit of Malta which looked more like a scapular. But, after all, what more natural in the case of a religious order and a ceremony which concluded with the recitation of an Ave Maria in the Quirinal chapel?

Afterwards, driving back to the Magistral Palace, Hercolani asked his companions what that strange tune had been which was played before Mameli's Italian national anthem.

"The Order's anthem," the chancellor explained.

"Dear me!"

It should be explained that this anthem, composed some twenty years ago in honour of Prince Chigi, was less familiar to the Grand Magistracy than to military bandmasters in Italy generally, and even abroad. When Giannantoni stepped out of the air liner in the Lebanon with his letters of credence in his pocket, he had been greeted by an atrocious cacophony which he had subsequently, and with a surprise equal to Hercolani's, understood to be the Order's anthem executed *à la libanaise*. However, the ancient anthem of Malta, believed to be lost, had come to light recently in a chest at the priory villa; but it called for instruments which were no longer to be found in modern bands or orchestras, and nobody had yet taken the trouble of having it transposed.

After these political splendours it remained for the lieutenant to make some display of the Grand Magistracy's religious glories in the same month. The Order had recovered its right of appearance at papal chapels and, by the same token, its precedence on those occasions. Cardinal Canali had been obliged to limit his aggression to pointing out that its delegations "normally composed of four members and raised to five without authority, must in future be reduced to the correct number owing to lack of seats."

Then, suddenly, came the news that Cardinal Leger, Archbishop of Montreal, paying a visit *ad limina*, would call at the Grand Magistracy and there receive the Cross of a Bailiff of Honour and Devotion. When this news broke, Cardinal Canali nearly had a fit. And the worst of it was that the man who was thus prepared to defy him could treat with him on equal terms.

He was protected in such a manner that Cardinal Canali was helpless—by Sister Pasqualina, to whom, indeed, he owed his Hat. Having appreciated the value of the knights' work in Canada, Cardinal Leger was anxious to congratulate the Grand Magistracy and had let it be understood that he would willingly accept the Cross of Malta.

Cardinal Canali moved heaven and earth to persuade him to give up this idea. Mgr. dell'Acqua actually went to the length of begging the lieutenant to "invite" His Eminence Cardinal Leger to cancel his projected visit "for reasons of protocol." Pecci informed him that the Order would not even answer this singular request. Cardinal Leger came *in fiocchi*, accompanied by the Canadian ambassador's wife, and made a speech extolling "the star of the Knights of Malta, shining in the heavens of history." Cardinal Canali was not even able to prevent the publication of this speech in the press.

Thus was "the Hercolani gang" honoured by the Republic and by a prince of the Church in quick succession.

# XII

TRUE TO ITS UNDERTAKING, the Grand Magistracy had not published its "interpretative" letter to the Secretariat of State. Nevertheless, it had communicated its contents to those governments with which it maintained diplomatic relations, and as a result had been confirmed in its opinion that it was of the utmost importance to do so. Peru, Portugal, and the Lebanon had informed the Grand Magistracy that had it not been for this explanation, they would have ceased to recognize the Order as sovereign and would have broken off diplomatic relations. And if other countries did not make the same point in so many words, they would nevertheless probably have acted in the same way. Shortly thereafter Nicaragua recognized the Order and, in its instrument of recognition, quoted the text of the letter as "proof of political freedom, the basis of sovereignty."

So that the Grand Magistracy's firmness and the good will of the Pope had together led the Secretariat of State into interpreting the judgment in a way which saved the Order's rights and its judges' honour.

True, there had been an "authorized" declaration printed in the Catholic *Courrier de Genève*, affirming that no document could be regarded as softening the severity of the special Court's judgment, the text of which had been published at the end of 1953 in the *Acta Apostolicæ Sedis*. The Grand Magistracy would, therefore, have been within its rights in publishing the letter of interpretation. But it made a strict principle of being more scrupulous than the Holy See and avoiding anything like a fanning of the flames. It confined itself, therefore, to having the existence of a "concordat" discreetly revealed by Senator Lando Ferretti, a sagacious member of the Order; and by Silvio Negro, the best-known journalist in Italy on matters touching the Vatican.

Apart from any other consideration, the Grand Magistracy was anxious to be as tactful as possible to avoid alarming the Secretariat of State, whose leading light was about to be removed from office in the Vatican government: Mgr. Montini was to be made to pay for his defence, albeit discreet, of the Order of Malta. The death of Cardinal Schuster provided the opportunity: the Pro-Secretary was elected to his archepiscopal see.

The Order had the melancholy satisfaction to its pride of realizing that it had given rise to the disgrace of the most able man in the Holy See. That it could have happened so must have seemed incredible to anyone who did not know of a remark made by Cardinal Canali to the other members of the Court of Cardinals, recalling what he had said to Mgr. Curatola on the road to Magione, to the effect that this business was "the most important that the Church had had to settle in this century, since it was directed against the élite of Catholic Christendom." He had his reasons for attaching importance to it and for persuading others that it was as important as he considered it to be.

Eminent jurists, among them Professor Cansacchi of Turin University, and Professor Oliver Farran of Liverpool University, having given importance to the letter of interpretation in reaching their conclusion that the Order was certainly sovereign, the Grand Prior of Rome once again sent a Jesuit into the lists. This time it was Father Lener, and a series of articles by him closed the Marian Year. He chose to be droll, seeking to show that, if the Order had, indeed, ever possessed sovereignty, it was the sovereignty conferred on it by the cardinals' judgment. The fact that he said not one word about the interpretation of the judgment was significant.

And since the "Soldiers of Christ" were thus being put into the vanguard, it looked as if the war was about to break out again.

# PART
# FIVE

# I

ON JANUARY 1, 1955, the venerable bailiff lieutenant launched an appeal "to all nations, religious orders, men of science, and that Catholic élite which constitutes the sovereign Order of Malta, for the social rehabilitation of lepers." He announced that he would summon a congress in the name of Christian charity with a view to studying methods of restoring lepers who had been cured but were still pariahs, to the bosom of society. The Holy Father congratulated the lieutenant on this initiative and promised that he would follow developments with the keenest interest.

But at the same time the Holy See was setting in motion a machine which was far from flaunting the flag of Christian charity, although covered by that of religion. On February 2, the Secretariat of State sent the Grand Magistracy a new pontifical chirograph, dated February 1: the Holy Father, wishing "to create favourable conditions for a return to normal within the glorious, sovereign, and Hierosolymitan Order of Malta," was setting up a committee of six cardinals "to assist and direct the Order at a difficult juncture, to revise its constitution and promote a new flowering of spiritual life within its bosom."

This text seemed to be an echo of the first letter from the Congregation of Religious, which had given rise to the Committee of Cardinals; and at the same time of the first chirograph, which had given rise to the Court of Cardinals. "Spiritual life" had always been the Holy See's war-horse; even, indeed, its Trojan horse by means of which it had tried to capture the *palazzo* in the Via Condotti. Surely, the Grand Magistracy must be forced to yield to such persistent zeal, a zeal which was best explained by reference to the composition of the committee: the same five names appeared, with the addition of Cardinal Valeri, Prefect of the Congregation of Religious. In four years, the guard had thus been doubled; but the number of the Order's friends had increased in a greater proportion. Some tribute was paid to that fact in the caution with which the chirograph, intended for publication, had been worded; and the cleverness with which this new interference was related to "anomalies in the Order's government." But these circumlocutions left it none the less clear that the cardinals were going to try to do and overdo what they had still not contrived to do at all.

On February 5, Pecci delivered to Mgr. dell'Acqua the most energetically worded of all the notes exchanged during the conflict. It did not even stop short of disputing the chirograph's terminology: the only "anomalies of government" derived from the prohibition to elect a grand master; the plan for reforming the constitution, deposited with the Secretariat of State in October, left the new Committee of Cardinals with nothing to do, since its labours could not be concerned with anything else without encroaching on the Order's sovereign rights; in view of the great danger in which these rights were again being placed, the delegates of national associations, entitled to express their opinion, were being summoned to Rome once again.

This retort exasperated Cardinal Canali, who had expected to throw down the walls and put courage to flight by his unexpected assault. The Grand Magistracy's arguments left him cold; not so the defensive manœuvre which had already proved so effective. The return of those eternal foreign delegates was henceforth as regular as the motions of the stars or cardinalistic outbursts of fury. The book of Berne was once more distributed to newspaper offices, but at this point the Italian government, considering that the Holy See was really going too far, took a hand. In view of the recent exchange of decorations, any new outburst of calumny must also be aimed at itself, and it took steps to prevent the resumption of that shameful campaign.

On February 11, the cardinals came up with a decree calling on the lieutenant to deliver to the committee, within ten days, the plan for reform drawn up by the Grand Magistracy: "No admission of new knights or dames of the Order, no promotions, nor the conferring of honours or rank will be valid unless approved by the Committee of Cardinals." Any "extraordinary" business operation must also be approved by it—"by extraordinary business operation should be understood any operation entailing an obligation in excess of 10,000 gold francs or gold lire." As regards routine business, the lieutenant would, from the date of the decree, be "assisted by and conjoined with" the Secretary of the Committee of Cardinals, Mgr. Scapinelli, himself to be advised by Prince Giulio Pacelli as juridical adviser (it was still being kept in the family), and helped by two Vatican clerks, one as administrative adviser, the other an accountant. "In emergencies" the powers of the committee could be exercised by its chairman, Cardinal Tisserant. Finally, all the committee's deliberations would be reported in the *Osservatore Romano*.

Once again no attempt at even a decent appearance of fulfilling the papal wish for a "spiritual flowering" had been made by including anything touching the religious life of the Order in this programme. As before, the cardinals were abusing the Holy Father's trust by reaching greedily for control of its business and decorations; and even its ladies. In signing the decree most of them had omitted the customary little cross before their names, and only Cardinal Tisserant had included his episcopal titles. Last of the list, "Nicholas, Cardinal Canali," seemed to sustain the whole pyramid of signatures with its broad shoulders and angry flourish.

The decree recalled certain earlier dispositions; but they had been perfected, and this time a veritable "commissariat" was being put in control, with Mgr. Scapinelli taking over the lieutenancy, Prince Pacelli the Chancellery, and their two acolytes the Treasury and business departments respectively. The new member of the Pacelli family was, incidentally, brought in almost despite himself: Prince Carlo, not having dared to appear again openly confined himself to giving advice and delegated his younger brother to represent him. Prince Giulio was, among other things, Costa Rican Minister to the Holy See.

The placing of the lieutenant in tutelage seemed designed to justify the epithet "provisional" with which the Dean of the Sacred College had formerly belaboured him. Forbidding the Grand Magistracy to confer honours without seeking approval in advance was intended as a deliberate insult to those most recently honoured. It was not merely a case of the Holy See revenging itself on the Presidency of the Republic and the Palazzo Chigi, but also of Cardinal Canali's personal spite against Cardinal Leger and Sister Pasqualina. Could it be because of that worthy nun, the Pope's housekeeper, that the cardinals were, for the first time, taking an interest in the admission of ladies to the Order? Certainly, they had not, hitherto, figured in the exchanges between the Holy See and the Order of Malta. Probably the six *Eminentissimes* were aware that ladies had to pay much more passage money, and could see a gold mine in the new facilities granted to them. The Order's bulletin, founded some months since to replace the review, had already given news, from Mexico, of the first dame magistral. And they were clearly in such a hurry not to miss anything that they had envisaged "emergencies" arising, urgent cases in which the Bishop of Ostia, of Porto and Santo Rufino could act alone. After his experiences as a member of the Court of Cardinals, Cardinal Tisserant would have preferred not to risk his dignity any further. But this typical Roman intrigue had served to rehabilitate him in the Pope's good graces and now Cardinal Canali, by whose means he had gained this advantage, required payment to the uttermost farthing.

At the via Condotti it was doubted whether, despite the terms of their decree, the cardinals would have the effrontery to flaunt these iniquities in the *Osservatore Romano*. But when, albeit belatedly, the Holy Father's chirograph was, in fact, published, the worst was to be expected. Publication of the decree would have disgraced its authors; but it would have been death to the Order. It must be prevented.

Thirty Roman prelates, all Knights of Malta, were assembled at the Magistral Palace, and the cardinals' decree was read to them. They were then told that if the *Osservatore Romano* published this text or any others deriving from it, the Grand Magistracy would publish a white paper or a blue book, or a red book or a yellow book, containing the entire correspondence between the Grand Magistracy and the Holy See since 1949. Even without comment it would, unfortunately, be the most damning act of accusation ever drawn up by Catholics against the Roman Church.

"Do not protest that we are contemplating sacrilege," the prelates were told; "we shall be doing no more than six members of the Sacred College, including its dean, are trying to do. We are fully aware that the Holy Father may suppress the Order of Malta entirely after publication of our white paper. But we would rather be suppressed by him than by them."

The Committee of Cardinals and the Secretariat of State were besieged by all thirty prelates, who knew only too much about the real facts of the case and the importance, for the Holy See, of avoiding any such revelations as were now threatened. The strategy was the same as that which had halted Cardinal Canali last June, but this time used more directly. The *Osservatore Romano* carried no word of the decree, nor anything else about this business.

The Grand Magistracy might come to regret having deprived themselves of a legitimate means of defence as the price of this silence; their consolation must be that they had not been obliged to show disrespect for the Church, or even for the purple.

# II

RENOUNCING PUBLICATION of their decree meant that the cardinals were not putting one of its articles into execution; but that did not, of course, mean that they would not put the others into operation—virtual seizure of the Order, its power to confer distinctions, its charitable works, and its property.

Pecci went to see Mgr. dell'Acqua and solemnly read him a *note* which deserved the name of *verbale*, to wit: "At this dramatic moment any discussion would be out of place. I beg Your Excellency to solicit an audience of the Holy Father to ask him, in my name, to grant what follows: temporary suspension of all actions whose consequences might be irreparable, consequences of such magnitude that the Order of Malta and the present dispute are trifles by comparison. I ask this not as a minister of the Order but as a son of the Church, in fear and trembling at what I see coming upon us, and seeing very clearly what the world-wide effects will be upon the Church, effects which certain people do not seem to have weighed."

Mgr. dell'Acqua assured him that he would be with the Pope within an hour. Nevertheless, the Grand Magistracy was bound to consider that this *démarche* might be ineffectual. While awaiting the cardinals' future decisions, it had to face up to the most pressing of those which had already been taken. Mgr. Scapinelli might turn up from one moment to the next, and there could be no question of limiting his powers by means of a bull, as had been done in Mgr. Alcini's case. To allow the lieutenant's "coadjutor" inside the Grand Magistral Palace would be allowing him to assume his office—and the lieutenant's. But how to prevent him entering? To use such means as would be an offence to his cloth would be giving occasion for those very censures which Cardinal Canali was so anxious to deliver.

A council of war was held at the Magistral Palace. All possible eventualities were considered, and the means of dealing with them. Either Mgr. Scapinelli would give advance notice of his visit, in which case the reasons for postponing it could be set before him; or he would come without warning, and the question would be how to get rid of him with due ceremony. There could be no hope of keeping him away indefinitely, but it might be possible to do so until the delegates arrived.

A plan was agreed to. The outer door would be left open only during office hours, and the wrought-iron inner gate, which separated the porter's lodge from the courtyard and the staircase, would be kept closed. Two clerks from the Grand Magistracy offices would take turns to remain on duty in the porter's lodge, ready to welcome the prelate domestic in suitable style and invite him to possess his soul in patience until they had informed their superiors of his visit. The chancellor, or in his absence, the vice-chancellor, would go down at once, to ask him what he wanted. If he replied that he wanted to see the lieutenant, it would be pointed out that etiquette required that he first ask for an audience. If he said that he wished to see the lieutenant immediately, he would be given the following declaration to read: "The Grand Magistracy, holding the measures adopted by the Committee of Cardinals to be an attack upon its sovereign prerogatives and long-established rights, has summoned to Rome representatives of the Order's various associations with voting rights, and cannot, until that vote has been taken, carry out any of those measures."

The chancellor and the vice-chancellor were aware that the one to whom this embassy fell would have to be sacrificed: the Holy See would require his resignation. But he would risk only his place: a professed member undertaking the task would have to suffer much more serious sanctions. And his sacrifice would enable the Grand Magistracy to hold out just a little longer.

But another eventuality must be taken into consideration. Mgr. Scapinelli might insist upon trying to make his way in despite this splendid declaration. He might march up to the gate, and while not, perhaps, attempting to climb it, since it was as tall as a man, might try to open it or to get it opened. Prince Giulio Pacelli, annoyed at having let himself be tricked into this business, had discreetly let it be known that he would act no more. But the other two laymen might well come with the prelate domestic. What would be their attitude? In short, might not a breach of the peace be provoked, giving occasion for accusations of outrage against a prelate, for seizing the Holy Office of the whole business, and rousing world Catholicism against the Order? The people whom Cardinal Canali's creatures had for so long been calling rebels would at last have given public proof of rebellion.

Taking precautions against possible false witness, the Grand Magistracy had the idea of recalling the carabinieri who were supposed to stand guard outside the palace but who, in normal times, were unofficially excused that duty. They would, in any case, be required, as usual, to provide guards of honour for the international assembly. Cattaneo was given the task of calling on the police authorities and asking them to put their men back on duty in the Via Condotti; and the men were to be urged to pay close attention to what happened in the event of a monsignore putting in an appearance.

"Are you expecting serious trouble?" the officer inquired.

"Not at all. We're not asking for strong-arm stuff. We want to be sure of impeccable witnesses in certain eventualities."

These precautions having been taken, the Grand Magistracy busied itself in trying to make them unnecessary. As it was presumed that, if he knew what to expect, Mgr. Scapinelli would show prudence, steps were taken to have him informed. Nothing, of course, was said of the moral support provided by the police: only of the firm and courteous reception awaiting him in the porter's lodge.

It was known that, before having received this information, he had made up his mind to come on February 18, without advance notice. On that day, so early that the outer door had not yet been opened, Cattaneo and Sersale, standing at a window, saw Cardinal Canali's volunteer, the flimsy distributor, waiting across the street, camera in hand, ready to immortalize the historic scene of the prelate domestic's arrival. He made off when he realized that he had been spotted, having photographed the closed door; shortly thereafter prints of his negative were making the rounds of editorial offices with the suitable caption: "Closed."

On the 19th, Mgr. Scapinelli sent a message to say that he would telephone the chancellor in one hour's time. That was probably to show that he was behaving circumspectly. Their dialogue, when the time came, was as follows: "Hallo. Scapinelli here."

"Hallo. The chancellor speaking."

"Good morning, Excellency."

"Good morning, Monsignor."

"You may remember that we have met before, Excellency."

"Of course, but I do not recall where it was, exactly."

"At your own legation, Excellency. It was on the outbreak of the war. We were all younger, then."

"Alas, how true!"

"Well, now, here it is, Excellency: I have to pay a call on His Excellency the provisional lieutenant, and I shall be along presently with two of the gentlemen appointed, with myself, by the Cardinals' Committee—you know all about that."

"I do. Am I to understand that you will be paying this call in conformity with the cardinals' decisions?"

"I am obliged to do so."

"In that case I must read you the message which I have been instructed to convey to you by His Excellency the Lieutenant and the Sovereign Council."

"Please read it slowly so that I can take it down."

The chancellor read the declaration at dictation speed, and when he had done so Mgr. Scapinelli said, "That is all?"

"That is all, Monsignor."

"Good-bye."

"Good-bye."

Mgr. Scapinelli sent for Pecci at once and told him that the declaration was unheard-of, scandalous, and offensive, and demanded an immediate apology. The Minister explained that the Order was under no obligation to bow down to a Mgr. Scapinelli charged with a mission which called for a cardinal *a latere*. "Let Cardinal Canali undertake it himself," he added, "and he will discover that we know how to receive him."

The substitute protested that the honour of the Holy See was involved. The minister's opinion—that a prelate domestic's pride was really in question—he kept to himself.

Another council of war was held in the Via Condotti. The delegations would be arriving within a day or two: it was surely better to dispose of an incident which might otherwise confuse the issue they would have to deal with. Hercolani consented to apologize to Mgr. Scapinelli: he would stoop; but only that the Order might conquer.

He called upon not only the chancellor to accompany him, but also the representative of the Grand Priory of Naples and Sicily. This Sicilian, Taccone's successor, trebly ducal by virtue of his names—Paterno Castello di Caraci—was the member of the Sovereign Council who had been least involved in the battle. He had been living in Catania, had only joined the Grand Magistracy after the signature of the "concordat," and had no part in those decrees which had annoyed the Vatican: a virgin knight. Hercolani could not, and had no wish to, become grand master or permanent lieutenant, and in his own mind had fixed upon the Sicilian bailiff as his successor. It was for this reason that he seized the first chance that offered to lull any suspicions the Holy See might entertain of the man.

At the Palazzo Sant' Calixtus he was generous with his apologies to Mgr. Scapinelli, but remained firm in his decision not to receive him at the Grand Magistral Palace until such time as the Assembly had given its formal consent.

"Do you not think, Excellency," Paterno said, "that Monsignor might come, if he undertook not to concern himself with the Assembly?"

Mgr. Scapinelli's face lit up with joy at this unexpected support. "But, of course!" he cried.

The lieutenant declared that he could not reverse a decision of the Sovereign Council. The prelate domestic cannot have felt his position to be a strong one, despite the support of six Eminences, for he offered to limit his visit to a few minutes, a mere formality, and thereafter to wait patiently until the Assembly had expressed its wishes. This visit, he explained, was a matter of saving his face with the cardinals and his colleagues. And, taking Paterno by the arm, "Excellency," he said, "you have shown that you understand my position. Try to convince the lieutenant that he must at least grant me that much satisfaction. He must understand that what is happening to me is without precedent in Vatican history. It kept me awake all night."

Paterno turned to Hercolani and urged, "Excellency, since Monsignor undertakes to stay only a few minutes——"

The lieutenant remained entrenched behind his plea of the Sovereign Council, although three of its six members were present. The chancellor, no doubt feeling that he had done his share of the talking on the telephone, held his tongue. But all three of them knew that the moment Mgr. Scapinelli stepped over the threshold of the palace of Malta, he would produce a new decree of the committee, ordering him to affix the seals which Mgr. Alcini had failed to set on its doors, and clear the house of its people.

They also knew why Mgr. Scapinelli did not back his request with threats: the Italian government had informed the Holy See that it could not lend its support to "unilateral operations" against the Order of Malta.

# III

A ROMAN CARDINAL who counted Cattaneo among his friends sent for him.

"My son," he said, "I have followed this business of your Order only from a distance, for it does not concern my congregation. But yesterday I was received by the Holy Father and, quite incidentally, we talked about it. You are held to be the man chiefly responsible for a resistance which has lasted nearly five years. I am not concerned to know whether that resistance was, or was not, legitimate. Your last exploits have not been your least: I am not concerned to know whether or not they were justified.

"What you have forgotten is that the Church can never be wrong—I mean that it cannot admit to being wrong. You have overlooked the Latin adage, *Roma locuta, causa audita*—and do not retort with the Italian one, *Ròma veduta, fede perduta*. Those who lose their faith when in Rome, never had any to lose. Of what use would be the power of the keys, even when delegated to unskilful or fumbling hands, if not to impose what appears to their custodian to be the truth—not the eternal truth, but the truth of the moment? Eternal truth needs no man's help to impose itself; you know it as well as I do, since you are a Christian and a Catholic. But there are, in the service of various interests, perhaps material, even sordid if you like, provisionally, temporarily, right ways of seeing and judging certain things. And if, with a view to ensuring the triumph of that right, the Church or its representatives use and even abuse its spiritual power, then they do well and we ought to give way to them. In such cases the Church is like a state which uses public force to apply an ephemeral, even an unjust, law. It acts in the name of reasons of state, the *raison d'Etat*, using all means available to it; and, before Christ, Socrates justified it by his death.

"What can the Church do, without its spiritual weapons? Dispatch its battalion of Swiss guards against the worker-priests of France or the noble Knights of Malta? No; it must brandish the lightnings of excommunication, invoke canon law, talk about offence to the purple. For, I repeat, the Church can never be wrong.

"The Church did well to set up the Inquisition in times which made the Inquisition necessary. (I will not, like one recent ecclesiastical author, say that people's nerves in those days were less sensitive than ours: it was the minds, not the nerves, which were different.) And today, the Church is the chief support of the spirit of tolerance. The Church did well to condemn Galileo, since Galileo was running his head against all the astronomical data of his day; and today, at Castel, Gandolfo, it possesses one of the most perfect observatories in the world. The Church is neither a progressive nor a retrogressive power, but an eternal one. It assimilates progress when progress has been tried and not found wanting. And it preserves from the past what is worthy of preservation. But its everlasting life is founded in the obedience of its sons. Whereas all the other powers are necessarily ephemeral, the Church, like God Himself, is and will be what it always was. Thus, a man is with it or against it; and if with it, then when the Church has spoken, he must submit. *Roma locuta.*

"It can never be wrong, yet nevertheless knows that it has been wrong more than once. And when that happens, we should not draw too much attention to it, but imitate the modesty of the son of Noah. You have made the three cardinals of the first committee ridiculous in their own eyes. Thereafter, working with the Order's lawyers who would not have been so bold without you, you have baffled and set at nought a tribunal of five cardinals. And now you have slammed the door in the new committee's face. All this parade of international forces which enable the Order to outface the Holy See and whose importance the Holy See had underestimated—it was not of your making, but it is your example, your inspiration, that is followed. Driven forward by each day's events, you no longer realized how far you were going, and, seeing only the cardinals, lost sight of the Church. It is the Church which now, speaking with my mouth, orders you to have done with it.

"Nor is that all: the Church owes it to herself to make an example. The lieutenant's case is settled in advance, since the days of his lieutenancy are counted: the election will not be long delayed. But it is considered that, in addition to yourself, there are two other people chiefly responsible: Apor and De Mojana. The three of you must go. The susceptibility of the Order will not be disturbed since its provisional leader remains in place until the election: but we require, as a sacrificial offering, the head of its government, that is to say, the chancellor; a knight of justice by way of warning to professed members; and the vice-chancellor as a lesson to the delegates. That is the price, my son, of the Order's salvation. *Roma locuta*."

It was a long speech and it brought the vice-chancellor sharply down to earth. Maybe he had admitted to himself that he would one day have to pay for the last measures of defence employed by the Grand Magistracy; he had not expected retribution to come so soon. But his friend had made no error of judgment in appealing to his feelings: his choice was instantly made. He had resisted the cardinals and their auxiliaries in the belief that by so doing he was serving the highest interests of the Church. He had advocated the acceptance of the judgment out of respect for the Church. Thus both faith and reason had prepared him for the argument he had just listened to and it did not even occur to him to plead not guilty. The sacrifice required of him was costing him less than he would have expected. It was the conviction that he was fighting the good fight which had kept him in the forefront of the battle. And at least the goal was attained: the election was in sight.

"Eminence," he said, "I had become so attached to the Order of Malta that I saw myself spending my whole life in its service. A knight of honour and devotion, it was the meaning I gave to those two words which governed my conduct.

Although I have done only what I thought honour required and devotion permitted, I shall not dispute your decision for a moment. You may take it that I shall leave the Grand Magistracy. I will convey what you have said to the chancellor and to De Mojana, and I shall be very much surprised if their decision is not the same as my own."

However, as his political flair did not abandon him even at a moment like this, he added, "They, and I, will seek the best way to make our resignations useful to the Order's cause. There is one thing I dare to hope: it is that Your Eminence had not been misled into giving us the assurances I have just received."

"What do you mean?"

"I say nothing of the Holy Father, who is above the quarrel. But the assurances we have so frequently received from the Secretariat of State, and even from the Court of Cardinals, have all too often been repudiated. Consequently we should like to feel certain that your assurances do really come from yourself, and have not been prompted by those whom we have learned to know rather better than you know them."

"I personally answer for what I have told you. Through me, you are face to face with your real judge."

Cattaneo bowed.

The next day he delivered to the cardinal a memorandum which, while making the requisite act of obedience, showed that the Grand Magistracy was in firm hands: it was to the effect that the Sovereign Council had considered it out of the question to allow two of its members and its vice-chancellor only to resign, since joint responsibility was its rule. They would, therefore, place the resignation of the whole Council and the vice-chancellor in the hands of the Order's future chief, "as soon as he has been elected." This sacrifice was not merely a matter of form: the government of that little aristocratic republic did not necessarily change when a new chief was elected, those who composed it having administrative contracts or mandates conferred by the several chapters. The cardinal smiled at this declaration which gave more than had been asked for on condition of receiving what had long been sought.

"I was not asked," he said, "to obtain your resignations. Only a promise of them."

"They are already written, Eminence, and addressed to 'the seventy-seventh grand master of the Order of Malta or to the tenth lieutenant of the Grand Magistracy.' Do you wish me to send them to you?"

"Your word suffices. My poor son, you are going to have to seek a new place."

"Who knows but what I might turn monk, that is become a professed member of the Order?"

"It would be a fine revenge, but I advise you to wait a while: you might not receive the necessary dispensations immediately."

# IV

CHAIRMEN AND DELEGATES of foreign associations had not set out on their journeys without first being besieged by the nuncios, cardinals, and bishops of their respective countries who were in touch or alliance with Cardinal Canali or Mgr. dell'Acqua. A concerted attempt had been made to convince them that nothing but the Grand Magistracy's intransigence endangered the Order's sovereignty, and that a victory for the Holy See would be a victory for the Order's internationality. The French were told that French influence would be given predominance; the Germans, German influence; the Spaniards, Spanish influence, etc. Favours, donations, and pontifical orders were lavishly promised.

Deaf to all these red-, violet, or black-robed sirens, the "rescue fleet" cast anchor in the Tiber, complete, and loyal as ever. Boldly, the Spanish galleon unfurled the flag of Malta at her masthead, since the concordat between Madrid and the Holy See had been concluded shortly after the signing of the more modest one between the Holy See and the Order. The new chancellor of the Spanish *diputación*, the Conde del Valle de San Juan, had replaced the Infante Don Fernando Maria. The

French association was in all its glory by reason of the agreement which had just been signed between its chairman and the Fourth Republic for the establishment of leper colonies in French Equatorial Africa. The Prince de Polignac was to go there himself, be officially received, would wear the Order's uniform with tropical head-gear, and, wearing white gloves, would shake hands with people cured of leprosy: the event was to be commemorated by a special postage stamp. It would be a prelude to the International Congress for the Social Rehabilitation of Lepers, to be held in Rome the following year.

However, the delegates were conscious of the responsibilities which were to be theirs in the new and decisive battle with the cardinals, and went off to sound their respective embassies. There, they were unanimously confirmed in their gratifying loyalty, the embassies having all been influenced by the energetic friendliness of the Italian government toward the Grand Magistracy. Even ambassadors not accredited to the Order, the Comte d'Ormesson for example, had already taken a hand and urged the Holy See to use caution.

On February 23, the Assembly passed two motions approving the Grand Magistracy's note to the Secretariat of State: the first referred the problem of reform back to the plans which had been adopted in October; the second declared that, "unfortunately, the measures adopted by the Committee of Cardinals must be considered incompatible with the rights and constitution of the sovereign Order." It went on to express "the hope that the Grand Magistracy would succeed, by an approach to the Committee, in removing this nullifying impediment."

On the morning of the 26th, Mgr. dell'Acqua held his daily diplomatic court. He played the same scene for the benefit of every ambassador or minister who happened to say a word in the Order's favour:

"Your good-will toward the Order of Malta is, naturally, based on the fact that you have never suspected it of being wanting in respect toward the Holy See. It has, in point of fact, been so wanting in respect that the provisional lieutenant was obliged to apologize to the Holy Father for his attitude toward the cardinals' tribunal, and again, more recently, to Mgr. Scapinelli di Leguigno for his refusal to receive him. But still, these things were done with the gloves on; the want of respect was in the spirit, never in the letter. But now, only yesterday evening, an absolutely unheard-of-thing has come to our knowledge: the chancellor and vice-chancellor actually called in the Italian police to prevent Mgr. Scapinelli from gaining entrance to the Palace of Malta. It is worse than unheard-of, it's a crime, from the Catholic and canonical point of view. So that you have been, all unwittingly, giving your support to anti-Catholics, enemies of the Church, canon law criminals."

And as he uttered these words Mgr. dell'Acqua waved a small photostat under their noses, crying, "Here is the proof of their crime! A signed document!"

To those curious to read this document, he replied that, alas! he could not allow them to do so: the matter was altogether too delicate.

Back in their own offices, these diplomats telephoned the Via Condotti. Not one of them had believed the story, but all affirmed that Mgr. dell'Acqua had done everything in his power to convince them that he did. Pecci, who had not attended Mgr. dell'Acqua's audience that day, went to the Secretariat of State at once, and came back with the same tale. But he, too, had been refused a sight of the document: "The matter was altogether too delicate."

The chancellor and the vice-chancellor immediately wrote identical letters in which they denied ever having called upon the Italian forces of public order to prevent Mgr. Scapinelli from getting into the Grand Magistral Palace. They demanded access to the document which claimed the contrary, with a view to prosecuting the author as a forger.

The fact was that whereas, thanks to a cardinal, a final peace had been secretly concluded between the Grand Magistracy and the Pope, the Committee of Cardinals and the Secretariat of State were resuming hostilities, their purpose being to sway the foreign delegates. Hardly had they been assured that the men behind the Order's resistance had given way, than they set about trying to drive them from office before the agreed date. At the same time, they were taking their revenge for the two motions and hoping to get them withdrawn. An accusation of sacrilege, supported by a forged or lying document, might have immediate effects.

The Sovereign Council thought it best to acquaint the delegates with this incident without delay. Their reaction was indignant: "What, accuse a man of a crime and refuse to produce the proof!"

One of the French delegates, Morierre-Bernadotte, was sent to see Cardinal Tisserant.

"My dear friends," he declared, when he returned, "the cardinal made me swear on the Gospels that I would not reveal the nature of the incriminating document he showed me. However, this I can say: I do not know what may be regarded as an incriminating document in Italy or elsewhere; but I do know that in France what I saw would be no such thing."

As a result, the Assembly decided that it "refused to take part in any discussion of the matter" and would conclude its labours on the 27th.

Before the delegates' departure Cardinal Tisserant wrote protesting against the two motions which had been passed. He leaned heavily on the "religious nature" of the Order as a justification of interference by the cardinals. The measure adopted in the matter of "appointment and decoration of knights and dames" was, he claimed, designed to "prevent abuse of concessions on the part of a provisional administration during a critical period." Now, Cardinal Spellman had been only too happy to get this same "provisional administration" to sanction his sixty-seven illegitimate appointments in 1953, and had followed suit with another forty-one candidates in April, 1954. A further thirty-seven already received in 1955 showed that the "Grand Protector and Spiritual Adviser" was by no means relaxing a zeal which reaped him such a rich harvest.

Cardinal Tisserant went on to complain that his colleagues and himself had considered the Assembly's second motion to be offensive, and demanded that it be "withdrawn or declared null and void." And he concluded by insisting, "in the most particular manner, on the gravity of the situation."

This letter did not produce the rift between the Grand Magistracy and the Assembly which the cardinals had hoped for. Morierre-Bernadotte who, henceforth, was given quasi-official status, was instructed to negotiate with Cardinal Tisserant, and managed the task with a skill which would not have disgraced an old hand.

The draft he submitted to the dean of the Sacred College was clever: "The Assembly asks the Grand Magistracy to withdraw the political motion, but reaffirms the same point of view." However, a great many comings and goings were required before the "Knight of Embassy" was able to announce, on behalf of Cardinal Tisserant, that the embargo on decorations, and control of both ordinary and extraordinary business, had been lifted.

The negotiator's efforts had been facilitated by Father Acacio Coussa, operating behind the scenes. General Giannantoni, who was still in touch with this monk in the matter of the Holy Places, had contrived, a short while since, a new mirage to dazzle the prefect of the Oriental Congregation. Knowing that his dream was the conversion of Russia, the General had conceived the notion of setting up a Russian association of Knights of Malta and entrusting it to Prince Dmitri Galitzin, Catholic representative of his illustrious house. The cardinal saw in these knights the first outriders of that army of *preux chevaliers* who, by way of the Holy Places, of Antonians, Basilians, Melchites and Baladites, Soarites and Maronites, would penetrate the Caucasus, there enrol the descendants of the only Russian princes to have taken part in the Crusades, and so make their way up into the heart of Russia.

Seduced by this prospect, the dean of the Sacred College approved the delegates' new motion, which withdrew the old one while not withdrawing it at all. Then came the struggle to get it approved by his colleagues. Cardinal Canali gave way only because his vengeance was already prepared: and its instrument was to be the man who had just made him yield.

# V

ON THE MORNING of March 3 the delegates were holding a most edifying meeting at the Magistral Palace. Mgr. Ferrero di Cavallereone was present, with some members of the Sovereign Council. The purpose of the meeting was nothing less than an investigation of a plan to produce a missal of the Order's feasts, with all the saints in question and a brief account of their miracles.

Apart from the founder, the Blessed Gerard, claimed by both France and Italy who were also in dispute over his successor, the Blessed de Puy, the various delegations had shared out their pious labour without quarrelling. The Spaniards sponsored St. Sophia of Caspe and St. Sancha of Aragon; the Portuguese, Blessed Niño and Blessed Garcia; the English, Blessed Fortescue; the Germans, Blessed Gerland; the Hungarians, St. Andrew, King of Hungary; the French, St. Flore of the diocese of Cahors, St. Vincent, one of whose femurs was presented to the town of Nice by the Grand Master Lascaris, St. Euphemia, whose left foot was given to the Sorbonne by the Grand Master Wignacourt, and Blessed Gourdon of Genouillac. The Italians had St. Ubalda and St. Toscana, St. Hugh of Genoa, Blessed Gerard of Florence, and finally Blessed Peter of Imola who had been Grand Prior of Rome, like Cardinal Canali. Mgr. Ferrero had reserved for himself two Hospitalers of unknown nationality, St. Nicaise, martyred in 1202, and Blessed Roger, by some considered to be the Order's second founder.

\*　　　\*　　　\*

While this seraphic business was going forward under the Archbishop of Trebizond's guiding crozier, the lieutenant and the chancellor had gone to the Vatican, whither an express message from Cardinal Tisserant had summoned them. The rendezvous given them was the plenary congregations room in the Apostolic Palace, which conjured up shades of the tribunal and the first committee of cardinals, both of which had used it for their sittings. The near neighbourhood of the papal apartments, on the other hand, evoked a more reassuring memory.

When the two visitors were shown in they thought they had strayed into a waxworks: three mute, erect, hieratic figures confronted them in the very centre of that vast hall. Cardinal Tisserant was in his red cassock, belt, and *cappa magna*. He was flanked on the right by Mgr. Scapinelli, violet cassock and *mantellone*; and on his left by Prince Carlo Pacelli in cutaway coat and striped trousers. Nobody came forward to meet the chief of the Order of Malta, who stopped, with the chancellor, when he was still a few paces away from this new Trimurti. Hercolani and Apor looked about them, almost expecting to see, in some corner of the room, a torch extinguished and reversed, as in certain scenes of medieval excommunication. The cardinal took a large sheet of paper from Mgr. Scapinelli's hands, and began without preamble to read it in his loud Lorrainese voice: it was simply the text of the papal chirograph which had appointed the last committee, and the object of reading it was to give the requisite starkness to what followed. He returned the sheet to Mgr. Scapinelli and received another, smaller, one in exchange; he read it aloud, pronouncing each word very clearly.

"Excellency, the Commission of Cardinals appointed to assist the sovereign Hierosolymitan Order of Malta, over which I have the honour to preside, has charged me to convey to you the following deliberations: *Primo*, the person fulfilling the functions of vice-chancellor of the Order will, for reasons known to the Grand Magistracy and to the chairmen and delegates now gathered in Rome, be removed from office and dismissed within twenty-four hours. *Secundo*, the provisional lieutenant will, within forty-eight hours, receive Mgr. the secretary of this committee at the Magistral Palace and put him in the way of exercising the functions entrusted to him.

"Before giving you a copy of the paper I am reading, I, Dean of the Sacred College, Cardinal of the Holy Roman Church, address myself personally to Your Excellency, reminding you

of your solemn vows, as provisional head of an institution
which, even though it be endowed with functional sovereignty,
is above all a religious order, to appeal to your sense of duty
and ask you to weigh carefully your responsibilities toward the
Church and toward history."

Impassive and haughty the lieutenant had listened, toying
with the wire of his deaf-aid to which he imparted the elegance
of a monocle cord; but the two deep lines on his brow, just
above the nose, grew deeper. He stepped forward to receive
the paper which the cardinal held out to him, and put it into his
pocket. To the chancellor he said, "Let us go."

But Apor had none of Hercolani's resources of disdain and
impassiveness. His Magyar blood was up and, advancing on
the cardinal, "Eminence," he said, in his croaking voice, "what
you have just done is unworthy of your purple, unworthy of the
Sacred College, and unworthy of a Frenchman."

What happened then had, perhaps, never happened in the
Vatican before. The dean of the Sacred College, his burly person bending forward to overwhelm his short, wiry challenger,
began, with clenched fists, to bawl at him, "How dare you be
disrespectful to me? How dare you outrage the Holy Father,
who has just spoken through my mouth?"

And, each louder than the other, and with voices broken
by sobs, Prince Pacelli and Mgr. Scapinelli broke into an outcry
of, "He is insulting the Holy Father."

"The only people who insult him," said the chancellor, "are
such as abuse his authority, and call upon us to let Mgr. Scapinelli
fulfil his functions after assuring us, not three days ago, that he
would not have to do so."

"Enough of these outrages!" the cardinal bellowed, as red
as his cloth. "Whatever has been done, said, or written no
longer counts. What I have just done, in the name of the Holy
Father, is what is called a canonical intimation, do you understand? It is canon law which has spoken."

The chancellor turned his back and rejoined the lieutenant.

"At your orders, Excellency," he said.

Whereupon both bowed to the cardinal and walked out.

\*          \*          \*

They reached the Via Condotti at the moment when the meeting about the Order's saints was ending. Their bearing, which still betrayed their anger and contempt, soon dissipated the haloes.

"We have just had a painful interview with Cardinal Tisserant," Hercolani explained. "Out of consideration for his character we shall not give you an account of it. But the chancellor will read you what was read to us."

Cattaneo listened to this reading without frowning, as if it were some routine decree of no importance. In the silence which ensued he thought of Cardinal Canali and the other members of the committee; but he thought also of another cardinal, whose friend he was and who was a true shepherd. He turned to Hercolani: "Since His Excellency the Venerable Bailiff Lieutenant is among us, it is his permission I ask to make a personal statement."

"It is granted," the lieutenant said; and withdrew.

"All honour to the vice-chancellor," Apor said; "he remembers our code even in the shadow of the gallows! It was a discreet way of reminding our chief that his presence was irregular."

"While," Cattaneo said, "as a Christian and as a knight, I protest against the outrageous treatment meted out to me by the Committee of Cardinals, I am placing my resignation in the hands of the Sovereign Council here and now, in order to avoid any fresh difficulties. In any case, as the Council is aware, I had already done so some days ago for other reasons."

His words were applauded by all; but all combined to demand that the Sovereign Council refuse his resignation.

"You are forgetting," Cattaneo said, constitutional to the last, if a shade ironical, "that the Sovereign Council must be influenced by nobody."

Cattaneo was the only victim of the intimation, which had spared the chancellor. But then, a cardinal had already told him that the Holy See held him, above the rest, responsible: it was another cardinal who carried that opinion to its practical conclusion.

In the afternoon, and at Mgr. Scapinelli's request, the delegates went to the Spanish Embassy, which had offered its good offices for a meeting. Smiling and mellifluous, he tried to reassure them on the subject of his visit. Some surprise might reasonably have been felt at his giving himself that trouble, when he had the authority of a canonical intimation. It looked rather as if the cardinals were afraid that the highly dramatic scene staged by their dean might not be entirely effective. Rather than suffer yet another failure, they were trying sweetness and light after the storm of violence. It was the usual Vatican technique.

But it was in vain that Mgr. Scapinelli repeated that his call would be a mere matter of form, a courtesy visit. The delegates knew, from the Grand Magistracy, what that word meant, and the language of the intimation had confirmed them in their distrust.

Passing to the subject of Cattaneo, the prelate domestic gave it as unquestionable that the vice-chancellor had called in the police to prevent him entering the Magistral Palace. But, less cautious than Mgr. dell'Acqua or Cardinal Tisserant, he added that the "incriminating document" was a report sent to the Holy See by an officer of the carabinieri. He did not mention the chancellor, who had sent Cardinal Tisserant a letter of apology for his outburst that morning.

That same evening the Sovereign Council decreed that it would "suspend judgment of the vice-chancellor's position until the Holy See had made known the text upon which had been based an accusation whose precise nature had not been made clear." By way of authority for this suspension the decree referred to the Order's constitutional code, according to which no disciplinary sanctions could be applied without proof of the misdemeanour being furnished.

A second decree asked that a date for the election of a grand master be fixed without further delay, at most within the next three weeks; and suggested a means of dealing with the difficulty in the matter of Mgr. Scapinelli. The Grand Magistracy declared itself willing to furnish the committee with a copy of all lieu-tenancy transactions. This would entail neither a derogation of sovereignty, nor a commitment for the future. By these two measures Hercolani hoped to avoid having to receive his "co-adjutor," without refusing in so many words; and to postpone

Cattaneo's departure, without openly opposing it. The canonical intimation delivered by Cardinal Tisserant, terrible in purple, had not disturbed his mind even if it had come as a blow to him.

Considering himself entitled to a little rest after such a day, he went off to the country near Rome, asking that he be left in peace, at least for twenty-four hours.

# VI

THE NEXT MORNING the chancellor told Cattaneo that he had just heard from the Secretariat of State that the cardinals would give up the second point in their intimation, provided the first be observed. In other words, they would accept copies of all Grand Magistracy transactions as a substitute for Mgr. Scapinelli's visit, provided the vice-chancellor be dismissed at once.

"My dear Cattaneo," Apor said, "the decision you have to take is a most moving one. If you take refuge in the Sovereign Council's decree, you will be saved for a little while; but there will be no election; and there will soon be no Order of Malta. You will have been playing the part of Samson—casting down the temple which you had been holding up."

Without a word, Cattaneo sat down at a table and, for the second time, wrote a letter of resignation. Handing it to the chancellor, "It's a pity the lieutenant isn't here to accept it," he said.

"That does not matter; he delegated all his powers to me. I will inform the members of the Sovereign Council and get the decree drafted. There are no words to express my opinion of your character." And, deeply moved, he seized the younger man's hands and pressed them.

"By St. Steven!" he swore, "I don't know where we shall find a man to replace you."

"Giannantoni."

"He knows nothing but Moslem affairs."

"Precisely: a specialist on the Arabs, he's the only one here who's on good terms with Cardinal Tisserant and that, for the moment, is all-important. I'm sure the lieutenant will be pleased with the proposal. Let us bless the Holy Places, the one chink in the cardinals' armour! I suggest that Giannantoni carry a letter announcing my resignation, from you, to the cardinal—and at once."

The Minister to the Lebanon, residing in Rome, was as surprised at the role he found himself playing as by Cattaneo's ideas for his future. He had held aloof from the struggle, but had nevertheless shown himself loyal. He condoled with the vice-chancellor, expressed his admiration for him, and took the letter which Apor had written. Cattaneo, for the last time, had affixed the Order's paper seal to the flap of the envelope—a white Maltese cross on a red ground, in imitation of the Holy See's. To Giannantoni, he said, "Tell the cardinal you're bringing him the skin of that obscene viper Cattaneo. Tell him you and the chancellor killed and flayed me."

Giannantoni set off for the Palazzo dei Convertendi and Apor went to see the delegates, who were in session. He read them Cattaneo's letter, then brought him into the room. He was received with an ovation: the hero of the Order, a shade more suppleness would have enabled him to avoid becoming its martyr. De Mojana, in the chair, hailed him as "a master exponent of Maltese ideals." Baron Twinkel, speaking for all the delegates, set forth all that the foreign associations and the Order itself owed to Cattaneo; and although he had spoken for the rest, they, too, each had a few words of the same kind to say. And if there were tears in their eyes, they were not only tears of sympathy, but of wounded pride.

*         *         *

When he had received the chancellor's letter, Cardinal Tisserant announced that, satisfied on the first point of the intimation, he was now waiting for the second to be executed. He knew nothing, he said, of any assurance given that morning by the Secretariat of State that his colleagues and himself would be ready to accept copies of transactions in lieu of Mgr. Scapinelli's visit to the Grand Magistracy. The lieutenant came hurrying back to headquarters and asked the French delegates to use their good offices once again. It had been one of their number who had brought about the agreement with Cardinal Tisserant which he was now repudiating; it was up to them to reopen the question with him.

Meanwhile, Hercolani was furious at Cattaneo's resignation and maintained that he was not going to accept it. Cattaneo's own arguments and his disinclination to any further discussion of something he regarded as settled, finally prevailed, however. The lieutenant signed the decree and appointed Giannantoni temporary vice-chancellor.

The French delegates—this time Morierre-Bernadotte was accompanied by Guy de Polignac and the Comte d'Harcourt—had to reconcile the grand magistral decree rejecting Mgr. Scapinelli's visit, the Secretariat of State's assurance that it would not take place, and Cardinal Tisserant's injunction that it was to be carried out within the next forty-eight hours. They contrived a rough and ready settlement whereby the Committee of Cardinals were to accept the copies of transactions and the Grand Magistracy to allow Mgr. Scapinelli to pay his "visit of courtesy." The lieutenant had every reason, in view of the canonical intimation, to question the value of all these conflicting agreements and promises. He knew that the alternation of unyielding severity and a more accommodating tone had only one purpose—the imposition of unyielding severity. Taking refuge in the Order's constitution, which made it his duty to defend its sovereignty and independence, he refused to ratify an agreement botched up in a few hours by the French delegation; the day ended in tragic gloom and the shadow of the Church's anathema.

In this extremity, the Prince de Polignac begged the French Ambassador to come to the rescue. His Excellency did so wholeheartedly, and the propiatory role which he played at the Secretariat of State was brilliantly repeated before the Committee of Cardinals. He had no difficulty, furthermore, in winning the support of his fellow ambassador, Mameli, who like himself was a knight magistral grand cross of the Order. Together, they gave their guarantee, both personally and in their capacity as ambassadors to the Holy See of France and Italy respectively, that Mgr. Scapinelli's visit would really be no more than a visit of courtesy. From Mgr. dell'Acqua they obtained a further concession: the copies of the lieutenancy's transactions were to be delivered to the cardinals on neutral territory and under supervision of an international commission. They then called at the Magistral Palace to testify to this double agreement before the delegates; and won the gratitude of everyone involved excepting, perhaps, the cardinals.

Only one member of the Sovereign Council—Gudenus, the man who had refused to accept the judgment—declared himself unable to subscribe to the agreement. It was not, he said, that he had no confidence in the two ambassadors, but that, despite his piety, he no longer had any confidence at all in the princes of the Church. And echoing the Spanish bravado at the first assembly, he proclaimed that "the venerable Grand Priory of Austria would, if need be, detach itself from the Grand Magistracy, to maintain the Order's sovereign status." There were smiles, and he departed to calm his ruffled spirits by a meditation in the chapel on the Aventine, as before.

Gudenus notwithstanding, the Order's sovereignty had never been so safe, since, indirectly, it was now guaranteed by both Italy and France. And this was the result of all the efforts made by Cardinal Canali and his colleagues to destroy it. There was one other result for them to dwell upon: the humiliation of having to get their word of honour underwritten by two laymen.

# VII

THEIR EXCELLENCIES Messieurs d'Ormesson and Mameli had devised the following elegant formula, which certainly revealed nothing of the storms which had produced it: "On March 5,

Mgr. Scapinelli will call on the lieutenant, returning the visit
paid him by the latter at the Congregation of Religious on
February 19."

Mgr. Scapinelli, his bearing modest, in due course presented
himself at the Magistral Palace. He hurried past the iron gates,
as if to seek asylum from the carabinieri, climbed the stairs,
was introduced into the red salon, and sat down beneath the
portrait of the Grand Master Thun Hohenstein in the very spot
once occupied by the Marquis Macdonald. There he was joined
by the chancellor. They recalled their meeting at the Hungarian
Legation, when they were younger, and seemed not to recall
their more recent meeting in the hall of plenary congregations.
Seeing the Prelate Domestic glancing furtively at the objects
around him, the chancellor thought of the "Master's" remark:
the American had thought his money had paid for the things;
today's visitor had once expected to sequester them. At the
moment, however, his one idea seemed to be to get out of the
place as quickly as he could. The lieutenant only kept him a few
minutes, like the Marquis Macdonald.

On March 7, Cattaneo and Giannantoni signed a thirteen-
page procés-verbal countersigned by De Mojana; Cattaneo
then left the *palazzo* where he had played so great a part. His
successor's first care was to go bail for his own good behaviour
to the Cardinals' Committee: to insure that his appointment
would be welcomed by Mgr. Scapinelli he sent him the lieutenancy transactions without waiting for the international
commission. There were two advantages to be expected from
this excessive zeal: it ensured the good will of the cardinals
and their secretary toward a man who had every intention
of sticking firmly to the Order's policy line; and it was a guarantee that the copies had not been tampered with—a common
practice among diplomatic archivists. There was a good deal
of surprise, however, when Mgr. Scapinelli called, on Cardinal
Canali's behalf, for a file which had nothing whatever to do
with current lieutenancy business: the proofs of the Tsar Paul
I's conversion which were such a thorn in the side of Rome's
Grand Prior.

Despite his esteem for Giannantoni and his desire to be

accommodating, the lieutenant could not countenance such irregularities. The Paul I file, at least, must be returned at once. But Cardinal Canali refused to give it back. Giannantoni being henceforth *persona grata* with the Holy See in any case, Hercolani thought it would be a clever move to pretend that Apor was responsible for handing over this file: by sacrificing him, he might save him. He called for the chancellor's resignation. Thus, as with Giannantoni and Paterno, the Order was preparing for the future.

Since a promise that the election would be allowed at last was the tacit implication of all these agreements, it seemed that it could not, now, be long delayed. From day to day the delegates awaited the brief which was to authorize it. But Cardinal Canali succeeded in holding it up again, for the Pope's health, which was failing again, made him a prisoner of the Trimurti. By way of consolation, Cardinal Tisserant promised the French that he would celebrate the St. John's Mass in their own church of Ste Elizabeth du Temple in Paris, and might even be present, the day after, at their procession in Villedieu-les-Poêles, where a confraternity of the Most Holy Sacrament, founded under the Order's aegis, would be celebrating its tercentenary.

On March 11 the cardinal who was Cattaneo's friend was able to have an audience of the Holy Father and to raise the question of the Order of Malta. His Holiness discovered that he had been kept in the dark concerning the latest developments; and that the decree containing the "rose of candidates" had never been delivered to him. He had been put off with a tale to the effect that no election was possible, for want of eligible candidates. Very annoyed at the way in which he had been misled, he instructed the cardinal to go directly to the Secretariat of State and have the necessary brief drafted at once.

"And be on your guard," he said, "for the Order of Malta is not the only victim of their tricks."

Despite which, the brief still failed to arrive. Warned by Mgr. dell'Acqua, Cardinal Canali was again busy forcing the Pope to retract his decision. On the 15th, De Mojana, alerted by the other cardinal, asked the lieutenant to remind the Secretariat of State that the Order was impatiently waiting for authority to hold the election. On the 18th, Cardinal Tisserant informed Hercolani, officially, that there would be no election and that his colleagues were again considering the idea of a regency. He also ordered the lieutenant to reinstate Baron Apor forthwith, which was some consolation. The chancellor's letter of apology and Cattaneo's resignation had whitewashed him. Tricks might be played on the Holy Father and even on the Order of Malta; but the Order of Malta might occasionally play one of its own on the cardinals.

"Reinstate Apor as chancellor?" Hercolani cried. "Never! What he did may recommend him to my successor, but not to me."

"Very possibly," the cardinal retorted.

It would seem that currents and cross-currents of influence within the Holy See were numerous, but the Holy Father's emerged in the end as the most powerful. On the day after Cardinal Tisserant had officially announced that there would be no election, Mgr. dell'Acqua wrote to say that it had been authorized. However, Cardinal Canali had managed to get it confined to the election of a lieutenant; it seemed that for all his eighty-four years he had not lost hope of soon adding the Grand Mastership of Malta to that of the Holy Sepulchre. Mgr. dell'Acqua added that the names of candidates must be chosen by mutual agreement. The Grand Magistracy replied that their list had been submitted long ago. After a short delay, the substitute wrote again, saying that the Holy See approved only one name on the list: Melzi d'Eril, Cardinal Canali's candidate.

Giannantoni showed himself worthy of the confidence which the Grand Magistracy placed in him, even to the extent of overlooking his initial excesses of zeal. He suggested Paterno's name to Father Acacio Coussa, and Cardinal Tisserant set about persuading Cardinal Canali that Paterno was no more to be feared than Melzi d'Eril. Mgr. Scapinelli, who had not forgotten the Sicilian Bailiff's attitude during the lieutenant's visit, was ready to vouch for his deference toward the Committee of Cardinals.

Cardinal Canali, however, determined to have an election free from risks, would not give way. He was told that the plenary

Council of State would not consent to vote at all unless there were at least three candidates. He was also assured that Paterno had not the slightest chance of being elected. He proceeded to investigate on his own account, came to the same conclusion, and raised his veto on a name which gave him nothing to worry about. On the 23rd, the Secretariat of State advised the Grand Magistracy that the date of the election was fixed one month hence, that the only name approved in the list of professed knights was that of the Bailiff Paterno Castello di Caraci; and that dispensation would be granted, in the event of their election, to "Don Flavio Melzi d'Eril, of the ducal house of Lodi," who had taken novice vows, and to the Dutch baron, Speyart van Woerden, who had taken no vows.

But as the Dutchman had requested that his particular petal be removed from the rose, there were, in effect, only two candidates, or, rather, one, Melzi d'Eril, on whom all the favours of the Holy See and all Cardinal Canali's hopes were concentrated.

# VIII

ON THE MORNING OF SUNDAY, April 24, 1955, the courtyard outside the priory villa was a scene of great animation. Motorcars were queueing up to pass through the wide open main gates under the watchful eyes of uniformed guards. Each car stopped at the lodge, where its occupants were received by the Marquis Pallavicini, Master of Ceremonies, Chairman of the Hungarian association.

Among the knights in red uniform, professed knights in black habits, the English and the Spaniards in black robes with white borders, were the twenty-eight electors who were about to choose the new head of the Order of Malta: they were—the eleven chairmen of the European associations, and seventeen professed knights, delegates of the grand priories or members of the Sovereign Council.

Once again were to be seen Baron Twinkel's tall figure, Graf Henckel's gleaming monocle, the long nose of the Conde d'Alçaçovas, the Infant Don Fernando's square countenance, the Hibernian spareness of Wilson Lynch, the noble brow of Colonel Elwes, the Caesarian profile of Count Czapski, the imposing bearing of Baron Van Voorst, the Prince de Ligne's powerful jaws, and the prominent cheekbones of the Prince de Polignac who was to obtain the Grand Cross of a Bailiff of Honour and Devotion for Cardinals Feltin and Grente, but only a Collar of Merit for President Coty.

There, too, was the Bailiff Thun, but the memory of the trouble he had caused was quite swamped by pity: half paralysed, he was supported by two footmen; he had even lost his beard in the long battle. The Venerable Bailiff Franchi de' Cavalieri was there, Dean of the Roman chapter; and another delegate of that grand priory, Don Filippo "of the ducal house of Caffarelli," who was not even a knight of justice but who, for the occasion, had received a dispensation from the Pope. Cardinal Canali, himself an elector in his capacity as grand prior, had insisted on this in order to ensure an extra vote for Don Flavio Melzi d'Eril, of the ducal house of Lodi. Don Filippo was heir apparent to Prince Ruffo in the chairmanship of the Italian association, and his was the new name with which Cardinal Canali was trying to dazzle Roman Society. As for Prince Ruffo himself, he had no vote, the Italian association consisting, apart from its military charitable works, simply in a combination of the three grand priories. Besides, he had grown weary of his role as Cardinal Canali's champion. When the cardinal had wanted him to return to the charge, he had replied, like his ancestor Cardinal Ruffo when he had been required to resume command of the armies of the Santa Fede, "Such things can only be done once."

Finally, the Colonna Sciarra Barberini *versus* Sacchetti Barberini case being still *sub judice*, the bailiff of St. Sebastian on the Palatine, only hereditary elector in the full Council of State, was absent.

Electors and guests made for the chapel, where the Lieutenant Hercolani was already installed on the throne which he was occupying for the last time. He was tranquil and serene, never having had any ambition but to do his duty and achieve the result which he now saw in process of accomplishment.

He knew that Cardinal Canali had scored a final point. The Holy Father, in the brief which would approve the election result, would announce that the Committee of Cardinals was to be retained "to collaborate in the measures of reform"; and would express a wish that those members of the Sovereign Council "whose term had expired" be replaced by new men. It was a polite hint that those whose mandates were still valid, such as Hercolani's in the Grand Priory of Rome, must give up their places. But Cardinal Canali had nevertheless failed to deprive him of the right, which he had enjoyed for twenty years, to sit on the Sovereign Council: the Pope had agreed that he be appointed to an honorary place, at present filled by a professed chaplain, as Commissioner of the Magistral Church. Thus in the Palazzo di Malta as in the Church of Santa Maria del' Aventino, Hercolani would still occupy an honourable place.

By way of celebrating his triumph in advance, Cardinal Canali was to celebrate the Mass. His partisans, spies, and minions were all of one opinion: Melzi d'Eril would be elected. Cattaneo's downfall had cleared the air. The professed electors had certainly made up their minds to toe the line; the chairmen of associations, indoctrinated by their nuncios and brainwashed by the cardinals of the Curia, were ready to perform an act of obedience. The Grand Prior of Rome rejoiced, and his rejoicing was apparent in his flashing eyes, wide gestures, even in his blessings. And he seemed to be wearing a new wig, so shiningly black did it gleam.

It was a great day, too, for the other two members of the Trimurti, who sat side by side on the bench: Prince Carlo Pacelli and Count Galeazzi had not come as Knights of Malta, although both were members of the sovereign Order; nor were they attired as Knights of the Holy Sepulchre, although both were high dignitaries of that equestrian order. Beside them, the Marquis Travaglini di Santa Rita sat smiling. He was about to be appointed director of tourism, with the task of preparing for the Olympic

Games in Rome; it was being whispered that he had had the original notion of suggesting to the Pope a new dogma to enhance the prestige of that sporting event: the dogma of the co-redemption of Mary.

Beyond them, Melzi d'Eril, in his white-lapelled uniform as a knight of justice, affected a careless indifference. Mgr. Alcini was there, beside Father Castellani; and Mgr. Scapinelli with Father Arcadio Larraona, that terrible missionary son of the Immaculate Heart of Mary having decided to relax, for once, and breathe the air of Maltese vanities. He had, indeed, let it be known that he would not refuse the Magistral Grand Cross were it to be offered him. Father Acacio Coussa, recently appointed Chaplain of the Order *ad honorem*, was there as a greeting incarnate from the Oriental Congregation.

Cattaneo was not there but, far from the Magistral Palace, he had continued discreetly working for the Order and earning its gratitude. The chairmen of associations had recently given him a silver tray engraved with their names as a memento of his work for the Order under the Hercolani lieutenancy. Also absent was another of the Order's champions, Baron Apor. Although certain of being restored to his place, he wished to avoid compromising it. Pecci, wearing his Cross of Profession for the first time—it was an honour just conferred on him by the lieutenant as a reward for his services—was recalling all the steps he had taken to bring about this memorable day's work. Mgr. Ferrero di Cavallereone was reading his missal, and probably thinking of the missal of the Order's saints in preparation. Mgr. Rossi Stockalper might, perhaps, be remembering his mission to Paris, "to unmask a Freemason of the thirty-third degree" who happened, also, to be the Order's minister. Together on the back seat Ferrata, Corsanego, Snider, and Gazzoni looked like four angels of justice contemplating their handiwork.

The office of the little hours terminated, Cardinal Canali took his seat on the faldstool, his back resting against the altar, and made a long speech. "Before the holy sacrifice, illustrious knights, I wish to offer you, from this holy altar and in the presence of Our Lord and Divine Redeemer Jesus, my fervent and fraternal greetings. At the same time I shall express my sincere hope and belief that grace abundant and heavenly aid be granted you at this historic juncture which is one of particular value to our militant body."

After this handsome exordium, in which certain words rang strangely enough to suggest what was coming, one might have thought that his speech was an exercise in irony. When, for example, he expressed his "complete satisfaction" in the fact that the grand priories and national associations had "responded in such exemplary style to the Grand Magistracy's appeal by sending their distinguished delegates," he can hardly have expected them to have forgotten that he had been keeping them waiting for two years. As they were in the paschal season, he went on to quote "the sweet and gentle word with which the Saviour accompanied the manifestation of his adorable person during his first appearance to the holy apostles: 'Peace be with you!'

"Peace be with you," he repeated to his listeners. "This internal peace indicates to the man of piety what must be his line of conduct in order to co-operate with the Divine Will. In a moment we shall read together a magnificent page of St. John's Gospel which, in this second Sunday after the Resurrection represents Jesus as the Good Shepherd giving His life for His sheep, knowing each one of them, asking nothing better than to expend Himself for their good, and sending out His faithful disciples to seek for the lost sheep, so that there may be but one flock and one shepherd."

The irony was so rank that even the Spaniards and the Irishmen smiled. An Italian muttered a line from Dante: "Habited as shepherds, ravening wolves. . . ." But the sheep themselves, the innocent sheep, might they not be infectious, passing on that Malta fever which, at the Vatican, Cardinal Canali was said to be infected with, and which is so difficult to cure?

Fearful lest all these broad hints might still not be clear enough, the grand prior did not hesitate to make use of the last papal chirograph: sure of the election, he foreshadowed its outcome; it was to be "a generous response" to the Holy Father's expectations. And to make assurance doubly sure he borrowed the supreme authority for a sort of supreme intimation: "Our mandate as electors is one of the greatest responsibility. We shall exercise it after the Holy Mass, imploring enlightenment and guidance of the Holy Ghost; and it will be the conclusion of that Mass."

By way of epilogue he repeated the prayer from the Acts of the Apostles, in which they, being gathered together, have to choose one of their brethren: "And they appointed two, Joseph called Barsabas, who was surnamed Justus, and Matthias. And they prayed and said, Thou, Lord, which knowest the hearts of all men, show whether of these two thou hast chosen. . . ." It was a reminder that the elect of the Holy See, the Lord's elect, was Melzi d'Eril.

And when, in the course of the Mass, he saw the whole congregation come forward to take communion, he could no longer doubt that such good Catholics would shortly bear witness to the Apostolic and Roman quality of their faith.

Leaving the church, the electors posed on its steps for the press photographers. The cardinal was in the middle, in red cassock and cape, lace rochet, pectoral cross, and wearing his bailiff's ribbon about his neck. On his right stood Hercolani and next to him, Paterno.

Footmen in nut-brown coats and red breeches served a collation in the villa's summerhouse. The cardinal, his cup of coffee in his hand, moved from group to group, as if still intent on canvassing for votes, just as his friend and colleague Cardinal Spellman took the plate round at the banquets of the American Knights of Malta. The bonds uniting the two cardinals made it quite natural to glance across the terrace and juxtapose the dome of St. Peter's rising above the horizon and the humble roof of the Bambino Gesù Hospital, hidden behind the Janiculum.

The members of the full Council of State returned to the church and there sang the *Veni Creator*, formed in procession behind the Order's standard, borne by Gudenus, and made their way up to the council chamber in the villa. Portraits of all former grand masters, from Blessed Gerard to Prince Chigi, covered the walls. Their frames, all identical, seemed to reduce the joys and sorrows of all these great men to a single level.

The Venetian glass lustre which hung from the ceiling, with its corollas and garlands, was poised, in fragile ornamentation, above nine centuries of history.

The electors placed themselves in order of seniority about the long table which was covered with a red cloth. Giannantoni, as vice-chancellor, and Sersale, as interpreter, remained with them. The cardinal, in the name of all present, pronounced the Order's ritual formula: "I swear to keep secret, for the sake of the rule, what it is proper to keep secret and especially not to reveal the votes of the councils, so help me God. In which, failing, may it be to the damnation of my soul."

The voting was according to a rather special usage reminiscent of that employed in the ancient Venetian Senate. The first round was simply to indicate the names of candidates. In the second—the balloting—electors voted for or against the diverse candidates named in the first. White or black balls were used in balloting, papers for the first round. To be elected a candidate had to receive half plus one of the total number of votes.

Each elector wrote the name of a candidate on a slip of paper, rolled it up and put it into an oval case, and placed the case in a bronze vessel. The cases and their contents were then examined: Paterno had one vote, Melzi d'Eril two, Hercolani fourteen, and De Mojana thirteen. The cardinal flushed angrily at this manifestation, albeit platonic, seeing in it a twinge—possibly even an outburst?—of revolt.

The first names to be balloted on were those which had received most votes in the first round. Hercolani came first: he again received fourteen votes, De Mojana again thirteen. It was a manifestation of friendship, of good will, carefully kept within the limit of the figure which could have elected them. The cardinal breathed again: it was not a revolt. His homily had gone home to them. The straying sheep had strayed for the last time. Paterno seemed to have received only one vote, in any case, presumably his own. Melzi d'Eril not being able to vote for himself, since he was not an elector, the cardinal knew that, apart from his own vote, he had received Thun's. That bailiff and he exchanged smiles of good omen; it was pleasant to know that victory must fall to their two votes. Nevertheless, they were a good deal surprised that Caffarelli had not voted with them from the start.

Melzi d'Eril's name was next for the ballot box. He got his two white balls; he also received twenty-six black ones. As it would have been safe to give him twelve whites in addition to his faithful two, without electing him, that extra fourteen black balls clearly meant something more. Livid, the cardinal glanced across at Thun, who looked stupefied, and at Caffarelli, who was staring at the ceiling. The ballot box went round for the last name: Paterno was elected with seventeen votes.

He had been accorded a majority which was adequate without being too obviously overwhelming. The first round had been the Order's retort to the Secretariat of State's exclusions from the list, and a tribute to Hercolani and De Mojana, one of the most active members of the Sovereign Council and, as such, one whom the Holy See was anxious to be rid of. The ballot, that is Paterno's election, was the retort to Cardinals Tisserant, Micara, Pizzardo, Aloïsi Masella, Valeri, and Canali.

The Grand Prior of Rome did not know that on the evening before the election the chairmen of associations had met in council at the Hotel Plaza and there worked out their tactics according to a plan already adopted by the other electors. For, afraid that the cardinal would raise up yet another obstacle, all had competed, during the last few weeks, in fostering his illusions and misleading him; not one of the conspirators had any feeling that he was involved in anything underhand or reprehensible. There had, however, obviously been a certain amount of malice in giving Paterno only one vote in the first round with a view to enhancing the shock of the final result. On the other hand, nobody had thought of bringing Caffarelli into the plot, for it was assumed that he was under an obligation to vote against them. Why, then, had Melzi d'Eril received only two votes? Apparently, either in the council chamber or in the priory church, Caffarelli had realized that from what he had heard everyone was firmly against the grand prior, and consequently against his candidate. It was the first time any candidate had been so contemptuously treated in a ballot, but the affront was not intended for the man who had suffered it: it was aimed at his patron.

At the announcement of the result the cardinal had risen unsteadily to his feet. He cast a glance at the brazier in which Sersale was burning the first-round voting papers, hastily congratulated Paterno, and made for the door, without even taking leave of Thun.

"Your Eminence will allow me to remind you that the *Te Deum* is at six this evening," Giannantoni said. The grand prior walked out without answering. Melzi d'Eril, waiting in the courtyard, hastened toward him with a smile on his lips.

"You had everything but votes," the cardinal said, and left him standing there, gaping.

He snatched his red hat with the golden tassels from Mgr. Curatola's hands and, followed by that faithful secretary, flung himself into his car, which had been moved forward at a signal from the porter.

Mgr. Curatola did not say a word. He saw the cardinal furiously revolving the great ring on his finger, and he felt one of those storms of rage, which nothing could calm, approaching. The chauffeur, also aware of the sultry atmosphere, had sensed that he was to drive fast. At the foot of the Aventine the motorcar crossed the Tiber and emerged into St. Peter's Square. The Swiss under the belfry arch presented arms and the Palatine guards hastened to throw open the barrier. Getting out of the car outside the *palazzina*, Mgr. Curatola ventured a word of consolation: "Eminence, St. Paul himself was shipwrecked on Malta."

The cardinal shrugged, and swept into the hall like the first gust of a gale. He threw his hat down under the baldachin decorated with his coat of arms, in which a "winged dog" was depicted trying to bite the sun.

Mgr. Curatola hovered, uneasily alert, outside his master's door, which had been violently slammed in his face. He was moved by the old man's grief when he heard him sobbing. He was accustomed to the cardinal's terrible outbursts of anger, but he realized that today's performance was an access of despair: five years of undermining, of stratagem and wiles, of perfidy and calumny, of committees and tribunals, of extortion of chirographs and threatening displays of the purple, had all come to nought.

The secretary sat down on a chair and took out his rosary, to help his cardinal at least by prayer. But his paters and aves were shot through and across by epic charges of chivalry, by sea fights, and the fluttering of a red flag with a white cross. Banks and newspapers, too, distracted his attention, sessions of the Trimurti, and visits from Christian Democrat Senators and Deputies, whose escutcheon displayed the same colours reversed, a red cross on a white ground. When he heard the cardinal blundering about in a kind of hysterical passion, anxiety overruled discretion, and he silently opened the door a little. He saw the old man stamping on his skullcap; his wig had fallen off and his snow-white hair, no longer concealed, made him look as if he had been suddenly aged by the touch of a wand. Mgr. Curatola recalled the tale of the Grand Vizier Palaeologos tearing out his beard and trampling his turban underfoot when the armies of Mohammed II were forced to raise the siege of Rhodes, driven back by the valorous Knights of St. John; and he remembered the epitaph which the sultan had decreed be engraved on his tomb: "I tried to take Rhodes and Italy."

The major-domo announced that luncheon was served. Mgr. Curatola knocked on the door, entered the room, picked up the wig and the skullcap, dusted them off, and set them back tenderly on that venerable head.

"Eminence," he said, "you have not taken Malta; but you still have Italy."